PRIZES *of* OPPORTUNITY

BOOK EIGHT

JACO JACINTO AGE OF SAIL SERIES

MARC LIEBMAN

Publisher:

Rotorhead Media, LLC
Savannah, TX

Proofreaders: Cheryl Carathers, Rose Gault
Cover Images from: Vectezzy
Book Cover, and interior design by – Deena Rae; E-BookBuilders, adaptation for ebook

BISAC Subject Headings:
FIC – 014000 – FICTION/Historical
FIC - 032000 – FICTION/War & Military
FIC – 047000 – FICTION/Sea Stories

File version: 202601001.017

CONTENTS

OTHER BOOKS

JOSH HAMAN SERIES

Cherubs 2
Big Mother 40
Render Harmless
Forgotten
Inner Look
Moscow Airlift
The Simushir Island Incident

AGE OF SAIL SERIES

Raider of the Scottish Coast
Carronade
Death of A Lady
Last Battles
For A Few Francs
Predators
Fight We Shall

DEREK ALMER SERIES

Flight of the Pawnee
Failure to Fire
Insidious Dragon

STAND ALONE

The Red Star of Death

DEDICATION

We, the United States, are a maritime nation. We have been one since we were Thirteen Colonies strung up and down the eastern seaboard of North America. We were then, and are today, dependent on the sea which is both a moat and a highway to our trading partners.

The United States is blessed with having much of our northern border on the south shore of the Great Lakes, our southern border on the Gulf of Mexico. To the east, we have the Atlantic Ocean and to the west, the Pacific and north of Alaska we have the Arctic Ocean.

Beginning with the American Revolution, in every war we fought, control of the sea and the lakes was critical to our success and our ability to prevail against all enemies. That hasn't changed in 2026 and will never change because the geography of the earth will not change.

Therefore, this novel is dedicated to the men and women of the Continental and U.S. Navies who, without their courage, dedication, perseverance and sacrifice, the United States would not be the great nation that it is today.

HISTORICAL BACKDROP

Prizes of Opportunity takes place after the end of the Barbary Pirates War in 1805 and into the War of 1812. In that period, the Founding Fathers as well as every citizen were finding their way to make this new country called the United States of America work.

If there were talking heads on social media in Europe in the 1790s, they would have scoffed at the idea that regular citizens could elect their leaders and those chosen could rule in the best interests of their fellow citizens. Clearly, the experts of the period held the opinion that in order to govern the unruly masses, one needed to be "high born," i.e., a member of the nobility. Even better, one needed a king or queen or at least a duke to provide the necessary leadership.

One can easily imagine the talking heads opining about how preposterous an idea it was to have the people elect a president every four years. To have the president's power different from that of each half of a bi-cameral legislature, each with different responsibilities, they would say, is novel and probably wouldn't work. Add in a judiciary that would rule if decisions by the president or laws passed by Congress were in line with the written document called the Constitution.

This concept behind our republic was not novel, it was revolutionary. And, from the beginning, we as a nation, were breaking new ground as we struggled with how to make it work.

Yet immigrants from Europe, the Caribbean, and South America were flocking to the United States. Census data shows in 1780, there were 2,780,369 residents in the Thirteen Colonies. According to the U.S.

Bureau of the Census, by 1790, the first official U.S. government census, the population had ballooned to 3,929,214. By 1800, our population was 5,308,483, and in 1810, it was 7,239,881.

Immigrants were flooding into the country, and our government had to deal with the answers to three key questions.

Who do we let in?

How do we vet them?

What is the path to citizenship?"

Besides immigration, our Founding Fathers began to pass laws to restrict and ultimately abolish slavery. The first is in the Articles of Confederation that was signed on October 20th, 1774.

Paragraph two of the Articles of Confederation reads *that we will neither import nor purchase any Slave imported after the first Day of December next, after which Time we will wholly discontinue the Slave Trade, and will neither be concerned in it ourselves, nor will we hire our Vessels, nor sell our Commodities or Manufactures, to those who are concerned in it.* Unfortunately, under the Articles of Confederation, the Continental Congress did not have the power to enforce the laws it passed.

However, during the 1st U.S. Congress, lawmakers passed, and Washington signed into law an act that banned slavery in the Northwest Territory. Many more followed that prohibited U.S. citizens from participating in the slave trade. Granted, it took until 1865 and the bloodiest war in U.S. history to end the practice, but the point is that almost from day one of the Federal government, the march to end slavery in the U.S. began.

From 1792 to 1815, Europe was aflame with a series of wars that affected our foreign policy and our economy. Both France and Great Britain pressured the U.S. to pick a side. President Washington declared that we were neutral. His successors Adams, Jefferson, and Madison steered clear of becoming entangled in the French Revolutionary Wars and then the Napoleonic Wars.

But we were involved. England was by far our largest trading partner. Food, raw materials, and some manufactured goods flowed to England, which shipped us manufactured goods. From France we imported wine, clothing and furniture in exchange for what we sent east.

The British were trying to force us through trade restrictions – tariffs, duties, policies – to side with them. The Royal Navy was authorized to stop and seize U.S. ships headed to ports in countries either controlled by the French or allied with France. Contraband was defined as military supplies, and bills passed by the House of Commons included almost everything useful to an army or navy.

In blatant disregard of the 1783 Treaty of Paris that gave us our independence, the British Army did not leave U.S. territory. It maintained small forts in the Northwest Territory from which it incited and equipped the Native Americans to resist the settlers moving west. England offered to help them create an independent nation whose territory was largely in the U.S.

In addition, the Royal Navy was desperate for men. It faced a desertion rate of 20 – 25% so the House of Commons authorized Royal Navy captains to stop ships to look for deserters and English citizens. The captains were also allowed to "impress" anyone on board thought to be an Englishman. Impressment is really kidnapping. While press gangs roamed England where it was legal, in international waters, it was not.

There were several incidents, the *Chesapeake-Leopard* and the Little Belt Affairs, in which U.S. and Royal Navy ships fired upon each other. Sailors were killed, taken off their ships, and impressed into the Royal Navy even though they had papers documenting their U.S. citizenship. Any one of these incidents could have precipitated a war.

Between 1800 and 1812, the Royal Navy impressed approximately 25,000 American seamen. Only 5,000 returned to the U.S. after the War of 1812.

Thomas Jefferson did not believe in standing armies or navies. Immediately after taking office in 1801, he ordered the Secretary of the Navy to reduce the size of the U.S. Navy to three frigates and eight smaller vessels. Then, during the fight against the Barbary Pirates, the Navy expanded. Within six months of signing the treaty that ended the war, the Navy was again reduced to a small coastal defense force. As a result, it could not protect American merchant ships outside U.S. territorial waters. When the War of 1812 began, the U.S. merchant ship fleet was second in size to the British in terms of number of ships and tonnage.

To be fair, Jefferson's attempt at convincing the British to change their economic policies fell on deaf ears. There were many in the House of Commons and House of Lords who wanted the U.S. government to fail so the country could be "encouraged" to rejoin the empire.

Jefferson tried several different acts. One - The Embargo Act of 1807 - was a disaster. He pushed through the Non-Intercourse Act of 1809. Combined, they caused the U.S. economy to contract. Some say 10%, some say 20%, but it is clear that the economy went into a recession.

Madison, who was Jefferson's Secretary of State, inherited a foreign policy mess and an economy going in the wrong direction. He also faced a growing demand to get the British to change their policies, by force as necessary.

Out of the need for manufactured goods, Americans started to look inward. In this period, Fulton built a steam-powered boat that started passenger and cargo service from New York City to Albany. Eli Whitney began a process that developed interchangeable parts for firearms.

American entrepreneurs, many of whom were immigrants, began taking advantage of the abundance of natural resources. The trade restrictions began to awaken the country, and the United States became, after the War of 1812, one of the drivers of the Industrial Revolution.

Today, many historians, as does this author, believe that the War of 1812 was the U.S.' second war for independence. Out of it, European leaders, including the British, realized that the U.S. was here to stay and that we would aggressively defend our freedoms.

So, in the period between 1805 and 1814, there was much going on for the Laredos, Jacintos, and Smythes. It presented business and family challenges as well as those to their country. Hopefully this short overview of the period will help you enjoy *Prizes of Opportunity.*

Marc Liebman
December 2025

PRIZES of OPPORTUNITY

M

CHAPTER 1

DEATH OF A FORMER FRIEND

21 MILES WEST OF CAPE TRAFALGAR, SPAIN, MONDAY, OCTOBER 21ST, 1805

Everyone on board *H.M.S. Tonnant,* 74 guns, knew the battle with the French and Spanish Navies was coming. Lieutenant Jack Shelton slid out of his compartment well before dawn and ate in the small mess for the lieutenants and warrants just aft of the upper gun deck.

Shelton was *Tonnant's* Second Lieutenant, which was as high as the American believed he would ever rise in the Royal Navy. Shelton had served with Jaco Jacinto on the Continental Navy frigate *Scorpion,* 20 guns, before becoming the de facto chief of staff of the Continental Congress' Marine Committee. After the war, he joined the business that ultimately became U.S. Industries.

His position as what could be called American Shipping & Passenger Lines (AS&PL)'s chief operating officer came a cropper when the Jacintos discovered that Shelton was stealing from his employer. He was letting merchants inflate bills so he could skim off money to pay his gambling debts.

Out of work and wanting to escape fellow gamblers who wanted their money, Shelton joined the Royal Navy. The service offered him a commission, and he served on a series of third- and fourth-rated ships of the line. Royal Navy captains quickly learned that he was a superb seaman and an excellent officer who proved his mettle time and time again. As *Tonnant's* Second Lieutenant, Shelton was sure he would not be promoted to commander. However, the Royal Navy provided him with food, a place to live and a modicum of money.

Unfortunately, Shelton's poor skills as a card player now put him in debt to two of his fellow lieutenants whom he owed over £200. Unless *Tonnant* took a prize or two, Shelton wouldn't have the money to pay them back. While he walked down the starboard row of sixteen 18-pounders, he chatted briefly with each gun crew to encourage them. They were ready for whatever would come, as was Shelton. In the back of his mind, the fear of being charged as a debtor by his fellow officers and ultimately being sent to debtor's prison was greater than dying in battle.

Last night, Charles Tyler, *Tonnant's* captain informed his officers that Shelton would be in charge of the guns on the main deck during the anticipated action with the French and Spanish fleets. In the past, Shelton had been the officer in charge of either the lower- or upper-gun deck. His reasoning was that he wanted someone near the quarterdeck who could take charge if either he or the First Lieutenant fell in battle.

For days, the fleet under Admirals Nelson and Collingswood had been stalking the combined French and Spanish fleet. For the battle, Nelson divided his ships into two groups. In one, Nelson would lead 16 ships in *H.M.S. Victory,* 100 guns. In the column to Nelson's windward, Collingwood, in his flagship *H.M.S. Royal Sovereign,* 100 guns, would lead 11 ships. *Tonnant,* 80 guns, was the fourth ship in Collingwoods's line.

Tonnant was originally built for the French Navy in St. Nazaire and commissioned in 1790. It managed to survive a pounding at the Battle of the Nile in 1798 where it was captured and then sailed back to England where it was repaired and re-armed.

Below where Shelton was walking, *Tonnant* had thirty-two 32-pounders on its lower gun deck. On the main deck, where Shelton would be when the cannonballs started flying, there were thirty-two 12-pounders between the forecastle and the quarter deck.

Royal Navy shipwrights ringed the quarterdeck with fourteen 32-pounder carronades. These short-barreled cannon were lighter than the standard 32-pounder and were known as "smashers" for their ability to turn bulwarks into splinters. In the forecastle, there was another battery of four 32-pounder carronades.

The tones from three bells on the Forenoon Watch were dying away when Shelton came up on deck. Without a spyglass, he could see the ships of the French and Spanish fleets. The last sighting taken at the beginning of the Middle Watch (about midnight) showed *Tonnant* about 30 nautical miles west of Cape Trafalgar on Spain's southwest coast.

Light winds made it hard to keep in a neat line which allowed those on deck to have an unobstructed view of the top and mainsails of the Spanish and French ships several miles ahead. Nelson's plan was simple. Their flagships would punch through the French and Spanish lines disrupting their battle line. With the enemy ships forced to either wear downwind or tack into the wind or be raked from the bow or stern by a Royal Navy ship, the battle would dissolve into a series of ship versus ship actions.

Maneuver, as Shelton and his former captain Jaco Jacinto preached and practiced was out of the question. The Royal Navy captains would rely on weight of broadside and rapid fire to overwhelm the enemy. Or as Nelson said when he had all his captains on board *Victory* several days ago, "England cannot fault a captain who lays his ship alongside that of the enemy."

While this tactic had stood the Royal Navy well, Shelton thought it had caused unnecessary casualties. But he was not the captain, Tyler was.

Shelton looked at the enemy ships and then at the quarterdeck where the ship's First Lieutenant was waving at him. "Shelton, at five bells, the captain is going to order the ship to clear for action. Then, once that is done, he will order a ration of rum for the crew."

Nodding, Shelton smiled, "Aye, our men will be ready to give the Frenchies hell."

"Excellent, Mr. Shelton. The men like you and will follow you. With luck, we will take a fat French or Spanish ship as a prize. Should we both survive, I expect my chits that total a hundred and twelve pounds will be paid when we return to Portsmouth and collect our prize money."

Touching his forehead with the back of his hand, Shelton responded. "That you will." *It will be a miracle if we survive. If I do, I will cross that bridge when I come to it.*

THE SAME DAY, 11:08 A.M. LOCAL TIME

As *Tonnant* approached the battle, the Royal Navy and French and Spanish ships ahead of it were obscured in gray-white smoke. Their masts and topsails poked above the cloud, and from where Shelton stood in the ship of the line's forecastle, he could see occasional flashes of red-orange flame. All on board could hear the incessant crash of cannons being fired that drowned out the breaking of wood and the screams of those injured.

Shelton knew it was almost their turn. Captain Tyler had picked out the fourth ship in the French and Spanish line. By counting the gunports and looking at the ship, he figured it had at least 74 guns making it close to equal to *Tonnant. I wonder if this ship is one of* Tonnant's *sisters?*

So far, the ship flying the French Tricolor had not yet either fallen off the wind to the east, nor tacked to force a passing engagement. Shelton was looking at the French third-rated ship-of-the-line when the Third Lieutenant appeared next to him. "'Good God man, I wish the wind would pick up so we can get on with it!"

"Soon you'll wish you'd we'd waited longer." The young man that had just reported on board *Tonnant* two months ago, was not a card player, and Shelton could not remember his name.

When *Tonnant* was less than a mile from the French third rater, it began to wear ship toward the east. As a seaman, Shelton marveled at how well the ship's crew pulled the yards around and then began to shorten sail.

While he couldn't hear the commands on the quarterdeck, the change in the wind on his face told Shelton that Captain Tyler had made a course adjustment to come alongside the French ship.

A quartermaster's mate came up to where the officers were standing. "Mr. Shelton, captain plans to take the French third rater down the starboard side. Range should be inside two hundred yards. Captain says he believes name of the Frenchie is *Algeciras.*"

"Thank you, Spence." Turning to the Third Lieutenant, Shelton suddenly remembered his name. "Mr. Gibbons, I think it best you take your station on the upper gun deck."

The man left leaving Shelton alone, watching *Tonnant* close on *Algeciras.* The rate of closure told Shelton that if he had the carronades on the forecastle fire the moment they could, by the time the ships pulled even and Captain Tyler yelled to have the sails slackened to maintain *Tonnant's* position relative to *Algeciras,* they might have their guns reloaded and could get off a second ball before the French do.

Cupping his hands around his mouth, Shelton yelled as he walked aft, "Lads, fire as soon as your guns bear!"

He'd just reached the aft end of the main deck and turned to stride forward, trying not to look at the French Marines in the rigging of *Algeciras.*

They were there to fire down on gun crews on *Tonnant's* main deck with particular emphasis on officers in their blue wool coats.

Even though they were well within range of the French smoothbore muskets, Shelton believed that they were not the real danger. If he was killed, he was sure it would come from being speared by a splinter or gored by a piece of shrapnel. The chance of being hit by a musket ball at 200+ yards was purely bad luck.

Shelton stood in the center of the forecastle, directly behind the forwardmost 32-pounder carronade. He was about to yell, "Fire" when the gun captain yanked the lanyard. Flint scraping on steel sent a shower of sparks into the touch hole igniting the powder. Milliseconds later, the gun fired.

The noise was deafening even though Shelton had his hands around his ears. Moments later, the second carronade fired. As the smoke dissipated, he could see large gaps in the bulwarks on *Algeciras'* quarterdeck where bodies were writhing from wounds. Shelton watched as the French captain ordered his helmsman to turn the wheel to angle toward *Tonnant* and hopefully, collide with the enemy ship to start a boarding fight.

Shelton turned back to the guns thinking *Captain Tyler, if you had let me, I would have the bow carronades double shotted with canister and when the smoke cleared, there wouldn't be anyone standing on* Algeciras*' quarterdeck!*

Walking aft, Shelton yelled encouragement to the 12-pounder gun crews as musket balls from the French Marines' muskets and swivel guns hissed past him and smacked into the deck or the far bulwark. Thankfully, at least so far, he hadn't heard the sickening sucking sound of an ounce of lead entering a human being.

His well-drilled and disciplined crews went through the loading drill – sponge out, shove the powder bag down the barrel, tamp it home, then shove in the wad, followed by the 12-pound cast-iron ball. Once the gun was pulled back into battery, the gun captain poured fine gunpowder down into the touch hole, made sure the gun lock was in position, and looked around to make sure none of his crew were near the carriage.

Aiming was not necessary since the target was less than 200 yards away and roughly the same size and height as *Tonnant.* Then, the gun captain yanked on the lanyard, and approximately 3,000 pounds of cast iron and wood leaped back on the deck.

Beneath his feet, Shelton could feel the vibration and concussion as the 18- and 32-pounders beneath him fired. While he could not hear the thuds from the same size cannonballs from *Algeciras* his feet could feel their impact.

Shelton was almost at the end of his walk aft, when he saw an orange flash, and a fraction of a second later, he staggered as a three-pound chunk of cast iron slammed into his chest. He saw his blood soaking his royal blue coat and knew he was mortally wounded.

Sagging to his knees, the dying Jack Shelton's last conscious thought was the only good thing about dying is that I won't have to pay my gambling debts. Two seamen carried his body down to the orlop deck where he was placed with the other bodies.

ON BOARD GOTHENBORG, 5°W, 46° 30° N, FIRST WEEK OF NOVEMBER 1805

Like her three sisterships to *Malmo* in the Laredo-Fonseca Shipping Fleet, *Gothenborg* was built during the American Revolution in 1780. Having been at sea for the better part of 25 years, *Gothenborg's* owners were reducing the 1,150-ton merchant ship's workload. Instead of carrying 800 – 900 tons, *Gothenborg* now was loaded with less than 500 on voyages from the United States to Europe. On the return trips, her cargo holds were filled with temporary decks and 200 – 250 passengers who slept in hammocks along with enough food and beverages for eight weeks.

Fonseca-Laredo Shipping posted bills in Amsterdam and learned from passengers that the notices made their way to Rotterdam and Antwerp. The posters said that Fonseca-Laredo Shipping would carry passengers wanting to immigrate to the new United States for a modest fare of £5/person over 13 years of age, £3/those under 13.

First choice was given to those who had the cash. Those who did not, were told that upon arrival in New York, they would be interviewed by U.S. Industries and a determination would be made as to where they would work. Over a period of two years, their fares would be deducted from their pay.

When Eric Laredo, the company's agent in Amsterdam, proposed the idea in November 1781, the board approved it but was skeptical of Eric's estimate. By June 1782, one ship a month was leaving Amsterdam with 200 or more future immigrants, of whom U.S. Industries was hiring five to 10.

For those who didn't have the cash and who weren't hired, they were required to sign a note saying that they would pay U.S. Industries within three years. So far, only a dozen had defaulted.

Since the United States had declared its neutrality during every administration since Washington, the board chose not to send ships to French ports to take on passengers. French citizens were required to journey to Amsterdam or London. To get there, the Fonseca Laredo agents in Brest and Bordeaux helped them find transportation.

What began as one or two ships every two or three months had become one ship a month leaving Amsterdam and/or London with just passengers.

Gothenborg, along with its sister ships, *Malmo, Stockholm* and *Helsingborg* were making the trip westward loaded primarily with passengers. On this voyage, *Gothenborg* left Amsterdam between storms. Once it was in the North Sea, it proceeded so' west toward the English Channel before it emerged into the Celtic Sea, a week after leaving the Netherlands.

The winter storms and their cold rain that pummeled the ship forced its 26-year-old captain Jeremy Harris, to slacken sail to minimize losing a mast or worse. During the First Watch, *Gothenborg* emerged from the storms. The clearing skies let the first officer fix the ship's position.

When it was plotted on his chart, Harris believed they were approaching the point where they would not encounter any Royal Navy frigates stationed to stop and search ships headed into the English Channel or directly to France carrying what the British Parliament called "contraband." Other than munitions, the definition of contraband was left up to the ship's captain.

The other risk was that the Royal Navy needed people, and U.S.-flagged ships were prime targets. Fonseca-Laredo's policy was that if one of its ships were approached by a Royal Navy or French Navy ship and could not outrun it, they were to stop. Each captain was provided with a sheaf of documents on its cargo as well as the citizenship of its crew and passengers.

There was enough light streaming through his cabin windows to let Harris snuff out the lantern that was providing the light needed for him to write in his log. A single dull boom that Harris instantly recognized as a cannon being fired caused him to stop writing in his log. He blotted his last entry, corked his ink bottle, and headed to the door of his cabin. He pulled it open leaving a surprised seaman knocking on air.

On the quarterdeck, the officer pointed to the yellowed canvas sails of a frigate bearing down on *Gothenborg.* The puff of smoke from the fired cannon was dissipating as it drifted aft.

"We will slacken sail so we are making steerageway and maintain our course of so' by so' west." Harris felt chilled by the wind. "Mr. Sonderstrom, ensure our passengers have stowed their hammocks and ask them to gather on the berthing deck. There's no need for them to be chilled in this air. I will take the deck until you return."

Jan Sonderstrom, *Gothenborg's* First Officer nodded, "Aye, aye, sir. You have the deck." The 22-year-old went down the companionway to where the passengers were. He was born in Stockholm and had walked into Fonseca-Shipping's office in Stockholm in 1798 wanting a job. With the company's support, Sonderstrom became an American citizen in 1799.

With Sonderstrom gone, Harris ordered the sails let out to slow the merchant ship from about six knots to three. The actions allowed his annoyance at being stopped by the Royal Navy for no reason to dissipate. Ships going westbound weren't trying to run their blockade of France.

As *Gothenborg* sailed so' by so' west, *H.M.S. Success,* 32 guns, sailed on its leeward side which made it easier for the longboat to row the 100 yards that separated the two ships.

Harris elected to put on his dark blue tri-cornered hat that had the logo of Fonseca-Laredo Shipping embroidered on the corner. With the hat and the dark blue heavy woolen coat that kept him warm, the New Haven, Connecticut native who began his career at Fonseca-Laredo as a 12-year-old midshipman, waited by the mainmast for *Success'* captain to climb up the ladder.

Those passengers who elected to come on deck, were gently held back by members of *Gothenborg's* crew. Much of the formal and informal training given to Fonseca-Laredo Shipping's officers were about their ship's and crew's legal rights under Admiralty Law. In terms of dealing with captains of warships, they were taught to be polite and deferent, but not obsequious, when answering questions.

Once the Royal Navy captain was standing on the main deck, Harris strode forward and touched his right fore and index finger to his hat. "Welcome to the United States merchant ship *Gothenborg.* I am Jeremy Harris, the ship's captain. Pray tell, what can we do for the Royal Navy today?"

A slight nod and the man who looked as if he was in his 40s said, "My name is Scott and am commander of His Majesty's Frigate *Success.* You have been stopped so we can search *Gothenborg* for contraband and English citizens who have escaped doing their duty for King and country."

Harris smiled. If he didn't know better, the words Scott spoke were almost verbatim to those that Captain Smythe used in a role play. At the Fonseca-Laredo Marine Academy, those officers promoted to first officer and captain had to attend a one-week course. In it, one of the classes was on what to do when boarded by a ship from a foreign power. Given that the British and its Royal Navy were blockading French ports all over the world, the focus was on what the Royal Navy captains were authorized to do.

"Captain Scott, *Gothenborg* has approximately 50 tons of Dutch cheeses, smoked fish, and meat along with 246 passengers. Any moment, that number may grow by one or two. That means we have nothing that the British government would consider contraband."

"We'll see about that. Now, Captain Harris, show me your ship's papers. Meanwhile, my third lieutenant will inspect your hold. Any resistance will be dealt with harshly."

Harris spoke to his First Lieutenant, "Mr. Sonderstrom, please show the Royal Navy whatever they wish to see." Then he gestured with his hand toward his cabin. "Captain Scott, there is no need for threats."

Scott said nothing as he, along with a Marine armed with a musket and a fixed bayonet followed Harris to his office. On the table, he had laid out the ship's charter, its insurance certificate, cargo manifest, list of passengers by name and citizenship along with a separate sheet that had the names of his crew, their date and place of birth, their citizenship if not American, that was notarized by the State of New York. For those not born in the U.S., he also had certificates of U.S. citizenship.

Scott went to the crew muster list after quick looks of the other documents. His tone of voice was condescending. "Harris, you do realize that anyone born in one of Britain's American colonies before May 12th, 1784, the day the Treaty of Paris went into effect is considered by my government to be a British citizen. As such, I can induct said persons into the Royal Navy."

Clasping his hands behind his back to keep himself from punching the arrogant British officer. "Captain Scott, I would beg to differ with you on that point. We fought the British for eight years and four months to win our independence. Whether you choose the signing date of September 3rd, 1783, or May 12th, 1784, either way, everyone living in the former British colonies at time of the signing they became United States citizens. So, unless they renounce their citizenship, which I suspect precious few have done, England… meaning your country… " Meaning neither you nor England, "…has no jurisdiction nor claim on their persons."

"Are you always this impertinent with your superior officers?"

"Captain, under Admiralty Law, we are both captains of ships, and I submit that in tonnage and size, *Gothenborg* is larger than *Success.* And to answer your questions, I was taught by my parents and superiors to be polite and provide well-reasoned answers to questions. Doing so is not impertinent."

Holding up Gothenborg's muster sheet, Scott looked Harris in the eye, "You know under current British policy, I could take about half your crew."

"Captain, it would be a grave miscalculation should you attempt to do so."

"How so?"

Harris pointed to the door of his cabin. "Shall we step out onto the deck, and I'll show you why?"

There, Captain Scott saw the last few moments of the ceremony in which four of the eight sailors and two of the six Marines were being sworn in as U.S. citizens. The others, including his third lieutenant were standing along the port bulwark, near the hatch below which their longboat was tied to a ring on the hull.

While they were in the office, Sonderstrom had let *Gothenborg* close the gap so there were less than 50 yards between the frigate and merchant ship.

Irate, Scott started toward the six members of his crew, shouting, "Deserters, I'll have you hung, all of you!"

Harris put a hand on Scott's shoulder to restrain him. The Royal Navy captain whirled toward the American, "Take your hand off me, you impudent wretch. How dare you touch me! One word from me and I will turn *Gothenborg* into splinters and feed you all to the fish!"

"I doubt that, Captain Scott. Within a few moments, I will have witnessed statements from your former crew members stating that they asked to join Fonseca-Laredo Shipping, something my First Officer Mr. Sonderstrom is authorized to do. Second, before you can give the order to fire, you will be dead, and *Gothenborg* will be alongside *Success* which will be boarded by over one hundred heavily armed men who are willing to die to be independent from the former rulers and do not want to be British citizens. It will be ugly, but like during our revolution, we will prevail. Now, sir, I suggest you go back to *Success* and allow *Gothenborg* to continue westward."

"You rebel bastard! You're all a bunch of undisciplined rabble!!!"

"Maybe, Captain Scott, but you left out an important word. We are independent. And one last word, I suggest you not write a fictitious account, since if this should come to a case before a judge, we will have many statements from witnesses attesting to what really transpired. Now, please leave my ship so we can continue to the United States."

NEW YORK, THIRD WEEK OF NOVEMBER 1805

For late November in New York, the weather was pleasant. When Jaco walked crosstown to the offices of AS&PL from his house on West Avenue and Barclay Street, he actually worked up a sweat. Waiting for him in the office that Darren and he shared was a stack of English and French newspapers that just arrived the night before last on *Tradewinds.* Depending on whether the paper was printed in Paris or London, they were about two to three weeks old. Yet, the content provided valuable insight into what was happening in Europe.

The headline in *The Times of London* screamed Victory at Trafalgar Costs Lord Nelson His Life. In the *London Gazette,* the headline stated Royal Navy Destroys French and Spanish Navies. On the front page of *The Morning Post,* the headline was more subdued because the paper was favored by King George III. It proclaimed, Britannia Still Rules the Waves.

Of these, Jaco preferred reading the *London Gazette.* The writing was terse and factual, and the paper rarely had opinion pieces or analysis. Its editors preferred to leave that to the other papers and simply record the actions and decisions by His Majesty's Government.

After reading the account that stated that the Royal Navy captured 17 Spanish and French Navy ships, it said that 458 officers and men of the English fleet were killed, and another 1208 were wounded. Only the officers were listed on the casualty list, and his subconscious drew him to the casualty list.

He'd met several Royal Navy officers who served with Darren, as well as others on his travels so he began to run his finger down the names listed by ship. His finger stopped when he saw the name Jack Shelton, Lieutenant under *H.M.S. Tonnant.*

Jaco's eyes watered. As much as he was hurt and disappointed by Shelton's dishonesty, seeing his name as someone killed in action caused his heart to skip a beat. Jack and he and been through a lot on *Scorpion.* He looked out the window and into the blue sky and said what was on his mind, "God bless you, Jack. Your troubles are over, and may you rest in peace."

CHAPTER 2

CATCHING UP

MILTON, NY, SECOND WEEK OF JUNE 1806

Girard Fontaine stood back as he watched his grandson Hugo Radcliffe tie grape vines to the rope that went along each row. At 66, the work in the fields was getting harder and harder for Girard Fontaine. With his two sons – Didier, Yves, their wives, and children - there was enough labor to work what was now 200 acres of grapes and 125 of apples.

They also had another 50 acres on which they grew corn and vegetables, and a fenced field of 25 acres for their cows. All in all, the Fontaines were self-sufficient and kept to themselves.

The grapes produced a fruity red wine that sold well in New York and Boston. In the fall, they could sell all the apple cider they could make. The family was living comfortably, and profits enabled them to pay off the initial loans from the New York Bank of Commerce. Their only debt was for the additional land purchases, and the Fontaines had enough money deposited in the bank to cover their notes. The land itself, Girard Fontaine said, was where the real wealth was.

For the past three summers, Hugo, Sophie Fontaine's oldest son from her marriage to Edmund Radcliffe, had been spending his summers with his grandparents and uncles at the Fontaine family farm. This past winter,

Hugo announced to his mother that he wanted to learn how to be a winemaker and live with his grandparents to learn the trade. Only after her father promised to ensure that Hugo continued with his schooling did she relent to the move.

For Sophie, who often joked that she was dangerous to marry, this meant one of her children was on his way, so to speak. This left 12-year-old Alain, who wanted to go to sea on a Fonseca-Laredo ship, and eight-year-old Rose living at home with Sophie's third husband, Greg Struthers.

Sophie's first husband Louis was a young noble from nearby Libourne, France who was picked by her father due to his noble birth. However, when Louis supposedly was visiting his parents, Sophie learned that he was sleeping with another woman. Fortunately, the young man caught what the French called *la pest noire* or the black death on his way back to the Red Rapier winery and died alone in an inn. For him, this was probably a good thing because he would have had to face Girard Fontaine's wrath when he returned.

On the ship that carried the Fontaines to Martinique, Sophie met Edmund Radcliffe and the two fell in love. This time, Girard allowed his daughter to marry for love. When Edmund was killed in a battle during which the privateer *Rapier* was captured by *Osprey*, the frigate captained by Jaco Jacinto, Sophie was pregnant with Rose.

Sophie came to the United States to claim Edmund's estate and had a letter of introduction from Jaco to U.S. Industries. In Charleston, she met Greg Struthers along with Shoshana Jacinto, Reyna Laredo Jacinto and Emily Smythe Muir.

In the end, Sophie decided to move to New York and married Greg Struthers. Along the way, U.S. Publishing Company, owned by Shoshana and her lover Naomi Moreno, published her romance novels as well as three novels written by Edmund Radcliffe. Each of her books were now into their third printing, and she was writing a new one every year.

Sophie was at her writing desk when she heard Rose calling. She let Rose know that she was at her writing desk. "Where's Alain?"

Alain's job was to walk Rose back and forth to school. "In the kitchen pigging out on some apricot tarts Herr Hoffman made."

Turning in her chair, Rose took the invitation and sat on her mother's lap. Looking at the sheet on which there were only a few sentences written, "What is this book about?"

"A princess whose father insisted that she marry a young prince she did not love."

"In France?"

Sophie nodded.

"What happens?"

"The princess runs away, and her family casts her out because they believe she embarrassed them."

"Then what?"

"She comes to America and falls in love with a sea captain."

"Like my real father and you?"

"Yes."

"Does he die like my father?"

"No, not in this story. They live happily after."

"Good."

Satisfied, Rose slid offer her mother's lap. "I'm going to get one of those tarts and some chocolate milk."

NEW YORK CITY, SECOND WEEK OF SEPTEMBER 1806

Every year, the leaders of each business that make up U.S. Industries meet to review the past year and to plan for the coming year. The tradition started when they were all living in Charleston, and the meeting would start the day after Rosh Hashanah and would end the day before Yom Kippur.

The event served three other purposes besides business. One, it allowed the families to socialize. Or as Perla Jacinto and Adah Laredo would often say, their nests were full.

Second, the dinners, which included spouses and children, helped strengthen the bond amongst the founding families as well as outsiders such Darren and Emily Smythe, Rafer Muir, and Greg Struthers, all of whom were now members of the inner circle was strengthened. And third, it enabled the extended family to celebrate the Jewish High Holidays together.

When the annual planning sessions were held in Charleston, they would alternate between Max and Ada's house, or the one owned by Javier and Perla Jacinto. Now, with U.S. Industries headquartered in New York, the meeting was held in one of the large private meeting rooms in the New York Hotel.

To get to the first floor of the hotel which had been expanded from the original 50 to 100 rooms, one walked into the main doors and then up 10 steps to the lobby. The hotel now had two dining rooms, one ballroom, and two bars and smaller meeting rooms which could be booked for special events.

Run by Ester Baez, one of the late Miriam Bildesheim's granddaughters, the Hotel New York was a perfect place. Those from Charleston could stay at the hotel during the week and enjoy catered lunches and dinners.

Shoshana was following her brother Jaco who was holding hands with his wife, Reyna, as they climbed the steps. She marveled that now, after 23 years of marriage, you'd have thought the two of them had just started dating. They were just as in love with each other as when they were teenagers.

Naomi Moreno, Shoshana's lover and partner, would come later in the day to talk about U.S. Publishing. Only what were unofficially called principals – Javier Jacinto (Chairman of the Board); Max Laredo (Chief Executive Officer); Amos Laredo (New Technologies and Investments); Laura Fonseca Laredo (Fonseca-Laredo Shipping), Reyna (American Medical & Industrial Products) and Jaco Jacinto (Managing Director, American Shipping & Passenger Lines); Darren Smythe (Managing Director, American Shipping & Passenger Lines); Greg Struthers (U.S. Industries Financial Services) and Emily Muir Smythe (Chief Financial Officer); Gento Jacinto (U.S. Industries Imports and Exports); and Shoshana Jacinto (General Counsel and U.S. Publishing) – were allowed in all the meetings.

Others such as Nathan Jacinto, (U.S. Wine Imports), Naomi Moreno, (President, U.S. Publishing), Rafer Muir, (President, U.S. Bank of Commerce), Ester Baez, (General Manager, New York Hotel), and Luke Giffords, (President, Bank of South Carolina) would come in later in the afternoon.

Once they were all seated, Darren held up his hand, "Mr. Laredo, before we begin, I have an important announcement to make. It will take just a minute and will reduce the workload of the wives of many of us in here."

Reyna jabbed her husband in the ribs as if to ask, "What is he going to say?"

Jaco squeezed her hand as if to say, wait.

"This past Saturday evening, I managed to find the courage to ask Miss Marijke Kopf, whom many of you know as U.S. Publishing's Editor, to marry me. Much to my relief, she said yes. Wedding date to follow, but hopefully by the end of the year."

Grinning, Javier said, "Captain, you are hereby ordered to bring Marijke to every dinner and social function this week."

"Aye, aye, sir. I gather Miss Kopf does not have a choice in this matter."

"You, sir, don't have a choice but to insist on bringing Marijke. Your mission is to convince her."

Renya leaned over as they were all laughing. "Why didn't you tell me he was getting ready to propose?"

"Because I didn't know. I knew he was getting close, but you know Darren, some things he likes to keep to himself."

"She's a wonderful woman."

American Shipping & Passenger Lines went first. Jaco went through the required topics, profits for this year, forecast for next, and what he and Darren saw as "storms at sea," i.e., challenges that would affect profitability. The most difficult one to deal with was the Royal Navy and the British policy of impressment. That topic would be discussed later in the week, along with expanding regularly scheduled passenger service to other European ports.

The other big news was that they were ordering three more ships for the packet service to bring the total to eight. This was being done to accommodate their recently renewed postal contract to service New Orleans, which was approximately 1,300 nautical miles and five to six days around the tip of Florida from Savannah.

The new packets were 20% larger than the ones in service. Ultimately, the new builds would replace the ones now in service. This brought Laura whose comments included stating that the ships returning from Europe are full, either with passengers wanting to escape the war in Europe or cargo. And, that cotton was becoming a bigger export item from both Charleston and Savannah. Fonseca-Laredo was building new ships to replace those that were old and tired and now had 20 in its fleet. According to Laura's plan, the firm would have 30 by 1812.

Gento briefly covered the increase of cotton exports but also of manufactured goods from New York, Boston, and Philadelphia that were now a larger portion of what was carried by their ships. The cargo mix going eastbound was now about 20% cotton, 20% manufactured goods, 20% wood, and 40% food. Returning westbound from England, the ships were filled 70% manufactured goods, mostly cloth, and 30% immigrants. From Amsterdam, it was mostly immigrants, and from France, 60% wines, 20% manufactured goods, mostly fabric, and 20% immigrants who were often smuggled aboard.

Gento noted, "Thanks to Cousin Nathan and Philippe, we can sell all the wines we can import at a healthy forty percent profit. The expensive wines we bottle here, make us fifty!"

He announced that their agent list in Europe now included men in Algiers, Genoa, Marseilles, Naples, Rabat, and Tunis and Venice in the Mediterranean. In Europe, U.S. Industries and its subsidiaries had offices and representatives in, Amsterdam, Antwerp, Brest, Bristol, Bordeaux, London, Stockholm, and Malmö. In the Caribbean, they had agents in St. Ignatius, Havana, Willemstad, Grenada, Martinique, and Nassau. They had more calls for cargoes of rum, molasses, sugar, coffee beans, and cacao to Europe than they had hulls, something Laura was working on, ships they could charter or acquire. However, chartering ships was more expensive and they do not have as much control over the crews. She is looking at buying used ships, but so far, what she has found belonged in a breaker's yard.

Gento concluded by saying, "We're losing seamen to impressment, and that must stop."

Javier held up his hand. "Save that thought. We – Congressmen from states that have many ship owners – have made that very clear to both Secretary of State Madison and President Jefferson. Max and I have some ideas that may solve that problem that we will share later in the week."

By the end of the day, the financial performance had been reviewed. U.S. Industries was healthy. Around five, the meeting broke up and adjourned to another larger room where dinner would be served.

It was in these private settings amongst friends and family members that Shoshana and Naomi, along with Nathan and his lover and partner Phillipe Dubisson, were allowed to hold hands. Kissing was forbidden, but as the years have gone on, the restrictions on gestures of affection had lessened.

The fear was always adverse publicity, given that both Shoshana and Nathan were members of one of the wealthiest and most powerful families in New York. Legally speaking as Shoshana was fond of saying, what Nathan and Philippe, and Naomi and I do in private as couples was our business. If it was in public, then it was U.S. Industries' business.

In 1797, New York State modified its sodomy laws in that if two men were convicted of buggery, the death penalty no longer applied. She suspected that Nathan was not the only male homosexual amongst the employees of U.S. Industries just as Naomi and she were not the only lesbians. Philippe, although most considered him part of U.S. Industries really ran Dubisson Wine Imports of New York. This was the company that paid his salary and commissions and was 40% owned by U.S. Industries.

NEW YORK CITY, TWO DAYS LATER

Javier waited until the principals had taken their seats, which were not assigned. As the event went on, he noticed that no one other than Max Laredo and he were sitting in the same place as they were on the first day.

"The day before I came to New York, Jacob Crowningshield, the Democratic Republican who chairs the Manufactures and Commerce Committee, and I, as the co-chair, met with Secretary Madison and President Jefferson to discuss the British government's policy that allows the Royal Navy to stop our ships and impress seamen who they claim are British citizens. They assured me that our ambassador, James Monroe, has met several times with the British Foreign Secretary James Fox. To be blunt, Fox was polite but uncooperative suggesting we have several choices. One is to continue to pressure Jefferson to use the U.S. Navy to convoy ships going to and from Europe."

"Choice two is to convoy them ourselves. Remember, Naval Escort Services owns the frigates *Osprey* and *Kestrel* and six corvettes. Currently, they are still based in Naples and escorting ships to ports in Italy, Spain, and Tunis."

"Or we can do nothing and continue as we are and hope the British win the war and stop impressing our men."

There was silence around the table until Jaco spoke, "Father, I think convoys are our only option. Armed vessels accompanying our merchant ships or a group of merchant ships will give a Royal Navy frigate pause."

Laura Fonseca Laredo leaned across the table. "Jaco, you used the word vessels. Are you suggesting more than one per convoy?"

"Yes. It depends on the size of the convoy. The minimum number would be two which we would have to have built unless we can convince Jefferson to let us borrow the frigates the Navy has in ordinary for a fee. That would save us time to build new frigates."

"The cost of a longer voyage will raise what we have to charge."

"Aye, Laura, it will. However, a message must be sent to the British Parliament not to trifle with the United States. Impressment is kidnapping, and kidnapping is against our laws, against British law, and against Admiralty Law. It also sends a message to our crews that we will protect them."

"Jaco, it could also create an incident if two captains want to show who has the bigger balls, as in cannon balls."

There were smiles around the table. None of the women were offended, and some of the men laughed.

"Yes, it could. However, the best way to deal with a bully is to punch him in the face or show you are ready to fight. It will be hard for a Royal Navy captain to return to port with a battle-damaged ship. When asked, assuming he doesn't lie, he must say that he got in a fight with a neutral American ship. To do this, we would need bigger frigates because *Kestrel* and *Osprey* only carry six weeks of food and the merchant vessels often need eight weeks to make the transit. Re-victualling them in England or France could be a problem. I don't think we can resupply our ships in either France or England."

"Actually, we can…." Shoshana answered before Jaco could continue. "… Under Admiralty Law, warships from neutral nations stopping in a port of one of the belligerents can stay for a short period to take on food and water. If you need to take on powder and shot, it becomes much more difficult. This is what we are doing with the Naval Escort Ships when they stop in Gibraltar, to wait for a convoy, is it not?"

"Yes, it is usually only two or three days. Shoshana, define a short period?"

"A week, no more. We can make a legal case for the resupply, and then the frigate leaves when the merchant ships in the convoy depart. This is allowed under the Admiralty Law concept of maritime neutrality."

"A week is plenty of time, especially if we know about when the ship will arrive in port, so we can alert the agent. However, we will have to teach our captains how to deal with the Royal Navy."

Max Laredo, who had been silent for most of this discussion, spoke, "Jaco, I think Darren and you should, assuming we decide on this convoy policy, take command of *Kestrel* and *Osprey* and test the resolve of the Royal Navy. Then, we can instruct your replacements."

The two Navy captains looked at each other. They had just heard an order that they would have to execute, assuming the U.S. Industries board decides to begin convoying ships across the Atlantic.

Javier agreed to sound out the Secretary of the Navy as to when *Kestrel, Osprey,* and the six corvettes would be released by the U.S. Navy and returned to Naval Escort Services.

Whether or not AS&PL should begin service to other European ports besides London and if so, which ones was the next agenda topic?

Darren, with Jaco's support, suggested that they start with Amsterdam. It was only about 24 hours from London so the ship could stop, unload in London, go to Amsterdam, unload any passengers and cargo and take on whatever cargo and passengers and return to London before sailing back to the U.S.

On the westbound leg, Max and Javier wanted to know what were AS&PL's responsibilities for the passengers when the ship stops in London for three days? Confining them to the ship was unreasonable.

Or does the ship sail directly to the United States from Amsterdam? That adds time to the London – New York passengers.

Or do they have a ship that shuttles between Amsterdam and London so that it arrives the day before departure to New York?

Shoshana was tasked to find out what the legal issues were of bring citizens from another country into England for a few days. Already, everyone at the table didn't want to assume the risk of keeping track of them disappearing into the English countryside. Gento was told to have his agent find out what it would cost to book hotels in London.

Once they knew the answers, then they could begin making decisions. Until then, people wanting to emigrate from Europe had to ride one of the merchant ships from departing from a port where we have agents.

BORDEAUX, SECOND WEEK OF OCTOBER 1806

Ness II, the younger of the two, a two-masted schooner, made the New York to Gibraltar trip in 16 days. This was two days longer than normal because it slowed for two days to ride out a storm. In Gibraltar, Nathan Jacinto and Phillipe Dubisson stayed on board while the ship was re-supplied.

Five days after leaving Gibraltar, *Ness II* docked five days later in Bordeaux. Either *Ness I* or *Ness II* would return in the first week in November to pick-up and bring the two men back to New York.

Although Philippe brought letters from his sister Angelique who had married Didier Fontaine and was living in Milton, NY, Hugo Dubisson peppered his oldest son with questions about his daughter and grandchildren that now numbered four.

The big difference on this visit from the last was that there were now two newcomers at the Dubisson dinner table. One was Marie-Louise Morin, the daughter of a dressmaker in Bordeaux who was now Sebastien's wife and very pregnant. She was due according to her husband, any day.

The other woman was Anne Remy who had just married Phillipe's youngest brother, Henri. Her father was a candle maker.

Hugo Dubisson went through all the appointments he had arranged for Nathan and Philippe. The order was now two thousand barrels of wines from different wineries. Some Hugo Dubisson and his sons would age, others would be aged at the winery where the grapes were grown, and the aging process would be monitored by Henri and Sebastien.

Barrels earmarked for Dubisson et Fils were marked and numbered with paint provided by Hugo and his sons. Each barrel would have its own log so they could monitor the progress of the wine.

The wineries would get one-third of their payment when they signed the contract with Dubisson and were guaranteed by U.S. Industries Import and Exports. Then, when the wine is ready for shipment, U.S. Industries would pay Dubisson, who paid the wineries. Since the first year they began this venture, the number of barrels has increased, as has the number of wineries participating.

Neither woman had been more than 50 kilometers (30 miles) from Bordeaux, and they were interested in what life in the United States was like, particularly as Marie-Louise said, pointing with her index and little finger at Nathan and Philippe, "pour deux sodomites."

Nathan was the first to speak. "We have our friends who we see at parties and other social events. For the most part, Philippe and I are not bothered, but we keep to ourselves."

Marie-Louise nodded as she spoke in a serious tone. "Napoleon maintained the French Revolutionary governments policy that began in 1791 through which being Sappho or a sodomite was no longer a crime. Now, they are everywhere, and you don't have to hide. I think that is a good thing."

Phillippe used his only arm to caress the cheek of his lover. "See, there are some good things in France." The other had been ripped off by a piece of shrapnel in the Battle of Zurich in 1799. He managed to survive the fever and infection and return to Bordeaux from where he and Sebastien had been kidnapped by the Republican Army. Turning back to Marie-Louise, he asked, "Why are you telling me this?"

"Because when you meet my mother Julienne, and my older sister Jeannette, you will know. They are both Sappho and they will never bear sons Republican soldiers can draft for their stupid war. I was ten when I watched them beat my father and rape my mother and older sister Jeannette. They were raped after they tried to stop Republican soldiers from drafting my two older brothers. They will not touch a man, ever again."

Mary-Louise took Philippe's hand and put her thumb and index finger on the gold ring. "My mother Julienne, sister Jeannette, and I applaud you for doing this. In my eyes and those of my mother and sister, you are married, just like Sebastien and me."

Taking her husband's hand, Marie-Louise held it up, "My mother and sister each have lovers who share their beds now that my father is gone, but no priest will marry them or even bless their relationship as what I heard a rabbi did for Nathan and you."

"When did your father die?"

"Weeks after he was beaten." Mary-Louise paused for a few second while she remembered the pain her father experienced in his last few days. "To make money, my mother and my sisters took over my father's business and make clothing for men and women."

Nathan smiled and looked at Philippe. Neither said anything. Mary-Louise looked at Nathan and nodded. "You like wearing dresses, no?"

The slight nod answered her question. "Tomorrow morning, I will bring dresses from my mother's shop along with some things you can wear to make you much more feminine. You can wear them in this house or anywhere in Bordeaux you choose. Before you set out to visit the wineries, we will take your measurements, and while you are out in the countryside, we will make you a wardrobe that will make you the envy of New York."

NEW YORK CITY, FIRST SUNDAY IN DECEMBER 1807

The venue Darren and Marijke chose for their wedding was the Middle Collegiate Church on Nassau Street. Built in 1731, the stone church and its attendant schoolhouse were used by the British as a prison and hospital during the American Revolution.

After the war, the Reformed Dutch Church which was formed by Dutch immigrants in 1624 took the building back. Among the original group of settlers that came from Rotterdam were the van Rensselaers from whom Marijke van Rensselaer Kopf was descended.

Both Darren and Marijke wanted a low-key wedding, but the guest list – the leadership of U.S. Industries - and the Rennsalaers connection to the colony and now state of New York's history made it difficult to keep the event out of the society pages of New York's newspapers. Shoshana, through her relationship with the publishers of *The New York Evening Post* and the *New York Gazette,* gave the editors facts they could use as opposed to rumors and gossip. The editors promised that any coverage of the wedding that mentioned Darren's service in the Royal Navy would note that he renounced his British citizenship and was now a citizen of the United States of America.

Before the ceremony, Darren went into a small room off the sanctuary. In this moment of privacy, he looked through the glass at the clear blue sky and told Melody that finally, 10 years after her passing, he is doing what she told him to do with her last breath.

In the ceremony, Jaco acted as the best man while Marijke's oldest son, 23-year-old-Kurt escorted his mother down the aisle. After the short Sunday afternoon ceremony, the wedding party and their guests adjourned to the New York Hotel where they had a celebratory dinner.

CHAPTER 3

STUPID DEFENSE POLICY

WASHINGTON, D.C., SECOND WEEK OF JANUARY 1807

Outside the president's office in the new White House, the weather was cold, even for those who lived in the new U.S. capital. In the U.S. Constitution, Article I, Section Eight states that a capital "District (not exceeding ten miles square) as may, by cession of particular states, and the acceptance of Congress, become the seat of the government of the United States.

The question facing members of the First U.S. Congress was where to locate the nation's capital. Since 1776 and the Declaration of Independence, eight cities – Annapolis, MD; Baltimore, MD; Lancaster, PA; New York, NY; Philadelphia PA; Trenton, NJ; and Yorktown, VA – had served as the country's capital.

Where the nation's capital would be located was the matter of serious debate in both houses of Congress. The two sites that were most favored were near the town of Wrightsville (now Columbia, PA) on the Susquehanna River. The other site was on the Potomac River where Georgetown, MD is today.

The decision was a compromise. First, the Assumption Act of 1790 was passed, which authorized the new Federal Government to assume all the debts of the Continental Congress and the 13 original colonies that became states after the Revolutionary War. This agreement, brokered by Alexander Hamilton, Thomas Jefferson, and James Madison, enabled the 1st U.S. Congress to pass The Residence Act of July 16th, 1790, to establish a capital district ten miles square.

Washington named the capital area the District of Columbia, and the 6th U.S. Congress was the first to hold sessions in the yet-to-be-completed Capitol Building in November 1800. President John and his wife Abigail Adams were the first residents of the White House in 1800, and Jefferson moved into the White House when he took office in March 1801.

Thomas Jefferson wrote in his weather log after his first reading of the day which was just after sunrise that the wind was out of the east, the skies were clear and the thermometer said it was 34° Fahrenheit. He was blotting the entry when his secretary knocked on the door.

"Mr. President, Mr. Smith, the Secretary of the Navy, is here for his appointment."

Robert Smith needed no introduction. He had been Jefferson's pick for the position because when he was appointed, he was leading an Admiralty Law practice for a law firm in Baltimore.

The two men greeted each other warmly, and Jefferson pointed to the other seat in front of the fireplace and its roaring fire. Coffee was offered and accepted. Besides milk, lumps of raw, light brown Jamaican sugar were dropped in by a pair of silver tongs.

"Mr. Smith, are the Barbary states living up to our treaty?"

"Yes, Mr. President. The last dispatch from Commodore Preble is that there have been no violations."

"Excellent, Mr. Smith, then let's bring all our men and ships home."

"Mr. President, it behooves us to leave a small squadron in the Mediterranean to ensure the corsairs controlled by the Barbary States on the northern coast of Africa stay at home and don't threaten our ships."

"Mr. Smith, they have proven their worth. Once all of them are home, put the men on half pay and the ships in ordinary. We no longer need a large Navy. In my new budget, the Navy will have funds for three large frigates and eight smaller vessels for coastal defense."

Smith put his cup of coffee down on the saucer to give him time to think. "Sir, I think this is an unwise decision. There will be no navy to protect ships owned by merchants whose ships ply the Mediterranean and sail to Europe. I can tell you with certainty that within a year or two, we will need the Navy again."

"Mr. Smith, my belief is that countries with large standing armies and navies tend to use them to create mischief. By not having a large army or navy, we will not be tempted to involve ourselves in a foreign war. Should we be threatened or worse, attacked, then I will reconsider. You can inform Naval Escort Services that they can keep the frigates and still fly the U.S. flag. Merchant ship owners who wish to continue to use their services can continue to do so. In the meantime, I want Commodore Preble's squadron back in the United States no later than May 1st of this year. Please inform me when the letter is sent, and I will so inform the Congress."

NEW YORK, SECOND WEEK OF JANUARY 1807

The documents that just arrived from Washington were laid out on the small table in Gento Javier's office. Most of the time, it was used for meetings with only a few people, but today, in front of Gento were bills of lading for shipments from 1805 and 1806.

He was trying to determine what goods he could import from England and which ones would lead to fines under the Non-Importation Act passed on April 16th, 1806, by the 9th U.S. Congress. The legislation was an attempt by President Jefferson to put pressure on Great Britain, the U.S.'s largest trading partner, and the U.S. was England's biggest.

The list of goods not to be imported from England was long, many of which were carried on Fonseca-Laredo ships contracted to U.S. Industries Import & Exports. Banned under the Non-Importation Act were: any items made from leather, silk, hemp, flax or that contained tin or brass; woolen cloth for which his customer would charge more than £5/square yard; glassware of all types; silver articles, both solid and plated; paper; nails and spikes; hats; beer and ales; paintings and prints of engravings; and the one item he wondered why it was added, playing cards.

The penalty for importing any of these items was a fine of three times their retail value. For Gento, U.S. Industries could manufacture nails and spikes at the plant that made axes, hatches, saws, and medical instruments. Beer and ale were plentiful in the U.S., and U.S. Industries wasn't involved in brewing either.

Shoshana had found paper mills in New York and Massachusetts that used the latest processes to make paper. Again, not a concern.

There were enough glass blowers and windowpane makers in the U.S. so they weren't a concern. Products made from leather, silk, hemp, flax, tin or brass; woolen cloth; glassware; and those made with silver articles were very troubling. Together, they accounted for more than 50% of the value of the cargoes carried by Fonseca-Laredo Shipping for U.S. Industries Imports and Exports from England.

Since the bill was enacted, the value of the cargo from England to ports on the East Coast had dropped by about 30%. Dropped value translated into less revenue, which further translated into less profit and, for him, the size of his bonus.

When he saw his father at the annual U.S. Industries planning conference in September 1806, his father said that he voted against the bill, but Democratic-Republicans passed it over the stringent objections of not only the Federalists, but also those of Albert Gallatin, Jefferson's Secretary of the Treasury.

In a moment of dark humor, Javier Jacinto said to his oldest son, "Jefferson and his policies are simply economic crosses we must bear. My fervent hope is that he does not destroy us."

When the Non-Importation Act was passed, Gento sent out letters to U.S. Industries agents in Algiers, Bordeaux, Brest, Amsterdam, Genoa, Naples, Stockholm, and Venice, looking for potential suppliers who could replace those in England. At one end of the table were samples of glass from their agent in Venice, and in front of him were the prices. They were better than what they were getting from England and cheaper, even with the added shipping time and distance.

Other samples of leather goods from Italy matched what they had been buying in England. Again, the prices were better. The only two items he could not replace were woolen cloth and flatware, platters and pitchers made from silver.

His next step was to portion the orders to suppliers to minimize the delivery risk. Once that was done, he planned to turn over his notes to one of his subordinates to write out the orders which would be delivered to Gibraltar by a Naval Escort Services schooner and then taken to each of the ports by either merchant ship or one of the escorting NES corvettes.

His next task was to find an alternative to English woolen fabric. Where he could find sufficient quantities in Europe, which was being torn apart by war, he did not know.

WASHINGTON, D.C., THIRD WEEK OF JANUARY 1807

Upon learning of Jefferson's order to bring Preble's squadron home from the Mediterranean and then disband it, Javier Jacinto requested a meeting with the Secretary of the Navy, Robert Smith. As the ranking minority member of the Commerce and Manufactures, he informed Jacob Crowninshield, the committee's Democratic-Republican chairman, who endorsed the meeting.

Crowningshield was from Salem, Massachusetts, and his family were also ship owners. He approved of the two topics Javier wanted to discuss with Smith but declined the invitation to go out in the cold air since he was already suffering from tuberculosis.

Robert Smith offered Javier Jacinto a drink of Scotch, which Javier accepted. "I gather this is not on the list of items we cannot import!"

Smiling, Smith responded, "That is correct. If it were banned, I fear there would be rebellion. As good as the whiskey that comes from Kentucky and Tennessee is, it doesn't hold a candle to a good Scotch."

Javier held up his glass, "On that, I wholeheartedly agree." He took a sip to give him time to frame what he was going to say next.

"So, Mr. Jacinto, I suspect I know why you are here and so let me save you some words. Mr. Jefferson is not going to rescind his order to reduce the Navy. We should be happy that he will allow the Navy to keep some frigates. I am pushing for eight, the President wants only three so I suspect we will meet in the middle. However, he did agree to allow me to rotate crews so that we can retain a cadre of trained officers and men so if we should need to expand the Navy rapidly, we can. Ships, on the other hand, don't grow like weeds, so having some sort of reserve fleet is my problem."

Looking at the man, he'd worked on and off with for years and who was a highly respected member of the House of Representatives, Smith knew where Javier Jacinto's interest lay. The Congressman from South Carolina wanted a strong Navy so it could prevent the Royal Navy from stopping U.S. merchant ships on the high seas and impressing sailors. A strong Navy would deter any European power from attacking the United States or from forcing it to pick sides in the ongoing war in Europe.

While Smith didn't know the exact number of sailors kidnapped, he was sure Jacinto did because he was well-connected amongst the ship owners up and down the U.S. Atlantic Coast. The last number he had seen was that it had passed 10,000 since the British government authorized this policy.

"Mr. Smith, you do know that not having a Navy will embolden the British and its Royal Navy."

Nodding, the Secretary of the Navy, replied. "I do. But may I remind you that President Jefferson is adamant so let us not argue about something that cannot be changed."

Another sip of the Scotch. Javier enjoyed the smoky aroma that filled his nostrils as the alcoholic beverage made its way to his stomach.

"The second reason is a request that I hope you can grant, given the President's desires to reduce the Navy."

Smith didn't say anything to let Javier Jacinto continue. "As you know, Naval Escort Services provided a squadron of two small frigates and eight corvettes. While Naval Escort Services paid for them to be built and equipped, the President agreed to allow them to sail under the United States flag as part of the Mediterranean squadron. As part of the Navy, the government was kind enough to pay for their maintenance, supplies, and any repairs. Those ships are still in the Mediterranean, and Naval Escort Services would like them returned. Once the government had paid off the crews, Naval Escort Services will offer the men new contracts and recruit men to fill out the crews."

"Pray tell, what do you plan to do with the ships?"

"Naval Escort Services will provide escorts to ships sailing to Europe just as we did before. Under Admiralty Law, ship owners are allowed to defend their property, and by providing armed escorts, we are doing just that."

"Under whose flag will they sail?"

"The United States, of course. We would like to sail under our Navy's ensign with written orders to protect the ships they are escorting, not to capture warships or merchant ships of other nations unless threatened or attacked."

"Or if they are operating under a letter of marque."

"Mr. Smith, as you know, to be a legal letter of marque, two conditions must be met. One is that the issuing nation must have declared war against another nation, which will be named in the letter. Two, ships operating under a letter of marque cannot capture any ship under any flag unless it is either in or departing or entering the port of a belligerent nation." The entering, departing, and even en route, was open to interpretation. That, Javier said, would only come if the U.S. entered the war in Europe or was attacked.

Smith crossed his arms and looked at the ceiling. "I see no reason why the ships should not be returned to Naval Escort Services when they arrive home. I will grant this request in writing under one condition."

A nod from Javier Jacinto told the Secretary of the Navy to continue. "My condition is that in time of war, the ships will return forthwith to the

U.S. Navy. At which time, the Navy will decide who shall remain on board, who shall be their officers, and how the ships will be employed."

"Understood, but since you have read Commodore Preble's and before him, Commodore Decatur's reports, both men were very complimentary of the quality of Naval Escort Services' crews and their ability to operate independently to accomplish whatever mission they were assigned. If it were not for the small Naval Escort Services squadron, the Navy would have been spread much thinner than it was."

"Yes, I am aware of the reports. However, I must warn you that President Jefferson and I will take a very dim view of the captain of any of your ships who creates an incident. You shall have my letter documenting our agreement delivered to your office in the morning."

Javier held up his glass of Scotch, tilted it toward Smith. "Thank you, Mr. Secretary."

ST. GEORGES CHANNEL, FOURTH WEEK OF FEBRUARY 1807

When the lookouts spotted the frigate two points astern, port side, *Sirius'* course was nor' by east. The ship, according to its lookouts, was three miles behind the merchant ship. By its location and the rigging, it was assumed to be a Royal Navy frigate. The steady west so' west wind was coming over the port aft quarter, pushing the 1,500-ton merchant ship along at a spritely seven knots.

The ringing of eight bells told Captain Caleb O'Brien that the Forenoon Watch was coming on duty. He would come on deck when he finished the entry in his log stating the midnight sighting showed them to be 52° N, 70° 30' W or in layman's terms two days from their destination - Liverpool, England. After looking at the frigate which was under full sail. Its royals, along with its top gallants, top and mainsails were all sheeted home. O'Brien concluded that *Sirius* and the Royal Navy frigate were sailing on roughly the same course.

Sirius was corkscrewing gently in the three-foot seas under partly cloudy skies. O'Brien looked at the setting of his ship's sails and decided that setting its royals wouldn't give them enough additional speed to justify the strain on the masts and rigging. Another quick look at the yellowed canvas sails of the Royal Navy frigate, and Caleb O'Brien left the quarterdeck to make his morning inspection of the ship's three holds.

He was starting down the forward companionway when he heard a cannon fire. O'Brien, who had served on the Continental Navy frigate *Trumbull,* 30 guns, first as a midshipman and then as its Second Lieutenant, knew the sound of a naval gun when he heard one.

Forcing himself to remain calm, the 30-year-old O'Brien climbed up the companionway just in time to see smoke billow out from a gun on the port bow of the Royal Navy frigate. A second later, he heard the report and saw the splash of the ball about 300 yards astern of *Sirius.*

Running from the frigate was not an option. The two shots were signals for him to slow down so the frigate could come alongside. Other than small arms, *Sirius,* like all the other Fonseca-Laredo ships, was not armed. Company policy was when approached by a warship from any navy, stop, be courteous, but be adamant that the ship is not carrying contraband of any sort and is flying under the flag of a neutral nation.

O'Brien already knew what words he would write in his official log and report. He'd been stopped in 1805 and had eight men taken by the Royal Navy. As a first-generation Irishman, he had little love for the country that occupied his native land.

"Bo'sun, slacken all sails and slow us down to about three knots to make it easy for the Royal Navy to catch *Sirius.* When you are done, prepare a warm welcome for the Royal Navy. Quartermaster, hold steady on our course of nor' by east."

The warm welcome was two rows of seamen lining the gap in the bulwark on the port side of the main deck where the Royal Navy officers would board. His bo'sun would offer a sling chair if the officer was unwilling to climb the ladder made from blocks of wood and cast-iron grab bars screwed into the ship's hull with screws.

Once he was confident that his orders were being carried out, O'Brien returned to his cabin and took the ship's papers – manifest, certificate of ownership, insurance certificate and a list of each crew member containing their full name, place and date of birth. None of his crew were born in the United Kingdom of England, Ireland, Scotland and Wales as the country liked to be known. Of the 140 officers and men, about a third were born in European countries and the rest in the United States.

"*Sirius,* standby to be boarded and inspected."

O'Brien thought it interesting that the speaker on the Royal Navy frigate did not use the name of his ship. "Aye, have your boat come alongside our port ladder. Will the officer need assistance?"

He didn't need to hear what the officer with the speaking trumpet said to one of his officers. O'Brien could tell by his body language.

The Royal Navy frigate's boat had an officer in a blue uniform coat with two gold epaulettes telling O'Brien that he was the captain. Another officer was sitting just forward of the captain, along with four Royal Marines with their muskets and fixed bayonets. Eight sailors rowed the boat the 200 feet that separated the two ships.

Built in 1796, *Sirius* was the second of six large merchant ships designed specifically for the North Atlantic and Mediterranean trade and could cruise with decent wind at six to seven knots with a full load. Like its sisters *Orion, Polaris, Canopus, Capella,* and *Antares, Sirius* displaced 1,500 tons, had copper plating to ward off seaworms, and at 171 feet long and 50 wide, it dwarfed the *Richmond*-class *H.M.S. Boston* that was only 127' 5" long, forecastle to stern, 34' 4" at the beam.

The frigate, commissioned in 1762, displaced only 676 tons and carried twenty-six 12-pounders as its main armament. It had two 6-pounders mounted on the forecastle and four more on the quarterdeck. On a good day, with a clean bottom, it could make seven knots, maybe eight.

Once tied up, the captain was the first to climb on board. He stopped on the main deck, surprised by what he saw. First was a line of 12 sailors, six on each side. O'Brien was at the end next to his bo'sun who blew the whistle in what is known as "still." That *Sirius* sailors knew meant pay attention.

Sirius' bo'sun announced in a loud, clear voice, "Royal Navy frigate Captain, arriving."

By the look on the cluster of Royal Navy men by the entrance to the main deck, they were not expecting this welcome. O'Brien strode forward wearing his light blue coat with pewter buttons. "Good morning, sir, I am Caleb O'Brien, captain of the Fonseca-Laredo ship *Sirius* and headed toward Liverpool."

He extended his hand as he stepped forward. The Royal Navy captain kept hands clasped behind his back "Reginald Preethy, captain of *H.M.S. Boston."* He scanned the rigging before returning his attention to O'Brien. "Do you know why we stopped your ship?"

"Frankly no. We are headed for Liverpool and are carrying no contraband. And we are registered in the United States which is a neutral nation."

"What are you bringing to England?"

O'Brien knew his ship's cargo. "15 tons of indigo; 100 of cotton; 50 tons of logs; 40 tons of salted fish; 60 of salted beef; and 60 of salted pork."

Preethy pursed his lips. "His Majesty King George the Third believes that every ship from your country has Englishmen on it. And, as such, they are required to do their duty to King and country in her time of need. As such, the Royal Navy has been ordered to stop all ships and determine if there are any English citizens are on board. If so, then we are authorized to enlist them in His Majesty's Navy."

O'Brien tried to sound conciliatory. "Captain Preethy, I can assure you that there are no Englishmen on *Sirius.* We are all citizens of the United States."

"Hogwash. You're Irish. What year were you born?"

"1777 in Salem, Massachusetts."

"See, you are English by birth."

"No, Captain Preethy, I am not. We declared independence on July 4th, 1776, a year before I was born, and it took eight years and four months to kick you British out. I am no more Irish, or worse, English than my second officer who is Dutch and my bo'sun who is Spanish." *My parents left Ireland because they didn't like an English parliament making laws for Irishmen who had no say in the matter. They were some of the first members of the Sons of Liberty, and my father was wounded twice in his eight-plus years in the Continental Army.*

"So, you were a rebel?"

"Aye, Captain Preethy. I was a wee lad during our war for freedom, but had I been old enough, I would have joined the Continental Navy. If that makes me a rebel, so be it."

"Then, if I wish, I could take you into the Royal Navy. You could start at the bottom, and maybe, after twenty years, you might qualify as a bo'sun."

"I've already done that, Captain."

"Well, Captain O'Brien. Time's a wasting. I want ten men, do you pick them, or do I ask for volunteers, or do I just take them."

"Neither sir. If you take them against their will, it is kidnapping, which is, by the by, against the law in England as well as the United States."

"The Royal Navy calls it impressment, and it is blessed by King George and Parliament which makes it quite legal, I'm afraid."

"With each man you take, Captain Preethy, England inches closer to war with the United States."

"We fought you once, and we can do it again. This time we shall prevail."

O'Brien stepped between his crew, mustered along the bulwarks forward of the main mast, and Captain Preethy, "I doubt that. This time you'll face a united population bound together to maintain our independence and freedom. I submit, the end result will be the same, only England will lose even more sons."

"I doubt that." Preethy faced the crew. "You, you, you…." By the time he finished the "you's," he had pointed to 10 members of *Sirius'* crew. "Step forward so I can have a look at you."

The men refused at first until one of the Royal Marines started prodding them with the tip of a bayonet. After having them all open their mouths and lift their shirts, he said, "You'll do. Off you go into my boat."

By now, a second long boat from *H.M.S. Boston* was tied alongside *Sirius*. As the 10 men were herded to the hatch in the bulwark, O'Brien said loudly, "Fonseca-Laredo will ensure your full wages from this voyage will be paid to your families and if needed, provide employment. Be assured, your families will be cared for in your absence."

O'Brien had to say it because he wanted to give the men comfort that their loved ones will not starve or be cast out of their homes. "Captain Preethy, will you please do me the favor and get off my ship. Be advised, my government will be notified of your actions."

Preethy started down the ladder, and when just his head and shoulders were visible to those on deck, he said, "Your government can piss off. Next time I stop an American ship, I might take ten or fifteen."

Sadly, later in the day as O'Brien wrote his report, he believed that none of these men will ever see their homes again. He wondered how many American seamen were impressed into the Royal Navy and vowed that when he returned home, he would volunteer to serve in the U.S. Navy, if only to have a chance at teaching arrogant Royal Navy officers like Reginald Preethy a lesson.

PORTSMOUTH, FIRST WEEK OF MARCH 1807

The Duke of Somerset preferred to be referred to as Vice Admiral of the Red Stacey Davidson and had, at the first of the year, taken command of the Channel Fleet. Those close to Vice Admiral Davidson knew if asked, Stacey would say that his title was given to him at birth, but he believed he'd earned his admiral's flag.

The Channel Fleet had its headquarters at the large Royal Naval Base at Portsmouth, and its ships were charged with blockading the French Channel Ports of Brest, Cherbourg, Le Havre, Lorient, and St. Nazaire, as well as protecting His Majesty's merchant vessels. Should the French fleet come out, the Channel Fleet would be the first to engage.

The overriding mission of the Channel Fleet was to ensure that no nation could invade England. This had been its traditional mission going back to Elizabeth I and Drake when England fought the Spanish Armada in 1588.

This was the first time Davidson had been back in England after spending three years in Port Royal, Jamaica as the commander of the Jamaica Station. Ships assigned to him were there to protect British possessions as well as its merchant ships from marauding French frigates and privateers in the Caribbean.

After Napoleon's disaster in Haiti cost the French Army a reported 75,000 dead and killed another 25,000 French colonists, the French Emperor decided to pull his army out of the Caribbean. The defeat also caused him to sell what was known as the Louisiana Territory to the United States.

From the British perspective, the Royal Navy now controlled the Caribbean, and the British Army was at home. This provided some relief for the Royal Navy so it could now concentrate on ensuring that the French Fleet stayed at home.

For Davidson, he elected to house his staff on the base rather than sail about on a flagship. This way, the reports come to a fixed location, and he could issue timely orders without frigates and sloops carrying dispatches to try to find the flagship.

Laid out in a row on the polished oak desk were reports from six frigate captains on their recent patrols. In each, they detailed what they saw in each port as well as the ships they encountered. While he had more reports to read, synthesize, and decide what to do next, these six caught his attention.

Earlier in the day, he went to the Admiralty Charts that were tacked to his wall in such a manner they covered the French coast from the Spanish border south of Bordeaux up to the entrance to the port of Antwerp in Belgium. With each report, he went to the location in the frigate captain's report where he stopped each merchant ship.

Only *Boston* seemed to be out of its patrol area but to be fair to the captain, he was headed for Bristol where he was going to turn *Boston* over to a yard and shift the crew, and ammunition to another frigate, take on supplies, and re-deploy to whatever patrol area he was assigned

After adding up the number of seamen taken off their merchant ships against their will, he had a total of 59. Divided by six, it was, as a practical matter, enough men to man 10 guns.

Question one in his mind was did these captains really need the men they impressed?

Question two was this tactic justified?

He had already heard from Jaco Jacinto on his last visit to London that the Americans were not going to stand for this tactic much longer. He wondered how many Americans were impressed against their will. He took a clean sheet of paper and began writing.

Eldon,

You are far better than I at reading the tea leaves amongst the MPS. I cannot ask you this officially, but I would like you to enquire as to the PM's position on the continued impressment of American seamen who are taken off ships flying flags from neutral nations.

I know not how many Americans have been taken over the past few years, but I suspect it is a considerable number, i.e., in the thousands, not hundreds.

From the papers, I gather Mr. Grenville's hold on power is bit tenuous since he has failed to negotiate a peace with France or get the emancipation bill through the house that gives Catholics equal civil and political rights as enjoyed by the Anglicans.

Would you please have a chat with Baron Grenville or with whom you think will be his successor? I'd like to know the sense of Parliament before I barge into the First Naval Lord's office and ask him to end impressment.

Stacey

He folded the sheet of paper and sealed it with his Duke of Somerset stamp. He asked one of his staff members to put in the red Royal Mail box, whose contents were picked up daily and delivered to London addressees the next afternoon.

WASHINGTON, D.C., SECOND WEEK OF MARCH 1807

Spring was in the air when Javier Jacinto walked into Secretary of State James Madison's office. Outside, trees were starting to leaf out, and Javier expected one more cold snap before spring replaced winter.

The two men were old friends, having both served in the Continental Congress together and had been members of the Constitutional Convention. Since then, Javier, a member of the Federalist Party, has been one of South Carolina's members of the House of Representatives. James Madison, one of the founders of the Democratic-Republican Party, and Javier Jacinto had their differences, but have always managed to come up with a compromise.

Before he poured a drink, Madison pointed to a chair in his office and then handed Javier a glass of Scotch. Once he sat down, both held up their glass and toasted the United States. "Before we begin, how is Jacob Crowningshield?"

"Not well, Mr. Secretary. His consumption has become noticeably worse. I fear he may not be with us much longer."

Madison nodded. "He is such a young man. What is he, mid-thirties?"

"Thirty-seven, Mr. Secretary."

"Javier, I invited you to come a half an hour early so I could hear what you were planning to say to the British ambassador."

"My message is quite simple. England is the United States' largest trading partner, and we are England's largest trading partner. However, they are passing laws in the House of Commons without regard to the impact it has on our economic relationship. It reminds me of the Intolerable Acts of the 1760s. Admittedly, they were a wonderful excuse for our revolution. However, requiring every U.S. ship to stop at a British port, be inspected, and pay duties is absurd. Couple them with their continued impressment of our seamen, it appears the British want a war with us."

"It is worse than just on the oceans. The British Army never left their forts in the Northwest Territories, and they continue to equip and encourage the Indian tribes to attack our settlers. We are, for all practical matters, already at war with the British."

"How serious is it?"

"Enough to force our President to keep a standing army deployed and fighting. You know how much Mr. Jefferson likes armies and navies."

Madison's comment about Jefferson made Javier smile. "Yes, I am aware. I plan to tell Mr. Erskine that we intend to start escorting our ships with armed vessels of our own. Admiralty Law allows us to defend our property. If a Royal Navy frigate captain decides to stop and board one of our ships, he may have a fight on his hands. Any attempt to stop or board is sufficient cause for the escort to engage."

"Please don't make it sound like a threat. Those words or any similar words would have to come out my mouth. If you can, please just stick to the facts."

"Understood."

"By the way, Mr. David Montagu Erskine likes to be called Baron Erskine. He's actually the second Baron Erskine, and I've seen him get a bit stuffy. He is married to General Caldwater's daughter."

Javier was visibly surprised. Caldwater had served in the Continental Army and was now a trustee of the University of Pennsylvania.

Madison's secretary knocked on the door to say the British Ambassador was here. Both Americans stood, and when Baron Erskine entered, he walked straight to Madison, ignoring Javier Jacinto, who stood smiling.

"Baron Erskine, this is Javier Jacinto, co-chairman of the House of Representatives Committee on Manufactures and Commerce. He is also chairman of the board of United States Industries, which owns a decent-sized fleet of ships."

A curt nod in his direction. "What kind of name is Jacinto?"

"Spanish, Baron. My family came to the South Carolina Colony from the Netherlands in the early part of the last century."

"What part of Spain?"

"Malaga."

There was an awkward silence which Madison broke. "A taste Baron?"

"Please." He pointed to the partially emptied glasses, "I'll have what you are having."

"It is an Islay Scotch."

"Excellent."

The three men sat in the armchairs arrayed in front of a fireplace, and Madison thanked Baron Erskine for meeting with the two of them.

"Baron, as one of the co-chairs of an important committee, Mr. Jacinto would like to share some information that we wish you to convey to the House of Commons and the P.M."

Baron Erskine took a sip of his Scotch and nodded as if to say, please begin.

Javier took a last sip of scotch and then leaned forward. "Baron, I do not know if you are aware that England is our largest trading partner.

And, by studying the cargo manifests from about two dozen trading companies, we think we can make a case that we are also England's largest trading partner. Suffice it to say, trade between our two countries is good for both of us."

"Larger than India?"

"We believe it so. The turnover of several trading companies in which I am involved with in another venture is several times larger than the British East and West India companies combined."

"I agree, trade is good for both countries."

"Baron, are you aware that several recent laws passed by the House of Commons has reduced that trade by at least twenty percent?"

"Please explain."

"First, American ships headed to other ports in Europe are now required to stop in British ports, pay duties, be inspected before proceeding. My fellow traders have simply stopped buying or selling goods to England. They prefer to do business with countries that allow us to sail directly to their ports...."

"But Britain is at war with those countries."

Javier waited a few seconds to make sure the British Ambassador was finished. "True, but the United States is not. We are trying to stay neutral, but the House of Commons is making it very difficult. Those same British merchants who used to trade are struggling to sell their goods to other customers. This means their turnover, and I suspect their profits are less, which means they may not be able to pay their taxes."

Baron Erskine took a deep breath. "What do you wish me to do?"

Madison held up his hand. "Convey Mr. Jacinto's point to the Foreign Secretary in the strongest possible terms."

"Understood."

"Baron, if I may, there is one more issue that I ask you to carry forward to the P.M."

"And that is?"

"The Royal Navy must end its practice of stopping our ships and impressing sailors they claim are English citizens but who are not."

"It is my understanding that it is only a few hundred sailors."

"Quite the contrary. As of our last accounting, the Royal Navy has taken over 12,000 men in the past ten years. Again, through my contacts with other ship owners, we can provide a list of the men taken. Should this continue...." Javier let his voice trail off.

"So, Mr. Jacinto, what happens if it continues?"

Madison spoke before Javier Jacinto. "The United States will consider taking action. It could lead to a war neither one of us wants. Mr. Jacinto and several of his fellow ship owners will start sailing in convoys escorted by frigates and other armed vessels. They have the right under Admiralty Law, to protect their property and their crews."

"I shall convey your message to the Foreign Secretary, but I feel obligated to inform you that both the P.M. and the Foreign Secretary do not respond to threats."

Madison held up his glass. "Oh Baron, we are not making threats. We are merely telling you what has happened and what might happen again if Britain continues its current policies. We have had this conversation about Britain's failure to honor the terms of the Treaty of Paris by keeping soldiers on our sovereign territory. Each time a Royal Navy ship kidnaps some of our sailors, it just adds fuel to the fire. I suggest that you impress on the P.M. and other leaders in Parliament not to underestimate our desire to maintain our independence and freedom."

"The Royal Navy will sink or capture any of your ships that it encounters. You were lucky in that Lord Cornwallis and General Howe made some mistakes. That won't happen again."

Javier Jacinto held up his hand. "Next time you are in England, I suggest you visit the Admiralty and ask some of its more senior officers, such as the Duke of Somerset, Admiral Davidson, about a frigate *Scorpion* and my son Jaco Jacinto."

After Baron Erskine left, Javier asked his friend. "Why do I think our words fell on deaf ears?"

"Because they have. He is like talking to a stone. Now you know what I have been dealing with since I took this position in 1801."

Javier Jacinto walked out of the meeting more determined than ever to build frigates large enough to go toe to toe with those in the Royal Navy. U.S. Industries can afford the expense, but they must be owned and operated by Naval Escort Services.

CHAPTER 4

A WORLD FREE OF THE WIND

NEW YORK, FOURTH WEEK OF MARCH 1807

Back in January, the Naval Escort Services board decided to leave one of the frigates – *Kestrel* and three of the six corvettes – *Rattlesnake, Cobra,* and *Copperhead* – in the Mediterranean. The reasoning was that Hackett's shipyard could not handle all eight ships at one time.

All eight needed a major refit, and the other half of the decision was where they would base the squadron in the U.S.? New York, Boston, and Philadelphia were the preferred options. Naples would remain their Mediterranean base.

Compared to the new frigates constructed by the Royal Navy, *Osprey* and *Kestrel* were much smaller but could carry enough provisions for 10 weeks which was more than enough for a transatlantic crossing. The corvettes were designed to carry six but could carry eight if needed.

The other issue was size. New Royal Navy frigates were now being armed with 32 to 36 cannons usually a mix of 12- and 18-pounders, and displaced close to 1,000 tons.

The N.E.S. frigates, even with twenty-four long 18-pounders, were at a distinct disadvantage in weight of broadside. While faster and more maneuverable than the typical Royal Navy frigate, the weight of broadside mattered. At around 650 tons, the board was concerned that in a one-on-

one fight with a Royal Navy frigate in which *Osprey* or *Kestrel* was forced to trade broadsides, the American frigates would come off second best.

During the Barbary Pirate war, the squadron was based in Gibraltar. The Royal Governor of Gibraltar turned a blind eye to having neutral warships based in his harbor because N.E.S. bought supplies as well as ammunition.

Given the tensions between the British and U.S. governments over impressment, continued presence of British Army soldiers in the Northwest Territories, and the restrictive trade rules and additional duties, the men in the room all believed they were on their own to protect their ships from the Royal Navy.

The U.S. board debated whether they should offer escorts to ships owned by other companies. They proved they could do it against the Barbary Pirates, and ship owners who joined the convoys would be charged a fee.

The answer to this question would drive the decision on what types of ships they needed. From a sailing perspective, they needed to be faster, more maneuverable, and more heavily armed than the typical 36-gun Royal Navy frigate. However, the consensus was that they needed provisions for at least three months, assuming that they couldn't take on food supplies in an English or continental port and had to go to Naples.

At the end of the meeting, the N.E.S. board minutes showed four decisions were made. One, the corvettes be refitted to carry eight weeks of provisions and would be based in Naples. They would continue to do the convoy work in the Mediterranean.

Two, *Kestrel* and *Osprey* would be based in New York and accompany convoys to English ports, Amsterdam, Brest, and if needed, ports in Northern Europe.

Three, they would contact the ship owners who were customers of N.E.S. during the Barbary Pirates War to offer an escort service and develop pricing.

Four, they would approach James Hackett in Kittery and Joshua Humphreys in Philadelphia to submit designs for a larger, maneuverable frigate mounting 32 to 36 heavy guns, either long 18- or long 24-pounders that could cruise at nine to 10 knots. And contain enough provisions for three months at sea.

PORTSMOUTH, FIRST WEEK OF APRIL 1807

Vice Admiral of the Red Stacy Davidson stood facing the chart that dominated the wall of his office opposite his desk. On it, there were small pins pushed through a scrap of paper with the name of the ship or ships at that particular location. While Davidson had no way of knowing exactly where the ship or ships were at the moment, the pin locations represented where they were assigned to patrol.

Where the ship or ships were physically mattered less to Davidson than their assignments. The assumption was that the captains and commodores were carrying out their orders.

On the table below the chart, there was a sheaf of papers, each page had an estimate of the ships based at a particular French naval base. Just before a frigate departed its station off a French port, weather permitting, it would dash in as close as it dared, and an officer in the lookout platform would call down what ships he could see.

One of Davidson's first decisions as commander of the Channel Fleet was to reduce the number of first through third-rated ships of the line positioned off the French Coast. His rationale was that after the Battle of Trafalgar, for all practical purposes, the French Navy was decimated. He did not believe French admirals were about to come out to have another "go" at the Royal Navy.

Also factoring into his decision was that the war against Napoleon had devolved into a land war. Most of the fighting was in Eastern Europe, and the British Army was, for the most part, at home. Therefore, he had one decent-sized squadron of one first rater (ships with 100 or more guns), three second raters (vessels with 90 – 98 guns), and three third raters (ships with 64 to 88 cannons plus three frigates positioned between 6°W and 8°W and 49°N and 51°N.

This box off the tip of the Brittany peninsula enabled any frigate captain knew where to find the nearest flag officer. And this task force could quickly sail to intercept any French fleet sortieing or intercept a Spanish squadron coming north or be brought back into the Channel.

Ships stationed off French ports and in what he called his "Quick Reaction Squadron" were rotated every month. Blockade duty was boring, and the frigates watching the French ports were authorized to take prizes only if it did not interfere with their primary mission of watching the French fleet.

To that purpose, frigate captains were specifically ordered to "show the flag" once a week to the French, weather permitting. At no point were they allowed to let more than seven days pass between the times when they sailed close enough to the port so that French lookouts could clearly see the Union Jack flying from the mizzenmast and they could look into the port.

Davidson was contemplating the latest report from a frigate off St. Nazaire that stated that the spars on all the French warships in the port were clean. What this meant, other than that the French had removed the sails, he did not know.

They could have been taken down for replacement or to prepare the ship to be hauled out of the water to have its bottom cleaned, or to have the spars replaced, or even to break up the ship. He could think of several more reasons why the sails were removed and didn't have an answer when his secretary, a young lieutenant named Bevins knocked on his door. "Admiral, the post has arrived, and you have several letters, one of which is from your brother. May I bring them in?"

"Please. Put them on my desk, and after I have perused them, I shall call you to dictate my answers."

"Sir, I will, if I may, bring you yesterday's *London Gazette, The Times,* and *The Morning Post* from London."

"Yes, it will be interesting to see what is going on in our capital."

"One more thing, sir. You have an appointment with Captain Preethy at 11. Do you want me to have lunch brought up?"

"I think not. Please remind me of what ship he has?"

"*H.M.S. Seahorse,* 38 guns. His prior command was *H.M.S. Boston,* 32 guns. *Seahorse* just came out of the yards in Bristol and is here in Portsmouth to finish fitting out."

"Ah, yes. The meeting with Preethy will be short and I will have lunch afterwards."

"Shall I close the door, sir."

Davidson shook his head. "Not necessary." He waited until Bevins left and sifted through the stack of official letters until he found the one from his brother.

Stacy,

I would prefer not to speak with the new P.M. or the Foreign Secretary since I know quite well what they will say about impressment. To them is a tactic to put pressure on the citizens of our former colony. Unless the First Lord of the Admiralty comes forward and says it is hurting the Royal Navy, neither the P.M. nor the Foreign Secretary will not change, nor are they interested discussing the matter.

For the record, I find impressing citizens of a foreign country a dangerous and disgusting tactic. And, if a bill banning impressment came up for a vote in the House of Commons, I would vote for it. Should I bring up a bill banning it, I would be flying in the face of the P.M.'s wishes.

And, as I am up for an appointment as either Home Secretary or President of the Board of Trade and Master of the Mint, I do not wish to endanger either appointment.

I know this is not the answer you wished to hear, but it is my sense of the leadership. And our cross to bear.

Eldon

Like me, Eldon believes improving our relations with the United States is a priority, unlike many of the senior members of the Houses of Commons and Lords who want to bring the United States back into the empire, by coercion or force, if needed. We could never win another war with the Americans. It will be just like the last one, and in the end, the Americans will win and emerge stronger than they are today. We need to find a way to make them our ally, not our enemy.

Davidson was reading a report from the Admiralty on shortages of key items, including quality oak. Most of which was being imported from Sweden and Russia, and the reports noted that the wood was inferior to that which had been imported from the United States.

When he read that part of the report, he smiled. Then, Lieutenant Bevins knocked on the door. "Admiral, Captain Preethy is here."

"Please send him in and then bring in some tea."

Preethy entered wearing his royal blue coat and gold epaulets and carried his hat under his left arm. He came to a stop in front of Admiral Davidson's desk and nodded sharply. "Admiral, I am Captain Reginald Preethy of *H.M.S. Seahorse,* reporting as ordered."

Davidson, who had stood when Preethy came in, debated whether he should sit, stand, or both should sit. He pointed to a chair by the desk. "Please, Captain, take a seat."

"Tell me about *Seahorse.*"

"She's a fine ship. Built in 1794, *Seahorse* has new copper on her bottom, twenty-eight 18-pounders on the gun deck, twelve 32-pounder carronades, four on the quarterdeck, six on the main deck and two on the forecastle, along with two 9-pounders. With these cannons, we can pound any Frenchie into splinters."

"Are you fully manned?"

"I should have between three hundred and three hundred and fifteen, but I only have two hundred and ninety-one. I will take what I can from the barracks ships and then get the rest when we go to sea."

"How so?"

"Find an American merchantman or two and take what we need."

"Like you did on *Boston?*"

"Aye, sir. We enlisted ten just before we arrived in Bristol. May I ask how you know?

"I read your report, and it mentioned taking ten men from the American merchant ship *Sirius* at the southern end of the Irish Sea. So, as seamen, how good are these Americans?

"Actually, they are excellent seamen who know what they are about. I wish the Royal Navy had more men like them. However, they cannot be trusted."

"Why not?" The words came out of Davidson's mouth before he had a few seconds to think of how he should phrase the question.

"One deserted in Bristol. Went over the bloody side at night and swam ashore. The other did the same here in Portsmouth. When we catch them, they will be hung as deserters."

"Captain Preethy, if you were kidnapped from your ship, taken into the Navy of a foreign country, pray tell, what would you do?"

Preethy pursed his lips. "I would not be happy."

"But what would you do?"

"I would do my best to get away and return to the Royal Navy."

"Which is what those two men did or are trying to do. So, where are the remaining eight men?"

"On board *Seahorse.* We have them under an unofficial watch so they don't desert."

"How does that increase their willingness to serve the Royal Navy?"

Preethy didn't answer. Davidson spoke formerly. "I want those eight men and their belongings delivered to this headquarters by the end of the afternoon watch. They are to be clean, unharmed, and have any possessions they may have since they were taken. Do you understand?"

"Aye, aye, sir. That will leave my crew even more undermanned."

"I suggest you scour the barracks ships and the waterfront. And, while *Seahorse* and you are under my command, you will not, repeat, not take any men off any ship flying the flag of a neutral nation that has papers to prove its ownership and the citizenship of its passengers and crew. Do I make myself clear?"

"Aye, aye sir. But Royal Navy policy authorizes me to impress men."

"Aye, it authorizes you to impress Englishmen, not citizens of another country. Your sailing orders, as well as all those I have issued, make this abundantly clear."

"Yes, sir."

"Sir, may I ask what you intend to do with the Americans?"

"Send them home."

"How?"

"My problem, not yours."

"Yes, sir."

"The victualling officer says you will be fully supplied and ready for sea in two days. When you are ready, I will have your sailing orders ready."

When Lieutenant Blevins returned from escorting Captain Preethy to the door, he knocked on the door. Davidson waved him in.

"Mr. Blevins, I have a task for you. Go find a sloop that you, in my name, can borrow for no more than ten days. Stock it with food and beverage for that time and find a small crew. Use my name for authorization and direct any questions to me. By then, Captain Preethy will have delivered eight American seamen to this office. You and the crew are to take them to an address in London along with a letter to the Managing Directors of American Shipping & Passenger Lines, both of whom I know. These seamen are going home to America. It should take about three days to sail from Portsmouth to just outside London."

"Sir, who will pay for their transport?"

"I will out of my personal funds."

Smiling, Blevins said, "Aye, aye sir." The more he worked for Vice Admiral of the Red Davidson, the more he enjoyed it. Every day, there was a new challenge.

WASHINGTON, FOURTH WEEK OF JUNE 1807

While listening to the account by the Secretary of the Navy, Robert Smith, while the latter addressed a rare, joint session of the Congress, Javier Jacinto was seething. Smith was reporting, as asked by the President of the United States to tell its elected representatives what happened on June 22nd, 1807, when *H.M.S. Leopard,* 44 guns stopped *U.S.S. Chesapeake,* 38 guns in order to search the American vessel for the Royal Navy deserters.

Leopard's captain, Salusbury Pryce Humphreys was under orders from his commander, Vice Admiral Sir George Barkley to search any U.S. vessels for Royal Navy deserters. Many Royal Navy ships had made port-calls in Norfolk and Hampton Virginia and at least half a dozen seamen had deserted. Barkley instructed all seven ships in his squadron which was off Norfolk to blockade two French third-rated ships-of-the line anchored in Chesapeake Bay.

Chesapeake, under the command of John Barron, had just left Norfolk. Many of its supplies were still on the main deck and being taken below when *Leopard* fired its bow chaser at *Chesapeake.* Barron was under no obligation to stop nor was the ship ready to fight since it had not cleared for action. Worse, many of its cannons were not properly restrained so they could not be used.

Humphrey's 1,055-ton ship then came alongside Barron's 1,244 frigate and ordered his crew to fire a full broadside – eleven 18-pounders and eleven 24-pounders into *Chesapeake.* Four men were killed and 17 of *Chesapeake's* crew were wounded, one of whom was John Barron.

The wounded Barron allowed Humphreys to take four men: Daniel Martin who was a man of color, John Strachan and William Ware who had deserted from *H.M.S. Melampus* and Jenkin Ratford, formerly from *H.M.S. Halifax.*

Of the four, only Ratford was at the time of desertion a British citizen having been born in London. The other three were American citizens who had been serving on Royal Navy warships but wanted to serve in the U.S. Navy. They joined the crew at the Gosport Navy Yard as *Chesapeake* was being fitted out.

Learning of their desertion, the British consul in Washington sent a letter to Secretary of the Navy Smith ordering him to return the men to the Royal Navy. Smith refused and responded saying they were U.S. citizens and concluded his report to the Congress saying that Barron had been relieved of his command and will face court martial. When asked, he said the U.S. has sent a letter of protest to the British Ambassador and will also protest directly to the foreign ministry in London.

Secretary Smith concluded his briefing by saying that President Jefferson has sent a note to the British Ambassador to the U.S. ordering the Royal Navy to leave U.S. territorial waters. Smith was not surprised by the derisive laughter from many of the Congressmen.

After hearing what Smith had to say, Javier Jacinto and many other members of Congress were angry. The Royal Navy had fired upon and then boarded a U.S. warship and kidnapped four American sailors.

Javier waited until he was recognized by the Secretary of the Navy who gave him a chance to speak. Already, the Secretary could not answer questions such as "do we know if the Royal Navy hung any of the men?"

"Mr. Secretary, what does President Jefferson plan to do besides diplomatic protests? *Leopard's* firing on *Chesapeake* was an act of war. The British, through their Royal Navy are interfering with our ability to trade with countries in Europe, are impressing our seamen, and in this case, blockading an American port and they have kidnapped over eleven thousand American sailors. I am outraged this is happening and it is high time the United States acted to defend its citizens and their property. It is high time that President Jefferson come to this body and ask us to fund rebuilding our Navy."

There were shouts of "hear, hear" to Jacinto's statement. However, deep inside, he knew that Jefferson wouldn't ask to rebuild the Navy or the Army because he didn't believe in standing armies or navies.

He vowed he would not let this happen to any more Fonseca-Laredo ships or those who were members of the N.E.S. consortium. *By God, if Jefferson won't build frigates, then we will!*

ON THE HUDSON RIVER, AUGUST 17TH, 1807

Jaco Jacinto and his friend and business partner, Darren Smythe stood near the forecastle of the steamship *North River Steamboat* as it passed the cliffs known as the Palisades. The tops of the rocky bluffs towered over the masts of the 142'-long ship that was making four miles knots against the one and a half knot current of the Hudson River.

North River Steamboat was built in the Charles Browne Shipyard located between Stanton Street and 4th Street on the East River. The steamship was 18' wide and drew a little over seven feet. On each side, just forward of midships, each of the paddle wheels of the 121-ton ship was 15' in diameter and four feet wide. The ship had a fore and mizzen masts which could, if needed, hold enough sails to push the vessel.

What Jaco and Darren had learned from Amos Laredo was that Fulton had built a smaller version of the *North River Steamboat* in which he steamed up and down the River Seine. Why Paris? His friend and benefactor, Robert Livingston, was the U.S. Ambassador to France at the time. Amos Laredo's role in U.S. Industries was to look for new businesses, industries, and technologies that might warrant an investment by the firm. Hence the invitation to ride on the steamboat.

While *North River Steamboat* was being built, Robert Livingston had approached Amos about investing in his venture that would carry passengers and cargo between Albany and New York in less than two days. In turn, Amos brought Darren and Jaco to the Charles Browne shipyard to see the progress being made on building the ship. When completed, the *North River Steamboat* would have three private cabins and berths for 54 passengers, a kitchen, a larder where meat was preserved by being covered in fat, a pantry, and a bar and dining room.

Besides marveling at the scenery, they were also enjoying the ride in the ship headed for Robert Livingston's estate on the east bank of the river near Tivoli, NY that they would reach in 32 hours. There, the two men were told the ship would remain for 20 hours before proceeding to Albany.

The stop at Clermont Manor was a chance for Livingston and the designer of the ship, Robert Fulton, to entertain their guests who they regarded as potential investors as well as to show off his estate. Also, during the 20-hour stop, *North River Steamboat's* captain Andrew Brink and his officers could inspect the two paddle wheels and the Bolton and Watt steam engine that had been imported from Birmingham England on one of Fonseca-Laredo's ships.

Amos Laredo came forward from where he had been speaking with several other passengers and put his arms on their shoulders. Amos was much taller than Jaco and a few inches bigger than Darren. "Gentlemen, are you enjoying the trip?"

Speaking for the two of them, Jaco answered his brother-in-law's question, "Aye, Amos, we are enjoying sailing on a ship that is not dependent on the wind. I am curious as to how well the paddlewheels would do in a moderate sea, and many other questions. But I can see that steam power is the future. How we make it practical and efficient must be carefully considered because the wind is free. Coal costs money and large quantities will have to be stored on the ship."

"Jaco, that is the conversation Mr. Livingston would like to have with both of you in his cabin."

Darren brushed back a lock of his unruly blond hair that now had streaks of gray. "Splendid. Jaco and I have more questions than answers, but we both see the possibilities of how a ship like this could revolutionize our business."

"Which is why he would like to chat with you. Mr. Livingston understands that you are not competitors to his license to carry cargo and passengers up and down the Hudson."

Immediately after Darren and Jaco returned to N.Y. on the *North River Steamboat,* they sat in their office and composed a report that concluded that steam powered ships will replace sailing ships in AS&PL inventory but to do so, they must (a) be as fast if not faster than the schooners they are currently operating; (b) be able to carry more passengers and cargo; and (c) make the transit from New York to London or other European ports without breaking down. Coal, already used in manufacturing and in homes, was plentiful and only needed to be stockpiled in sufficient quantities to replenish the ship.

PHILADELPHIA, FIRST WEEK OF SEPTEMBER 1807

The frame and almost completed hull towered over Darren Smythe and Jaco Jacinto as they accompanied Joshua Humphreys around the slipway. From where they were below the ship, they could see the copper plating had been installed, and the rudder on what would be a 1,200-frigate was in place.

Humphreys led them back to a stairway that the three men climbed to get to a platform that enabled them to look down into the hull. The orlop decks in the forward end of the hull and the stern had been built, and planking the berthing deck was underway.

The eight diagonal riders that went from the main deck diagonally across the ship to the keel and then up the far side were still visible. These were pioneered on the *U.S.S. Constitution* to add stiffness and prevent the center of the ship from sagging, or the more common term, hogging.

They climbed down a ladder onto the berthing deck and walked forward so they could see into the bilge. Already the bulwarks that went from one side of the ship to the other to divide the holds were in place and helped support the berthing deck.

After their tour, Jaco asked the obvious question. "How soon will she be ready for sea trials. "With luck and an average winter, Captain Jacinto, next June. The second ship, about a month or two later. The gun deck will be stout enough to support eighteen long 24-pounders on each side. In the stern, we'll have two long 18-pounders and two more as bow chasers."

Darren's eyebrows went up at the mention of the long 18- and 24-pounders. They'd just come from the foundry making the cannons and were impressed by their accuracy at 200 yards as well as the force of impact when they hit the simulated ship's bulwark.

After inspecting the logs that would become the ship's masts and spars, they were in Humphrey's office, where he offered a glass of wine. He had Madeira, port, and a dry French red wine. Or whiskey. The two naval officers chose Madeira.

Humphreys asked where they planned to base the ships whose keels, when fully loaded, would extend 23 feet below the waterline. Darren looked at Jaco, who answered, "Not sure yet. We will pick a port that the Royal Navy would not normally blockade, and that gives the ship quick access to the sea. We are thinking New York at first, but maybe Kittery if there is a war, but no decision has been made yet."

"Kittery is a good choice except for the winter weather."

"Aye, there's that."

While they were standing on the dock waiting to board the AS&PL packet for the overnight trip to New York, Darren said, "You know the oak they are using is better than anything the Royal Navy had."

"Yes, and it does a wonderful job of repelling Royal Navy cannon balls."

"Aye, now I know why."

"If it comes to it, are you willing to give the Royal Navy a bloody nose?"

"I am an American citizen now. My wife is American, my children are Americans, my sister and her children are Americans. While I might sound like an Englishman, I am no longer one. Would I be happy fighting a Royal Navy ship? No. But, I would take great pleasure in defeating one."

"Darren, I am not a fortune teller or a soothsayer, but I fear that in our lifetimes, we will again have to fight Britain. Maybe sooner or later."

"I agree, my good friend. There are members of the House of Commons and the House of Lords who are still smarting from the revolution that brought this marvelous country into existence. I suspect they wake up every morning thinking of new policies and laws that will put pressure on us, hoping that at some point we will bend to their will and rejoin the empire. What they don't see is that they are cutting off their nose in spite of their face. Your father says that the U.S. does three times as much business with England as it does with France. One would think England would be happy with that, but no, they can't stand anyone who trades with France. It has been that way since the 100 Years' War, and I fear, it will continue long after we are gone.

"Darren, I agree and think many in Parliament believe we want to be Englishmen. However, I see them as bullies. And the only thing bullies understand is a good punch in the nose to back off."

"It will take more than one punch, but that my friend, is what we will have to do."

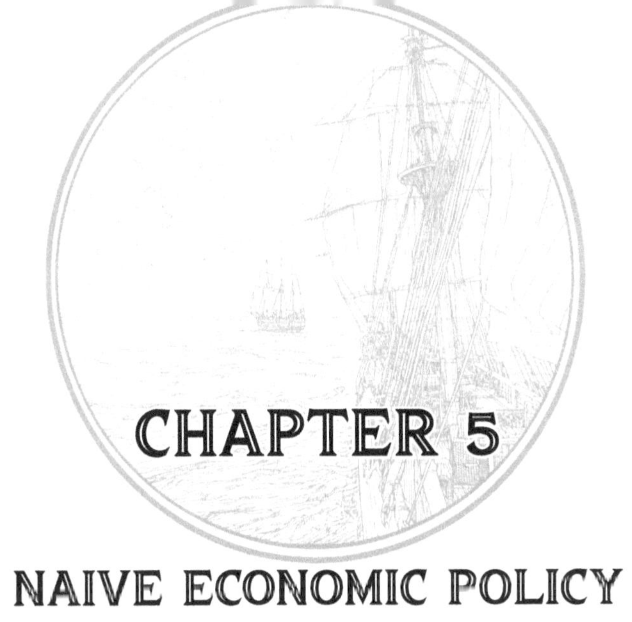

CHAPTER 5

NAIVE ECONOMIC POLICY

BORDEAUX, FRANCE, THIRD WEEK OF OCTOBER 1807

When Hugo Dubisson came into his office and saw Magistrate Moreau, he had flashbacks to June 1793. On that ugly day, his wife was murdered by French soldiers when she tried to stop them from raping his 13-year-old daughter Angélique. They then drafted, a better word would be forced, his two sons, Sebastien and Philippe into the French Army and sent Hugo to prison.

After having been beaten and tortured for almost a full year, Hugo Dubisson was released. While in prison, he refused to tell his captors the names of the members of the nobility who he helped escape and often wondered why they didn't kill him. Once out, surviving his prison ordeal made each day with Angélique and Henri precious.

Almost six years later, Didier Fontaine returned to Bordeaux to make a covert visit to what used to be the family winery. While in France, he fell in love with Angélique despite what happened and despite the nasty scar on her cheek caused by the tip of one of the rapist's bayonets. The soldier had wanted to leave her with a souvenir of their visit.

Captain Eduard Beauchamps, the man who killed Angélique's mother and let his men rape her, tried to stop Didier and Angelique from leaving Bordeaux on *Mademoiselle Celeste,* a ship owned by Cyrille Robillard of

Martinique. Beauchamps and Didier fought with swords on the deck of the merchant ship as it was pulling away from the pier.

The fight ended when Didier ran Beauchamps through with his rapier. As the French Army officer was holding his bleeding midsection, Angélique grabbed the bayonet from one of the muskets the French soldiers brought on board and were now in the hands of the crew of the *Mademoiselle Celeste.* Angélique shoved it into Beauchamps' throat and stared into his eyes as he died. Beauchamps' body was dumped at sea, and the other soldiers who didn't want to leave France were taken ashore in one of the ship's boats.

Seeing the French Magistrate Martine Moreau in his office caused Hugo's stomach to turn in knots. By the look on his 25-year-old son Henri's face, he could see that he was having the similar flashbacks. Henri was just eleven when he watched helplessly as his mother was killed and his older sister raped.

With Hugo taken off to prison, Angélique and Henri managed to keep Dubisson et Fils in business until their father was released. Henri had no love for the Republicans or Napoleon and only wanted to continue to run his father's business along with his older brother Sebastien.

When Sebastien and Philippe were drafted into the Republican Army in 1793, neither Henri nor Angélique thought they would ever see their brothers again. Only Hugo held out hope that one day, they would return, alive.

Philippe was the first to return in June 1800 after losing most of his left arm to shrapnel in the Battle of Zurich in September 1799. Sebastien had been in Napoleon's army that surrendered in Egypt and returned to Bordeaux in November 1801.

If Hugo Dubisson had a pistol handy, he would have had trouble resisting the urge to shoot Moreau, who loved to visit and threaten Dubisson with more prison time. Seeing only Henri and Sebastien, Moreau looked directly at the head of the household. "Citizen Dubisson, where are the rest of your children?"

"Angélique is married and is living in America and is now an American citizen. The same with Phillipe, who is also my agent in the United States."

Moreau shook his head. "No, they will always be French citizens."

"I am afraid not, Magistrate. They renounced their French citizenship and swore allegiance to their new home."

"Does Philippe ever come to France?"

"Occasionally."

"What does that mean?"

"Once a year." He wanted to add *he does not like his native land because of people like you* but held his tongue.

Moreau pursed his lips and then spoke, "Citizen Dubisson, do you know why I am standing here?" Magistrate Moreau waved his arm and smiled after he spoke. Behind him were six French soldiers.

"No." Dubisson wanted to say get out, but that would only anger Moreau, who thought he was, law unto himself in Bordeaux. Who could Dubisson appeal to? There was no one, and Moreau knew it.

"The French Republic is fighting for its life against our traditional enemies, the Germans and the English. To fight this war, the republic needs money, and Frenchmen are prohibited from doing business with our enemies. It has come to my attention that you are exporting hundreds of barrels of French wine every year, and some of it is shipped to England. Worse, you may not be paying your full share of taxes."

"I pay what I owe and have the receipts. I have manifests and contracts that prove that my wine goes to customers in Martinique and New York. What they do with it, I do not know."

Moreau's head went up and down. "Your tax payments show you are exporting two thousand barrels of wine a year. That makes you the largest exporter in Bordeaux."

Saying nothing, Dubisson believed, was the safest thing to do. Anything he said to the snake Moreau would be twisted and used against him.

"Who is your customer in New York?"

"U.S. Industries Imports and Exports."

"And where are the profits from the wine sales?"

Ahhhhh, Moreau wants to know where I keep my money so he can connive a way to get it.

"My profits are modest. As you know, I am a *negociant.* I take the grape juice and make it into a wine. Sometimes the wine is good, sometimes not so good."

Looking around, Moreau said, "I see you live modestly. Your sons, have they done their duty?"

You bastard, you know the answer. "They have. Philippe is *blessé,* and Sebastien, as you can see, is right here. He was left by Napoleon in Egypt. I have their certificates of service if you would like to see them."

Moreau waved his hand. "No, not necessary. What about Henri? Has he served?"

"No. He is exempt because when Sebastien and Philippe were in the Army, he was my last surviving son and therefore did not have to serve."

"Ahhhhh, but Sebastien and Philippe have returned home, so now it is Henri's turn to serve his country."

I think not. He and his family will be spirited out of the country before the draft gangs come. There's a N.E.S. ship coming any day, and I will put them on that ship with a note to Philippe.

Moreau pointed at Henri. "An Army officer will be here next week when I send several wagons to collect two hundred barrels of wine. The Americans have not come to the aid of France in her time of need. That is unlike when they were fighting for their independence. As I am authorized to do, I am imposing a fine of one hundred livres and 200 barrels of wine, which you will turn over to the French Army. When I return to collect the wine, I expect you to have the livres, in gold preferably."

"And if I don't have the livres?"

"Then, it will go badly for you. You are clever, Dubisson, so I suspect you will find a way to give me one hundred gold livres."

Arguing with Moreau was a mistake. Dubisson had the money, but this was extortion. He doubted that the government would get half of the money, if that.

He would, however, ask for a receipt. Hugo Dubisson stared at Moreau, trying to hide his dislike, even hatred. In the back of his mind, a plan was forming that would rid Bordeaux of this monster who was extorting money from him and other Bordeaux businessmen.

NEAR TALENCE, FRANCE, THREE DAYS LATER

Moreau liked to ride and fancied himself as a horseman. He had a house and barn just outside the perimeter road that ran around Bordeaux. Nearby was the road to the town of Talence.

On Sundays, Moreau would saddle one of his horses and gallop through the woods and fields, not caring what the horse's hooves tore up. If, on his rides, he saw something interesting, he would come back to visit the owner. If he liked it, he would assess a tax or fine for some obscure infraction. If the owner had the temerity to fight, then to Moreau, he was a marked man and would see more visits from the magistrate.

The magistrate was riding fast down a trail through the woods near Talence. He was partially hunched over as he gave the horse his head, so to speak.

Seeing Moreau coming, two men by the side of the trail pulled on a half-inch thick rope. Moreau saw it at the last second and raised his head, just as his shoulders touched the rope.

Moreau was flung off his horse and landed on his back. With the wind knocked out of him, he lay on the ground for a few seconds. Seeing a man emerge from the woods with a mask on his face, Moreau started to get up, suspecting the man to be a robber. What he did not see was the man behind him, also wearing a mask, who slammed a large rock into the back of Moreau's head. The wound was fatal, and Moreau was left where he fell with his head next to the rock, something that wouldn't be out of place on the trail.

Later that morning, Henri and his wife, Anne Remy boarded *Ness I* for the four-day trip to Gibraltar. There, the ship would take on provisions before setting out on the 14-day journey to New York.

NEW YORK, FOURTH WEEK OF DECEMBER 1807

Outside the windows of U.S. Industries, a heavy, wet snow was falling. Looking out the window of the conference room, Javier Jacinto could see there were already a few inches of snow on the street. How long it would snow, no one knew. The good news was, however, that it was 30° Fahrenheit (-1° Celsius) outside. In the evening, it would get colder, but at least the window wasn't blowing.

Lying on the table behind him was the latest bill passed by Congress on December 23rd, 1807, called The Embargo Act. It was, in his mind, another weak attempt by President Jefferson to put pressure on the British.

The terms of the act forbade U.S. ships from leaving port to go anywhere in the world. Only President Jefferson could approve a voyage in which cargo would be carried. There was no restriction on passengers, meaning AS&PL ships could ply their trade without cargo, which represented about 20% of their revenue.

Ships flying foreign flags could come and go as they pleased. Through Laredo Shipping, which had a license to fly under the Swedish flag, theoretically, they could re-register all their ships in Stockholm. But other ship owners didn't have this option.

Just to go between ports in the U.S., the ship owner was required to purchase a bond before leaving that the owner would forfeit if his ship called on a non-U.S. port.

He was sure that the bill, drafted by the Senate at the urging of President Jefferson, was insane and that many U.S. businesses would suffer. Worse, the country would suffer. While the bill was aimed at trading with England, it hurt everyone.

"Javier, what is it that you wanted me to see?"

The speaker was Gento Jacinto, his oldest son, and the man who was running the import and export business for U.S. Industries. "Read this and tell me what you think.

Javier could see Gento's index finger following the text as he read it a second time. When his son finished, Gento looked up. "Father, is this a joke?"

"No, I am afraid it is the work of our president and his allies in the Senate. We, that's all the Federalists and some of the Democratic-Republicans in the House tried to kill it, but we couldn't. Most of those who supported it are from cities like Atlanta and Richmond in the south. But their constituents will care when they find they cannot sell their indigo, lumber, dried fruit, fish, or salted meat. Then they will care."

"Father, whomever wrote this doesn't understand how much of our trading we do with Europe. It is insane and will mean the ruin of many companies."

"What you are telling is exactly what Max and Greg Struthers said. Shoshana thinks it is unenforceable because how will the government stop ships from leaving or know where they have been?"

"Do you have any advice, father?"

"Other than to tell Greg to get ready to buy our competitors who fail. Start looking where we can sell what we have in our warehouses here in the U.S. We need to hoard our cash until this falls apart and the president comes to his senses."

"How long do you think it will take?

"Three months for the screams from our competitors and us to be heard, another three months before the Congress gets off its arse, and three more before we repeal it. So, plan for a year, maybe eighteen months."

Gento pushed the copy of the bill aside. "I need a stiff drink."

"Make it two. Tomorrow, we will have a board meeting to make some difficult decisions."

WASHINGTON, SECOND WEEK OF JANUARY 1808

In the weeks since President Jefferson signed the Embargo Act of 1807, the legal department of U.S. Industries was churning out documents. One set was a bond for the American Shipping & Passenger Lines schooners that sailed up and down the Atlantic Coast and then around Florida to New Orleans.

The Embargo Act did not assign responsibility for enforcement or provide guidelines for compliance. To Shoshana, this was an opportunity to operate in a gray area because it would be illegal for the government to fine a company for violating a policy that didn't exist at the time of the violation. She had her staff prepare bonds with an attached schedule so one bond covered the first six months of 1808.

Then, there was another stack of applications to register all 22 of Fonseca-Laredo Shipping's and the six American Shipping & Passenger Lines' vessels in Sweden. Three – *Malmö, Stockholm,* and *Gothenburg* – all built during the American War for Independence and were still registered in Sweden. They were nearing the end of their service lives, but now that the country was independent and recognized by Sweden, she believed the Swedish ambassador in Washington could approve them or recommend approval. Then, they would be carried by either *Ness I* or *Ness II* or one of the corvettes to Stockholm and brought back to New York.

While still cold, the weather in Washington was noticeably warmer than in New York. Her father was waiting for the *Zephyr II* to dock with a carriage that would take Benjamin Jacinto, Gento's youngest son, who was a graduate of the Litchfield School of Law, Laura Fonseca Laredo, Jaco, and Shoshana, to his house in the Capitol District. A wagon carried their luggage to the modest three-story house on the Potomac River in the northwest portion of the nation's new capital. From the front porch, one could see an island in the middle of the river and rapids, which marked the northernmost navigable point in the river.

One of the two rooms facing the front of the house was Congressman Jacinto's office. The other room in the front was the U.S. Industries office. And, behind them was the dining/meeting room and the kitchen. Upstairs, there were one large and two smaller bedrooms on the second floor, and the third had three small rooms.

The day after they arrived, the first stop was Albert Gallatin's office. Born in Geneva, Switzerland, Gallatin emigrated to the United States at 19 during the War for Independence. He'd served in both the House of

Representatives and the Senate when Jefferson asked him to be his Secretary of the Treasury.

Javier knew him well, and Gallatin, as did Javier, opposed Jefferson's Embargo Act. But now that it had passed the House and the Senate, it was the law of the land.

After introductions, Gallatin looked at Javier. "Sir, you have brought me a conundrum. While every one of us in the room can read the Embargo Act, there is not one whit of direction as to whom to bring the documents you have prepared and what we should do with them."

Shoshana, always ready with a legal argument, piped up, "Then, Mr. Secretary, the law cannot be enforced, or if the Federal government is unwilling to enforce it, then the Supreme Court should declare it unconstitutional."

Gallatin raised his hand, "Miss Jacinto, I suspect I know where you are going with your argument, but Mr. Jefferson has given the Revenue Cutter Service the task of enforcement. They report to me, so I shall pass the documents on to them. They appear to meet the intent of the law, and knowing the quality of your legal work, Miss Jacinto, they will be sufficient. If not, I shall contact Congressman Jacinto."

"Thank you, sir, for your kind words. I can then assume that American Shipping & Passenger Lines can continue operations which, by the way, includes carrying U.S. Mail."

"That is correct. I shall have my secretary deliver a letter to Congressman Jacinto's office today to that effect."

In the carriage, Shoshana asked, "Father, that was much too easy. I am suspicious. What did I miss?"

"Nothing. Neither Secretary Gallatin nor the Revenue Cutter Service have figured out how they will enforce the act. And second, Mr. Gallatin thinks, as do I, that it is an act of lunacy that will fail to achieve its objective which is pressuring the British. While in force, many businesses will fail. God willing, it may even cost the Democratic-Republicans the White House."

They rode in silence back to the house near the border of Georgetown, MD, and the Capitol District. There, they had lunch before setting out for the Swedish embassy.

Baron Gustav Nilsson was waiting in the parlor of the house that was both the Swedish embassy and his residence when the delegation from U.S. Industries entered. Shoshana strode directly to the Swedish diplomat she first corresponded with during the American Revolution, inquiring about whether Laredo Shipping could register its ships in Sweden, and if so, how. The Swede was as tall as Shoshana, gave her a tight hug before gently pushing her back so he could look at her. "The years have been kind to you, Shoshana."

"And you, sir, as well. You are as handsome today as you were as a dashing cavalryman who came to the U.S. to be an observer during our war for freedom. It appears that you like the United States because you never left. I am sorry to hear of Count Olafsson's passing." Shoshana was referring to Count Olaf Olafsson, who was Sweden's chargé d'affaires beginning in 1777 and had returned to Sweden in 1793.

"Aye, the years have passed quickly. The count had a good life. He was eighty-eight when we lost him."

Nilsson turned to Jaco. "It is good to see you again, Captain. We didn't spend much time together because you had a ship to run. I have read about your exploits in the book *Frigate Captain,* which I believe was published by your sister."

"It was. I think the author exaggerated way too much about what we did."

"You, Captain, are way too modest. I suspect, no, I know, there are British admirals and captains who lost many a night's sleep over you."

Shoshanna put a hand on Laura Fonseca Laredo's shoulder to signal that she was next to be introduced. "This is Laura Fonseca Laredo, the president of Fonseca-Laredo Shipping."

Baron Nilsson bowed slightly and bowed until his mouth was just above Laura's hand. "It is a pleasure to meet you. If you are the head of a large shipping company, it proves that you are an astute and skilled woman who can be successful in a man's profession, as well as being beautiful."

Laura nodded and smiled. Barron Nilsson turned to Benjamin Jacinto. "Welcome. It is an honor to meet you."

Last, he turned to Javier, and as they shook hands, Baron Nilsson put his left hand on top of the handshake. "It is always good to see you, my good friend. Come, let us have a drink before we get down to business."

He turned to a man in his 30s. "May I present Lars Persson from our Ministry of Trade." The blond-haired young man bowed slightly and shook each person's hand, stopping for a moment to look at Shoshana who, at 6' 2", was as tall as he.

A servant appeared with a tray, and Baron Nilsson spoke, "I know Javier likes Madeira. Laura and Shoshana, what say you?"

"Madeira is fine."

"And Benjamin?"

"Madeira."

A toast to the two countries and their rulers. Back in 1777, King Gustav III of Sweden sent several Swedish officers to observe the war from the Continental Army's side. He then recognized the new country later that year and sent Count Olafsson to be his representative to the Continental Congress. On April 3rd, 1783, Sweden became the fifth country to officially recognize the new United States. Their recognition came four months before the Treaty of Paris was signed. Then, in 1803, Sweden sent three large frigates to the Mediterranean to serve with the American Navy in the Barbary Pirates War.

As a member of the Commerce and Manufactures Committee in the House of Representatives, Javier called on every ambassador and chargé d'affaires in Washington. Those relationships were not only good for the United States because they opened doors for other U.S. businesses, but also for U.S. Industries.

The group was led to a large dining room with ornate furniture. The Americans sat opposite the two Swedes. Baron Nilsson looked at Shoshana. "I suspect I know why you are here, so I will spare you the details. As of July 1807, Sweden is no longer a member of the British-led coalition fighting the French. However, that may change. If we should again be aligned with the British against Napoleon, then I think if your ships are flying a Swedish flag, they will be less likely to be stopped. Technically, they will not be flying the flag of a neutral country. The French Navy, such as it is, and French privateers in the Caribbean will look at them as prizes and Sweden cannot protect them."

Lars Persson smiled at Shoshana, with whom he clearly had an interest despite noticing the gold ring on Shoshana's left ring finger. "Miss Jacinto, may I ask how many merchant ships are in the Fonseca-Laredo fleet and how many you wish to register in Sweden?"

Laura answered. "Twenty-two, not including those being built. Three, as you know Mr. Persson, have been continually registered in Sweden since 1778. The registrations are renewed every year, and we would do the same for the new ships and for others we deem necessary to re-flag. Should Europeans stop killing each other, then we would probably bring all but these ships back to U.S. registry."

"Yes, Ms. Jacinto, the war against Napoleon is unfortunate. There are many kings and dukes who do not like Napoleon or his ideas. So, unfortunately, I fear these wars will continue for years to come. The alliances, we call the coalitions, seem to change like the wind. My government fears we may have to fight the Russians of all people! But that is not your concern."

"So, will the Swedish crown continue to allow us to register our ships? We have the documents needed with us.

"Excellent. Yes, I believe that to be the case. I shall provide a letter to the court endorsing the registration." No one spoke for a few seconds until Baron Nilsson said, "I think so. But I fear the registration fee has gone up considerably."

Laura knew that it was currently £100 per year per ship. The fee was more than made up on the first voyage of the year. In the past, they had sent a draft to Amsterdam, where Erik Laredo delivered it to the Swedish Embassy, which arranged for it to be sent to Stockholm. This was, oddly enough, the fastest route given that the number of ships going back and forth to Swedish ports was limited. It also gave Fonseca-Laredo "control" over the draft for the entire voyage. "Baron, may I ask what the fee is for 1808?"

"Two hundred and fifty pounds. I am sorry, but we must pay for our wars!"

"Done." Laura couldn't get the words out of her mouth fast enough. Negotiating to save £20 or £30 per ship wasn't worth it. It was her profits she was spending, but having ships sailing to Europe with cargoes and returning with people and cargoes was more important.

"Would the three of you go through the documents with Lars while I have a private word with Captain Jacinto and my friend Javier?"

Lars took Benjamin and the two women to another room. When they were gone, Baron Nilsson closed the door, and before he sat in the same chair, he topped off his guests' glasses. "I fully expect in a year or two, Sweden will rejoin another coalition against the French. Who will we be allied with I do not know, but the war or wars will continue."

Nilsson took a sip of his Madeira. "I admire the United States' desire to remain neutral in the conflict in Europe, but I fear your country may be forced to choose sides. The question is which one. We know that your president is a fan of France but does not dare declare he supports Napoleon. Sweden would prefer to side with the English. So, what do you think President Jefferson will do?"

"Despite my disagreements with President Jefferson, I can almost guarantee you that he will only pick a side if the United States is attacked by one of the warring powers. However, I believe that most European nations perceive us as weak because we do not have a large army or navy which is President Jefferson's policy. However, we have an election this year, and there will be a new president who may have a different view."

Nilsson smiled. "Do you have a prediction?"

"No. I suspect it will be either Madison or Monroe. I know my fellow Federalist and South Carolinian Charles Pickney intends to run, but I fear he does not have the support needed to win. He is not well known in the northern states."

"Do you have a preference amongst the candidates?"

"No. As you know, we have our differences with the British over trade, their continued presence in the Northwest Territory, and over impressment. I submit we are continually trying to get the British to discuss these important matters, but from what we have been told by Secretary of State Madison, speaking to the British Foreign office is akin to speaking to a stone. Madison is no shrinking violet and believes we need an Army and Navy to defend ourselves. The question I cannot answer is will Congress be willing to pay the bill?"

"Ah yes, the joys of a democracy. The people get a vote and a say."

"Aye, we fought for this right and privilege and will not surrender it lightly."

Jaco sipped his Madeira and then put the glass on the table. "Father, may I add something."

Seeing Baron Nilsson nod, Javier said, "Please."

"Sir, we demonstrated what we can do during our fight against the Barbary Pirates where we fought and won four thousand miles from our shores. Sure, they were not the British or the French, but we have shown our mettle in the past against both countries. So, sir, if you are passing information on to your government, you can tell that we will, if needed, defend ourselves. I believe Mr. Madison and Mr. Monroe differ from President Jefferson in this regard in that they will support expanding our Army and Navy."

The Swedish diplomat nodded to convey his understanding, but Jaco was not finished. "Sir, I think a war with the British is a matter of when, not if. Why? Because I believe the British will not change their policies toward us until we force them to stop. We will, if needed, do it by force of arms."

Baron Nilsson tapped the table several times with his forefinger. "Does that mean that if it comes to war with the British, you will ally yourselves with France?"

"No, Baron Nilsson it does not. We will not need French help. We are quite capable of defeating the British, and quite frankly, I do not trust the French. Twice during our fight for independence, France betrayed us."

Nilsson looked confused and Javier began to explain "Baron, what my son said is true. First, they signed the 1779 Treaty of Aranjuez in which they committed to helping Spain capture Gibraltar. Then, while we were negotiating with the British, after they lost badly in the Battle of St. Vincent in 1780, the French secretly approached the British without telling our delegation they wanted out of the war. In both situations, they violated the Treaty of Friendship and Alliance we signed with them in 1778. My son didn't mention that when France signed the contract for the Louisiana Territory in 1803, they knew they didn't have title to the land. It took them weeks to get it from the Spanish."

Baron Nilsson laughed. "I knew none of this."

"Aye, when dealing with the French or the Spanish, be very careful."

"Our traders have learned that painful lesson many times over."

"As have we."

CHAPTER 6

STARE DOWN AT SEA

EASTERN ATLANTIC, 45° N, 20° W, THIRD WEEK OF MAY 1808

Kestrel was riding easily in the long Atlantic swells under what her new captain, Micah Jacinto, described as her cruising rig – two jibs and all three gaff topsails raised. In this configuration, the quartermaster mate cast the log and determined that she was making 10 knots.

Not bad, Micah thought, as he stood on the quarterdeck of the three-masted schooner that mounted 24 long 18-pounders. He had proved himself in action during the war with the Barbary Pirates in several actions, but in particular, on board the corvette *Viper.*

At the end of the war, Micah chose to remain with Naval Escort Services and retain his reserve commission in the U.S. Navy. After the Barbary Pirates War, he was promoted to lieutenant and then given command of one of the corvettes. Now that Naval Escort Services' new frigates *Eagle* and *Goshawk* were about to be commissioned, two captain slots came open.

When it became clear that Micah was under consideration for one of the captaincies, Jaco walked out of the room. As he did, Jaco told the selection board chaired by Darren that he didn't want to be privy to the deliberations about his son and would accept, without comment or protest, its decision. Micah was chosen for one of the two.

The small frigate's mission was to sail to the Azores, take on supplies, and then patrol a line between 40° and 50°N along 2°W. The area was selected because it was where the shipping lanes to Europe began to converge, and Royal Navy frigates patrolled, looking for ships bound for ports in French-occupied Europe.

His sailing orders allowed him to escort any ships to a port in Europe that requested such service. When he left, his father pulled him aside and said, "Trust your instincts, but don't do anything stupid."

Micah could recite verbatim his sailing orders which stated:

> *Kestrel is authorized to assist any U.S.-flagged vessel or any other ship under a neutral flag to prevent U.S. citizens from being impressed into the Royal or any other Navy using the means at its disposal..*

His orders did not give him any guidance on how he should execute them. N.E.S. regulations authorized him to protect any ships under his care, i.e., ones he was protecting, and others that were endangered by the actions of a foreign navy. He also couldn't initiate an attack on an enemy warship but could defend his ship and those he was escorting if needed.

The question of how he would do this was the topic of many discussions over glasses of port in *Kestrel's* small captain's cabin. As per N.E.S.'s policy, he didn't choose his three officers and midshipman, they were assigned to him. All were junior to him and had graduated from N.E.S.'s school in King's Point, NY.

Like him, they were all young. His midshipman, Norman Sampson, was 14, and Emanuel Cobb, his First Lieutenant, was 19. Bart Conner – he hated being called Bartholomew – his Second Lieutenant and his Third Lieutenant, Jacob Kahn, were both 18. The "old men" on the crew were his quartermaster, Josiah Givens, a freed slave who thought he was 28, but wasn't sure, and Bo'sun Francis Beauregard from New Orleans, who was 30.

They'd left New York in the first week of April, stopped in the Azores to replenish their supplies, and then began patrolling. Micah kept *Kestrel* out for a month before returning to Ponta Delgada for supplies. The frigate was working its way north along 19°N by taking nor' west until it crossed 20°N and then would head nor' east until it reached or crossed 19°W. His plan was to repeat the process until he reached 50°N and then return south.

So far, it had been boring. On different days, they sighted a French ship headed west, but no Fonseca-Laredo or American ships. To keep his crew sharp, Micah would have the crew clear for action and run out but not load. Today, to add some spice, while the men were clearing the ship for a gun battle, he was going to pick out men and tell them they are dead and see how the rest of the crew worked. Yesterday, he ordered Bo'sun Beauregard to tack the ship with only half the number of men he would normally have.

Seeing his First Lieutenant Bart Conner on the main deck, Micah moved to the front railing of the quarterdeck. Two bells on the Forenoon Watch had just rung, meaning it was about nine in the morning, and he was about to give the order to clear for action. Once it started, he would walk around the ship creating casualties.

"Deck, two ships close together, two points off the port, three miles."

Micah walked to the forward corner of the quarterdeck on the port side. As he did, he took a spyglass from the rack. All were copies of the Dollond spyglass with achromatic doublet lenses that eliminated distortion and were much clearer than other types. Dollond's patent had expired in 1772, and now spyglasses with high-quality achromatic doublet lenses were about half as expensive as in the 1790s. Each N.E.S. ship had at least five, two for lookouts, two for the quarterdeck watch, and one spare.

Micah studied the two ships, once he found them in the narrow field of vision. All he could see was the tops of their masts, and it appeared that their sails were loosely hung, signaling that they were moving slowly. The yellowed canvas told him that one ship had spent a lot of time at sea which also suggested a Royal Navy warship.

"Lookout, can you make out the type of ship?"

"One is a frigate, for sure. The other is a merchant vessel."

"Captain, aye." Adrenalin started to flow. "Mr. Conner, clear *Kestrel* for action. Load ball, but do not run out."

Bart Conner put the back of his hand to his head and began to yell out a series of orders. "Bo'sun Beauregard, we will alter course to nor' by nor' east. Trim the sails accordingly for maximum speed as soon as we are steady up."

"Aye, aye, captain."

Micah put the spyglass to his eye and began to slowly search the horizon. The circular view only covered a small portion of the ocean, and when he found the two sails, he rested his elbow on the railing to steady his arm. He couldn't make out the flags. Standing up, he collapsed the glass and began to work out the geometry of how he would approach the two ships.

"Deck, I can see a boat going from the frigate to the merchant ship. I'll bet a ration of rum that the frigate is Royal Navy."

"Captain, aye." *So, the frigate captain is sending a boarding party to the merchant ship. Why? There is no other reason except to inspect the ship for contraband and impress a few sailors.*

"Mr. Conner, pay my respects to *Kestrel's* officers and have them, along with Mr. Beauregard join me on the quarterdeck once the ship has been cleared for action and we are ready for a fight."

Micah was leaning against the back railing when his officers gathered, facing him. "Gentlemen, my assumption is that the Royal Navy frigate is impressing, I prefer to use the word kidnapping, some of our countrymen. I intend to get them back without a fight, but as you know, *Kestrel's* order allow us to protect the lives of our citizens. So. here's my plan..."

ON BOARD *KESTREL*, 9:28 A.M.

Neither H.M.S. Mermaid nor the merchant ship Narragansett attempted to get underway as Kestrel approached from the starboard quarter. She was downwind and Micah planned to luff his ship's sails to stay in position. Surely, the lookouts on Mermaid had reported the approaching frigate. The angle of the view would have enabled them to count the 12-gun ports to let them know a frigate with at least 24 cannon was approaching.

Now that *Kestrel* was within a hundred yards of where Micah intended to tack and then luff the sails, he could clearly see the American flag hanging from a halyard that went from the quarterdeck to the top of the mizzen mast. The Union Jack was streaming in the breeze.

"Mr. Beauregard, on my command, we will tack to port. New course, Mr. Givens will be nor' by nor' west. Once we are steady up on the nor' by nor' west, luff the sails so we take station aft of *Mermaid* and *Narragansett.*"

After hearing acknowledgements, Micah gave the command to tack. *Kestrel's* bow came through the wind and Beauregard gave a stream of orders to let out the sails. *Kestrel* glided to a stop so that the first two gunports were even with the stern of *Mermaid.* So far, Micah was amazed that no one on either ship had hailed them. His plan was that, if needed, he could accelerate, fire into *Mermaid's* stern from point blank range and then fall off the wind. This would let him get away from the bigger frigate and enable him to use *Kestrel's* speed and maneuverability to either re-engage at a time of his choosing or escape.

He walked forward to the bow with a speaking trumpet in hand when a Royal Navy officer appeared at the railing of *Narragansett.*

"What ship are you?"

"Kestrel."

"State your business!"

"Sir, if you have kidnapped American citizens against their will to serve in the Royal Navy, I suggest you return them to *Narragansett* at once."

"His Majesty believes they are Englishmen who need to do their duty."

"Sir, I am not here to argue with you. Again, I strongly suggest you leave *Narragansett* forthwith and return any American citizens immediately."

"On whose authority?"

"The United States Government. I am authorized to defend American property and citizens."

"And if I don't?"

"I shall open fire." Micah turned so he could yell down the forward companionway. "Mr. Cobb. You may run out the starboard battery." Before the Royal Navy officer could speak, Micah yelled out through the trumpet. "Sir, you have less than a minute before my first 18-pound ball will go into the stern of your ship. At this range, all twelve will cause considerable damage and by the time you get underway, your ship may be a floating wreck."

"You're bluffing. Firing into one of His Majesty's Ship's is an act of war."

"So is boarding a neutral warship and kidnapping some of its sailors. In my country and yours, it is called piracy and if memory serves, England as does the United States hangs pirates. Sir, what is it going to be? Do you want to call my bluff?"

"May I have your name for my report which will say that you threatened a King's officer."

"Jacinto. Micah Jacinto." He then spelled it out letter by letter. "You might want to know that my father's name is well known by many of your admirals. Now, sir, leave *Narragansett* and return any U.S. citizens immediately then sail away."

"I shall comply, Captain. However, should we meet again, you may not find the event to your liking."

"I look forward to it, sir. And may I have your name?"

"Joseph Hightower."

A second boat left *Mermaid* and those on *Kestrel* noticed it left *Narragansett* with fewer people. A man wearing a blue coat appeared on the quarterdeck of the merchant ship. "Thank you, sir. All eleven of my men are back on board. Your ship?"

"*Kestrel,* we are owned by Naval Escort Services and authorized by our government and Admiralty Law to protect American ships from unlawful actions such as you experienced. Who owns *Narragansett?"* Micah wondered if his answer satisfied the captain of the merchant ship.

"Bay Colony Shipping out of Boston. Denis Smithson, commanding."

"We will note the event in our log. Good day, sir."

Micah had *Kestrel* fall off and trail *H.M.S. Mermaid* until sunset and then headed back to its patrol area. Dinner that night in *Kestrel's* cabin was quiet. Toward the end, Bart Conner asked, "Sir, were you really going to give the order to fire on *Mermaid."*

"Mr. Conner, if the question is, was I, as captain of *Kestrel* prepared to give the order to open fire, then the answer was absolutely. My orders are clear in that *Kestrel* is to protect our ships and fellow citizens by the means at my disposal. At the time, those means included my brain as well as *Kestrel's* crew and their ability to fire our long 18-pounders rapidly and accurately. It is clear that Captain Hightower didn't wish to learn how good we are at our job."

NEW YORK, FOURTH WEEK OF MAY 1808

For those who knew Nathan Jacinto, his slight build and effeminate gestures were accepted. They didn't affect anything he did at work. For his lover, Philippe Dubisson, they were one of the "things" about Nathan that attracted him.

Now that they were living together, Nathan's desire to present himself as a woman was in full bloom. Once they returned from work, Nathan went up to the third floor of the house where they lived to change into a dress.

The two were living as husband and wife, with Philippe being the male in the relationship and Nathan the female. When Philippe and Nathan told their parents about their relationship, it was accepted, and they allowed them, just as Shoshana's and Naomi's was, to be blessed by a rabbi. On weekends, Nathan was *en femme* the entire time and preferred to be called Natalie, something he was forbidden to do at work. For those who didn't know Nathan, his slight frame and light complexion made it easy for him to pass as a woman.

Gento, Nathan's father, took an idea to the U.S. Industries board. He approached Shoshana about changing U.S. Industries' policies toward those who preferred others of the same sex. Eventually, the board came around and published its policy that every employee in the firm is entitled to live with whom they choose, practice what religion they prefer, as long as their choices do not adversely affect their work. Promotions were to be made based on work performance.

That new set of rules was known as the "Free Choice" policy and was written by Shoshana and would "officially" take effect on the first Monday of June 1808. To celebrate, Nathan/Natalie and Philippe went to Southport, their favorite molly house, on the corner of Grand and Suffolk Streets.

Southport had an excellent restaurant and bar on the main floor, along with a ballroom where couples could dance from eight p.m. to one a.m. when the facility closed for the evening. Couples could rent one of the 12 small rooms for an evening.

It was one of the largest molly houses of the dozen such establishments in New York, and a private club exclusively for gay men and crossdressers. Memberships were expensive and also ensured privacy for its members.

Nathan/Natalie was wearing a pale pink dress with a sheer layer covering her bodice and a white shawl that draped over her shoulders. It was one of those made on their last trip to Bordeaux. The dress's sleeves were short and gathered with a white button on top of her shoulder, and she was wearing a pair of elbow-length silk gloves, despite it being summer. Her flat shoes had pointed toes with ribbon fashioned into flowers and attached to the leather.

After dinner, they danced for a few hours before deciding to walk up Suffolk Street. The weather was pleasant, and they were followed by their carriage, which was driven by a U.S. Industries employee.

Suddenly, three men darted out from between two houses. One slammed a club into the back of Natalie's legs, sending her sprawling on the ground. Another man hit Philippe in the stomach while a third man ripped Natalie's purse from her arm.

Before Philippe could stand up, the assailant hit him in the stomach and then on the back of the neck. The blow sent him sprawling to the ground. By the time the driver of the carriage could react, the thief who hit Philippe found his wallet, and the three thieves went running into the darkness.

Sensing they were just bruised, the driver helped them into their carriage, and once Philippe and Natalie were safely in their home, he went to fetch Dr. Reyna Jacinto.

NEW YORK, THE NEXT DAY

The day after the attack on Nathan and Philippe, Jaco Jacinto and his older brother Gento watched as the constable looked over the area where they described the attackers came from. It was a gap between two houses that, Jaco could tell, would allow the attackers to hide in the shadows. No one would see them until they emerged on the street. There were no lanterns to light the street or the narrow wooden walkway.

"Constable, I presume that this is not the first attack that occurred here. Am I correct?"

"This is not the only place from which thieves make their move. In the past two months, the number of attacks has increased. Men are losing their jobs because companies are cutting back."

Jaco, who was standing with his hands clasped behind his back, asked, "What can we do to catch these men and stop the attacks?"

"Get President Jefferson to ask Congress to repeal the Embargo Act."

Both Jaco and Gento laughed. "Yes, that would help us all but not help us catch the thieves. What are you doing to catch them?"

"Sir, not much. We do not have enough men to watch all the places where likely attacks are taking place. They see us and go elsewhere. Local residents are supposed to keep watch, but apparently, no one saw the attack."

"Have you thought about laying a trap and catch some in the act. Then, the courts can make an example of them."

"They only attack when there are a man and a woman. They think the woman won't fight. They grab what they can and then run. And we do not have any women constables. And, sir, it would not be helpful if you took matters into your own hands."

"Aye," A plan that was forming in Jaco's mind, but he changed his approach. "Is the number of constables a money problem? If so, I can speak to the mayor."

"That would help, but then Mayor Dewitt Clinton will want to raise taxes to pay for more constables, which the poor cannot pay."

"I understand, and you are telling me that there is little you can do?"

"Unless we catch them in the act, you are correct, Mr. Jacinto."

"Thank you, sir." Jaco turned away, followed by his older brother, Gento. Once they were in the carriage, Gento faced "Jaco, what are you thinking?"

"Having one of us walk with our wives is too great a risk. However, I was thinking of a small flying squad of men from one of the ships to flush some of these thieves out into the open."

"Then what? Unless you can prove they committed a crime, you can't arrest them. I doubt that you will scare them."

"Gento, you have a point, but I don't like having a cousin and his lover robbed. It is not about the money, it is about the principle."

Neither said anything as they rode back to the U.S. Industries office.

CHAPTER 7

MEETING OF THE NAVAL MINDS

PORTSMOUTH, FOURTH WEEK OF AUGUST 1808

What started as a letter signed by both Jaco and Darren to Vice Admiral of the Red Stacey Davidson asking who they should speak to in the Admiralty and the House of Commons generated an invitation to visit Portsmouth. Secretary of the Navy Smith agreed to let both newly launched frigates, *Eagle* and *Goshawk*, each with 36 long 24-pounders on their gundecks, two long 18-pounders as bow chasers and two more in the captain's cabin as stern chasers, visit England with the U.S. government's and the Navy's sponsorship.

They were to be listed as "reserve" ships and could fly U.S. Navy ensigns. The crews were all "reservists," some from the Navy as per Smith's direction, along with half the officers. Darren would captain *Goshawk* and Jaco *Eagle*. *Osprey* would accompany the two larger frigates, which would spend five days anchored in Portsmouth Harbor, during which they would host a visit from the Admiralty.

Eagle was launched as scheduled during the first week of June and *Goshawk* followed after the July 4th holiday. Shakedown cruises of both ships confirmed that they could make 10 to 11 knots under full sail and could cruise in a moderate breeze at eight. Not as fast as the smaller schooner frigates that routinely made 12, but they were much bigger at 1,200 tons and carried bigger guns.

The trip to England was uneventful, other than Jaco, and Darren practiced one-on-one duels to test the ship's handling, the crew's ability to sail the ship, and tactics. In Ponta Delgado in the Azores, they met *Kestrel* and sailed north. When the visit was over, *Kestrel* would return to its station and in November, be relieved by *Osprey.*

With *Eagle* flying a commodore's flag, the first boat headed toward his ship, the second toward *Goshawk,* and a third to *Kestrel.* Once they anchored, signal flags adorned the rigging, and a large version of the Stars and Stripes was hung between the fore and mainmasts. The *Don't Tread on Me* flag flew from the mizzenmast.

The crew of *Goshawk* rendered honors to the Royal Navy captain who climbed on deck. Jaco recognized Drew Rathburn, who was Vice Admiral of the Red's Davidson's Flag Captain. The two officers shook hands, and Drew put one hand on Jaco's shoulder. "We are delighted that you accepted our invitation. It is, as you can imagine, a bit tense around here."

"We know. We are here to try to talk some sense to some of your senior officers, unofficially, of course!"

Grinning, Rathburn said, "Absolutely!!! We are just Naval Officers having a friendly chat over several glasses of whiskey, which is much better than shooting at each other."

"Sir, with all due respect, let us get to shore so Darren and I can see a very old friend."

"After you, sir, but please do not arrest Darren because he is wearing a different uniform."

Rathburn's eyes got wide. "I had not thought of that, so yes, it will be a bit of a shock."

The three Americans were ushered into a large office where a grinning Vice Admiral of the Red Stacy Davidson was waiting. A servant was standing behind a bar, and another behind a table with sliced meats, cheeses, and bread.

Even though he was the senior officer, Jaco encouraged Darren to be the first to greet Davidson. The manly hug that followed showed there was more than a professional relationship between the two. When, Jaco introduced his son, Vice Admiral of the Red Davidson said, "Like father, like son. You have already made it into one of my reports. I must ask, Captain Hightower noted that you threatened to fire on his ship. Is that true?"

"Admiral, my orders were to prevent ships of foreign navies from harming U.S. citizens by the means at my disposal. Thankfully, Captain Hightower chose the right course of action."

Davidson looked at Jaco. "So, your son is a diplomat as well as a skilled naval officer."

"Admiral, he gets that skill from his mother, not me."

Davidson laughed. "So, this evening, I hope the three of you can join Belinda and me for dinner. Your lieutenants have been invited to dinner with ours at our mess on base. It is not formal. Then tomorrow, we have lunch with the First and Second Naval Lords who are already here on other business. Unfortunately, young Captain Jacinto, it will be just your father and Captain Smythe, and me. Then, in the afternoon, I believe we are taking a tour of one of your ships. I presume that is acceptable."

Jaco nodded after glancing at Darren. "Captain Smythe has personal business tonight and will join us for dinner and lunch. His father is not well, so Darren is going to spend as much time with him as possible. *Goshawk* and *Eagle* are as identical as we could make them, so the tour will start on *Eagle*. If you wish to see *Goshawk*, we can arrange that but I propose that Captain Micah Jacinto give you a tour of *Kestrel* which routinely cruises at 12 knots and is capable of 14."

"Excellent." The Admiral turned to Rathburn. "Captain Rathburn, please make those changes to the schedule."

Facing Darren, "I am sorry to hear about your father. I lost mine many years ago, and it was not a pleasant experience."

"Aye. And, I need to have a discussion with brothers that I hope, will not be painful."

PORTSMOUTH, TUESDAY, AUGUST 23RD, 1808, 12:23 P.M.

Captain Drew Rathburn was waiting at the pier for Darren to arrive on the boat from Gosport when the longboat from Eagle delivered Jaco. When he climbed up the stairs from the landing, Darren had a grim look on his face that brightened when he greeted his former subordinate and his friend.

Jaco made a mental note to ask Darren after lunch. His assumption was that the news about his father was not good.

On the way to the officer's mess in the building where the unmarried officers lived, the Royal Naval officer started to prepare the Americans for who they were about to meet. "First Naval Lord is Sir Richard Bickerton, 2nd Baronet. He had numerous commands and was Nelson's number two at Trafalgar where he commanded one hundred gun first-rater *Royal Sovereign*. He became First Naval Lord in May of this year."

Earlier, Rathburn explained that Bickerton was, as the First Naval Lord, the most senior officer in the Royal Navy. Pausing, Rathburn then added. "Second Naval Lord is Admiral Sir Thomas Pasley. Like Bickerton, he has been in the navy since the Seven Years War. He lost a leg during an action with a French ship back in 1794 which has limited his commands at sea."

He took a quick breath, "Since we are all naval officers, ranks are the proper form. Both men will listen to you, but neither will tolerate poorly formed arguments. The fact that they are meeting with you is the result of Vice Admiral Davidson's urging. And, Darren, be prepared for questions on why you are wearing an American uniform."

Darren laughed. "Splendid. Their lordships may not like the answer."

Jaco added, "I presume someone has told them that even though I may be considered a rebel, I have decent table manners and know how to eat with a knife and fork."

Rathburn chuckled. "Aye, I learned my manners at the Royal Naval Academy. Darren, given his proper English parents already knew."

They were the first to arrive and helped themselves to a glass of the King's port from the crystal decanter on the table at the end of the room. They noted the nametags where they wanted each man to sit at the round table.

Jaco was opposite the First Naval Lord with Darren on his right and Drew Rathburn on his left. The Second Naval Lord would sit to the left of the First Naval Lord with Vice Admiral Davidson next to the man who was the operational commander of the Royal Navy.

The Second Naval Lord's focus was recruiting and training men for sea. Recruiting also included impressment of sailors taken from other ships. Jaco took the letter from Secretary of the Navy Smith and placed it on the plate in front of Admiral Bickerton's chair.

Seeing the note, Drew asked. "Jaco, what is that?"

"An official letter from the Secretary of the Navy, who is a civilian, to the head of your navy, with the hopes he will pass it on to the appropriate MPs in the House of Commons." Both men knew that the First Naval Lord was Britain's equivalent of the Secretary of the Navy. It was also diplomatic and policy cover for the Royal Navy flag officers to meet with two American

Navy Captains who were on active duty for the purpose of this voyage. It was also a way around the diplomatic deaf ears, as Smith called them, of Britain's foreign ministry.

Vice Admiral Davidson followed the two senior officers into the room. Both were wearing their working uniforms rather than full dress. Davidson wanted an informal meeting and conversation that the two Naval Lords could take forward.

After introductions, Drew Rathburn stepped back. Bickerton was the first to speak. "Captain Jacinto and Captain Smythe, I have read the Royal Navy's reports on both of you. Captain Jacinto, if we were meeting before 1783, I would want to find the most remote dungeon to put you in. Then, I would toss the key into the ocean and order any man that let you out to be hung immediately."

Smiling, Jaco said, "Sir, I take that as a compliment."

"It is. I have also read our reports on your actions against pirates in the Mediterranean and applaud your work. I would like to know more. Perhaps, Darren and you could meet with Captain Rathburn to share what lessons your navy learned."

"Aye, sir, it will be my pleasure."

"Excellent." The First Naval Lord turned to face Darren. "Captain Smythe, the Royal Navy's loss is the American Navy's gain. Putting you on half-pay and the retired list was not one of the Royal Navy's brightest days. Nor were its actions against all our rules justifiable. Neither I nor the Second Naval Lord bear you ill will, but I fear there are others in our service who do not share our opinion. Should you run afoul of a naval officer who does not share our views, contact any one of the three flag officers in this room, and we shall straighten that individual out, forthwith."

"Thank you, sir."

Admiral Bickerton opened his arms. "Excellent. Gentlemen, shall we break bread with each other and share our experience as naval officers."

The waiters held out the chairs for the three flag officers. The three captains waited until the flag officers were seated before they sat. Their glasses were either topped off or filled. The First Naval Lord held up his glass. "I think it is appropriate to toast to our national leaders, then our individual navies, which I propose will be followed with one to a growing friendship, and then the most important toast, which is to the friends we have all lost in the service to our countries."

"That is most generous and agreeable, and to add a touch of humor, First Naval Lord, I'd be willing to drink to those toasts."

Smiling, the First Naval Lord, spoke. "To the President of the United States, Thomas Jefferson."

Glasses were raised, and each man said, "President Jefferson."

The next toast was to King George III and the same process was followed as it was for the toast to the Royal Navy, the U.S. Navy, and their growing friendship. Then, for the last one, the First Naval Lord asked them all to stand for a moment of silence after they drank their port.

As the appetizer was served, the First Naval Lord said to Jaco, "Captain, when I visit *Eagle* tomorrow, I intend to climb up the side. I do not, even at my advanced age, expect or want a bo'sun's chair."

"Sir, it should not be a problem. The blocks of wood are eight inches wide, and there are iron handles along the side."

"Excellent. Vice Admiral Davidson has asked me to ply you with enough drink to get either you or Captain Smythe to reveal how you build ships that are impervious to cannon balls."

Jaco laughed. "I would submit that the secret starts with American wood, which the Royal Navy is importing to build its new ships. And friendly trade policies might make it cheaper and easier to obtain."

The Second Naval Lord had been studying Jaco as if he was sizing up an enemy before a swordfight. "Captain, that's an interesting reference. Could you expound on your thoughts?"

"Sir, the House of Commons has passed laws that are attempting to restrict the United States' ability to trade with other nations. One example is that any ship coming to Europe, must stop in an English port, be inspected and then pay a duty before proceeding to its destination. My family is one of the shareholders in a very large import and export company that buys and sells goods to customers in Amsterdam, Bordeaux, Brest, Genoa, Malmö, Marseille, Naples, Tunis, and Venice to name just a few of the places. To say this is an inconvenience is an understatement. The United States has publicly refrained from taking sides in the current series of wars in Europe."

He stopped speaking for a few seconds. "Plus, the Royal Navy stops our ships to see if they are carrying contraband which they are not. Then, in the process, they impress seamen who are U.S., repeat, United States citizens. Some, like my friend Darren have formally renounced their citizenship, others have not but have formally sworn allegiance to the United States. We provide proof of their new allegiance as part of the ship's papers, something that Royal Navy captains ignore. Between 1792 when the end of last year, by my government's count, over eighteen thousand have been impressed into Royal Navy service. Sir, to put it another way, assuming your average Royal Navy frigate has a crew of two hundred and fifty officers and men, that's enough to crew seventy-two ships."

The First Naval Lord started speaking as soon as Jaco spoke the word ships. "Captain, we have been using press gangs since the days of Queen Elizabeth. English courts have upheld the process."

Jaco held up his hand, "Sir, with all due respect, those court decisions were in regard to citizens living in England, Ireland, Scotland, Wales, and British colonies. May I remind you, sir, that as of September 3rd, 1783, we are no longer an English colony. My sister Shoshana, whom Vice Admiral Davidson has met and I think seen in Old Bailey a few years back, has looked deeply into the matter. What you do in the home islands is England's business, but when warships stop neutral merchant ships on the high seas and take seamen off against their will, another word applies, and that is kidnapping. it is a crime in England and the United States. We just had an incident when our frigate *Chesapeake* was fired upon, and four men were taken off, supposedly as deserters. Three of them were U.S. citizens, one had just enlisted. Whether or not they deserted from the Royal Navy or not is moot, they were U.S. Citizens. My point is this practice must end, or it will lead to a situation which I think everyone in this room would like to avoid."

Bickerton responded quickly, "Very diplomatically put. I take your comments to mean another war between the United States and Great Britain may be in the offing?"

Nodding, Jaco said, "Aye, sir. And if I may, before I came to England, I did a bit of research. History shows that, since 1702 and today, England and France have been at war for 52 of the 106 years. It is no wonder that the country is short of men!"

No one at the table said anything for several seconds. To Jaco and Darren, it felt like an eternity, then the First Naval Lord spoke. "Whether I approve of impressment or not is moot, as is England's position on trading relations. I don't make foreign policy; that is the purview of King George III and Lord Bentwick, the Prime Minister. However, England and its Navy are not in the least worried about the U.S. Navy. We have the best ships, the best-trained crews, and the best captains. The Royal Navy has, so far, been able to take the measure of every naval force arrayed against our island nation. So, Captain Jacinto, spare me any assertions that the U.S. Navy will be a threat to the Royal Navy's control of the seas."

Darren spoke up. "Sir, if I may be bold to speak for my good friend and at one time, my mortal enemy. If you were to visit his house in New

York, the halls on the first floor are lined with the bells of Royal Navy ships he either sank or captured. I believe there are an even dozen, and they include at least six Royal Navy frigates and one sloop-of-war. We, that is the U.S. Navy, may be small, but between 1803 and 1805, we conducted an expeditionary land and sea campaign against the Barbary Pirates four thousand miles from our shores."

He was nodding as he spoke. "I was taught Naval history just a few hundred feet from where we sit at the Royal Naval Academy. To my recollection, even the Royal Navy has never executed such campaign, even off India. From it, we now have a cadre of officers and other ranks who have this experience. *Eagle,* the ship you will visit tomorrow, as is *Goshawk* is crewed with fifty percent experienced hands and fifty percent new recruits. So, while President Jefferson has forced the Navy to be small in terms of budget, we are training crews who will be the nucleus of new ships as we build them."

The former Royal Navy captain could see the First Naval Lord was about to speak, but Darren put up his hand as a signal to say, "Sir, I am not finished." He swallowed. "Unlike Royal Navy sailors who are often motivated as much by fear of punishment as King and country, sailors in the U.S. Navy are motivated by their desire to protect the freedoms that we all enjoy and will not allow any country or leader to take from us. Freedom, sir, is a powerful motivator and is why thousands of men and women from all over Europe and England itself are flocking to our shores. In the United States, we have the freedom to choose what profession we want to enter, where to live, and can buy as much land as we can afford. We, the people, vote for our leaders, and anyone who is a citizen can vote." He almost said that must live under the thumb of those who are born to privilege.

Darren took a deep breath. "I didn't understand the attraction of the United States and its freedoms of choice until I began living there. It is one of many reasons why I renounced my English citizenship and swore allegiance to the United States."

No one at the table spoke for a few seconds. It gave the waiters a chance to clear the table of the main course and place small bowls of English Toffee pudding before each of the diners. Their glasses of port were refilled.

The former British captain wanted to make another point. "Sirs, tomorrow, when you visit *Eagle* and *Kestrel,* remember they were bought and paid for by a consortium of U.S. companies, just one of which is U.S. Industries. The firm that Captain Jacinto and I have shares in through our ownership of American Shipping and Passenger Lines is the first venture of its kind. We carry passengers, mail, and cargo from New York to London on an average of twelve days. We guarantee fourteen. Before we left, Captain Jacinto and I rode on a vessel that went from New York, up the Hudson River to Albany without sheeting home a sail. It was powered by a steam engine and paddle wheels. Like Captain Jacinto said, it would be a mistake to take the United States lightly."

Bickerton picked up the letter that was in the center of the table. He again read the addressee. "I presume that this letter is asking Britain to reconsider its policy of impressment and you would like me to pass this to the First Lord of the Admiralty and ask him to give it to the Prime Minister."

"Aye, sir. That is the wish of our Secretary of Navy Robert Smith."

Smiling, the First Naval Lord, said, "I gather that your government has tried going through the normal diplomatic channels and the results were not satisfactory."

"To use Mr. Smith's words sir, speaking with the British Ambassador to the United States on this matter was akin to speaking to a stone. Mr. Monroe, who before he returned last year, was our ambassador to the Court of St. James said similar words." Jaco's comment generated chuckles from both the First and Second Naval Lords.

"Captain, it may surprise you, that as the First Naval Lord, I have also run into that rock wall on numerous occasions. I take your point."

Those at the table could sense the First Naval Lord had something else to say. "This cannot leave this room. While this may not help you, note that I am not a fan of impressment and will forward this letter with those sentiments. Neither is Vice Admiral Davidson. The Second Naval Lord doesn't like it, but since Admiral Paisley's job is to fill out muster rolls, he will ask what is the replacement policy that will enable him to keep Royal Navy ships manned. However, until the PM tells the First Naval Lord that the House of Commons no longer supports impressment, my hands are tied."

Bobbing his head, Jaco said, "Understood, sir."

"Good, one more point which shall also not leave this room. We, and I think I speak for everyone at this table, could do without another war. One day, we will rid ourselves of the menace called Napoleon. If I had a magic wand, I would do what I could to avoid a war with the United States, but there are those in the House of Commons who want our former North American colonies back. You and I know that will never happen, but they have a voice, and some are still in positions of power. But like you, Captain, we follow the orders from the civilians to whom we report."

Sir Richard Bickerton stood, telling everyone at the table that lunch, or at least the First and Second Naval Lords participation in the meal, was over. Vice Admiral Davidson left the three captains.

All of them kept quiet for a few seconds. "Darren, how is your father?"

"Not well. He only has a few weeks before the illness kills him."

Jaco looked at his friend. "Darren, we can appoint a temporary Captain for *Goshawk* so you can stay here until the end and then catch one of our schooners back to New York."

"Thank you, Jaco, but let me work through this. Tonight, I am having a discussion with my brothers about Emily's and my shares in the firm. I want to hear my father's wishes if he is coherent without my brothers in the room."

Neither of the other two officers said anything. They could see the pain on Darren's face. "Shall we talk about fighting pirates? It is much more interesting than my family's troubles."

PORTSMOUTH, ENGLAND, WEDNESDAY, THE 23RD OF AUGUST 1808

Once the lookout spotted the long boat leaving the Royal Navy base with two flag officers on board, he called down to the deck. Jaco took a spyglass from the rack and studied the boat. Vice Admiral of the Red Stacy Davidson was sitting next to the First Naval Lord, Admiral Richard Bickerton.

Before he could say anything, *Eagle's* bo'sun began giving orders causing the crew to pour out of the fore and aft companionways. The ship's two drummers started beating out a rhythm similar to the beat when the ship clears for action.

Once the bo'sun stopped issuing commands, Jaco went to the forward end of the quarterdeck, "Mr. Howard, the two flag officers are Vice Admiral of the Red, Stacy Davidson. He is the Commander of the Channel Fleet. The Admiral is Richard Bickerton, First Naval Lord. And there is a Royal Navy captain whom I presume will come aboard first."

A touch with the back of his hand told Jaco that Howard understood. Jaco stood at the quarterdeck railing watching his men assemble. The mates had them in position before he climbed down from the companionway to where he planned to greet the two flag officers.

Each of the sailors was dressed in his "dress" uniform which was a blue and white striped shirt and white trousers. The mates wore dark blue coats with pewter buttons and white pants. The officers had the same coats, but with gold buttons, and the midshipmen wore a red vest under their blue coat. Lieutenants had one epaulet on their left shoulder, Jaco as the captain, had epaulets on both shoulders, gold buttons along with gold embroidery along the collar. All his officers were wearing tri-corner blue hats, and Jaco's had gold embroidery around the top.

While the uniforms conformed to the standards set by the Secretary of the Navy, they were not perfect matches. They were close enough and were approved by Secretary Smith.

His bo'sun stood at the end of two rows of six side boys that went from the bulwark to almost where Jaco was standing with his three lieutenants and midshipman, ship's surgeon, and quartermaster arrayed behind the captain. *Eagle's* carpenter, sailmaker, and cooks were all mustered with the men lined up in neat rows that made up a U around the area where the two Royal Navy flag officers would come aboard.

Drew Rathburn was the first officer through the bulwark. He stood at attention while Bo' sun Howard blew All Call and then announced in a loud clear voice, "Captain, Royal Navy, ahhhhhhrrrrriving."

Once that command was finished, Drew touched the brim of his hat, faced aft at attention for a count of two, and then walked toward Jaco. Coming to attention, he said, "Captain, it is an honor and a pleasure to be your guest."

"Welcome and we shall have an enjoyable morning." Rathburn stepped to the side just in time for Bo' sun Howard to bellow out, "Commander, Royal Navy Channel Fleet, ahhhhhhrrrrriving!"

Davidson nodded to the bo'sun, faced aft for at least two seconds then marched toward where Jaco was standing. Jaco Jacinto and Drew Rathburn as the junior officer, initiated his salute and Davidson responded. When the admiral dropped his hand, so did the captains.

The process was repeated when Admiral Bickerton stepped onto *Eagle's* main deck. The only difference was that the two drummers did a drum roll as the admiral walked amongst the side boys.

With the honors rendered, Jaco said to Admiral Bickerton, "Sir, if you allow me, the tour will start in my cabin, where I will introduce my officers. Then we shall tour the ship."

"Excellent, please proceed, captain"

Pointing with the palm of his hand, Jaco said, "Aye, aye, sir." Then he turned to his First Lieutenant, Oliver Arnold from Norfolk, Virginia,

"Mr. Arnold, dismiss the men. Have them at their stations for the tour as needed."

A nod of Arnold's head was complemented by a touch of the brim of his hat. The 23-year-old was so thin, one would think he would get blown over by the wind. However, Jaco noticed that Arnold could climb the rigging as fast as *Eagle's* topmen and was constantly visible to the crew, either watching the work without interfering or being intrusive or asking questions.

Once in the cabin, *Eagle's* officers stood in a row at the forward end of the cabin so Jaco went down the list – First Lieutenant Oliver Arnold, Second Lieutenant Cyrus Brooke, Third Lieutenant Alden Browne, Midshipman Malachi Cohen, Quartermaster Linus Turner, Bo'sun Harold Howard, and Dr. Gideon Maxwell. As each man was introduced, each touched his hat and nodded.

Laid out on the table was a side view of *Eagle* given to Jaco by Joshua Humphreys before the frigate was commissioned. "Admirals, *Eagle* displaces just over 1,500 tons, is 180 feet long, and has a beam of 49 feet. It has, as you will see, three decks: main, gun, and berthing, plus a divided hold which we shall not enter. Forward, just below the berthing deck, is the surgeon's cockpit, which the Royal Navy calls the orlop deck."

"*Eagle* is armed with thirty-six cannons and easily cruises under tops, mains, and top gallants, in a decent wind, at nine knots. It can go faster. During sea trials, in a moderate breeze from the port quarter, our log showed us making twelve knots. We have stores aboard to stay at sea for two months."

Jaco stopped. Bickerton was the first to ask, "Captain, I noticed there are no cannons on the main deck except for several small six-pounders. May I ask why?"

Smiling, Jaco said, "You may. If we are to engage in battle with another ship, we intend to fight with our main armament and have the crew inside the ship, protected from splinters and cannister balls."

"And the small enclosure around the wheel? Pray tell what is that for?"

"We only have the sides up here in port, but in bad weather, it is enclosed and protects the officer of the deck and the quartermaster from wind and rain. If we are to engage an enemy ship, it is strong enough to stop musket balls and cannister."

They left the captain's cabin and went down the aft companionway to the gun deck. The gratings to the main deck were all open as were the gun ports. Lanterns hanging from the ceilings provided additional light.

Waiting by the mizzenmast, Second Lieutenant Cyrus Brooke, stepped forward. "Admirals, as you can see, we have thirty-two large cannons mounted here. In the captain's cabin, you saw the two stern chasers, and up forward, we have two more of the same cannons as bow chasers."

"No carronades?"

Brooke answered, "No sir. We think carronades are a waste of space because of their short range."

Bickerton looked surprised and turned to Jaco. "Pray tell, is that a common belief in your Navy?"

Jaco nodded. "Aye, sir it is. Tactically, we believe maneuver and accurate, rapid long-range fire will carry the day. I believe Admiral Davidson can speak to that better than I since he was on the receiving end."

Bickerton looked at Vice Admiral of the Red Davidson, saying he needed to speak up. "Sir, when my squadron engaged *Scorpion* during the American War for Independence, Captain Jacinto used his frigate's speed, handling qualities, and cannons to engage and hit our ships regularly at six to eight hundred yards. In the space of an hour or so, he put two frigates, larger than *Scorpion,* out of action and damaged my ship, *Puritan,* before sailing away. Captain Smythe had a similar experience when he had *Gladius* which, along with *Hasta* and *Pilum,* were specially modified to hunt and engage *Scorpion.* When he did, *Scorpion,* under Captain Jacinto, put them all out of action and escaped."

Looking at Jaco, Admiral Bickerton said, "What type of cannon do you have?"

"Very large ones."

Bickerton laughed. "Is that why they are all covered with canvas?"

"Aye, Admiral."

"And the gunports closed?"

"Aye," *And so you cannot see how the hull is built.*

At the bow of the ship, Second Lieutenant Brooke showed the British officers the wheels which enable the bow chasers to be swiveled through a larger arc giving them a wider field of fire. Both British admirals nodded their understanding.

From the surgeon's cockpit, the Admirals could peer into the first hold. There, they could see the bulkhead that went from one side of the hull to the other and was bolted to the ribs and the overhead beams. From their vantage point, they could not see the diagonal cross members that provided added strength to the hull and helped prevent it from hogging, or sagging.

Back in his cabin, the ship's cook brought in a tray of freshly baked oatmeal and sugar cookies. The admirals clearly enjoyed the sweetness of the treats. As he sipped a glass of wine, Admiral Bickerton noted, "Captain, I can see you run a very clean ship that is also very tidy. Your men appear to be cheerful. What kind of desertion rate do you suffer?"

"We don't have any deserters, sir. Our men are all volunteers, and if I wasn't afraid of your press gangs, I'd let a quarter of my men go ashore each day. Typically, the last boat back is at four bells on the First Watch. Each boat that goes ashore has a mate who is responsible for mustering the men at the landing. If someone is missing, then he has to find him. And if a man goes missing, then shore leave ends. No one in the crew wants that!"

"Captain Jacinto, that works well when you are at peace, but England is at war, and our men often have had a bellyful of life on a Royal Navy ship."

"I beg to differ, sir. We never had that problem either in the Mediterranean or against the French or when we were fighting England. I submit, sir, that our motivations are much different. We go to war when our freedoms and rights are in danger. I mean no disrespect when I say this, Admiral, but you go to war when your king and several other monarchs decide they want to put a Bourbon king back on the throne in France. The average Englishman doesn't care a whit about who sits on the throne of France. All he wants is to be able to feed his family and put a roof over their head."

Admiral Bickerton looked at Jaco, started to say something, then paused. "I am not at all offended, Captain. There is much truth to what you say. Thank you for the tour and the excellent cookies. I wish you fair winds and following seas. Again, this shall not leave this cabin, neither the First Naval Lord, nor I, nor Vice Admiral Davidson want to go to war with you."

As they were shaking hands, Jaco said to Admiral Bickerton, "Sir, neither do we, and this time it will be different. Back in 1775, we didn't have a navy. Today, we have one small, but I think you saw in your visit, competent Navy. So, it would be wise to remember that in a dog fight, what counts is not the size of the dog, but the size of the fight in the dog."

Admiral Bickerton smiled, "Captain, I will keep that in mind. It has been a pleasure."

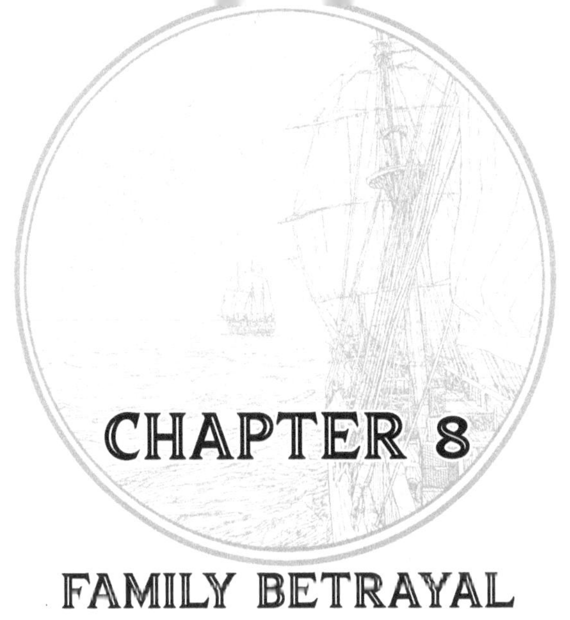

CHAPTER 8

FAMILY BETRAYAL

GOSPORT, ENGLAND, WEDNESDAY, AUGUST 23RD, 1808

Around the same time that the admirals were coming on board *Eagle,* Darren was skipping the steps he knew creaked as he went upstairs to the second-floor bedroom where his father was lying in bed. To be sure he was not seen, Darren entered by the kitchen door.

His two brothers were in the offices at the factory located about a block away. Darren put the single chair next to his father, who looked pale and weak in the early morning light. Sitting down, he said softly, "Father, tell me what is going on. Something is not right."

Lester Smythe was in his 78th year and turned his head slowly. "Your brothers are always arguing, and I fear they have run the business aground."

"You know this how?"

"Esau Labatto. I brought him into the business after he graduated from Oxford. He is a very smart boy who is very good with customers. The workers in the factory adore him, and he knows contracts. Apparently, the Royal Navy contract is coming up at the end of the year, and neither Bradley nor Gerald has bothered to go to London to discuss the renewal. We have new instruments, new medicines, and yet, all they do is argue."

"What do you want me to do?"

"First, things first. We need to secure the renewal of the Navy contract. It covers all our expenses, and with the expansion of the Navy, it will be even more profitable. Also, we should approach the Army, but neither Bradley nor Gerard has done so. Then, I need someone to go through the ledgers and tell me the truth."

Darren listened and was saddened because these were things he could not do. Before he could say something, his father continued. "Emily should be here tomorrow. Make sure she is given access to the company's ledgers. And, today, go find Dr. Labatto. He is still practicing and brings his son Ezra to me."

"Isn't Bradley treating you?"

"He is, but I think he is killing me rather than letting me die of old age. I stopped taking the medicines my son prescribed and feel much better."

There was a sadness in Darren's father's voice that he had never heard before. His father was always proud of his children and would do anything to help them. *Even though I have not visited as often as I should, my father accepted that, and we cherished the moments we had together. He does not deserve this!*

"Darren, both Gerald and Bradley want the money in the banks so they don't have to work. I am not going to let that happen."

The naturalized American citizen wanted to ask how much money, but hesitated thinking it wasn't his business. Lester told him. "In my accounts at Barings Bank and Bank of England, there are about one hundred and fifty thousand pounds (~£16,934,491 or $ 21,337,548 in January 2026). They know to the penny because Bradley's wife keeps the books and has seen the account books. In my new will, Bradley and Gerald will get fifteen thousand each which is a princely sum, but that is all. They are not to get a copper more than what is in my will."

Lester stopped talking and sipped a glass of wine. "My attorney, Austin Barlow works with your Henry York at Scoons. He is also the Smythe & Sons attorney, and he redid my will. When it is read, Bradley and Gerard will be surprised."

"In what way, Father?"

"I named Emily as the executor of my estate with you as her alternate. She, with your help, will decide what to do with the business and the money. Each of you will also receive fifteen thousand pounds. If we close Smythe & Sons, each worker will get three thousand pounds from the estate."

Lester leaned forward and pulled a letter from underneath his pillow. "Emily should be here today or tomorrow on some sort of *Ness* ship. I don't know what that is. I am hoping she is bringing her new husband Rafer, and their son Laclan."

"Father, she is. *Ness I* and *Ness II* are fast schooners that we, or Naval Escort Services and U.S. Industries, use to carry mail, dispatches, people back and forth across the Atlantic."

The scion of the Smythe family leaned back against his pillow. "It is good to see you, my son. I have, through Henry York and your letters, learned of your accomplishments, and I am proud of you. Who knew the little boy who used to watch Royal Navy ships on the stone by the dock would be so successful."

"Thank you, Father. You and mother brought me up well."

"Thank you. And how are my American grandsons?"

"Darryl is following his father's footsteps. David is a medical doctor and practices in Charleston. He is courting a lovely young woman. Jonah who was part of the Lewis and Clark Expedition that went to the Pacific Ocean, has written a book about his experience. He lives, at least for the moment, in New York, but I can tell he is itching to go west. He wants to explore the shore along the Pacific Ocean."

Lester nodded. "Go, do what I asked. I do not have much time left."

PORTSMOUTH, THURSDAY, AUGUST 24TH AUGUST 1808

Early in the morning, as in just after four bells on the Morning Watch, there was a soft rap on the door to Darren's cabin at the aft end of Goshawk. "Captain, sir, Ness II has just entered the harbor and is approaching the Gosport Dock. Our longboat is ready for you."

"Splendid, have Midshipman Cowan accompany me to my parent's house so the crew will know where I can be found. Should I go anywhere, I shall send a boat out to *Goshawk* with a note."

By the time *Ness II* started to turn around, one of its boats was in the water and Darren's beat it to the town landing. *Ness II* slowed long enough to take on board a representative from the Naval Base and give them copies of its papers and a note saying that two of the ship's passengers, Emily Smythe Muir and Rafer Muir had gone ashore. It gave the Smythe & Son office as the address where she could be found.

Emily's two chests of clothes were laid in a neat row along with one for Rafer Muir. "Where's Laclan?"

"Staying with Reyna in New York."

"How's father?"

"Not well and not happy with our brothers. He thinks they are trying to kill him. Dr. Labatto senior and Dr. Labatto junior think the medicine being given to father has large quantities of arsenic in it and is slowly poisoning him. They took the bottles home where they tested it. I don't know how, but we have known the Labattos for many years, and I do not think they will lie.

"I'm not surprised. That gives us a criminal element. Do Brad and Gerald know I am coming, errrrr, rather, I am here?"

"No. You need to look at the ledgers. I met with Esau Labatto last night, and he paints a pretty dark picture in that the business is just hanging on."

Emily pointed to a bench in the park near the dock. "Let us sit and talk. Rafer, would you please give the wagon driver an extra quid, telling him we must talk for a few minutes."

"I am sorry that you have been put in the middle of this, but Father and I have been corresponding about Bradley and Gerald for several months. He suspects that they want the business to die, Father to die, and they then split the money in the bank. Unfortunately, they have not seen father's most recent will. I have, as has Shoshana."

Emily sat turned slightly to her brother. In the beginning, Emily had her hands in her lap but as she spoke, she became more animated. "When I left New York, Shoshana, Max, and Greg agreed that there are two options. One, let the business go and divide up the money according to Father's will. Two, I am authorized by the board of U.S. Industries to acquire Smythe & Sons if I think it is worth saving. Or, let it go insolvent, pay off the debts, and acquire the licenses and patents. Max Laredo said that it would be nice to have a business in England besides the office in London. It will help us grow our English business. Max also thinks, as I do, that we can sell saws, chisels, axes, etc. that are made in America here in England for far less than ones made locally."

Emily thought for a few seconds. "If Dr. Labatto determines that Bradley and Gerald are poisoning our Father we can use that against them. If there is way too much arsenic in the medicine, they can be charged with attempted murder and I can threaten to cut them out of the will entirely. Remind me to discuss that with Mr. Barlow at Scoons."

"What do you want me to do?"

"I need moral support and your opinion. When are you leaving?"

"I'm not until this is over. I gave Jaco a précis of what I knew last night. He is going to take the two frigates to Amsterdam and then maybe to Malmö. *Goshawk* will be commanded by my First Lieutenant. Then, on the way back, *Goshawk* will pick me up, or if we are not finished, you and I will go home in style on one of our ships."

"Have you met with Austin Barlow from Scoons yet?"

"No, that is scheduled for three tomorrow."

"Where are we staying?"

"I have reserved a room for Rafer and you at the Portsmouth Inn. If you want to stay in the house with Father, that would be better, but I suspect it will not make Gerald or Bradley happy. I can cancel the reservation and pay whatever fee exists."

"Cancel the room at the Inn. Rafer and I will move into our house." Emily pointed with her hand at the wagon, "Shall we?

Rafer climbed into the back of the wagon with Darren letting Emily ride next to the driver. While it was only a short walk from the dock to Smythe & Sons, they needed the wagon for the chests.

When Emily walked into the office she and her mother once shared, she found it a mess. There were receipts in piles that had never been filed away. Invoices were missing notes on when and how they were paid. Worse yet, here it was the end of August, and July's books had not been completed. There was no note of profit or loss.

In the May books, she found notes indicating that two drafts, each for £1,000, were issued to Bradley Smythe and two more to Gerald Smythe. There were no notes indicating what the money was to be used for or if it was a loan to be repaid.

Emily's curt response to Darren and Rafer's queries on what she would like for dinner, or whether she would like to take a break for a few minutes, was an indication that a volcano was about to blow. Emily came into the sitting room with one hand on her hip and another holding a sheet of paper. "Just this year, Gerald and Bradley took eight thousand pounds out of the business over and above their salaries!"

She slammed the sheet of paper onto the table, poured a full glass of wine, and downed almost half of it in one swallow. "The bloody books are a God-awful mess. If either a bank examiner or worse, someone from the Exchequer's office saw what Smythe & Sons now call financial records, we couldn't afford the fines. And I just looked at this year. Lord only knows what I will find later."

She picked up the glass and was about to drink when they heard a soft tap on the door. It was the two Labattos.

"Emily, Darren, here is my official analysis. Ezra is writing a more detailed one that you will have in a day or two. Your brothers mixed in arsenic in the medicine at levels that are over a period of months, lethal. Do you know how long he has been taking this ….." Dr. Labatto, paused for a few seconds to search for the right word. He settled on "… poison?"

"No, but we can go ask him. Why?"

Ezra stepped forward. "If it has been less than two months, simply not taking this will let it pass from his body. Given his age, it will have an effect but will not kill him. Beyond three months, the damage is irreversible, and Mr. Smythe will live only a few more months."

Emily pointed to the door and followed the two doctors up the stairs. Rafer waited until his wife was out of earshot. "Darren, I'm a dumb Scotsman but if this happened in my clan, the head of the clan, or in this case, you or Emily could run them through."

"I was wondering what they would look like dangling from a yardarm, but I take your point."

"You know, Darren, life takes us to strange places. I fought wars in India and Canada before I arrived in the United States to quell a rebellion. After a few weeks, I wondered what the bloody hell I was doing. So, I went back to Merry Olde England, retired, and then came to Charleston. Who do I fall in love with and marry, an Englishwoman who had the same thoughts as me. Now, I am sitting in a parlor listening to a story about two brothers who don't have the brains God gave them. Greed, that's what it is, pure greed, has gotten the best of them, and they are trying to kill their father. For what? Some money that they will get when he passes away. All they had to do was wait, and they would get it all. Now, I fear, they have woken a sleeping tiger whose rage will cost them everything."

Emily suddenly appeared in the doorway of the room. "Are you talking about me?"

Rafer stood up and put his arms around his wife. "Not exactly, we were talking about the tiger who is about to devour two people named Bradley and Gerald."

"Tomorrow, we will take Dr. Ezra Labatto's report to Mr. Barlow at Scoons and ask him what we should do with it. Frankly, I think it is enough to cut Bradley and Gerald out of the will. Or offer them a token to avoid a lawsuit."

Darren was smiling, "Rafer says there is a simpler solution, which is taking them down the road and shoving the ruddy bastards over a cliff."

The Labattos came down and stopped. "Emily, I left Mr. Smythe with a bottle a medicine that will help him cleanse his insides. This will begin to flush the arsenic out and within a day or two, he will start to recover. How much, given his age, is yet to be determined. We are also taking the medicine, so if needed, we can have additional samples tested and use them in court, should we get that far. Bradley has violated his Hippocratic Oath and deserves to permanently lose his medical license. When you are ready, I will be happy to write that recommendation. "Good night, and I will come by late afternoon, if I may."

"Please." Emily held the door and then refilled her glass. Standing in the middle of the room, she said, "Tomorrow, I expect a visit from Bradley and Gerald and maybe even his wife Anne, who is responsible for the books. I want all three of us in any meeting with my brothers. Rafer, when we go to Scoons, I would prefer for you to stay here."

"To protect your father?"

"Yes. He has pistols and swords somewhere in the house, but I know not where. Darren, would you please go ask Father and tell him I will be up shortly to share what I just learned."

PORTSMOUTH, FRIDAY, THE AUGUST 25TH, 1808

When Darren and Emily opened the door, they heard Rafer's loud, command voice. "In the parlor."

Darren started laughing when he saw Rafer sitting in a chair on one side of the room. On the other side, Bradley and Gerald were facing him with their hands and feet tied to a chair and strips of cloth tied across their mouths, into which were stuffed another wad of cloth. Anne, Bradley's wife, was sitting between the two men, with her hands and feet tied, and had a terrified look on her face.

Emily was horrified when she saw her husband sitting in her father's rocking chair, wearing a kilt with his clan's plaid. Across his lap was a sword, and he had two pistols, one in his lap and the other on the small table next to the chair where her father put his glass of whiskey or Madeira in the evening.

"What have you done?"

"Nothing. It appears that Mr. Bradley had some medicine to deliver to your father. The bottle is on the mantle waiting for one of the Dr. Labattos to come to test it. Mr. Bradley does not understand the meaning of the word no and I am afraid, I had to cock a pistol and point it at his chest to get him to understand that neither he nor his brother Gerald is allowed to see your father. A rather detailed description of what a pistol ball does to a man's chest from a retired British Army colonel followed."

"Untie them, now!"

"As you wish, my love."

Emily stood with her hands on her hips. "Bradley, Anne, Gerald, once you are freed, you shall go sit into the dining room. We have much to discuss." Turning to Rafer, "Rafer, would you fetch some wine and glasses for all of us."

Darren sat next to his sister and helped arrange the papers in the order that they planned to discuss them. Her two brothers and sister-in-law Anne sat opposite the two siblings.

Before Rafer returned, Gerald who was the oldest of the Smythe's four children, held up his hand as if he wanted to speak. He had a degree in chemistry from the University of Edinburgh. Bradley was two years his junior and born in 1754. Emily was born in 1756, and Darren who had just turned 50 was the baby and born in 1758.

Emily was well past explanations. She had a plan and an agenda. Impatiently, she said in as courteous a voice as she could, "What?"

"I can explain…"

"What can you explain, pray tell? Taking money from the family business, the poorly kept books and records, the lack of new business, or the poison you are feeding our father?"

Gerald's jaw dropped. No words came out, giving Emily an opening to continue. She slid a copy of Lester Smythe's last will. "Have either of you read this? Note the date - May 25th, 1808 - on which it was notarized as his last will and testament."

Neither of her brothers said a word and looked at each other. "Let me save you the answer, which is yes. Here is the copy of the letter signed by you attesting that you were allowed to read Father's will. It is dated on May 26th, 1808."

"Two days later, on May 28th, Father visited Dr. Ezra Labatto complaining of chest pains, a headache, and a cough. Dr. Ezra Labatto came by the house on May 29th to see our Father and he was feeling better, and he recommended chicken soup. Then, when he returned on May 30th, you told Dr. Labatto, according to his patient record, that Father was feeling better. Yet, beginning that day, you began feeding him a concoction you made that contained arsenic. When father finished one bottle, you refilled it with another with a heavier concentration of arsenic."

Gerald laughed, "That's nonsense, you can't prove it."

"Actually, we can. All the empty bottles and some partially filled ones are now in Dr. Labatto's possession, and he's running tests."

"Please allow me to continue. This won't take long. I have started to go through the books, beginning with January of this year." Emily showed them the entries Anne made, noting that the money was given to the two brothers. She concluded by saying, "Give me a few more days and I will find more irregularities. Withdrawals such as these needed to be signed by Father and one other person. His signature is nowhere to be found, nor, I might add, is either of yours. So, one could presume that Anne might have taken the money for herself."

"I did not. The drafts were given to Gerald and Bradley to cash." Those were the first words the woman had spoken since Emily arrived.

"So, my brothers, where does that leave us?"

Emily took a sip of her wine as Rafer stood by Lester Smythe who then gingerly sat down at the head of the table. "Father, welcome. We now have all the shareholders of Smythe & Sons present. With your permission, I will continue."

Lester Smythe bowed his head slightly, "Please, but before you do, I would like to say something."

"Please, Father."

"When you bring a child into this world, you shower it with love, you try to impart values that will enable them to contribute to the world in some small way. Our goal was to leave you with more than what Olivia, may she rest in peace, and I had when I took over Smythe & Sons from my father. We didn't make it easy on you because life's best lessons come out of struggles and even failures. All we asked in return was that you return the love and bring children into the world that would continue to espouse the values and ideals that Olivia and I cherished."

He took a sip of wine, and no one said anything. "Two years ago, I could sense something had changed. That was when I learned that two of my sons, the ones I entrusted to carry on the Smythe & Sons tradition of making fine medical instruments and medicines and other cutting tools, had lied to me. In fact, I caught them telling me one thing and customers another. When I confronted Gerald and Bradley about two years of lower turnover and profits, they told me not to worry, everything would be fine. It was not fine. I had to go to the factory floor to reassure workers that we were not going out of business. I even called on customers to do the same."

Lester made a face and then pursed his lips. "That was when I realized I had to find another way because I was betrayed by my own flesh and blood. Yesterday I learned that you, Bradley and Gerald, are trying to hasten my death. I just don't understand why. You could have had it all had you waited until nature took its course. Now, you will pay the only way you understand. Emily…."

"One, all of Smythe & Sons will be acquired by U.S. Industries, Limited. It will keep its factory here but will open a new office in London which will offer products made in the United States as well as an expanded line of cutting tools."

Bradley spat out, "You can't do that…."

"Yes, I can. Father owns fifty percent of the shares, Bradley, Gerald, and I own fifteen, and Darren five. Father, Darren, and I control seventy percent of the shares, and we have all agreed that this is the best option. I am happy to note in the minutes any objections, but the majority of shares will win. Which brings me to number two."

Darren handed Emily two pieces of paper and slid one to Gerald and the other to Bradley. "These are your termination letters. The board will now vote either yes or no to accept them."

Emily, Darren, and Lester said, "aye" one right after the other. "That's seventy percent in favor. You are not to return to any Smythe & Sons office. Your salary up to the end of September will be paid in full, after which you will receive no additional compensation. You are also forbidden to contact any of our customers. Should you do so, Mr. Barlow from Scoons will file suit, and he will be supported by U.S. Industries' General Counsel, Shoshana Jacinto. Trust me, my brothers, you do not want to be on the other side when she decides to sue you. The copies of your termination letters are yours to keep. Darren and I have copies as shareholders, there is a copy in Smythe & Sons corporate books, and Scoons has a copy as well."

Taking a deep breath, Emily took another sip of wine. "Which brings us to the last will and testament of Lester Smythe, our father."

She let a few seconds pass, which seemed like an eternity. "Our father and I had a disagreement over what to do. However, since he is our father, we will follow his wishes. The will gives each of you a lump sum payment of fifteen thousand pounds, which our Father will honor through Darren and me as the executors of his estate upon his death."

Another pause, and then Emily continued. "Should either of you or your children contest the will or your termination, three things will happen. One, the payment will be forfeit, i.e., you will not receive the fifteen thousand pounds. Two, we will file charges against both of you for attempted murder. And three, Dr. Labatto will file an ethics complaint against Bradley with the Royal College of Physicians, asking them to terminate his license to practice medicine. Do you have any questions?"

Gerald stood up, put his hands on the table, and leaned forward. "You ungrateful bitch. Emily, while you went off to America to kowtow to your Jewish friends, we were left here. And for kissing their arses, they made you wealthy. You will never get away with this."

"I suggest, Gerald, that both you and Bradley look in the mirror. No one created this disaster but you and your brother. Good day, and I do not want to see either of your faces again. Now get out of this house and do not ever, repeat ever, return."

CHAPTER 9

SUCCESSION PLANNING

LONDON, FIRST WEEK OF SEPTEMBER 1808

Emily's first move after terminating her brothers was to appoint Esau Labatto as the new president of Smythe & Sons. Next, rather than hire a bookkeeper, she retained Scoons to keep the company's books and file its taxes.

Within days of taking the medicine prescribed by Dr. Labatto and no longer taking the arsenic-laced formula created by her brother Gerald, Lester Smythe began to feel better. With each passing day, he became more active and took on projects to help Esau Labatto.

Lester wrote letters of introduction to the Royal Navy, telling them of the change in leadership and asking them to meet with Emily and Esau. Getting positive responses, She, along with Esau and her husband Rafer, took a carriage to London.

Coming out of the meeting with the Royal Navy, they had a commitment to renew early, and the new contract and purchase order would be sent shortly. Then, while meeting with the British Army, they agreed to a large order to replace the kit that British Army surgeons were currently using.

While Esau was meeting with customers he already knew, Emily and Rafer went to the Bank of England. She left £10,000 (~£1,146,733 or $1,433,416 in January 2026) of the £50,000 (~£5,733,665 or

~$7,1267,081 in January 2026) in the account. Bradley's and Gerald's names were removed as signatories on the older one.

From the office of the Bank of England, Emily and Rafer went to C. Hoare & Co., a private bank for wealthy Britons established in 1672 that had an excellent reputation for wise investments that grew. She gave them £15,000 (~£1,720,099 or ~$ 2,150,123 in January 2026) of the £50,000. At the moment, only she would have the ability to authorize withdrawals and had the bank prepare papers for Darren to sign.

From C. Hoare & Co., the couple went to Barings Bank, where her father had £80,000 (~£9,173,864 or ~$11,467,330 in January 2026), which was £5,000 more than the latest bank book in Gosport showed. Again, she gave them the documents needed to remove Bradley and Gerald as signatories on the account, leaving her father and her as the only ones who could withdraw money. Another package of documents that would allow Darren to be added went into the briefcase Rafer was carrying.

Stop number four was at the newly established English branch of the Bank of Rothchild. Greg had encouraged her to set up an account there because the bank had branches in other European countries and duchies and a correspondent banking relationship with the New York Bank of Commerce. £25,000 (~£2,866,833 or ~$3,583,541 in January 2026) was deposited in a new account at Bank of Rothchild.

The process of moving money around took the better part of three days. When Emily was finished, she was confident that neither Gerald nor Bradley could gain access to any of her father's money. Before she left London, Emily placed an ad in two London papers advertising for a "sales agent" to be based in London for Smythe & Sons, Ltd. Sensitive to the fact that many Brits might resent the fact that the centuries-old firm was now a wholly owned subsidiary of U.S. Industries, no mention of the new owners was made.

She, Rafer, and Esau returned to London in the third week of September and chose Hiram Brookings to sell medical products, and Ralph Ham would sell the cutting tools. Samples of the cutting tools – axes, adzes, chisels, hatchets, planes, and saws - and a small inventory had already arrived. Drawings came with the tools, and Ralph Ham headed to shipyards.

With this done, Emily worked with Scoon's accountants to clean up the company's books. Their target date to return to the U.S. was a booking on the AS&PL schooner leaving London in the first week of October.

NEW YORK, FOURTH WEEK OF SEPTEMBER 1808

Jaco and Darren made it back just in time for the annual U.S. Industries planning event held between Rosh Hashanah and Yom Kippur. At the board meeting, the consensus was that the Embargo Act of 1808 was hurting U.S. Industries. Despite their efforts, revenue was down about 20%, as were profits.

Also agreed by those who ran the firm was that they would make no new investments unless there was a clear upside, such as acquiring Smythe & Sons. Construction of new ships needed as replacements would continue; however, no new orders would be placed. Older ships would be refitted whenever feasible and cost-effective.

Outside the firm, the leaders of U.S. Industries were convinced that their peers and competitors were also feeling the same pinch. Already within the Congress, there was a growing consensus between the Federalists and some of the Democratic-Republicans that the Embargo Act should be repealed.

Where the arguments began was what should replace it, if any legislation. Those who wanted it repealed did not want a replacement and wanted to trade with whichever country or customer they chose. As businessmen, it was up to them to determine business risk. There was also a strong, bipartisan consensus that the country needed a U.S. Navy to provide a deterrence to the Royal Navy to stop, by force, if needed, illegal stopping and seizing U.S.-flagged merchant vessels and impressment.

From a business perspective, the portion of U.S. Industries that was not off were the people wanting to leave Europe. Erik Laredo's letter to the board said that he could easily fill a ship a month with 500 people willing to pay to travel to the U.S.

Laura Fonseca Laredo committed to writing a letter to Erik saying that she could dedicate two to three ships to sail from New York to Amsterdam to meet a once-a-month schedule. These older, 1,000-ton merchant ships would be modified with temporary decks in the holds. They could carry 500 passengers in hammocks on three decks and, at a passage fee of £20 per adult and £10/child under the age of 12, the line could turn a tidy profit. Her plan was accepted.

On Thursday, Max Laredo opened the meeting saying that they needed to have a serious discussion about succession planning. He noted that Javier was 73 and he was 67 and it was a bittersweet but lighthearted comment when he said, "Miriam Bildesheim proved that we can't live forever but that we can live a long time." Then he said, "Neither Javier nor I are planning on dying soon, and Dr. Laredo says we are both healthy, but none of us know if we will be written into the Book of Life on Yom Kippur. So, each of us needs a plan.

Each member of the board was supposed to bring their succession plan and who they were grooming to be their replacements. The names on the list were presented and discussed.

When that was over, Javier said, "During this coming year, Max and I want to create a supervisory board of three who will work with us and who will eventually replace us. The three individuals will come from those in this room. And it will require the individuals selected to give up their current position. The plan is, at least for the moment, to make the selections in June 1809. While our families created this business and will always have a say in how it is run, it does not mean that all three will have a Jacinto or a Laredo or a Fonseca in their family tree. Your performance and that of those who work for you, not whether you are a man or a woman, is what will be the deciding factor."

Javier and Max, who were sitting at opposite ends of the conference table, could see the heads turning and looking at them and then at their fellow board members. Max then added, "Neither Javier nor I will tolerate any Machiavellian moves and attempts to undercut your fellow board members will be looked upon by both of us unfavorably and could result in your being removed from the board, or worse, fired from U.S. Industries."

WASHINGTON, FOURTH WEEK OF FEBRUARY 1809

It may have been cold outside the still-unfinished Capitol building, but it was hot on the floor of the House of Representatives. The debate was regarding the passage of the Non-Intercourse bill, which President Jefferson was pushing Congress to pass before James Madison was inaugurated on March 7th, 1809. The bill would ban all trade with France and the United Kingdom.

Even though Javier Jacinto was a Federalist and a member of the minority party, as the co-chair of the House of Representatives Commerce and Manufactures Committee, the members of the Democratic-Republicans listened intently to what he had to say. When he walked to the podium, he suspected that Jefferson had fewer votes for the bill than he thought.

Javier looked first at the Speaker of the House of Representatives, "Mr. Speaker, I, like my Democratic-Republican colleague, the Honorable John Newton, oppose the passage of Senate Bill 42, which we all know as the Non-Intercourse Act. It is simply a bad piece of legislation that replaces the Embargo Act of 1807, which, I and many of my colleagues, warned would harm the United States. Rather than saying I told you so, I will simply tell you that in many towns in this great country, business turnover has dropped significantly. Depending on which business and whom you ask, it is between ten and twenty percent."

Javier paused to look around. "Yes, everyone sitting in this chamber has had constituents give him the same figures. And yet, some of you support this bill that will forbid trade with France or England. Why? Because they are at war? This is akin to cutting our collective noses off our own faces."

Another pause. As he usually did, Javier had his notes on the podium, but rarely did he look down because he did not want to break eye contact with his fellow members of the House of Representatives. "France and England are our two largest trading partners. Our country, the United States, has the second largest merchant fleet in the world. That is correct, astonishing as it may sound. Many of my fellow members of Congress who either own ships or charter ours or other firms to carry their cargos to their customers. So, this bill again embargoes any trader in the United States from doing business with customers in France and England. How stupid is that?"

"Yes, there are risks in trading with France and England. The Royal Navy has blockaded almost every French port, but still, our ships get through. More ships are stopped going to England because *there are more ships going* to the United Kingdom."

Javier Jacinto was on a roll. "To arbitrarily end this trade is an act of lunacy. What will this act get us? I will tell you. More Americans will be looking for work, more will go hungry because they do not have jobs, more will be tossed out of their apartments because they cannot pay their rent, and many of you in this very room will have to look some of your employees in the eye and tell them you can no longer afford to pay them."

Looking around the chamber, Javier made eye contact with those who supported the bill. "One last point. Besides being conceptually ill-advised, the Embargo Act of 1807 is unenforceable. We didn't have the government departments that could attempt to enforce its clauses. The same is true of this bill. Who will enforce it and how? I do not want to pay the taxes needed to add to the size of our federal government so that it can further constrict our economy."

"While you are contemplating that question, realize that if this bill passes, it will not change England's position toward us one whit. Nor will Napoleon suddenly turn to the U.S. and say, it is O.K. not to trade with us. Neither Napoleon nor King George III nor any of their country's leaders care. To think that it will force the House of Commons to debate the impact is folly. This bill, if it passes, will continue to cause our economy to contract. As a result, I, as does Chairman Newton, urge you to vote no. Then, after the inauguration, we can have a discussion with President Madison and look at other options."

When Javier walked out of the House's chamber at the end of the session, none of his fellow Federalists were going to support the bill. He suspected that Jefferson had arm-twisted enough of his fellow Democratic-Republicans so the bill would pass.

CHAPTER 10

AVOIDING FIREWORKS AND LAWSUITS

VICINITY OF 50°N, 10°W, FIRST WEEK OF APRIL 1809

When the small squadron of four N.E.S. frigates sailed from New York in early February, their plan was that each ship would patrol a set of boxes using 10°W as its westernmost boundary and 51°N as its northern limit. The southern border was 47°N and to the east, 5°W.

This was, to the squadron commander Abner Jeffords, a lot of water to patrol, but their mission was deterrence by presence. N.E.S. allowed the AS&PL agent in London to be interviewed by *The Times of London* and the *London Gazette,* during which he casually mentioned that the U.S. would have a small squadron operating southwest of England. Their mission was to protect American-flagged vessels.

Jeffords had taken over command of *Eagle* as part of the planned rotation and was designated as the commodore. Cato Cooper was given *Goshawk,* and Colin Landry, *Kestrel,* and Brandon Grantham commanded *Osprey.* Each of these men had proven their worth as corvette captains against the Barbary Pirates and all had served under Jaco Jacinto during the American Revolution, the Quasi-War against the French, and the Barbary Pirates War.

This six-month cruise, as the two before it and those that followed, was part of a plan devised by Darren Smythe and approved by the Secretary of the Navy, Robert Smith. Half the crews were N.E.S., half the crews U.S. Navy seamen. While the commanding officers of the ships were all N.E.S., all the U.S. Navy officers were graduates of the N.E.S. officer course at the Fonseca-Laredo academy in Kings Point.

After the cruise, the Navy crew would be put on half-pay, and another crew would come on board while the ship was being refitted. The goal was to provide a cadre of officers and seamen who could become the nucleus of frigate crews should the United States have to go to war.

All the N.E.S. officers and seamen held reserve commissions or ranks in the Navy and, if needed, could be recalled. The agreement N.E.S. had with the Navy, was in time of war, the N.E.S. ships would join the U.S. Navy if Secretary Smith or his successor so desired. Smith referred to the N.E.S. squadron as his instant Navy. It was, he believed, a clever way to get around Jefferson's policy of not having a standing Navy.

The squadron put into the Azores to shelter from a storm that covered the ships with ice, then heavy rains and heavy seas. Once the storm had passed, the crews repaired any damage and took on fresh supplies.

While there, the Portuguese port captain invited the four captains to dine with him. During the dinner, he said that just before the storm, a small British squadron searched the Azores for American merchant ships and, at a dinner with Captain Felix Creighton, the Royal Navy commodore and captain of *H.M.S. Lively,* 46 guns, he said that his squadron's mission was to find American merchant ships and bring as many of their seamen into the Royal Navy as he can.

The Portuguese officer said Creighton had three other ships besides *Lively* with twenty-eight 18-pounders, fourteen 9-pounder carronades, and four 6-pounders. *H.M.S. Cleopatra,* with twenty-eight 18-pounders and six 18-pounder carronades, *H.M.S. Boston* with twenty-six 12-pounders, and *H.M.S. Juno,* which had the same armament as *Cleopatra,* filled out his force.

Ship for ship, the American captains thought they were evenly matched. Experience said *Kestrel, Osprey,* and probably *Eagle* and *Goshawk* were faster and more maneuverable. Combined with their long 24-pounders on *Eagle* and *Goshawk,* and the long 18-pounders on *Kestrel* and *Osprey, th*ey had an edge in range that would make up for the difference in the weight of broadside.

Just before they sortied from Ponta Delgada, they decided to sail north in a scouting line with each ship's top sails visible to the one next to it. *Goshawk* and *Eagle* would be in the center with *Kestrel* and *Osprey* on the wings.

Their sailing orders specifically allowed them to defend any ship from a firm that has either invested in or hired N.E.S. or one flying the American flag. Like Micah Jacinto's orders, the paragraph used the words *protect and defend American-flagged vessels stopped or being harassed by any means available.* They were not going hunting, but if they meet an American-flagged vessel, they will offer to escort it to its destination.

Three days out of Ponta Delgada, a green flare lit up the early morning sky. *Osprey* had sighted a ship. As per their doctrine, *Eagle* also fired a flare that was seen by the lookouts on *Goshawk* and *Kestrel.* Within minutes both were adding sail and turning toward *Osprey.*

At six bells on the Forenoon Watch, the lookouts on *Eagle* reported three ships close together, one of which was a Royal Navy frigate, all with luffed sails. Distance was two miles. The lookouts also reported three sets of sails in a line sailing on a course roughly so' by west which Jeffords thought was odd.

Jeffords looked at the closest ship and was sure he though they were American. "Lookouts, can you identify all three ships?"

There was a long pause during which Jeffords was sure his lookouts were confirming what they saw."

"Captain, the center ship is a Royal Navy frigate, and the ones on either side of it are ours."

"Captain, aye." He then leaned over the quarterdeck railing and ordered, "Clear for action, no drums. Load ball. Do not run out."

Then to the officer of the watch, "Signal *Kestrel* and *Osprey,* follow *Eagle.*" Then Jeffords added, "Next signal. *Goshawk* investigate three ships," then signal, "*Goshawk,* return any sailors taken."

Seeing the acknowledgement, Jeffords sent another signal, "*Osprey, Kestrel,* clear for action, do not run out."

More flags went up and down the halyards. When they were done, Jeffords cupped his mouth and yelled to the lookouts in the maintop, "Keep telling me what you see!" He resisted the urge to go to the lookout platform. Not because he was over 50, but because it would send a message that he didn't trust his lookouts.

"Royal Navy frigates shortening sails to just topsails. Continuing so by west."

"Boats are going between the Royal Navy frigate *Lively* and the two merchant ships. One is *Liberty,* and one is named *Freedom.*"

Damn, they are Fonseca-Laredo ships and he probably knows some of the crew. And we found Captain Creighton and his squadron.

"*Goshawk* is luffing up, just behind the British frigate.

ON BOARD *GOSHAWK*

Cato Cooper strode to the forecastle as *Goshawk* slowed to a stop. "Captain of *His Majesty's Ship Lively*, please come to the aft railing of your quarterdeck."

A young man with blonde hair looked at Cooper, who was over six feet tall, broad-shouldered, and bald as a billiard ball. He probably weighed well over 200 pounds but was not fat. "Sir, he is not on board."

"Where is he?"

"On one of the Yankee ships."

"Find him and tell him I want to speak to him."

The young man Cato Cooper thought might be a midshipman disappeared from sight, probably finding out what to say. He reappeared, "He doesn't want to talk to you."

"Tell him, if either he or the First Lieutenant doesn't appear within two minutes, I will fire a twenty-four-pound ball into his cabin. Also, tell your captain and first lieutenant that they are to return any seamen, repeat, any seamen they impressed to their ships immediately."

Another man appeared just as Cato heard the gun port pop open and the rumble of the gun carriage's wooden wheels rumble over the deck as it was pulled into battery. He was wearing a blue uniform with one epaulet. "You wouldn't bloody dare fire on a king's ship."

"I have in the past and would gladly do so again. My patience is running thin. Where is your captain?"

"On *Liberty*."

"I suggest he return immediately, or he won't have much of a ship to return to. Also inform him that he is to return all the men taken from *Liberty* and *Freedom* forthwith."

"And if he doesn't?"

"I will open fire. My sailing orders allow me the latitude to protect American citizens and property by any means available."

The gun ports for *Lively's* two 9-pounder stern chasers opened, and the cannons were run out. Inside the captain's cabin, Cato could see the gun crews aiming both cannons at *Eagle's* hull. At this range, they probably wouldn't penetrate, and he debated whether or not he wanted to wait for the Royal Navy to fire the first shot.

Thoughts of the *Chesapeake – Leopard* encounter ran through his mind. This time, *Eagle* was prepared for battle, and he'd be happy to exchange 9-pound balls for four of his ship's 24-pound ones. He had ordered the guns on the starboard battery to be double shotted.

A seaman ran up to Cato and tapped him on his shoulder. "Sir, lookouts report our ships are trailing the other Royal Navy ships. They have all run out."

"Thank you. Keep me informed." *Jeffords will never allow his ships to go broadside to broadside with the Royal Navy ships. At the moment, that's his worry.*

Cooper was turning back to the stern of *H.M.S. Lively* when he heard two loud bangs, followed almost instantly by two thuds followed by the bellow of the number #1 and #2 long 24-pounders firing. He forgot to cover his ears, and he was standing just above and forward of the #1 gun. The noise was both deafening and painful. His ears were ringing when the smoke started to clear.

Ball #1 from *Eagle's* #1 gun shattered when it hit the side of the muzzle of *Lively's* starboard stern chaser. Shrapnel from the broken ball and the gun barrel shredded the two gun crews. Ball #2 from the #1 gun cut a gunner in half, went down the pantry before slamming into the aft-most cannon on *Lively's* port side. The impact knocked the 4,000-pound barrel off the carriage, which landed on two men, crushing one to death and the legs of the other. Pieces of the ball and gun carriage wounded a half a dozen more men.

Ball #1 from the #2 gun went through the captain's cabin, through the thin wall at the end, and embedded itself in the center of the mizzen mast, just above where it goes down toward the bilge and keel. Splinters flew through the air, goring more Royal Navy sailors.

Ball #2 from *Goshawk's* #2 gun in the port battery hit about a foot above where the earlier ball had cut the mast in half. The impact was enough to break the mast which hung in space for a few seconds before it came down on the deck.

The second ball from *Goshawk's* #2 port cannon screamed down the length of *Lively's* gun deck before ripping open a two-foot wide by two-foot-tall hole in the bow planking, just to the right of its port bow chaser and splashing in the water, 50 yards in front of the frigate.

Slowly, with only the rigging holding *Lively's* mizzen mast in place, it began to teeter back and forth. Men scattered as it toppled to starboard.

Cooper bellowed. "Cease fire, cease fire!!!" he could hear the men below him shouting commands as they reloaded the two cannons. Within a minute the long 24-pounders were back in battery.

The lieutenant who spoke came to the railing. "Now, will you fetch your captain?"

"He's on his way."

"Is he still in a boat?"

"Aye."

"Send the boat around to my port side. We will bring him aboard so we can have a conversation. Trust me, I won't harm a hair on his Royal Navy head. Then signal your friends that we are meeting and that they should not engage. My fellow ships will not attack as long as yours don't."

The young man ran to the side, and a long boat came rowing around *Lively's* heavily damaged stern. Cato looked down at the man from the bulwark and then hastened to the hatch in the bulwark. His bo'sun bellowed after blowing all call, *H.M.S. Lively, ahhhhrrrrriving!"*

Captain Creighton charged forward looking for a *Goshawk's* captain. He ran past Cooper who tapped him on the shoulder, "Are you looking for *Goshawk's* captain?"

"I am. I want to know who I will charge in an Admiralty Court."

"Well, sir. You found *Goshawk's* captain. I'm Cato Cooper. And, you sir, committed a crime by stopping neutral ships and taking men off them. And your name is?"

"Creighton. They are English citizens and deserters."

Cooper rolled his eyes. "Oh, please. I know for a fact those ships are owned by Fonseca-Laredo Shipping, and in their papers, they have a paper for each sailor certifying that they are U.S. citizens."

"My King doesn't accept that. If they are born in England or in an English colony, they are British."

"Sorry, Captain, that doesn't hold water. About a third of the men aboard this ship were not born in the United States. Some of us were born when we were still an English Colony. Your ship needs help, and you will return every sailor to either *Freedom* or *Liberty*, immediately. Once they are safely aboard their ship, you can return to yours."

"And if I refuse?"

"You will watch me pound *Lively* into splinters. Then, any surviving officers, including the moron who ordered you to fire your stern chasers at my ship will ride with us until we return to the U.S. There, you will face kidnapping charges. In New York and most states, it is punishable by hanging. Your choice, captain."

Creighton walked to the bulwark. "Bishop, how many Americans are on board?"

"Sixteen, sir."

"Are any of them hurt?"

"No, sir. One has a minor splinter wound."

"Return them to their ships, now!"

"Aye, captain."

"Satisfied?"

"I will be when they are on their ships, and their captains say so."

Fifteen minutes later, both *Freedom* and *Liberty* were underway. Jeffords' squadron stood off at a distance from the Royal Navy ships, watching them as they clustered around *Lively,* whose mainmast was now teetering.

Cooper was asked to come aboard *Eagle,* and after hearing the story, Cooper's report, endorsed by Jeffords, was put into an oilskin and taken to *Kestrel* along with a modification to Colin Landry's sailing orders directing him to sail as fast as practical to London and ensure the report is given to the U.S. ambassador. He should be able to anchor in the river, deliver the message to the AS&PL dock, which will then have a carriage take the officer to the U.S. ambassador.

PORTSMOUTH, THIRD WEEK OF APRIL 1809

From his office window, Vice Admiral of the Red Stacy Davidson watched H.M.S. Lively limp into the harbor. Only the foremast was still its normal size.

It had taken seven days to cover the 550 nautical miles from where the incident occurred to the Royal Navy base. It spent two days repairing the damage and burying the 16 dead sailors. Three others died on the way, leaving 18 others who were wounded and would recover.

Davidson had already read the official complaint filed by the U.S. ambassador with the foreign ministry. The accompanying copy of Captain Cooper's report was as thorough, detailed, and clearly written by a naval officer. He had to smile when he read Cooper's version of the conversation between him and *Lively's* officers.

He, too, wondered who the idiot was on *Lively* who ordered the stern chasers fired and what he hoped to achieve. He'd seen *Eagle's* gundeck and believed she was armed with 24-pounders, maybe even 32s.

The First Naval Lord is the one who forwarded the American's complaint and report along with a note saying that Creighton works for you, you decide what you want to do, just don't court-martial him. He also sent a summary of Creighton's personnel record.

Captain Creighton went to the Royal Naval Academy at 12 and graduated when he was 14. He'd spent time on a second rater, then worked his way up the lieutenant ranks on frigates before being given the command of his first frigate in 1802.

While his record wasn't stellar, Creighton had taken several French and Spanish frigates as prizes. As Davidson was reading Creighton's record, the word "competent" leapt off the page.

Now that *Lively* had returned, he sent his aide to ask him to come to his office. When Creighton entered his office, Davidson still didn't know what he was going to say. Davidson stood behind his desk, and the first words that came out of Davidson's mouth were, "What happened?"

Creighton gave the Commander of the Channel Fleet a précis of what happened, from the moment he hailed the two American merchant ships until *Eagle* fell off and sailed away. He noted that after the American ships left, the ship's carpenter recommended that they take down the royal, top gallant, and top sail spars and then the upper two sections of mast, leaving only the mainsail yardarm. The rationale was that when the mizzen mast fell, it tore many of the stays to the mainmast, and that it might fall and bring down the foremast.

"Who ordered the stern chasers to be fired?"

"I believe it was my Second Lieutenant, sir. He was killed by one of the American's balls."

Interesting answer, and we cannot ask him. Nor can I say that I think impressing American seamen is stupid. No good will come out of it other than war.

"How many Americans were you planning to impress?"

"Twenty, ten off each ship."

"Do you know what *Liberty* and *Freedom* were carrying?"

"Aye, sir. Their captains showed me their manifests. In their holds were seven hundred and fifty tons of cotton, fifty barrels of rum, fifty barrels of sugar, and ten barrels of molasses."

"And their destination?"

"Liverpool, sir."

"We get most of our cotton for the clothes that you and I wear, and much of the lumber to build our ships from America. They ship us other goods we buy, and America is, despite our empire, our largest trading partner. Have you ever wondered why we harass their ships and take their seamen?"

"No, sir, I haven't. My sailing orders permit it if I believe I can fill my muster list. And, sir, if I may, many of their sailors are Royal Navy deserters."

"Frankly, Captain Creighton, I doubt that, since we don't allow shore leave for our sailors in most ports. And, how do you know an American ship is carrying Royal Navy deserters?"

"I don't until I board."

"And, then?"

"I ask them where they were born. On *Liberty* and *Freedom,* they had certificates of citizenship showing each man's birth date and where he was born. Anyone born in England is a likely deserter."

Davidson forced himself not to show his annoyance at Creighton's answer. "How can you conclude that?"

"Because the only reason they would be in America is that they want to avoid service in the King's Army or Navy."

"Captain, I suggest you cease believing that. Did you look around *Eagle* while you were on board? If you did, what did you notice about the crew?"

"Sir, their captain was an enormous black man, and those that I could see seemed to be a polyglot lot. By that I mean, there were black men, some of mixed blood, and many white."

"My point. If you stopped an American ship owned by Fonseca-Laredo sailing west, you would have found that it was full of immigrants wanting to go to America. And any ship owned by an American company will reflect that mix. So, sir, I suggest you come to the realization that stopping American ships and taking American citizens on the assumption that they are deserters or because they were born in England is sheer folly. The Americans are getting more and more pissed at our country, and I think we are on the road to war over this issue."

"Yes, sir. I understand your concern."

"Would you have liked to take on *Eagle* in battle."

"Aye, sir, I would. Given the chance, I think *Lively* would take *Eagle's* measure. Our rate of fire and discipline would carry the day."

"I admire your confidence. Tell me what you noticed about *Eagle* that is different than *Lively?*"

"Well, sir, there are no cannons on its main deck or any that I saw other than two that looked to be six-pounders on the quarterdeck. All the guns are on a deck below on the main deck."

"And they are?"

"I would bet either eighteen or twenty-fours, sir."

"And the hull?"

"Didn't notice anything other than the two dents my nine-pounder put in the hull. Our eighteens should do quite a lot of damage."

"I took a tour of *Eagle* when she was in Portsmouth last year. So, here are some things for you to think about. One, she is fast. The captain said she could cruise at ten knots and make twelve in a good wind. Two, having faced one of her predecessors, I suspect she is also very maneuverable. Probably more so than *Lively.* Third, if you were inside, it has four internal cross-ship bulwarks that support the berthing deck and give extra strength to the hull. It has a more sharply raked bow than our bluff-bowed ships, and the hull begins to taper just after the mainmast. And last, I believe it has 24-pounders that are superior to ours in range and accuracy."

"I take your point, sir. *Eagle* would be a handful in a fight."

"That, Captain Creighton, is an understatement."

"Sir, may I be so bold as to ask what is going to happen to me?"

"You may. The First Naval Lord has said how I handle this incident is up to me. For the moment, Captain Creighton, you are beached. The House of Commons believes that what happened to you is simply the cost of doing business. By that, I mean, impressment will continue until further notice, and the Royal Navy's view is you did nothing wrong to stop *Liberty* and *Freedom.*"

Davidson stopped for a few seconds to let his words catch up to his brain. "*Lively* needs extensive repairs, and until such time it is ready for sea, you sir, have no command. If *Lively* is deemed repairable, then you will resume command at the time it is ready for sea trials. Your crew, however, will be sent to the barracks ships along with your officers, the Second Naval Lord will use your officers and men to fill vacancies."

"However, in the interim, besides spending time watching your ship being repaired, you will report to me every day. I have some projects that need attending to. Number one is that I want you to spend some days thinking about how you, as a frigate captain, would fight a ship of the same size as *Lively,* which is two to three knots faster, more maneuverable, and can hit your ship repeatedly with twenty-four-pound balls from one thousand yards. Also, assume the crew is equal to the best the Royal Navy can offer, and its captain is innovative and clever in his tactics."

"Sir, that is a tall order, but I shall do my best."

"I expect nothing less. You might want to consult with my chief of staff, Captain Drew Rathburn, who may have some insight on how to fight the Americans. Like me, he has firsthand experience that wasn't pleasant. I am collecting papers on this problem."

NEW YORK, FIRST WEEK OF JUNE 1809

Shoshana Jacinto was looking at what she thought was an interesting letter from one of Henry York's associates at Scoons. The letter asked her if she thought there was a chance that the U.S. Congress could be convinced to recognize English copyrights. Feelers his firm had put out to the members of the House of Commons told him that Parliament would be favorable to the idea.

She wrote back, saying that there were two options here. One, English and American printers could recognize each other's copyrights. The laws were similar enough that they could work out an agreement. Two, use this agreement to gain legislative approval.

Arthur Haver-Brown, the Scoons partner who specialized in copyright issues under the 1707 Statute of Anne, wrote back asking whether he should come to New York or if Shoshana and Naomi should come to London to work out an agreement with the publishers Scoons represented.

The letter from Haver-Brown had just arrived, and she was waiting to show it to Naomi, who was meeting with a writer who submitted a manuscript that U.S. Industries Publishing, now known as U.S. Press, wanted to take to market.

Naomi walked into Shoshana's office. "How'd it go?"

"We went over the contract, and he wants to take it to a lawyer. I said fine. We'll see."

Shoshana picked up the letter from Haver-Brown and was about to show it to her lover and president of U.S. Press when Anita Hastings rapped on the doorframe to her office.

"Do you have a minute?"

"For you, almost always."

Anita Hastings smiled. She had been trying to get Shoshana into her bed ever since they met, and so far, had failed. It had become a standing joke between the two of them. Anita was, as Shoshana said, "in heat" ever since the six-month anniversary of the premature death after a short illness of her long-time lover, Dorothy Dinwiddie, a year ago.

"Last week, one of our two printers, Charles Wiley, put out feelers for investors who might want to back him in a publishing venture. He also had lunch three days ago with several writers offering to publish their books."

"Why did you wait until now to bring this to me?"

"Because I wanted to make sure. I am one of the investors in the consortium Wiley approached. She reached into the drawstring bag and laid a document on the table. It was labeled confidential."

Shoshana didn't touch it and gently slapped away Naomi's hand when she reached for it. "I don't want to see it or read it, and neither should Naomi. But if you want to tell me, off the record, what Wiley is looking for, I think we'd be interested."

"He's looking for twenty-five thousand to start and a commitment for another twenty-five if needed."

"Not enough, but he will learn the hard way as we did. Are there other printers that we can use?"

"I thought you might ask that. At a charity event, I was approached by the sister of a small printer who is looking for more work. He's got a press, a book binder, and is printing Bibles for churches. That is his bread and butter."

"Can he handle half of what we print?"

"I think so, but Naomi, I'd like you to meet him."

"Set up a meeting at his shop. We'd like to see it."

"Before you go, I want you to know that I slept with his sister. I told her after I set up the meeting, I will step away from any decision. He must stand on his own."

In dealing with Anita, there was always a "something else." "So, you like this woman?"

Anita's eyes brightened, "I do."

"Wonderful. We would like to meet her as well. Does she have any skills we can use?"

"She's his typesetter and helps in the shop with the printing. And she is working with the bookbinder to learn that skill."

"Perfect. One more thing. Is there a way we can get a message to Wiley that we don't mind a competitor but would if he starts poaching our authors and prints books under our imprint and our copyright."

"Through the consortium, we will let Mr. Wiley know that if he poaches authors under contract or violates a copyright, then the loans will be called immediately, and any additional funds will not be available."

"Thank you."

"By the way, Sophie Fontaine's reading this Saturday is sold out. We have two hundred and fifty reservations. The New York Hotel said we can squeeze in another fifty if needed."

Naomi said, "Excellent, Anita, Good work. We're looking forward to being there."

"Wonderful. So will Charlotte Ruys, she's the siseter of the printer Jany Ruys."

Anita left, and Naomi looked at Shoshana. "Do you think Anita is on the up and up?"

"Yes. She knows how hard it took to get us to this point. We now have contracts for paper along with contacts with bookstores in New York and they rest of the country to go along with our literary reading series for men and women. That took her years to create, and she gets good press from them. So, it would be stupid to walk away knowing that we, and that includes Anita, have a staff to run them. And, if she brings us a second printer, she's again put another trust marker on the table."

"I'm glad I'm your husband, not your enemy."

Shoshana smiled at the reference to their relationship. While she is a tiger in the business world, Shoshana was much more docile at home. "One more thought. Anita knows I'd cut her off at the knees if she turned on us. Being part of U.S. Press gives her, at least in her mind, status. It also lets her think she has access to our families and our money. To some degree, it does, but she must go through several layers, first you, then me, just to get an idea considered at U.S. Industries."

Then Shoshana slid the letter from Scoons across the table. "And now we have this. We may soon have an introduction to the English market and have our copyright protected."

NEW YORK, FIRST WEEK OF SEPTEMBER 1809

Naomi was smiling when she stuck her head into Shoshana's office. "Mr. Wiley is here, along with a man who I believe is either one of his investors or even his lawyer. They are in the conference room near my office."

Standing, Shoshana was smiling. "Well, this should be fun. Shall we?"

Charles Wiley and the other, well-dressed man stood when the two women entered. "Ms. Jacinto and Ms. Moreno, this is Avery Trent."

Trent shook hands with both Shoshana and Naomi, "I am pleased to meet both of you. U.S. Press seems to have figured out how to make publishing both possible and profitable."

Shoshana shook Charles Wiley's ink-stained hand, as did Naomi before sitting on the opposite side of the table. As she sat, Shoshana asked, "Mr. Trent, we've not met. What is your role in Mr. Wiley's successful printing business?"

"I am both an investor and a lawyer, like you, by profession."

Shoshana wondered what the "like you" meant. He could have, as Shoshana did, spent years as an intern/law clerk before taking the examination that would enable her to represent clients in court, or he went to one of the U.S. or English law schools.

"What firm?"

I want to know because U.S. Industries has long-term relationships with two law firms. One is with Soriano & Burrows, her old law firm in Charleston which now has a New York office, and the other is with late Alexander Hamilton's law firm.

"Griffiss and Lowe."

Shoshana nodded in response to the answer. It was a well-known law firm who had not approached U.S. Industries for work. "So, Mr. Wiley, what brings you to our office today?"

"Contracts for printing new books, or additional editions of ones that are already in print. More precisely, the lack of new contracts. I had not been informed if we failed to deliver on a contract in any way, so I am a bit puzzled."

Naomi began speaking. "Mr. Wiley, your print shop has been a vital part of U.S. Press's success. We have no complaints about your past performance, only that of your future plans."

"I don't understand, Ms. Moreno?"

"Sir, we have come to learn that you are looking for investors to create a competitor to U.S. Press. Let me be clear, we are delighted that you are doing so because I believe it will be good for both of us. However, we are uncomfortable helping you fund your new venture with profits from contracts from U.S. Press. Ergo, no more book printing contracts from us."

"Ms. Moreno, these are tough times. My newspaper printing business has fallen off because advertisers have pulled in their horns. I will have to lay off staff."

Naomi sat with her hands clasped and her wrists resting on the edge of the highly polished table made from eight-inch-wide planks of white birch. "We are all in that same boat, Mr. Wiley. U.S. Industries as a whole and each of our separate businesses are feeling the pinch from President Jefferson's Embargo Act, but you must understand our position."

Trent reached out and touched Wiley's arm. "Is there a middle ground in which Mr. Wiley receives some work from U.S. Press?"

"Sadly, Mr. Trent, I think not as long as he is involved in a competitive venture."

Both Naomi and Shoshana could see the sadness on Charles Wiley's face. He had been their printer of choice now for eight years, and both sides had shared information that helped them overcome obstacles, from paper supplies to book binding to selling the printed copies.

Again, Trent spoke. "May I ask how you came to know about Mr. Wiley's desire to become a publisher?"

Shoshana had anticipated this question. Her answer, at least in her mind, was almost rehearsed. "You may. Suffice it to say that between the New York Bank of Commerce which is primarily a commercial bank but also has an investment banking arm, and U.S. Industries which makes investments in technologies and new business ventures in which we take an ownership stake, we are continually having conversations with people in the local and even international business community."

When she saw her answer didn't satisfy Avery Trent, Shoshana added, "U.S. Press is the largest and probably most successful book publishing house in New York, and probably the United States. So, if someone wanted to start a competitor, it would be if not newsworthy, gossip worthy."

Trent smiled. "I take your point."

Shoshana decided to make a gentle reminder. "Rest assured that U.S. Press will not stand in Mr. Wiley's way because he knows the obstacles we had to overcome. Both Naomi and I think there is room for more book publishers and, more importantly, think there is a market for more books, especially those that are well written and well-presented."

"That, Ms. Jacinto, is good to know. However, is this the time you drop the hammer?"

"There is, Mr. Trent and Mr. Wiley, no hammer to drop. Only to keep one on a rack. Please note that U.S. Press will aggressively protect its copyright to the books that have been printed, those in work, and our relationships with our authors. All those rights are in the contracts Mr. Wiley signed."

"In other words, you will sue us."

"Yes. And as you know, Mr. Trent, lawsuits are economic warfare as much as they are about the law."

"Understood."

Charles Wiley looked at his attorney and then at Naomi and Shoshana, "There is no way I would knowingly violate a copyright. If it got out that I did, no author in his right mind would sign a contract with me."

Her eyes sparkled when Naomi spoke. "That is so very true."

NEW YORK, FIRST WEEK OF OCTOBER 1810

The hard part of the annual U.S. Industries get-together was over now that the annual reviews of each business unit's performance were complete. It was time for the session to shift to planning for the coming year.

During the reviews, the negative impact of the Non-Intercourse Act of 1809 on the lifeblood of U.S. Industries, international trade, was evident. To get around the provisions of the act and still support their customers in the U.S. as well as in Europe, they had taken to odd ways to circumvent the letter of the law, but not its spirit.

Fonseca-Laredo ships suddenly had cargoes that needed to be unloaded in Lisbon, Rabat, the Madeira Islands, Ponta Delgada in the Azores. From those ports, the ships would proceed to England or France. Returning trips had a mix of cargoes and immigrants, particularly when they stopped in Amsterdam.

The three ships sailing back and forth to Amsterdam were partly full of cargo sailing east, and full of passengers coming west. The immigrant transport business was good, and captains were instructed to stop in Amsterdam if they had room, which also added to U.S. Industries per voyage revenue.

Amos Laredo had, at the behest of Max and Javier, studied how the Non-Intercourse Act of 1809 and Macon's Bill #2 of 1810, passed back in May, helped U.S. Industries. It temporarily lifted the embargoes on trading with France and England, but, like its predecessor, the cost of compliance reduced U.S. Industries' revenue and profits.

Everyone around the table knew its negative effect, and Amos thought he had an idea that offered hope. Even though everyone around the table knew about his project, he was tight-lipped about what he learned.

On Thursday morning, while most of the cups of coffee, tea, and hot chocolate were still piping hot, Max Laredo said. "Before we begin planning for next year, I think we ought to listen to Amos. We all know what he was tasked to do, and would like to hear what he learned. And I am sure that the rest of you would as well. So, Amos, the floor is yours."

"In my role as the person who looks for new opportunities for U.S. Industries, I asked Max and Javier if I could flip the intent of Mr. Jefferson's Embargo Act of 1807 and its descendants on their collective heads and see how we, as a firm, could benefit."

"Oddly enough, when I turned inward, there are many products I think we could manufacture here in the U.S. at the same or better quality than what we get from English and French merchants and at a better price. I spent several days with Mr. Fulton at the Patent Office in Washington studying the patents he has granted and those awaiting review. You would be surprised at how many arrive each day and what they propose. Already in the U.S., we have invented the cotton gin. We now, thanks to Mr. Eli Whitney, build firearms with interchangeable parts. To illustrate my point, I have two examples that are part of a longer list I propose we investigate."

He looked down at his notes. "The first thing I did was take the top ten manufactured products we bring from Europe to the United States and ask, could U.S. Industries make them here? If the answer was yes, do we buy a business or start one?"

Amos slid the top sheet of paper off to the side. "What do we, U.S. Industries, make in the U.S. that we export? Answer cutting tools and medical devices. What is the common expertise? Working with metal, mostly iron and steel, but tin and copper are also metals with which our companies are familiar."

"What do we import from England?" He looked at the list, "Hinges, knobs for doors and cabinets, brackets to support shelves, cutlery, and bowls are at the top of the list. When I studied the prices we pay English suppliers and asked Asa Winters and Evyn Griffiths what it would cost to make them, I found the answer was startling. Think half price. In other words, if we paid ten shillings for a hinge, we could make it for five. They also think they could make them better and faster. And shipping costs would be less. On my list, metal goods are number one."

He looked at a second sheet. "Here are two more. One is cloth, not clothing. I have seen several patents and know that in Massachusetts and Connecticut, there are weavers who can turn cotton and wool into cloth. They all use water from rivers to power their machines, but I think steam power is the way of the future. It is not yet practical for ocean travel, but I believe we can invest in mills that will make cloth every bit as fine as we get from Manchester, England. And we might even be able to buy some of the equipment. Lord knows, there are probably men and their families who would love to come here."

Amos held up a sheet of paper. "The other is this, paper. There are new manufacturing processes that produce paper faster and use wood pulp, not cloth, so the cost per sheet is about a hundredth of what it is now."

"What I propose is that I be given a small budget and assemble a team that has an engineer or two, someone who is good at math and accounting and someone besides me who can visualize the possibilities. Then, we start with my list. If we think the opportunity is viable, we evaluate the investment. If not, we go on to the next item. People from this team will be part of the initial group of managers for these new businesses."

Max and Javier listened to the conversation, occasionally interjecting their opinions. Just before lunch, Max tapped the side of his glass with a spoon. The ringing caused the discussion to end. "O.K., first question, how many of you think we should proceed with Amos' proposal. All nine hands went up.

"Excellent. Javier and I support the idea. Question two: Who should work on this committee? Asa Winters is a given, but he needs help. Who?"

Jaco raised his hand. "May I make a suggestion on where the men and women should come from?"

"Please..."

"I think this is a wonderful opportunity for some of our best young people. Rather than we pick today, each of us nominates two or three, let Amos and Asa interview and select them. However, here is the caveat. They will, as Amos suggested, be the leaders of the new venture. This will enable us to offer our top people a chance for advancement and show their mettle."

Max looked at Javier, who nodded, and then at Amos. "Amos."

"I think Jaco is right. May I suggest that tomorrow, or before we break for Yom Kippur, everyone give me the names of their candidates. Then, I will choose after Yom Kippur, and the first task of the group is to figure out the first project, which we should have identified by Thanksgiving. One last point, while this is the core team, we may bring in others as warranted."

Max looked around the room. "Any objections?"

Seeing none, he said, "It is time for lunch."

CHAPTER 11

IMPRESSMENT

LONDON, SECOND WEEK OF JANUARY 1811

The terse letter from Admiral Bickerton, the First Naval Lord had Vice Admiral of the Red Stacey Davidson wondering as he rode in a carriage from Portsmouth to London. He could recite the words verbatim, probably written by one of Bickerton's secretaries was in a fine, English hand.

> *Vice Admiral Davidson,*
>
> *I wish to see you in person to discuss a delicate and very important matter. Pls. repair to the Admiralty as soon as possible.*
>
> *Richard Bickerton*
> *Admiral*
> *First Naval Lord*

He had no idea what the delicate and important matter was, and nosing around asking questions would probably incur Bickerton's wrath. In the back of his mind, he thought this may be the end of his Naval career since he had had several run-ins with the First Naval Lord earlier in his career. He thought the arguments were a result of a difference of opinion on how best to approach a difficult issue. Davidson's default position was always what was best for the country, then the Royal Navy and then the individual.

Belinda, his wife, rode with him in the carriage that arrived at their house in Mayfair well after dark. The servants, alerted that they were coming, had a meal prepared for them, and then it was off to bed.

When he walked into the Admiralty, the young lieutenant standing watch at the front desk came around the front. "Good morning, Vice Admiral Davidson, First Naval Lord is expecting you. I shall have someone walk you up."

"No need, I know the way. And, if he is expecting me, then I won't be rude when I show up."

The young lieutenant bowed, "As you wish, my lord."

Davidson stopped and looked at the lieutenant. He spoke in a soft, gentle tone. "Lieutenant, in this building or when I am wearing this uniform, I am a Vice Admiral in the Royal Navy, not the Duke of Somerset. As such, other than the privilege and duties of my rank, we are in the same service and share the same dangers. If you feel the need to acknowledge a request or an order from me, simply touch the back of your hand to your forehead and say, aye, aye, sir. Am I clear?"

The man put the back of his hand to his forehead, "Aye, aye sir. My apologies."

"No apology necessary, Lieutenant. Carry on."

Bickerton's secretary, a commander, saw Davidson coming down the hallway, and when he stood up, so did the First Naval Lord's other three. "Admiral, please go in. The First Naval Lord was wondering what day you would come."

Bickerton came around from his desk and shook Davidson's hand. "Stacy, please close the door. And what do you prefer this time of day, tea, coffee, or something stronger?"

"Coffee, sir. Maybe after you tell me what was so urgent, I may ask for something stronger."

Bickerton laughed and motioned to the couch as he poured coffee from a silver pitcher into a cup. "Sugar, milk?"

"Sugar, two spoonfuls, please."

After handing the Vice Admiral of the Red's cup to him, Bickerton took his cup of tea from his desk and placed it on the coffee table. On either end of the couch where Davidson sat at the end closest to Bickerton's desk, there were two overstuffed armchairs whose leather had seen better days.

"Glad you could come. First the news, then the task."

Davidson nodded affirmatively.

"On the first of June, I would like you to relieve Admiral Paisley as Second Naval Lord. He is not well and has asked to be relieved. We are keeping this hush-hush as you can imagine. I picked June because that is when, as First Naval Lord, the new flag assignments are announced."

"Sir, I am honored and, quite frankly, sir, am flattered and surprised. You and I have not seen eye-to-eye on several issues."

Bickerton cut Davidson off. "Which is exactly why I want you as Second Naval Lord. I don't want a yes man in that position."

"Sir, in me, you will not have one."

"The task. From a naval perspective, we are in a bit of a lull. Most of the fighting is in Central Europe by the British Army. The Royal Navy is not involved other than the blockade. What I want you do to visit the Jamaica and North American stations, and Gibraltar to assess the officers and our needs as a navy. I fear we may have another round with the Frenchies or worse, the Americans. I will give you letters of introduction you can show the commanders I want you to meet, just not why. Plan to be back by the end of April."

"Aye, aye, sir. I will do my best."

"If you need a few extra officers, take them. Your chief of staff, Rathburn, is getting a flag, and I would be most interested in where you would post him."

"Jamaica, sir. He knows the waters, and I think our main threat will be the Americans. Rathburn knows them as well as anyone and won't be intimidated. He also won't do something stupid, either."

"What ship should I take, sir?"

"Pick one. I'd take a heavy frigate mostly for speed but also because I don't want to send something that the French or Spanish may see."

"What about India, sir?"

"Leave that to me. You won't have time to go there and get back, and I already have someone in mind. When you come back, have a list of those who you think should be promoted and those who should be beached or retired. Then, as Second Naval Lord, you can execute your plan."

"Aye, aye, sir."

"Send your itinerary to me before you go so I know where to reach you. If I think it needs an added stop, I will let you know. Other than that, I shan't interfere."

"Yes, sir."

Bickerton held up his cup of tea. "To your success here and abroad. Being Second Naval Lord looks like a rose bush in full bloom, but trust me, Stacey, it is full of thorns."

Laughing, Davidson replied, "Yes, sir. I know because I have been one of those thorns."

"Exactly. Good luck."

The First Naval Lord's words meant the meeting was over. He was both elated and scared. He was tasked to poke around and learn the truth about the fleet the First Naval Lord commands.

VICINITY OF 48°N, 6°E, THIRD WEEK OF FEBRUARY 1811

For most of the voyage from New York, Darren thought the weather was decent. It was cold, windy, at times, but not stormy. He was on City of New York, one of AS&PLs newest ships, on its maiden voyage. Three others, City of London, City of Boston, and City of Charleston, were soon to follow.

Each of these ships had improvements that came about from passenger input and lessons learned from the line's decade-plus of operation. The *City-class,* as they were referred to in AS&PL and their literature, were much larger than their predecessors.

Each had 32 cabins, 16 on each of two decks, four owner's suites in the stern of the ship, and on the lowest deck, there were two dozen small compartments made from partitions in which four hammocks could be slung. They provided a modicum of privacy but did not have a door.

Meal service as well as the quality of the food kept improving and now included fresh fruits and vegetables that could be served almost every day. Along with a selection of wines, smoked meats, cheeses, freshly baked biscuits, and breads were part of the fare offered.

Passengers were fed in two shifts: those in the cabins and then those on the "berthing" deck. For those in the owner's cabins, room service was available.

City of New York was easily plowing through the long six-foot swells. Its up-and-down motion became almost rhythmic as on the up take, the bowsprit would appear to point at the sky and then plunge down, sending cold, 45° Fahrenheit (-7° Celsius) spray down the main or promenade deck.

For most of the day, *City of New York* was in and out of rain showers. Besides soaking those who were needed on deck to handle lines, the light rain made it hard to see any ship more than a half a mile away.

This was typical for this time of year. They were well east of where what Franklin called the Gulph Stream split. Part of the current flowed north and passed between Iceland and Scotland while the other continued east into the Bay of Biscay. Even though they were not in either current, when the warm air over the Gulph Stream mixed with the colder air coming off Greenland, it created clouds, fog, and rain.

Normally, when an AS&PL ship made its maiden voyage, either Darren or Jaco was the captain with the future captain acting as the First Lieutenant. On this voyage, it was Ezekiel Winters, Melody Winters Smythe's youngest brother.

Ezekiel had left Charleston with the British when they evacuated Charleston in 1782 and went to Barbados. From there, he joined the British East India Company as a midshipman. After making lieutenant, Winters learned he would, as someone born in the Thirteen Colonies, never captain one of their ships. He left and made his way back to the United States, where he joined AS&PL.

Like most of the other AS&PL officers, he held a reserve commission in the U.S. Navy. Born in 1764, Winters had been at sea for most of his life.

Darren was also on board because he had business in London. One was a meeting with Henry York, his attorney at Scoons, who sent him a letter inviting him to discuss some investments. York also wanted to introduce him to Arthur Haver-Brown, who will take over his practice when York retires.

While in London, he planned to ride from London down to Portsmouth to spend a day with his father while *City of New York* spent its five days in port.

Standing in an enclosed platform at the aft end of the three-masted schooner AS&PL, called the "bridge," Darren called a godsend. It protected the quartermaster and officer of the watch from the cold wind and spray. Arrayed on a board at the front of the enclosure were the compass, inclinometer, and thermometer.

Darren had returned to the captain's cabin which was just forward of the passenger cabins and aft of the crew berthing compartments in the forecastle. He'd gone on deck to get a sense of the weather which had turned very cold with the outside temperature now down to 36°Fahrenheit (-2° Celsius) both he and Ezekiel were afraid the cold rain might turn into freezing rain.

He was making notes on the trip for his report and evaluation when there was a firm knock on the door. "Yes?"

The door opened, revealing a young midshipman. "Sir, Captain Winters respects, sir. He would like you to come to the quarterdeck as soon as possible."

"Is there a problem?"

"Yes, sir, if you call a Royal Navy frigate captain being obnoxious, there is."

Darren grabbed his heavy woolen coat and followed the midshipman out the cabin door. On deck, Darren could see a Royal Navy frigate a quarter a mile ahead of *City of New York* beginning to tack to port to cross the schooner's bow. Through a spyglass, he could see that the frigate's 18-pounder guns were run out.

Ezekiel Winters had ordered the crew to wear the more maneuverable *City of New York* to port. Darren arrived on the quarterdeck in time to see *City of New York's* bow begin to turn so it would pass a safe distance behind the Royal Navy frigate, thus avoiding a collision.

"Where did he come from?"

"Sir, we saw the top of its masts and caught a couple of glimpses but continued on our course to enter the English Channel. The Royal Navy rarely bothers us. As a prize, we're not worth much!"

"Apparently, this ...."

The number 1 cannon on *the* frigate's port side bellowed. The ball screamed past the aft end of *City of New York* and splashed a half a mile away. The message to both Darren and Ezekiel was clear.

"Slacken all sails." The booms creaked as they were let out. Ezekiel wisely had the crew keep them taught enough to maintain steerageway. *City of New York* slowed to two or three knots and waited while *Minerva* finished tacking around to come alongside. Two boats were lowered into the water by the frigate's crew and began rowing the 100 yards that separated the two ships.

"Ezekiel, let us find out what the Royal Navy wants."

The Royal Navy captain was the third man to arrive on *City of New York* deck. He was preceded by two men with cutlasses hanging from their belts, into which each had stuffed two pistols.

"Are you the captain?"

Ezekiel Winters replied evenly, "Yes, I am Captain Ezekiel Winters of the United States schooner *City of New York.* Besides fifty-two passengers, our cargo is only U.S. and Royal Mail and baggage along with a few barrels of dried apples. We have no contraband."

Without introducing himself, the Royal Navy captain turned to a lieutenant who was the fourth man to board *City of New York.* Darren noted that in addition to *Minerva's* captain, one of his lieutenants and eight of his sailors were now on board the schooner.

"Search the ship!" The Royal Navy captain strode up to Ezekiel Winters. "How many men are in your crew?"

"Besides myself, there are three officers, thirty sailors, a chef, and two stewards. May I ask your name, sir?"

"Captain Everett Martingdale the Second. Captain Martingdale to you Winters."

Darren winced. He hadn't heard the name Martingdale in years. He served under Captain Martingdale on board *H.M.S. Puritan.* Martingdale refused Darren's suggestions on how to take the French frigate *Oiseau.* Martingdale's combination of stupidity and arrogance got his ship damaged and many of his crew, along with himself, killed. *He may be a relative or even a son.*

The lieutenant came up on deck. "Nothing but chests of clothes and provisions in the hold along with the mail."

Martingdale nodded. "Winters, line up your crew on the leeward bulwark."

Ezekiel Winters stood his ground, "Why may I ask?"

Martingdale drew his cutlass and shoved the point under Winters' jaw. "Because I said so. My ship is short-handed, and I am taking fifteen men. I will be polite, and if no one volunteers, I will pick them."

Darren had seen enough. "You will do nothing of the sort. This is a ship registered in the United States and flying its flag, and you have no right to take any man, woman, or child off this ship."

Martingdale turned toward Darren, waving his cutlass. "And who may you be?"

"To start with, my name is Darren Smythe, and I am one of the owners of American Passenger and Shipping Lines. I am also a retired Royal Navy captain and know the rules and policies under which you operate. What you are doing is illegal, and you and I both know it."

"So, you are English?"

"I was born in England, but now I am an American citizen."

"But you were born in England?"

"Aye, that I was."

Martingdale spun around and ordered, "Take this man by force if necessary and clasp him in irons. He is a traitor to his king, his service, and his country. I will deal with him later."

The Royal Navy officer went down the line of sailors and took a dozen who were prodded by pistol barrels and cutlasses to the waiting long boats. Once they were away from *City of New York*. Ezekiel looked at the relative positions of the two ships. The schooner had drifted slightly aft, so he ordered the sailors to pull in the booms, and as soon as the ship started to accelerate, he picked a course that would make it difficult for *Minerva* to bring its guns to bear.

Once clear, he had all the sails the ship could carry and Ezekiel had the quartermaster set course for the entrance to the Thames River. All the male passengers volunteered to handle lines and sheets. Guided by the bosun, they did well, and in less than two days, *City of New York* would dock.

On board *Minerva*, Darren was shoved down the companion way to the orlop deck, where manacles were placed around his ankles and handcuffs around his wrists. The ship's bilge smelled like rotten seawater that hadn't been pumped out. It probably hadn't been cleaned either.

In the dim light, he could see the barrels of food and beer, some of which were cracked. Rats were scurrying around, suddenly interested in the new resident of the orlop deck.

He leaned against the ship's rib and tried to make himself comfortable. The rough wood made it difficult. Darren closed his eyes and wondered what Ezekiel Winters was doing with *City of New York*. Smiling, whether he lives or dies, Martingdale does not know or understand the firestorm he has unleashed. He grinned when he thought about what Jaco would do once he found out the Royal Navy kidnapped him.

Darren could tell by the creaks and motions of the frigate that *Minerva* was again underway. He didn't have to wait long for Martingdale to make his appearance.

Two Royal Marines came below and undid the shackle that kept his manacles chained to the deck and led him up the forward companionway to the main deck and then aft to the captain's cabin. When he was ushered into the captain's cabin, only Martingdale was there.

"What's your story, Smythe?"

"After the American Revolution, I was put on half-pay, turned down the King's shilling, and retired. Along the way, I emigrated to the United States, married, and became one of its citizens. Today, I am the managing director and one of the owners of the shipping line that owns *City of New York*."

"Where were you born?"

"Does it matter?"

"Yes. If you were born in England, you are English. Once an Englishman, always an Englishman. The fact that you left is more evidence that you are a deserter and a traitor."

"I was born in Gosport. And I am neither a deserter nor a traitor."

"Then why didn't you accept recall?"

Darren was sure Martingdale didn't understand either process or care. "I wasn't eligible. By law, England is allowed only to recall English citizens, of which I am no longer one. I notified the Royal Navy that I had renounced my English citizenship and even had to defend myself in court. The Royal Navy, by the way, lost and was fined."

"So, you changed allegiance to avoid serving your king and country. That makes you a coward as well."

Darren forced himself to remain on an even keel. "No. That is incorrect. I did all this long before England was at war."

Martingale slid a sheet of paper across the table. "Read this."

Darren saw the seal of the First Naval Lord, which said that Royal Navy captains whose ships are short-handed may stop any ship on the high seas and remove, by force if necessary, anyone they believe is an English citizen. They are to enlist them in the Royal Navy or offer them a chance to serve in the British Army. The policy, the paper noted, was reinforced by Parliament in 1703, 1705, 1740, and 1779.

"This is preposterous!"

"Maybe so, Smythe, but what I did is well within my authority as captain of *Minerva.*"

Martingdale pulled the sheet back and put it on his desk. "So, did you ever serve with my father?"

"I did. I was his first lieutenant on *Puritan.*"

"Were you there when he was killed?"

"Yes." *The less said, the better.*

"Where were you when he was mortally wounded?"

"On the quarterdeck." Everything in his being was holding Darren back from telling Martingdale that had his father accepted Darren's advice and forced a maneuvering fight, they would have easily captured *Oiseau,* and his father wouldn't have been killed. Thanks to his father's arrogance and despite the crew's efforts, a boarding fight couldn't be avoided. The French frigate was old and badly damaged in the fight. It sank so there was no prize money.

"Then you saw my father die?"

"I did. He was struck by three balls from a swivel gun. He was dead by the time he arrived in the surgeon's cockpit."

"And then what happened?"

Darren gave a short summary, saying that he took command, ordered *Puritan's* crew to pull in its sails so it could accelerate and cross *Oiseau's* bow. The French captain anticipated the move and managed to ram *Puritan,* but the Royal Navy crew prevailed. Two days later, *Oiseau* sank.

"That is what the action report says. Did you write it?"

"I did."

"Well, Mr. Smythe, I still think you are a traitor. I am going to bring you to Portsmouth and let them decide what to do with you. In the meantime, I will write up my thoughts. You will be kept manacled and cuffed but will be given a lieutenant's compartment. You are not to speak with any member of my crew unless one of my officers is present. You are forbidden to speak with the men I took from your ship. Any violation, and I will throw every Article of War at you and watch you dance at the end of a yardarm."

With that, Martingdale yelled, "Guard," and instructed him to take Mr. Smythe to the empty gunner's compartment. A guard was to be posted outside it every hour of the day.

LONDON, TWO DAYS AFTER *CITY OF NEW YORK* WAS BOARDED

Once the passengers were gone and the schooner was being cleaned in preparation for the next group of passengers, Ezekiel took a carriage into London to meet the U.S. counsel. There, William Pinkney, interrupted a meeting to hear what happened.

Stopping U.S. ships on the high seas was nothing new to Pickney, who knew the British would not budge on the issue. They reserved the right to stop ships and take men whom they believed, rightly or wrongly, were English. These men would be forced to serve until the end of the wars against the French, whenever that may be.

There was no commitment by the British to care for a sailor who was crippled and could not serve or for those who survived, to be repatriated to the U.S. Pinkney feared that the longer the English were at war with the French, the more incidents there would be. There was, Pinkney told Winters, little he could do other than lodge another protest with His Majesty's foreign minister, which was, Pinkney said, akin to pissing into the wind.

As the young officer was leaving, Pinkney asked Ezekiel not to do anything rash, like try to burn London down. Winters had the carriage stop at Scoons' office in London and left a note for Henry York. He was assured that it would be delivered to Tunbridge Wells later that day or the next.

Riding back in the carriage to Perry's Dock and *City of New York,* Winters thought about Pinkney's words. Wryly, he smiled, thinking that he worked for the man who might just do that once he learns his best friend is probably now sitting in a jail in Portsmouth waiting to be tried for treason.

PORT ROYAL, JAMAICA, THIRD WEEK OF FEBRUARY 1811

When Vice Admiral of the Red Stacey Davidson arrived on H.M.S. Nexus, a sister ship of Lively, there were no Royal Navy ships anchored off the naval base at Port Royal. From Vice Admiral of the Blue Bartholomew Rowley office, both, the Commander, Jamaica Station, both Davidson and he see the forest green hills of Jamaica behind the town of Kingston.

To the Jamaica Station, the Royal Navy had assigned six frigates, two brigs, four sloops, and one ancient fourth-rate ship-of-the-line that was now en route to Portsmouth, where it would probably be broken up. The others were at sea, prowling for French privateers based in Haiti. His 12 ships weren't, Rowley contended, enough, something Davidson knew when he had the same post.

Jamaica Station had the responsibility for the Caribbean and given that the British had captured Martinique - again - in 1809 and Guadalupe in 1810, there wasn't much French Naval activity. When Davidson asked Rowley what he thought the primary threat to British interests in the Caribbean was, he quickly answered, "The Americans. They know these waters better than we do, and they're clever buggers."

Davidson nodded. His two conclusions were that, now that he had visited Bermuda and Jamaica, the Royal Navy had too many ships committed to blockading France and not enough in the Caribbean.

Two, a Vice Admiral was overkill for this billet unless more ships and squadrons were sent to Jamaica. It was a position for an aggressive rear admiral with a frigate background, which was something he could fix when he returned to London.

After two days of enjoying the lovely weather in Jamaica and *H.M.S. Nexus* replenished, the large 38-gun frigate sailed north to Halifax. Once they were at sea, Davidson debated for a few days whether they should make a port call in New York.

Even though he didn't have diplomatic permission for an official visit, he could claim that the ship was seeking shelter from a storm. And it would give him a chance to visit Darren Smythe and Jaco Jacinto and possibly gain some valuable intelligence.

PORTSMOUTH, FOURTH WEEK OF FEBRUARY 1811

The cold, raw wind from the north was almost enough to blow a man over, which is why Josiah Scranton was walking close to the brick wall of the cordage and sail maker's buildings. It was a roundabout route to the base's headquarters, but it kept him out of the cold, biting wind from the nor' west.

He'd been working in Scoons' Portsmouth office as a law clerk since it first opened. Neither he nor his family could afford to send him to one of the Inns of Court, so Scranton rose through the ranks of law clerks. While he assisted any partner who came to Portsmouth, York had enough clients and work to keep Scranton busy.

Scranton was walking toward the harbor when he saw two Royal Marines leading a man in manacles next to an officer who was followed by two Royal Marines with muskets and fixed bayonets. Immediately, he recognized the man in manacles as Captain Darren Smythe from his visits to the Portsmouth office and from the times he brought documents for then Lieutenant, then Commander, and then Captain and now American citizen Darren Smyth to read sign.

He nodded at the group as it passed him and was sure from the look in Captain Smythe's eyes that he recognized Scranton. This changed what Scranton planned to do.

In the pouch he was carrying, he had executed contracts from one of York's clients to provide iron fittings to the Royal Navy. Another was one from a victualer for supplies of salted beef, pork, and peas. A third was from a local brewery for casks of beer. All had been substantially increased by the Royal Navy's expansion and increased tempo of operations.

Once those were delivered, Scranton walked to the jail, which was across a narrow street from the judge advocate's offices. Trying to be innocent, he inquired of the Royal Marine manning the desk if there were any new prisoners brought in. His reason for asking was Scranton wanted to know if the prisoner would need a lawyer.

The Royal Marine sergeant looked at his log and spun it around. Pointing to a new entry, he said, "This man will need one. He's a bloody Royal Navy captain."

"Do you know what he is charged with?"

"No, but I was told to keep him in a cell by himself and treat him well!" The sergeant laughed. "We treat them all well, right up to the time they are hung!"

Emboldened, Scranton asked, "May I see him?"

The sergeant thought for a second, and Scranton put a gold Sovereign on the counter. "Alone, with no guards around."

Palming the coin, the sergeant nodded. "No funny business, Mr. Scranton or me and my mates will have our way with you.

Scranton and Smythe sat in the corner of the small cell whose floor was strewn with hay, facing the walls. In the corner, there was a wooden bucket that reeked of urine and feces.

Softly, Josiah Scranton asked, "Captain Smythe, do you remember me?"

Darren nodded. "You work for Mr. York."

"Aye, I do. What are they charging you with?"

After providing a short précis of what happened, Scranton stood up when he saw the sergeant approaching. "Mr. York will know you are here tomorrow morning when he arrives in Portsmouth."

Scranton left the jail and went down the street to the Judge Advocate's office. He knew several and asked one if he knew what Captain Smythe was being charged with. "No. He must have just been brought in. We don't have anything on him. I suggest you check back in a week. By then, I may have something for you."

Back in the Scoons' Portsmouth office, Scranton penned a note to Henry York summarizing what he knew that went into the pouch that went to Tunbridge Wells every night. York was scheduled to be in Portsmouth three days hence. He'd bet good money that York would be here sooner.

LONDON, FIRST WEEK OF MARCH 1811

The Right Honourable Charles Philip Yorke and the First Lord of the Admiralty was the last man to arrive. He was appointed to his position by Spencer Perceval, England's prime minister since October 1809. Yorke was a member of the House of Commons and the equivalent of the U.S. Secretary of the Navy. Waiting for him were John Scoons and Henry York.

Spencer nodded to John Scoons, whose great-grandfather acquired the firm from the Hooper family in 1759. The Hoopers could trace the roots of the firm back to 1570, when the founder, Nicholas Hooper, proclaimed in Tunbridge Wells, England, that he was a scrivener and creator of documents. Scoons thanked both York and Bickerton for coming and turned to Henry York, whom he had warned not to betray his anger at what the Royal Navy had done to one of its own.

After listening, Yorke said, "I don't know this Captain Smythe except for what I read in his file, and I find it hard to believe he is a traitor. He left the Royal Navy because we forced him out and chose not to take a pension. But I can't see what I can do. He was plucked on a routine stop by *Minerva* to impress men for his ship, and whose captain was acting in accordance with his orders. We can't release him without looking like fools. If he is charged, then Captain Smythe will have a chance to defend himself. What is done is done."

York struggled to contain his anger. "Sir, are you telling me you are going to go ahead with this trial?"

"We haven't charged Captain Smythe yet. Treason and desertion are a bit drastic, given the circumstances. Not following orders is where I land."

"You do realize the Navy lost a hearing in court and there is an injunction against the Navy forbidding it to recall Captain Smythe."

"I do." Yorke looked down his nose at York, who was, in his mind, just a commoner lawyer. His family had a barony, but as the second son, the title was not his. "And, sir, quite frankly, I don't think the Royal Navy in time of war needs to abide by a civilian court."

York was now tired of being polite and respectful. "Mr. Yorke, does the name Jacinto ring a bell?"

"No, can't say it does. Sounds Spanish. Was he one of ours?"

"Well, sir, 'twere I you, I would have one of your aides look up the name of Captain Jaco Jacinto, Continental Navy, and the ship *Scorpion.* Captain Smythe is Captain Jacinto's business partner, and I submit that when he learns that the Royal Navy is holding his friend on made-up charges, the Royal Navy will rue the day it arrested Captain Smythe."

Yorke pushed back and stood up to leave. "There is nothing the Colonials can do that will cause me to lose sleep. Good day, Mr. York."

York sat shaking his head after the First Naval Lord left. *Now I know why the Colonials rebelled!!!*

NEW YORK, SECOND WEEK OF MARCH 1811

Even with two-thirds of a crew, Ezekiel Winters pushed City of New York as hard as he thought prudent. In his mind, only cannon balls or snapped masts were going to stop or slow the ship. Despite adverse winds, City of New York was coasting to a dock 11 days after it left London.

What he didn't expect to see was Jaco Jacinto standing on the pier. He'd come with Micah Chaffetz who had a list of follow-on questions for Darren. Not knowing who Chaffetz was, Ezekiel asked if he could speak with Jaco privately.

In the midship's owners cabin at the aft end of *City of New York*, Jaco was standing when Ezekiel started speaking. When Ezekiel finished, Jaco was sitting in one of the padded chairs. His hands were shaking and. His voice quivered with anger when he asked Ezekiel to repeat what he had just said and leave out no detail.

When the officer was finished, he said, "Finish your duties today, and then go to the top floor of the bank offices. We will be expecting you."

On his way from the dock where *City of New York* was being made ready for its next trip to England to Wall and Pearl, Jaco stopped at the shipping company's offices. There, he confirmed which ships were scheduled to arrive and leave New York and which ones were undergoing maintenance.

Emily Smythe Muir was only told that she needed to join him in the large conference room on the fourth floor for a matter of grave importance. The same message was delivered to her husband, Rafer Muir, and his sister, Shoshana. He told Greg Struthers, who was in a meeting with Morton Geiger, that the company has a major crisis brewing.

With everyone assembled, Jaco nodded to Ezekiel Winters, who had just arrived. "Tell everyone what you just told me."

No one spoke when Ezekiel finished until Emily broke the silence, "Arrogant bastards. We can't let them get away with this."

"No, Emily, we won't." Jaco stood and leaned over the table, resting on his fingertips. "I am going to take *Zephyr II* to Southampton and then go to Gosport. Hopefully, Darren's father or Henry York knows where Darren is. If needed, I will burn London to the ground to get Darren back."

Shoshana stood, "Good, I need to go pack. Let me know when the ship is departing, and I will be on it. I will reach out to Henry York via letter that will be on *Westerlies* because it is leaving tonight. By now, York may know something."

Reyna entered the room. "Why does Reyna need to go on a ship with Shoshana?"

"The bloody British have taken Darren. We think he is being taken to Portsmouth, but we are not sure. Its jail is the logical place."

"And you are just sitting here talking about it?"

Jaco saw the fire in his wife's eyes and tried to calm her down. "We just found out about it when *City of New York* docked."

Rafer Muir slapped the table with his hand. "Since this is going to be a land campaign, count me in. Plus, I need to prevent my wife from wringing the First Naval Lord's scrawny neck."

"Captain Jacinto...." The new voice stopped conversation. It was Morton Geiger who was standing in the doorway. "You have the makings of a crew waiting downstairs. Mr. Jeffords, Mr. Cooper, Mr. Landry, and Mr. Grantham have volunteered and will find the men. They need to know how many and when?"

Without even thinking, Jaco was in planning mode. "Full crew plus about a dozen. Then there are those in this room who want to come along."

"Sir, we'll get *Zephyr II* to a dock and provisioned. By evening, I'll know when we can sail. If I were a betting man, I would guess sometime tomorrow morning."

When Morton Geiger left, Greg spoke matter-of-factly. "I support what you are going to do and will hold down the fort while you are gone. Jaco, I know you. Please do not create an international incident that I must explain to your father so he can explain what happened to President Madison."

"Given that the British would not end impressment in the Jay Treaty and have resisted all attempts at negotiation, even unofficial ones, I believe President Madison would approve, maybe not officially, of me giving the Royal Navy a bit of a black eye."

Gosport, where Darren's father and where Jaco assumed his brothers still lived, was on the other side of the bay from Portsmouth. Jaco did not want to involve them at all. Neither he nor Emily could trust her brothers.

"Reyna, you do not have to come."

"That my husband is not open to discussion. I am coming. I know the Smythes. Darren is your best friend and business partner. Besides, you may need a doctor."

The words "my husband" came out of Reyna's mouth only when she was not going to tolerate any discussion or a suggestion that did not align with what she wanted to do. Arguing would be pointless, and trying to keep her off *Zephyr II* would put his life and limb at risk.

PORTSMOUTH. THIRD WEEK OF MARCH 1811

Thanks to Josiah Scranton's quick thinking, the Judge Advocate at Portsmouth now knew that Captain Smythe had an attorney. Scoons was well known in Portsmouth and at the naval base. Several local businesses and many Royal Navy officers were its clients.

Captain Wesley de Montfort, Royal Navy Judge Advocate, had several problems on his hands. Problem one: he had a former Royal Navy Captain in the base jail accused of treason, desertion, and failure to follow orders, and no evidence to support any of the charges. Evidence was promised, but so far, none had been forthcoming. He was holding him because he was ordered to do so by the Royal Navy's senior legal officer.

Problem two. He had a copy of the injunction which was delivered by a Scoons messenger. Clearly, the Royal Navy was in violation of the court order. As an attorney and as a Royal Naval officer, he was aware that the Royal Navy reported to the Defense Council, which was all elected members of Parliament. Ignoring civilian oversight would float as well as a cannonball.

Problem three. His orders, which were in writing, were to hold Captain Smythe until trial. He was not, in any circumstances, to be released on bail. He was not allowed to be moved to empty quarters or a prison ship and not to be harmed.

Problem four. Technically, Darren Smythe was a civilian and therefore not subject to the jurisdiction of the Royal Navy. Therefore, to allow him to be tried by the Royal Navy, someone in the Second Naval Lord's office would have to order Captain Smythe back to active duty.

Problem five. Darren Smythe asserts he is no longer a British citizen which was supported by the injunction which again, supported the argument that the Royal Navy had no jurisdiction, nor the right to try in a court martial, former, and now retired, and U.S. citizen Captain Smythe, much less order him back to active duty. Bottom line, Captain Smythe has not committed a crime.

Problem six was sitting in his office in the form of an irate Henry York. He was demanding that either the Royal Navy charge his client or release him. If he was charged, York was there to arrange bail. York also brought with him sections of English law that, if followed, required him to release Captain Smythe immediately.

Exasperated at de Montfort's intransigence, York asked if Arundel would show him his orders to incarcerate Smythe until the Royal Navy decided how it wanted to proceed. The Royal Navy officer asked why.

"While you, sir, cannot press your superiors to change, I am under no such obligation. I am free to use whatever legal means necessary to free my client."

De Montfort thought for a few minutes, thinking that whatever actions York took, they might give him some answers. He rifled through a stack of papers and found his orders. "Mr. York, read these and you will understand why I am being difficult."

York noticed right away there was no signature over the name H.S. Perceval, Counsel for the Affairs of the Admiralty Board. Instead, there was a scribbled set of initials over where Perceval would have signed. The letters 'O" and "G" were discernible. York knew exactly who it was, Oliver Granby.

Trying to be helpful, de Montfort offered, "Mr. York, if it helps, I can have my secretary make a copy of the orders that I will initial as a true copy."

"Yes, that would be most helpful. And, also if you would, please add the initials of who signed it for Mr. Perceval, that would also be helpful."

De Montfort left for a few minutes and returned with the copy that he signed and added his seal. "Sir, do you know whose initials they are?"

"Captain Oliver Granby. He works for the Counsel for Admiralty Affairs. Do you know him?"

"Can't say that I do."

York left believing that, for the moment, Smythe was safe. What worried him was what would Granby do? By wording the orders the way he did, Granby knew that they would be impossible to follow, while at the same time, the RN could hold Smythe in perpetuity.

He also wondered if Perceval ever saw the orders or was even told about them. In his mind, besides being contradictory, they violated English law. Based on the new American Constitution, they were illegal to an American citizen, and another example of why the Colonials fought so long and hard for independence.

It would take some legal machinations and pressure from Parliament to get the Royal Navy to release him, but York believed he could. Once back in the Portsmouth office, he drafted a letter to Shoshana Jacinto and was assured by Josiah Scranton that it would be hand-delivered to the next AS&PL ship. Once Scranton had the letter, York believed that he would see Ms. Jacinto and probably others before the letter arrived in New York.

CHAPTER 12

RAIDER OF THE ENGLISH COAST

SOUTHAMPTON, MONDAY, MARCH 25TH, 1811

The prevailing westerlies were kind to *Zephyr II* as it crossed the Atlantic. They were steady, sometimes moderate but consistent in that they were coming out of the so' west, which meant that the schooner did not have to tack. All three booms were secured perpendicular to the wind coming over the starboard quarter.

While this wasn't *Zephyr II's* best point of sailing, the wind allowed the ship to follow a straight line from New York to the entrance of the English Channel. Eleven days from when the schooner passed through Narrows at the mouth of New York harbor to enter the Atlantic, it dropped anchor in the River Itchen, just inland from where it empties into the Solent River.

Within minutes of the boat with the Royal Customs officer pulling away from *Zephyr II,* a boat was swung out and over the side. Ezekiel Winters, Marijke Kopf Smythe, Emily Smythe, Rafer Muir, Shoshana Jacinto, and Abner Jeffords boarded it along with Cato Cooper. On the second trip, Jaco and Reyna went ashore with their baggage, along with a crate carrying a half dozen muskets, 12 pistols, six swords, along with powder and shot.

Once everyone was ashore, the Fonseca-Laredo agent hired two coaches and a wagon to take them from Southampton to the Smythe's house in Gosport.

While the shore party was en route to Gosport, Morton Geiger, who remained on board *Zephyr II* as its captain along with Abner Jeffords, would get the two-masted schooner reprovisioned.

On the way over, Emily insisted that her father would want to know that Darren was being held in a Royal Navy jail. She was also confident that her father would let them use the house as a base of sorts.

So as not to raise suspicions, the women rode in the carriages and the men in the wagons. As they rode, the verdant green countryside was just as Emily remembered. Neatly kept farms with fields bordered by stone fences and hedges brought back memories.

It was close to supper time when they arrived in front of the house in which Emily grew up. The sign out front still said Smythe & Sons. In his will, Lester authorized Smythe & Sons to take completely over the house and convert it into its offices.

"Emily. What a pleasant surprise. I had no notice you were coming." Lester waved in the direction of those in the street. "Who are all these people?"

"Darren's second wife, Marijke. You know Jaco and his wife, Dr. Jacinto and my husband Rafer!"

"Welcome. Please, all of you, come in."

Once inside, the carriage driver paid off, and the introductions were complete, Lester led them all into the sitting room. It was a place where Emily remembered many a conversation – some pleasant, some not so pleasant – took place.

A woman, probably in her mid-fifties, appeared, wiping her hands on an apron. Lester said, "This is Angelina. She takes care of the house for me. Please, we'll get some chairs. Angelina will bring us some port or Madeira. Decent French wines are hard to come by these days.

Lester Smythe sat in his rocking chair after he poured either port or Madeira into their glasses as requested and looked at his daughter. "So, my lovely daughter Emily, what brings you and this entourage to Gosport?"

Emily started with the punch line: the Royal Navy had arrested Darren, and he was being held without bail in the Royal Navy base's jail. Lester listened carefully, and when she finished, Lester said, "I am not surprised. The Royal Navy is desperate for men, and just last week, another press gang showed up at the factory. Again, Esau had the younger workers hidden in this house."

He took a long sip of his Madeira. "Emily, what are you going to do?"

"Get him out."

"How?"

"Father, after Shoshana returns from Mr. York at Scoons office here in Portsmouth, we will know more. Then, we will make a plan."

"Whatever you do, please keep me informed. My Darren doesn't deserve this."

"Father, the less you know, the better."

"My daughter, you didn't hear me. I want to help, and I do not want my son, who served his king honorably, to dance at the end of a rope. Even in my dotage, I can help."

Rafer came to his wife's aid. "Aye, sir, we shall do just that."

Smiling, Lester held up his glass. "So sayeth a Scotsman who for centuries wanted to do, but couldn't, what our colonial friends did."

PORTSMOUTH, TUESDAY, MARCH 26TH, 1811

At the Scoons office, Emily, along with Shoshana, Marijke, and Ezekiel, asked the nearest clerk if Henry York was expected. The man, whom she didn't recognize, said no, but his senior law clerk, Josiah Stanton, was.

This wasn't the first time Emily was in this office. Back in 1782, she made her offer to buy Francis Burdette, her boorish husband, out of their marriage. In the end, Burdette took the cash, knowing that it came with losing the Smythe account and that he would have to find a replacement for their billings.

That was an unhappy time in her life but once Emily arrived in Charleston, the independence and freedom she'd dreamed about became a reality. Emily flourished working for the Laredos and the Jacintos, and now, she was the chief financial officer of a company that had sales in the millions of pounds.

"Mrs. Smythe, my name is Josiah Stanton, and I am Henry York's senior law clerk. You probably don't remember me, but I helped Mr. Holcombe with your divorce and the paperwork with the matter of removing your brothers from Smythe & Sons."

"Yes, Mr. Stanton I do. With me is Ms. Shoshana Jacinto, Mrs. Marijke Kopf Smythe, and Ezekiel Winters, Darren's brother-in-law."

"Ms. Jacinto, I have heard so much about you and have had the pleasure of seeing some of your work."

Nodding to Ezekiel, Scranton said, "You are Melody Winters' brother, no?"

"I am that."

Stanton pointed down the hall, "Please join me in one of our conference rooms, and I will have some tea and coffee brought in."

Once inside, Stanton offered refreshments before he went to collect the files York kept in Portsmouth. When he returned, Scranton offered as he looked at Emily, "I presume you are here about your brother, Darren. May I suggest that I review what has transpired since he was taken, and then, I believe we can go see him. Mr. York will be here tomorrow and can provide the particulars on what work he has done at Tunbridge Wells and in London."

"That Mr. Scranton, would be excellent."

The walk to the naval base, officially known as the Royal Navy Dockyard, took less than 15 minutes from Scoon's offices. Shoshana asked, and Scranton agreed, that he would assign her an intern to assist her as she studied the documents Scranton had. What Shoshana wanted most were cases and precedents when Admiralty Courts came into conflict with English civil courts.

Portsmouth, Emily believed, hadn't changed much since she was a child. The only difference was that the harbor was full of warships being resupplied rather than anchored, bereft of sails and cannon. There was much more activity than she remembered, but after the American Revolution, the Royal Navy downsized as fast as men could be paid off and ships put "in ordinary," or broken up or sold.

Emily, Shoshana, Marijke, and Ezekiel waited outside while Scranton talked to the Royal Marine officer on duty. A few moments later, the Marine came outside, bowed slightly to Emily, and said, "I can give you fifteen minutes. Only two will be allowed inside. Two must wait outside."

Turning to Ezekiel, he asked, "Are you carrying any weapons?"

Ezekiel shook his head and raised his arms as if to say search me when he said, "No."

"Good." Looking at the Scranton, the Marine said, "Any funny business and I will ask Captain de Montfort to cease allowing Captain Smythe visitors."

"Sir, has my brother had any visitors?"

"No, other than Mr. York and Mr. Scranton. I suspect that now that you are here, you will want to come every day."

Emily handed the Marine a gold coin. Technically, giving the Marine officer on duty a gold sovereign might be considered a bribe, Scranton, with York's approval, said no, it was a gratuity given for their cooperation.

When the Marine guard with the key to the cell opened the door, Darren was lying on the plank bunk, staring at the ceiling. Seeing his visitors, he brightened. Marijke gasped at the sight of her husband, and Emily forced herself not to react. Darren's clothes were filthy, he hadn't shaved in weeks and was very pale.

Marijke stood by the door to make sure that no guards were hanging about while Emily and Darren sat on the bench. Emily faced the wall and talked softly, letting Darren know who had come to England and, one way or the other, his days in this cell were coming to an end.

While Emily and the others were visiting Darren, Rafer Muir, Colin Landry, and Jaco Jacinto walked through the town of Portsmouth. Seeing a second-hand uniform shop, Jaco walked in. What caught his attention were several headless mannequins lined up in the window and along the sides of the store with Royal Navy and Royal Marine uniforms.

The proprietor proudly said that he collected uniforms from retired officers who might need money to augment their retired pay and from families whose sons had died in the service of their king. These uniforms, he said, came from their personal effects, which were brought home on their ships.

A few hundred feet down the street, they came across two more of these stores. Inside, their owners said essentially the same thing. The uniforms and insignia were for sale. Buyers were officers who were newly promoted and who couldn't afford a tailor.

Back in the Smythe's house, the mood was upbeat. Darren was alive and, under the circumstances, doing well. Over dinner, the debate was what to do next. Shoshana was adamant, saying that they needed to meet with York, get his insight, and then decide.

She believed that York, along with Emily, should visit Captain de Montfort and plead with him to release Darren. What she learned in the law library at Scoon's office confirmed what she suspected. There were enough cases to provide precedent that the civil courts can, if it is not clearly a nautical matter, overrule an Admiralty Court. Or force the Royal Navy to abide by its rulings. However, she did note that all those precedents occurred in peacetime, and England is now at war, but not with the United States. The operative word was not because it was not a belligerent in the war raging in Europe.

Shoshana believed that they had a strong case that the roots of the case were civil, i.e., could the Royal Navy recall a citizen from another country and try him in court? Everything else, she argued, stems from this fact.

When Jaco crawled into bed at close to midnight, Reyna was not asleep. He had been studying two maps, one of the Royal Navy Dockyard and the other an Admiralty map of Portsmouth Harbor.

Reyna propped herself up on an elbow in what Jaco knew all too well as the "We need to talk" position. "You don't think the Royal Navy is going to release Darren, do you?"

"No, I don't." Jaco pulled her head down so Reyna's cheek was resting on his chest. "We're going to have to get him."

"Is that what Rafer, Ezekiel, and you were doing?"

"Yes. We have a plan that we all think will work.

"How?"

Jaco kissed his wife on the forehead. "That my love is our secret. Depends on what happens tomorrow with Captain de Montfort. If he is going to be released, then we will wait. If not, we go."

"You can't just fight your way into a Royal Navy Dockyard, take a man out of their prison, and fight your way out."

"We're not."

"Then how?"

"I said that was a secret. Suffice it to say, we are going to use the Royal Navy's own arrogance and complacency to our advantage."

His answer still didn't satisfy Reyna, who wanted to know more. Jaco resisted the interrogation as best he could. Frustrated, Jaco kissed his wife passionately, which led to a pleasurable outcome and a decent night's sleep.

PORTSMOUTH, THURSDAY, MARCH 28TH, 1811

That de Montfort agreed to see Emily, Shoshana, Marijke, and York on short notice was a surprise. Since he wasn't a "principal," de Montfort asked Ezekiel Winters to wait outside. Before he did, Ezekiel asked if he could walk around the Royal Navy Dockyard while he was waiting, and de Montfort assigned one of his lieutenants to act as Ezekiel's guide.

What wasn't a surprise to the three women and Henry York was that de Montfort was intransigent. He was adamant that he was to hold Darren Smythe, Captain RN retired, until advised by the Counsel for the Affairs of the Admiralty Board to release him. He showed York a copy of the letter he sent asking for guidance, but has not, at least as of the moment of the meeting, received an answer.

As they were escorted back to the gate, none of them said a word. It was in Scoons' Portsmouth office that York said he believes Captain Granby is still smarting from the injunction and will take his sweet time deciding what to do with Captain Smythe. York believed Granby could keep Smythe in legal limbo and in jail for as long as he wished.

Emily thanked York, who asked if he should force the issue in Parliament after pointing out that the firm has several partners who are MPs. By doing so, it could force the Royal Navy's hand. The publicity could be embarrassing to the Prime Minister, or worse, he could force a vote approving continued impressment. Emily asked York to wait and they will advise what they wish to do next.

All the Americans were worried that the Royal Navy would go dead in the water if York went to Parliament and could deny and delay releasing her brother. Worse, security around Darren would increase or the Royal Navy would move him. She was convinced that the way forward was getting Darren out, by force if necessary

While Emily and Shoshana were meeting with Henry York, Jaco and Rafer Muir were visiting the clothing stores. Jaco came out with two Royal Navy officers' coats and hats, while Rafer bought two coats worn by the Royal Marines.

Also perusing the second-hand uniform and military supply stores were Brandon Grantham and Colin Landry. Grantham laid on his Irish brogue heavily as they searched through bins looking for the buttons and other items that made up a Royal Marine's uniform. By the time the three men had finished shopping, they had the uniforms for five Royal Marines.

They met on the street near Scoon's office, where Grantham and Landry took the clothing and went back to the Smythe house in Gosport. There, they would assemble the uniforms.

Once they were all together and finished what the Americans called lunch, Jaco tapped on the table. "Shoshana, as you know, the consensus is we are about to discuss freeing Darren. Since you are our lawyer, I think it best if you do not know our plans this way, you can truthfully say you did not know what we are about to do and thus, were not involved in the planning or commission of a crime."

"Agreed. I think that is best, but I still want to help."

Jaco could see his wife was about to say something, and he cut her off. "Reyna, I know you want to help, but this time, it is best that you are on *Zephyr II.* I will brook no discussion about this. Rafer and I have decided that it is best that you and Emily are on the ship."

Reyna nodded her head, as did Emily. Then she said, "Jaco, you damn well better make it back to *Zephyr II,* or I will, by God, come after you, the Royal Navy be damned."

"Aye, my love, that is why you are going to be on the boat, and I shall be ashore."

Emily, who had heard stories about her friend, Dr. Laredo's fearlessness in battle, nodded before speaking. "What are we womenfolk to do?" Her tone when she spoke the word women folk was borderline sarcastic.

"You can help by being a crew member on *Zephyr II* and sailing it. Mr. Winters will be its captain and will be even more short-handed than on the way over. And, you can get the muskets and pistols loaded, just in case. Emily, Reyna, and you are going back to *Zephyr II* escorted by Grantham and Landry. Once you are safely on board, they will return with Mr. Geiger and four men. Now here's what Rafer and I think will work."

The meeting ended about an hour later, and a carriage with the women and their escorts left shortly thereafter.

PORTSMOUTH, FRIDAY, MARCH 29TH, 1811

Zephyr II glided to a stop late in the afternoon of Thursday and dropped anchor in what the Admiralty Chart said was 12 feet of water. They were just outside the Gosport side of the harbor and were less than 100 yards from the shoreline. The schooner was within sight of a battery of 24-pounders at a place called King's Bastion.

When Ezekiel Winters looked over the side, he could see the plume of dirt that the port anchor and then the starboard one caused when they landed in the mud. The wind was out of the nor' west and he waited until he was sure *Zephyr II* was not going to drift before he ordered the two longboats to be hoisted over the side.

Once they were in the water, the masts were stepped and the sails rigged so they could be sailed with a jib and mainsail. Just after dark, the two boats sailed for Gosport.

PORTSMOUTH, SATURDAY, MARCH 30TH, 1811

Once they were out of the house, Rafer Muir formed up his detail, which marched smartly down to the dock where two of Zephyr II's sailors were waiting by the two long boats. They, like the other two men, were dressed as if they were sailors in the Royal Navy.

The sails of both boats were flapping noisily as they luffed in the moderate breeze. Jaco, wearing the uniform of a Captain in the Royal Navy, boarded last and sat on the aftmost thwartship plank, just forward of the coxswain.

"Cast off, Mr. Jenkins, we have work to do."

"Aye, aye, sir."

A push from the dock and pulling in from the sheets caused the long boat to accelerate. From his seat next to Rafer Muir, who was resplendent in the red uniform of a Royal Marine Major, Jaco could see the four British Army Land Pattern muskets lying on the floor of the boat. They were loaded and ready to fire. The men dressed as Marines were sitting in pairs just forward of the mast.

At the pier, Grantham, wearing three V-shaped, red and gold stripes on his arm signifying he was, as he said, "a bloody Royal Marine sergeant!"

Jenkins said, "Captain Jacinto, we'll be waiting for you. Go get Captain Smythe."

Jaco turned around when he stepped onto the pier of the Royal Navy Dockyard. This was the crew of the second boat's cue to start for the same landing.

When he took his position in front of the four "Royal Marines," Rafer whispered, "Do not speak. Let me, the loud Scotsman, do the talking."

Ahead, Jaco could see the guardhouse where Darren was being kept. The four "Marines" took station outside the door while Jaco and Rafer went in.

In a commanding voice, Rafer addressed the lieutenant of Marines who, when he saw a major enter, came out from behind his desk. "Lieutenant, I am Major Rafer Muir here to pick up one each Darren Smythe, formerly a captain in the Royal Navy. We are taking him to London for trial."

Muir placed a folded sheet of paper on the desk that bore the seal of the Royal Navy. They had lifted it from one of the letters that Lester Smythe received from his son, who also left a few sheets of Royal Navy stationery used for official correspondence at the house.

The lieutenant popped open the seal and read the letter. "Major, this is most irregular. I must check with Captain de Montfort before I can release him."

"No, you don't." Muir turned to Jaco, who, up until this point, had been standing quietly off to the side. "Captain?"

Jaco reached into his coat and handed Muir another letter. Muir, in turn, handed it to the lieutenant. "This is from Vice Admiral of the Red Stacey Davidson, who is also the Duke of Somerset, giving you the authority to release the traitor Smythe into Captain Jacinto's custody. He will ensure that Smythe is delivered to the Admiralty in London for trial. The tide is ebbing, and we have a boat to catch. Now, time's a wasting, Lieutenant!"

The lieutenant read the letter from Davidson, written the day before. What neither Jaco, Rafer, nor the Marine lieutenant knew was that Davidson was, at the moment, somewhere in the Atlantic on his way back to England from Halifax, Nova Scotia.

"May I keep these letters for my records?"

"You may."

The lieutenant barked a series of orders, and two of his men disappeared down the hall. Both Jaco and Rafer could hear the clanking of iron bars. "Lieutenant, leave Smythe in hand irons, but I want the manacles off so he can climb a ladder onto Captain Jacinto's ship.""

Another set of orders were yelled. The door opened, and Jaco had to turn away. Muir remained in character and barked, "Sergeant Grantham, take possession of our prisoner."

Outside, the building, Grantham rudely pushed Darren into a position just in front of his four Marines, who now had their bayonets fixed and behind Rafer and Jaco.

Seeing Rafer Muir, Jaco Jacinto, Darren, and the four fake Royal Marines leave the jail, Morton Geiger waved at Colin Landry. Geiger was dressed as a Royal Navy Lieutenant. Landry, dressed as an ordinary seaman, was standing at the end of the Royal Navy Dockyard's Double Rope House.

Landry and three other sailors from *Zephyr II* had a wheelbarrow with 24 bottles filled with rum and "corked" with clothes soaked in rum and sprinkled liberally with gunpowder. In the wheelbarrow was a small coil of slow match.

Once Landry acknowledged his wave, they began to walk between the Double Rope House on their left and the Hemp House on their right. They could hear the bottles break as they hit the stone floor, and by the time they reached the end of the Double Rope House, smoke was pouring out the windows.

The Hemp House brewed up quickly, and with no more bottles to toss, Morton Geiger formed the four men into a detachment and walked to the landing. Behind them, fire was already spreading the length of the Double Rope House feasting on the tar-covered rigging, barrels of pitch, and dried rope.

With the fires burning behind them, no one took notice of the two detachments. Geiger stopped momentarily to order a group of sailors looking at the fire to go find buckets to help put the fire out.

Darren was put in one boat with the fake Royal Marines and Rafer Muir and one of the Marines used a pike to shove the boat away from the landing.. Jaco waited until Geiger, Landry, and the three others were in the second boat before he took his seat.

The strong wind that fed the flames also pushed the long boats along. With both the main and jibs taut, the boats knifed through the water and out of the harbor entrance.

Rising smoke from the long rope building was visible from *Zephyr's* main deck. The lookouts reported the fire was spreading, and at least two buildings were on fire. They also spooked the two long boats heading toward them.

Ezekiel Winters used Jaco's Dollond spyglass and counted noses on the boats. With him on the quarterdeck were three women who wanted to know what he saw.

"They're flying a blue cloth, which means they got Darren. Now we must get underway. Each of you has an assignment to haul in the sheets. Now, please, go."

Turning to the crew, Winters ordered, "Weigh the port anchor smartly. As soon as it is clear of the water, hoist the main sails, and once the starboard anchor is out of the mud, we'll fall off and pick up our friends."

The starboard anchor came up easily, but the port one was stuck in the mud. A capstan bar broke with a loud crack, sending two men flying into the men in front of them.

Reyna rushed to the fallen men, who were bruised but not bloodied or hurt. She then went back to her station as one of the line handlers on the foremast mainsail boom sheet.

Winters ordered, "Cut the hawser. We'll leave the Royal Navy a souvenir."

Zephyr II, freed from the bottom, surged ahead. Ezekiel ordered a course toward the English Channel. The booms for the main sails were let out so the longboats could catch the schooner.

First to come aboard was Darren. Men reached down and helped him climb up the side. Once on deck, he was led to where two men were waiting with a large block of wood, a hammer, and a chisel. Three loud bangs later, the cast-iron bolt cracked, freeing Darren's hands. Gleefully, he tossed the manacles into the channel.

Emily was the first to hug him, and she pulled back, wrinkling her nose. "God, you smell like a pig sty!"

"No, my sister, I smell like someone who spent months in one of his Majesty's Navy's jails. I do need a bath and a change of linen."

Longboat two was tied to the lines to hoist it aboard, and as it was being lifted, *Zephyr II* went through a swell which sent it smashing into the side of the schooner, breaking the boat's planking in two places. It would be repaired later when they had time.

With everyone back on board, Ezekiel ordered all the booms to be hauled in, the topsails raised, and both jibs flown. Abner Jeffords looked at the wake as *Zephyr II* left the Solent and entered the English Channel. Without casting a line, he was sure the moderate nor' west wind was pushing the three-masted schooner along at 12 knots.

Behind the schooner, the pillar of smoke rising from the Royal Navy Dockyard was getting darker and taller. Jaco glanced at the smoke and then turned his attention to captaining *Zephyr II.* His job wasn't done until his friend was safely home. To that, they had to dodge the Royal Navy.

40 NM WEST SO' WEST OF LAND'S END, SUNDAY, MARCH 31ST, 1811

After clearing the Isle of Wight, Jaco had the schooner under full sail, course so' by so' west. The sooner Zephyr II reached the vastness of the Atlantic, the sooner it could disappear. The waters in the Celtic Sea and the approaches to the English Channel were full of merchant ships, Royal Navy frigates, and fishing boats.

They all laughed as Darren asked to have a screen rigged so that the ship could pump fresh seawater all over him as he tried to wash the stink from sitting in the bilge of a ship and then a jail cell for two months. Once he felt clean, his teeth stopped chattering, and his body quit shivering from being washed down by 50° F water, he dressed and met privately with Shoshana as she recorded a formal statement. Once written out, it was witnessed by Jaco and Morton Geiger.

Now cleaner, but not clean, Darren asked for permission to come up on *Zephyr II's* small quarterdeck. While with an officer, two quartermasters, and a bosun's mate on the deck, it wasn't crowded; there wasn't a lot of extra space.

Jaco walked to the aft railing, thinking his friend had something important to say. "Jaco, thank you for coming to rescue me. Being a guest, albeit a well-treated one, in one of His Majesty's jails is not a pleasant experience. I do, however, believe that in the end, justice would prevail, and I would have been freed."

"Our sisters and I disagree. Henry York was running out of legal options, and the Royal Navy was acting as if it were above the law. It was planned to court-martial you on trumped-up charges and then hang you as an example to others. While the Royal Navy took its sweet time sorting out what to do, you, my friend, were rotting in jail. That's number one. Number two is that I would rather die than let you dance at the end of a rope because England is short of men to fight one of their stupid wars."

"You didn't have to set fire to the entire dockyard, did you?"

"No, just the rope and hemp sheds. If we had more time, we would have set the sheds with dried wood on fire. What we did was intended as a distraction so we could get away, but I also wanted to send a message. During our revolution, the flag we flew at the top of the mainmast with a coiled snake and the words don't tread on me is the same one we fly on the N.E.S. frigates and corvettes. And, if I am in command of a U.S. Navy ship, I will also fly it. The words still apply."

"Well, I guess I still had faith in the rule of law."

"I do too, but only when both sides agree to obey it. In this case, the Royal Navy didn't accept the injunction and went off on its own."

"Well, my friend, if you were in my shoes, I would have done the same. So again, thank you." Darren faced aft so his words would not be heard by the others on the quarterdeck.

"Jaco, if it comes to war with England, if not offered a captaincy of a frigate, I am going to demand one. I now have a score to settle with England and better understand why you fought us for so long."

A few seconds passed, "Darren, trust me, if war comes, getting you a frigate is not going to be a problem. We're both now fifty, and I do not want to fight another war. But, if needed, I will."

When night fell, the only concession Jaco made was to lower the top sails and drop the second jib and the staysails. The watch team was under instruction that unless there was a storm on the horizon, at first light, to fly all the sails the schooner could carry.

By staying close to the English coast, Jaco wanted to stay away from any prowling frigates. They were also sailing as close to the wind as the schooner could, which limited the directions a Royal Navy frigate could cut them off.

As they did on the way over, the two married couples, Darren and Marijke retired early to their cabin followed by Rafer and Emily. After the four bells into the first watch, Jaco joined his wife in their cabin.

Reyna snuggled close to her husband and asked, "Why was Emily so mad at Darren at dinner?"

"Darren naively believes that in the end, he would have been freed. It was just a matter of time and waiting the Royal Navy out."

"We would all be old and gray and maybe in our graves when that happened."

"Aye, Darren will come around. Think no more of it."

A sharp rap on the door of the captain's cabin woke Jaco. He unwound himself from his wife's arms. "Sir, lookouts have spotted a fleet of ships. All Royal Navy. Mr. Winters thought you'd better have a look."

Jaco pulled on a coat and tied his breeches. On deck, he could see clouds to the nor' nor' west. Behind him, the spring sun was just coming over the horizon. Morton Geiger handed him his Dollond spyglass. Two points on the port bow, Jaco counted eight ships, two of which were large two-deckers escorted by at least six ships.

He could not see any signals, nor had any of the ships turned in his direction. Above and behind him, he saw the U.S. flag streaming from a halyard that flew it from the top of the mizzen mast.

"Mr. Geiger, continue our present course. If any of his majesty's ships turn in our direction, then we will adjust accordingly. I do not think they are interested in us. And if they are, we shall alter course to run away and hide."

On board *H.M.S. Europe,* 64 guns, Vice Admiral Stacey Davidson was enjoying the warmth of the spring sun. He had decided to return on the fourth-rated ship of the line, thinking it would probably be the last time in his career that he would be at sea on a warship. When the lookouts called out the fast sailing, three-masted schooner to the north and east of his flagship, he was handed a spyglass.

Immediately, Davidson recognized the lines of the schooners owned by American Shipping & Passenger Lines. He turned to *Europe's* captain, Chauncey Enfield, "That's one of American Shipping and Passenger Line's schooners. They make the passage from New York to London in less than fourteen days. The passenger accommodations are quite nice.

Davidson watched the schooner for a few seconds, wondering where Darren was at this very moment. He was, he hoped, returning to England for his last assignment as Second Naval Lord before retiring. But, like all other officers and seamen in the Royal Navy, they were "in" for the duration. Duration means until Napoleon was defeated, no matter how long it took or how many lives were lost.

PORTSMOUTH, FIRST WEEK OF APRIL 1811

The smell of burnt rope, tar, and pitch was still in the air when H.M.S. Europe arrived. The wind from the nor' west blew the odor right down the harbor and out into the Solent.

Stacey Davidson wondered what caused the distinctive odor until he saw the Royal Navy Dockyard. The fire started in the Double Rope House, and the northernmost Hemp House had spread to four other buildings. He didn't know that about 80% of the Royal Navy's rope at the dockyard was burned along with the buildings and naval stores.

Nor did Davidson know about Darren Smythe and he had nothing to do as *Europe's* captain, Chauncey Enfield, conned the ship of the line to its anchorage. While he was watching, one of the midshipmen came to attention in front of him. "Sir, the base is signaling. The dockyard's captain wishes to come aboard."

Puzzled and wanting to go ashore as soon as possible, Davidson said pleasantly, welcoming the minor distraction. "Is it Captain Soames?"

The midshipman had his answer ready. "Aye, sir."

"Tell him to come over, forthwith."

Virgil Soames was piped aboard, and at the gap in the bulwark, a grinning Chauncey Enfield welcomed his friend and former shipmate on board. "Captain, Vice Admiral Davidson is waiting for you in his cabin."

"Captain Enfield, please join us."

"Aye, that I will once I make sure that *Europe* is well anchored and won't embarrass me by dragging an anchor."

Davidson, after greeting Soames with a handshake and a warm hug, asked straight away, "From what I can see from the poop deck, it looks like a fair amount of the Royal Dockyard was burned. Do you know what happened here?"

Soames took a deep breath and pointed to a chair. "Sir, it is best that the Admiral sit down."

The soon to be Second Sea Lord's manservant entered carrying a tray with a pitcher of strong Jamaican coffee and several cups. Vice Admiral of the Red Stacy Davidson took his coffee and sat down behind the simple wood table that was his desk on *Europe.*

"Aye, you will enjoy the tale of what I am about to tell you."

"Will I?" Davidson's voice was tainted by sarcasm.

Soames described the fire and the freeing of Darren Smythe along with what he learned from Captain de Montfort. He added that he went to see Henry York who was very circumspect and reiterated that the Royal Navy was enjoined from recalling Captain Smythe. Beyond that, York said nothing other than he was aware there was a fire at the Royal Naval Dockyard.

After listening to Soames speak, Davidson put his cup down with a loud smack. "If I were the Admiralty, I would take this as a warning to stop this stupid practice of impressing American seamen because the Royal Navy thinks but does not know if they are deserters. "

Davidson looked at the two officers. "'Twere I someone who played the horses, my bet is one each Captain Jaco Jacinto is behind this fire. I suspect the next time men from one of his ships are impressed, he might burn London down. If he did, England would have deserved it, and I wouldn't blame him."

As Second Naval Lord, Stacey Davidson assumed that when he began his duties at the Admiralty, he would have to sort out what caused this mess.

LONDON, THIRD WEEK OF APRIL 1811

Vice Admiral of the Red Stacey Davidson, the Duke of Somerset, was standing in his new office in the Admiralty. Outside, looking at the street below, one wouldn't know there was a war on unless one reflected on the ratio of men to women. He was now Second Naval Lord, and one of his first orders of business was to find a supply of hemp. There were a half a dozen new ships in Portsmouth awaiting rigging and another half dozen needing repairs to their rigging.

Captain Jacinto knew how to hurt the Royal Navy without firing a shot. England had no source of hemp on the island. Much of it came from North America, i.e., the United States.

Phineas Taylor, a Captain who lost his left foot and most of his left arm when he was captain of *H.M.S. Pilum* in a battle with *Scorpion,* was the chief of his office staff. Taylor endured fever, infection and several operations before the wounds healed. It took over a year before he was fit. Once he was healthy, the Royal Navy put him on half pay. He requested to come back on active duty as either a lieutenant or a commander to work on a staff, and the service brought him back as a lieutenant. Since then, he was again promoted to commander.

When Davidson was responsible for officer assignments, Taylor was working on the victualling board. As Second Naval Lord, he requested that Taylor become his chief of staff.

So engrossed in the activities of the street below, Davidson didn't hear the clump of Taylor's peg leg on the wooden floor. "Sir, you have two letters from Captain Jacinto. I thought you might want to read them straight away."

"I do." Davidson pointed to one of the armchairs after Taylor put the two letters on the desk.

"Before I read them, what do you make of the cock-up in Portsmouth?"

"Sir, if the Royal Navy had released Captain Smythe with a heartfelt apology and a few hundred quid, the fire would never have happened."

Davidson nodded. He agreed with his assessment but suspected there were several admirals in this building who might disagree with Taylor's assessment. He popped open the wax seal on one of the letters that was on a plain sheet of paper.

Dear Vice Admiral Davidson,

It is my understanding that you are now or will shortly be the Second Naval Lord. By writing directly to you I wish to take advantage of our cordial relationship and hope that my strong message does not destroy our friendship.

This letter is meant as fair warning to England and the Royal Navy. Do not stop either a Fonseca-Laredo or American Shipping & Passenger Lines ship and impress any repeat, any members of our crew or passengers, ever again.

If the Royal Navy stops another one of our ships and impresses any of our sailors, then, as English author William Congreve wrote in Mourning Bride, "Hell hath no greater fury than women scorned."

So, let the Royal Navy and England be warned.

Cordially,
Jaco Jacinto
Managing Director, AS&PL

Davidson held up his hand as if to say to Commander Taylor, "Don't stand up." He went around his desk to hand the note to Taylor thinking that Jacinto wasn't admitting that his men set the fire. By doing so, would make it a criminal act. And since no one saw Jacinto or his men set the fire, it would never hold up in court.

After reading the note, Taylor said, "Sir, this Jacinto chap is a cheeky bastard, but he has a point. My recommendation to the First Naval Lord would be to stop impressment altogether, but knowing the man, he won't. So, giving him this letter would be like pissing in the wind. You may feel better but will need to wash your clothes. Nonetheless, I would take Captain Jacinto at his word."

"I agree, so let's see what Captain Jacinto has to say in his second letter."

This one was written by someone different and was on American Shipping & Passenger Lines letterhead.

Vice Admiral Davidson,

It has come to my attention that the Royal Navy may be short of hemp needed for rigging as well as sufficient tar and pitch to caulk its ships. Through its agents, Fonseca-Laredo Shipping and American Shipping & Passenger Lines, have access to large stores of hemp already made into ropes of various diameters, as well as raw fiber. Plus, we have pitch, tar and other naval stores that might be of use to the Royal Navy.

We would be happy to sell and deliver the material promptly on our fast schooners which, as you know, make it from New York to London in less than two weeks. We have sufficient ships so we can dedicate one to sail directly to Portsmouth.

Should the Royal Navy be interested, our agent in London has the current prices and shipping rates and is authorized to conclude the transaction. We can have the first shipment at the pier at the Portsmouth Royal Navy Dockyard within three weeks of receiving your order.

Cordially,
Jaco Jacinto
Managing Director, AS&PL

Davidson handed the letter to Taylor. "What say you?"

"That's faster than any of our current suppliers. If we get into a battle and need to refit a large number of ships, we don't have the rope to do it. I say we take Captain Jacinto up on his offer."

"Agreed, if the price is reasonable. I'll let you, Commander Taylor, be the judge of that."

"Aye, sir. I'll meet with their agent today, and if it is, I'll have the order on their next ship to America."

"Next item of business. Have Rear Admiral Kubricks come to my office as soon as he can."

As Davidson scanned the *London Gazette,* it was clear that the War of the Fourth Coalition had ended. Even so, the Peninsula War was still in full bloom, albeit in a bit of a stalemate. The English and their Spanish allies have been unable to push the French out, and the French don't have enough troops to defeat the combined Spanish/Portuguese/British Armies. For the Royal Navy, it is business as usual in a war against France, i.e. blockade their ports to keep their navy at home, and transport supplies and men to the British Army.

Sitting on his desk was a report on whatever the Royal Navy could glean from the actions of the U.S. Navy against the French and then against the

Barbary Pirates. While he had read them before, he thought a refresher would be good.

Commander Taylor rapped on the frame of his door. "Sir, Rear Admiral Kubricks is outside, waiting to come in."

"Send him in, then please close the door."

Vice Admiral of the Red Stacey Davidson debated if he should be sitting down during this conversation or standing up. He decided that a fellow flag officer deserved the respect of a face-to-face conversation and stood.

The senior legal officer in the Royal Navy stopped in front of Davidson's desk. The Second Naval Lord got right to the point. "Rear Admiral Kubricks, it is my sad duty to relieve you of your duties as the senior judge advocate officer in the Royal Navy. I expect your letter of retirement on Commander Taylor's desk by the end of today. You will turn over all your current tasks to your deputy. That is all."

"You can't do to that to me, Admiral Davidson. The First Naval Lord will not stand for it. We are at war."

Davidson held up his hand. If the First Naval Lord overruled him, he would retire and live in the country. But he knew Bickerton wouldn't because he'd already told him he was going to relieve Kubricks. If he retired, Belinda and he would visit America. Kubricks was the perfect scapegoat for the disaster at Portsmouth.

"Aye, Rear Admiral Kubricks, we are at war. And your decisions almost added another enemy to what is already England's long list of enemies. Your retirement letter on Commander Taylor's desk by the end of the day. I suggest you do it. If not, you might wind up leaving the Admiralty as a captain or a commander once you are charged and convicted under Article 12 for dereliction of duty, Article 32 for behaving in a cruel, scandalous, and oppressive manner and Article 35, which covers any crimes not covered elsewhere in the Articles of War. Now, get out of my office, you have a letter to write."

The clock on Westminster was reading four p.m. when Phineas Taylor knocked on his door to report that the order has been placed with U.S. Industries agent in London, he had Kubricks resignation letter, and Kubricks will be on the retired list effective immediately.

NEW YORK CITY, FIRST WEEK OF MAY 1811

Darren was sitting in the office he shared with Jaco, looking out the window. The weeks since his rescue had caused him to rethink some of his beliefs. Now that he was back in New York, Darren believed that the Royal Navy had betrayed him. All the honor and traditions that made the service the pride of England had been warped by men who disagreed with his decision to emigrate to the United States. More than ever, he now understood why men like his friend Jaco had fought England for over eight years.

One of the clerks appeared in the doorway with bundles of English and French newspapers. "Captain Smythe, I have the mail, and on top, there is a letter from a Royal Navy admiral."

Darren thanked him and put the newspapers on the table between their desks. The handwriting on the letter was familiar, and he noted that the letter was sealed with the stamp of the Second Naval Lord. When he opened it, the hand was not one of the secretaries used by senior admirals. Davidson had excellent penmanship with a distinct style.

Darren,

As you know by now, I am now the Second Naval Lord, at least for a few more days. As such, I wish to offer my personal apologies as well as those of the Admiralty and the First Naval Lord for the behavior of our service towards you.

The Royal Navy's treatment of you was unconscionable as well as illegal. And, for your incarceration, again, on behalf of the Royal Navy, I apologize.

Unfortunately, the policy of His Majesty's government and reiterated to me by both the Prime Minister and the First Naval Lord is that England and its Royal Navy reserve the right to stop any ship on the high seas and inspect it for war materials. In doing so, its captains are free to impress any sailors on that ship who are believed to be Englishmen.

How that determination is made is left up to the individual captains. We cannot willy-nilly impress citizens of other countries into the Royal Navy. Doing so is kidnapping and is against English law. Impressment is a policy I find abhorrent and cannot in good conscience support, and therefore, I must lower my flag rather than issue orders to captains authorizing them to carry out this policy.

My request to be placed on the retired list has been delivered to the First Naval Lord. I have been instructed to continue to fulfill my duties as Second Naval Lord until such time my replacement arrives.

So, my career in His Majesty's Navy is ending, not the way I would have wished. Even in these difficult times for England, I believe, as you do, that one's principles and values, along with one's integrity, come first.

On a happier note, Belinda and I plan to sell our house in London and move back to our estate in Somerset. Once that objective is achieved, Belinda and I would like to visit America to see what all the fuss was about. Boston, New York, Philadelphia, and Charleston are high on our list.

We hope you will be gracious enough to see us. Should you want to answer, address it to me, Glastonbury, Somerset, England. The postman knows where our estate is located.

God bless, fair winds and following seas.

Stacey Davidson, Duke of Somerset

Second Sea Lord

Vice Admiral of the Red

Darren read the letter a second time and was not sure how to react. Davidson, for all his connections within the government, was willing to resign over impressment. There was something more to this issue, and he, Darren Smythe, Captain Royal Navy retired, was a pawn to be sacrificed. Maybe, just maybe, Jaco was right. The Royal Navy needed to be taught a lesson.

LONDON, FIRST WEEK OF SEPTEMBER 1811

Henry York had decided to make a case out of what he called the Darren Smythe Affair. He believed, as did members of his law firm as well as several Members of Parliament that no one, including the king, was above the law. There were plenty of cases to support Darren's wrongful imprisonment case.

York was convinced that the Royal Navy was wrong when they imprisoned Darren Smythe and let him languish without charging or trying him. If the Royal Navy had just put Smythe on a warship as it did for all the other impressed seamen, the imprisonment wouldn't have happened. He believed that the injunction against recalling Smythe made him untouchable. Yet, out of a sense of vengeance, the Royal Navy acted.

There were two paths open to York. He could take the Royal Navy to civil court and ask for damages. Or he could take his case to Parliament. Neither option precluded the other.

Going to court will take months just to get on a court docket. York believed if he went to Parliament with the argument that Smythe was wrongfully imprisoned because the Royal Navy violated a court order, he thought that he might get a bill of goodwill and money from the Royal Navy's budget. There was always the chance that Parliament would vote against his bill and order the Navy to try Captain Smythe.

York knew that Darren was wealthy. His stock in AS&PL became shares in U.S. Industries. Shoshana said when she came to England that money to defend Darren was not an issue, and his annual share of the U.S. Industries' profits exceeded £10,000.

The question in York's mind was how much England should pay. While he was canvassing members of Parliament, he was told to get enough support for a resolution and then let the MPs pick the number. As part of the process, he could provide suggested amounts but let them decide.

Since York was not a member of Parliament, he could not introduce a resolution, but he could ask one of Scoons' partners to do so. This led to a meeting with an MP who was encouraged by the Duke of Somerset's brother, who was also an MP, to introduce the resolution.

Today was the day it would be debated and voted upon. Stacey Davidson sat down next to York and whispered. "My brother says it will pass; how big a cheque His Majesty will write is what will be debated."

The resolution was read. Most of the MPs saw the Royal Navy's actions as a usurpation of power. The first number that was floated was £50,000 to come out of the navy's budget. Numbers were floated back and forth before Parliament settled on £25,000, along with the agreement to pass a law clarifying that the Royal Navy and the British Army must abide by any decisions or rules made by civil courts.

It took a week for the money to be transferred to Darren's account at the Bank of England. Once it was, Henry York wrote Darren a letter. The letter he received in return did not surprise Henry York. Besides a thank you for his support, it contained instructions to withdraw all but £1,000 from his Bank of England account. Three-quarters of the money was to be transferred to his account at the New York Bank of Commerce and one-quarter to his account at the Dutch private bank Van Lanschot Kempen.

Henry York complied with his instructions. In his note back to Darren, he said he was retiring but would be available for the next year, to handle any other legal affairs in England.

CHAPTER 13

PREPPING FOR WAR

WASHINGTON, FIRST WEEK OF DECEMBER 1811

Javier Jacinto sat quietly in his seat in the House of Representatives as he listened to the Secretary of War William Eustis speak. The topic was the recent battle in the Indiana Territory near Prophetstown.

Apparently, an estimated 600 men, mostly Shawnee, but there were also others from several native American tribes who attacked a group of militia and U.S. Army troops. The Shawnees were led by Tecumseh's brother Tenskwatawa a.k.a. The Prophet. After several hours, the Indians retreated, leaving behind 32 dead. According to Eustis, how many others were wounded was not known.

The Americans, under the governor of the Indian Territory, William Henry Harrison, suffered 62 dead and 126 wounded. After the battle fought on both sides of a creek, the Shawnee called *Keth-tip-pe-can-nunk* in central Indiana, the Americans burned Prophetstown, which was the Shawnee capital.

Eustis concluded by saying that Tecumseh and Tenskwatawa were opposed to the 1807 Treaty of Fort Wayne and further U.S. settlement in the region. Tecumseh was, at the time of the battle, believed to be in Canada speaking with the British."

This led to Javier's question, "Was there any evidence of British involvement?"

"No, Congressman. In Governor Harrison's official report, there is no mention of British Army soldiers or agents. However, all the arms captured had the King's crown stamped on the lock plate with the year the musket was manufactured. While I don't know the specific dates, Governor Harrison mentioned that all were made after 1807. This again proves that the British Army or British agents are selling munitions to Tecumseh and his allies to use against us."

Javier, who was one of the 36 members of the Federalist Party in the House of Representatives, sat quietly in his seat after Secretary Eustis left. His thinking about the implications of the battle was interrupted when Henry Clay, the Speaker of the House of Representatives and a representative from Kentucky, sat down next to him.

In 1811, Javier was one of the most senior members of the House. He had been a member from South Carolina since the First U.S. Congress convened on March 4th, 1789. Before that, he was a member of the Continental Congress.

Clay, who was born in 1777, was only 34 when he was elected to the House of Representatives and was younger than any of Javier's children. However, Javier Jacinto was respected for his insight, and Clay realized that even though the Democratic-Republican Party had an overwhelming majority with 106 of the 142 seats, he wanted Javier as an ally.

All the other members of the House had left the two men sitting alone. "Javier, what say you about this battle?"

"As battles go, it was a skirmish. Where it leads, I do not know. However, it is another indicator of British interference in our country. They are putting pressure on us economically with their trade policy. They are impressing our sailors into the Royal Navy, and they refuse to leave our land. This cannot continue much longer."

Henry Clay looked at the ceiling. "If I were a gambling man, I would bet that there is a war with England coming. When I do not know, but I can tell you that President Madison is at his wits' end on what to do."

Facing the Speaker of the House, Javier said, "If that is the case, we need to start preparing now. That means appropriating money for a larger Army and getting the Navy back to sea, which is something that I, as well as all the Federalists, will support. Let us get a bill on the floor to do this when we reconvene in January. We can use the time between now and then to get something to put on President Madison's desk sometime in February."

Clay held out his hand. "However, before we start working on a bill, I suggest you and I meet with Secretary of the Navy Hamilton and

Secretary of War Eustis to hear their thoughts. You pick the members from your party as I will, and tomorrow, we will give them instructions. However, it must be done in complete secrecy, lest the British get wind of our plans."

Javier took it, "Aye, I agree. You do realize that we are extending an olive branch to President Madison. We are in this mess because his predecessor would not allow the Congress, led by your party, to fund an Army and Navy of sufficient size to defend our country."

"Mea culpa, Javier. But, I was not a member of the House until this past election, so please don't pillory me on the actions of my predecessors."

ON BOARD *ALACRITY II*, THIRD WEEK OF DECEMBER 1811

The month-long, end-of-the-year Christmas break allowed Javier Jacinto and his wife, Perla, to travel to his beloved Charleston to see friends and visit with his constituents. He would return to Washington by the time the House of Representatives reconvened on January 6th, 1812.

The trip on *Alacrity II,* one of AS&PL's ships, gave him a chance to read the pile of British and American newspapers as he tried to get a sense of what was driving the two countries closer to war. Within the house, the factions were made up of both Federalists and Democratic-Republicans.

One faction wanted to take England to task, a.k.a. the name War Hawks. Another wanted to ally with France, citing that Napoleon controlled much of Europe and that France helped the United States win their independence. Then there were those, like himself, who feared a war with England would destroy their businesses.

It was also clear that President Madison, who had been Jefferson's Secretary of State, and James Monroe, who had been Jefferson's Ambassador to Great Britain, were fed up with British intransigence on issues of trade, impressment, and their continued presence on U.S. soil. Both men, Javier believed, were convinced that the only way to get the British to change their behavior was a war.

Something, Javier believed, was behind the British position that we either didn't understand or the British were unwilling to admit, much less negotiate. He was looking at a map in the *New York Evening Post* that showed where it was believed British soldiers or agents were based.

Javier blurted out the deck of *Alacrity II*, "Oh, my God, this isn't about customs duties, impressment, this is about control of the North American continent. The bloody British don't want us to control most of North America now that we have bought the Louisiana Territory. They are afraid we will take Canada, something the War Hawks have been touting."

With that revelation, he went to his cabin and began writing a note to Max Laredo to share with the leadership of U.S. Industries. While U.S. Industries ran profitable businesses, one of the things it did not own was large tracts of land for factories with access to the major rivers within the boundaries of the U.S., the Great Lakes, and the Atlantic Coast. His letter asked Max to put the topic on the agenda for the January board meeting.

NEW YORK CITY, SECOND WEEK OF JANUARY 1812

In the conference room dubbed "The Board Room," the nine members of the U.S. Industries Board of Directors sat around the table. Outside, the wind howled, blowing snow almost horizontally. No one at the table paid attention to the 200 Fahrenheit outside temperature, thanks to the roaring fireplaces at each end of the room. Inside everyone was dressed warmly, and only the top of the polished oak and maple table was cold.

Javier Jacinto, who sailed on one of the AS&PL packets from Washington, was in New York, just for this meeting. As the chairman of the board, Max Laredo sat at the head of the table. Gento Jacinto and Laura Fonseca Laredo were asked to attend because their businesses – shipping, importing, and exporting goods – would be affected by any decisions made.

Darren and Jaco were invited because not only would AS&PL be affected by a war with England, but they would probably be recalled into the U.S. Navy. Last was Emily for her knowledge of U.S. Industries' finances and Greg because he ran the financial services – two banks plus what would be called in the 21st Century, a private equity firm.

Coffee, hot chocolate, and tea were supplemented by freshly baked traditional crusty rolls and sweet-smelling cinnamon rolls. Javier waited until everyone at the table had served themselves and looked to make sure the door was closed.

"What I am about to share is known only by a few leaders of the country. I have Speaker Clay's permission to share our conversation with

President Madison. When I return to Washington, we will bring a bill to the floor to significantly expand the Navy and to increase funding for the state militias and the Army. The President says he will consider signing it if, in his words, the bill is within reason."

Javier looked around the table. "President Madison believes that war with England is coming. There will be several laws passed by the Congress that will garner most of the attention, but the increase in the Army and Navy will not be publicized."

"We, that is U.S. Industries and Naval Escort Services, will be affected. One, we must plan to run our businesses without any English customers. That means AS&PL will stop its service to London for the duration of the war. Emily, I need you and Greg to meet with Max and me so we understand our finances."

Grimly, Emily nodded. Greg said, "We have plenty of cash and can probably sustain our operations for three, maybe four years with zero revenue. I just hope it is not necessary."

"Excellent, but Max and I want to see the figures. I almost forgot, the Secretary of the Navy wants to keep two of our fast schooners at the disposal of the Secretary of State to take diplomats and documents to and from Europe."

"Father, that is not a problem. We can tie them up in the yard across the river in Brooklyn. And we can sail two down to Washington so they are there when needed."

Nodding, Javier faced his son. "Javier, Darren and you will be offered commissions to captain frigates and AS&PL, Fonseca-Laredo Shipping and N.E.S. will be asked to contribute crews. I have already met with the members of the board of N.E.S. and part of our agreement with the Department of the Navy is that in time of conflict, N.E.S.'s ships and crews become part of the Navy. Gento, I will give you a list of ports where we will start asking our agents to begin acquiring powder and shot. If our ships stop in a neutral port, legally they cannot procure munitions. However, since N.E.S. owns the ships, our agents can provide whatever military stores they need. Max has already sent a letter to Asa to triple our factories production of cannonballs."

When Javier finished, Jaco raised his hand. "Father, how much time do we have?"

Shaking his head, Javier said, "Sadly, my son, I don't know. What I do know is that Darren and you will be summoned to Washington in the next month or so to meet with Secretary Hamilton and the Commodore. A war with England is something nobody wants, but the English have rejected our attempts at diplomacy and President Madison believes this as the only way we can get them to change their policies."

War in Europe was good for U.S. Industries if the U.S. was neutral. War with England, their largest trading partner, was not.

VICINITY OF 45°N, 8°W, THIRD WEEK OF FEBRUARY 1812

The blustery cold wind of the day before that had buffeted Fonseca-Laredo's newest and, at 1,500 tons and 180 feet long, largest merchant ship, Confederation, had died down. They were replaced with puffy white clouds, blue skies, and a steady wind from the so' west which forced the ship to sail nor' west.

Over breakfast, Roger Hornsby, *Confederation's* captain, told his sole passenger, Philipe Dubisson, that he would sail on this course until they reached the 12th meridian so he could tack to the south and start tacking back, and until they were off the coast of Africa and could take advantage of more favorable winds.

Hearing the words during a meal, Hornsby could have been speaking Greek. Shown the planned course on a chart, it all made sense to Dubisson, who was on board because *Confederation* was carrying 1,800 barrels of wine in its hold, weighing 800 tons.

Before the wine barrels could be loaded, Dubisson went through the calculations of how much each wine barrel weighed. From there, Hornsby could tell him how many barrels his ship could carry.

Each precious barrel contained 59 gallons (225 liters) of wine that had been aged six months in his father's warehouses. The barrels weighed 90 pounds (~44.5 kilograms), and the wine, at 13.5 pounds (~6.12 kilograms) per gallon. Philippe's calculations showed that the wine in each barrel weighed 796.5 pounds (361.3 kilograms), so the total weight of each barrel was 886.5 pounds (406.1 kilograms).

The wine in the casks was *vin ordinaire* or table wine and came from five vineyards near Bordeaux. It had been aged for six months in the two Dubisson et Fils warehouses in Pauillac, a town 56 kilometers down the Garonne River and thus closer to the Atlantic from Bordeaux.

Dubisson et Fils, of which he was the North American agent and based in New York, had much riding on this shipment. For years, they had been smuggling wines into England. In the past two years, the French government forbid exporting French wines to England, and British customs duties on the wine made it exorbitantly expensive in England. This left the United States as Dubisson et Fils primary customer.

The good news was that the growing American market could take all the wine Dubisson could produce. The bad news was that if they could not get the wine to America, Dubisson et Fils would be in serious financial trouble. As a *negociant,* Dubisson bought the freshly squeezed grape juice, and in his warehouses, he turned it into wine. He also owned wine that was being aged at the vineyard so if he could not sell the wine, he was out the cost of buying the wine.

While in Bordeaux, Philippe bought four books to add to his collection. He'd found an original copy of Voltaire's *Candide* published in 1759 along with a copy of *Candide II* released in 1760. The other two were *Gil Blas* by Alain-René Lesage published in 1750 and *Anti-Justine* by Nicolas-Edme Rétif that was published in 1799.

On the way home, he decided to read *Gil Blas* which was a story about a stable hand and a maid in Spain who manage to shed their humble beginnings and become wealthy. Philippe was sitting in a chair abeam the main mast reading when he heard the lookout yell just after the tones from five bells on the Afternoon Watch had died away. If he had seen the chronograph in Captain Hornsby's cabin, he would have seen that it was just after 2:30 p.m. "Deck, ship, three points aft of the starboard beam at about four miles. Looks like a brig!"

Hornsby, who was on the quarterdeck, hollered back. "What course?"

There was a few second pause. "Looks like she's headed our way."

Looking up, Hornsby saw the Swedish flag that would tell any Royal Navy ship that they were from a neutral country. However, that never gave Royal Navy captains desperate for men to fill out their musters pause.

And a brig? The Royal Navy used frigates to watch over French ports. They had slipped out of the Garonne at night without showing a light. When they arrived, *Confederations'* lookouts hadn't seen a Royal Navy frigate. Bordeaux was not a major French naval base which is why, Hornsby believed there were no Royal Navy ships around.

Leaning over the railing, Hornsby saw Philippe walking aft. "Mr. Dubisson, we are going to bend on more sail and ease off a bit to make us more difficult to catch. If we are lucky, it will be dark before they catch us and we can slip away."

Philippe waited until Hornsby gave out the commands that led to the setting of *Confederation's* top gallants and royals along with an additional jib. He could feel the merchant ship heel a bit more and had no way of knowing if they were going faster.

Hornsby came down from the quarterdeck and on his way to his cabin, he said, "Mr. Dubisson, please join me in my cabin, if you will."

Confederation's captain let Philippe enter and then closed the door behind him. "If you will give me a moment or two, I would like to make an entry into my log."

Phillippe walked to the aft end of the captain's cabin which was at the stern of the ship and looked at the wake. If this ship was taken by the British or worse a privateer, his family would be out the money they paid for the juice that they had turned into wine.

As Philippe stood there, he held the bottom of his left arm with his right hand and gently massaged the soft tissue, something he would do when under stress or thinking about a major decision. *What could* Confederation *or he do to keep the wine?*

"Mr. Dubisson, please allow me to share my thinking about our situation."

Captain Hornsby's voice brought Philippe back to the moment. "The brig could be Royal Navy, but I doubt it. In my experience, the Royal Navy only uses brigs in auxiliary roles such as part of a larger group frigates escorting a convoy. Or, to carry mail or messages so my assumption is that it is probably a British privateer. On the markets in London, what is in our hold represents a small fortune. *Confederation* will add to the coffers of the consortium that own the privateer."

"What do we do?"

"Fonseca-Laredo's policy is that we do not resist foreign navies or privateers. We are supposed to let them stop us to inspect our cargo. Wine is not contraband so there are no worries about that so we should be let go. My ships have had men taken off to be forced to join the Royal Navy, but I have never lost a cargo or a ship and I do not intend to do so today."

"Sir, what do you plan to do?"

Hornsby started by stating they have a store of muskets, pistols and swords for use in port. Then, he outlined his plan on how to prevent *Confederation* from being taken given that it will take two to three hours for the brig to overtake the merchant ship.

VICINITY OF 45°N, 8°W, ON BOARD *RATTLESNAKE*, 2:46 P.M.

The corvette was under every sail that its captain, Micah Jacinto could conceivably hang on the three-masted schooner. It was, according to his quartermaster, making 12.8 knots, which, given that she didn't have a clean bottom, was, in Micah's mind, better than he expected.

He was in a hurry because *Rattlesnake* was late leaving Porto, Portugal where he had stopped to fix a leak from a plank that had come loose. The repairs and replacement of the spoiled flour, oatmeal, and dried peas had taken three long days. His mission was to meet *Confederation* and escort her back to the United States.

Had all gone according to plan, *Rattlesnake* would have patrolled off the French coast, waiting for *Confederation* to exit the Garonne River. His sailing orders were clear in that he was not to allow the corvette to be blockaded in a French port.

Micah knew that his chances of finding *Confederation* were slim once she left Bordeaux. But what he had from Fonseca-Shipping's operations center was the course Hornsby would normally follow this time of year. That alone narrowed down the amount of ocean he would have to search.

"Deck, Two ships alongside each other dead on the bow, four miles."

"What type ships?"

"One large merchant ship and a brig."

"Captain, aye." *Four miles at twelve knots equals at most 18 minutes. I'll bet it is* Confederation. Micah leaned over the railing. "Bo 'sun, clear the decks for action. Load ball, but do not run out."

ON BOARD *CONFEDERATION*, 3:17 P.M.

Hornsby had slowed the merchant ship so it was making about four knots, down from the six it was when the brig pulled alongside within hailing distance. The six gunports on its port were run out, and Hornsby could tell they were 9-pounders.

A man on the quarterdeck wearing a blue coat yelled through a speaking trumpet. "We are the privateer *Drake*, and my letter of marque from the British Parliament allows me to take ships trading with France as prizes.

Slow *Confederation,* so I can send a prize crew aboard. If you refuse, I will open fire."

Philippe Dubisson was standing on the quarterdeck next to Hornsby when *Confederation's* captain responded. From where Dubisson stood, only a few men were visible since most of the crew were below decks, armed and ready. "*Drake,* we're from a neutral nation not at war with England. Letters of marque only allow you to seize ships from countries on whom England has declared war. So, is England at war with Sweden?"

"Sweden, bloody hell. You're as much Swedish as I am French. You're a bloody American. Slow down!!!"

"In this sea, *Confederation* is a bit unhandy below four knots. I don't want to risk a collision."

"Damn your rebel eyes, hove too, or I will fire."

"Aye, I will luff my sails."

Once the order had been given, *Confederation's* captain stood on the forward end of the quarterdeck when a bo'sun mate stopped just below the railing. "Captain, the lookouts have spotted what they think is one of our corvettes at about two miles. Don't look."

Hornsby nodded, "Please prepare the polite reception for the boarding party. Let's keep them occupied on their prize. Have the lookouts keep me informed quietly."

A stocky, bald man in a blue coat climbed on the deck, followed by another similarly dressed man. Eight other men followed, all armed with two pistols and a cutlass or sword. The last man bent over the bulwark and yelled, "Shove off and bring the prize crew."

Striding forward, Hornsby did not hold out his hand. He had no love for the British, having spent two years as one of their "guests" on a British prison ship in New York Harbor. Over half the men died from disease and poor food. He told his wife that he would rather die than go through that experience again.

"We can go to my cabin where you can inspect my ship's papers. May I have your name?"

"Gilbert Fitzmaurice."

Hornsby turned to go aft, "Roger Hornsby." Fitzmaurice was followed by two of his men. When they entered, Philippe pointed to the sheets of paper laid out on the table. When Fitzmaurice bent over to look at them, *Confederation's* Third Officer pointed two pistols, one at Fitzmaurice and one at the sailor who raised their hands. Philippe disarmed both men and then held the weapon while the two men were tied up and gagged.

On the main deck, the second boat with 12 men had climbed up and were looking around for their comrades. They were below, all trussed up and sitting on the floor against the starboard bulwark so that if *Drake* fired, their bodies would be the first to get shredded.

Back out on deck, Hornsby was greeted by one of his sailors. The Swedish flag was lowered so the Stars and Stripes could be raised. By now, *Rattlesnake* was less than a mile away. "Officers of *Drake,* we have captured your boarding party. If you fire on us, your shipmates will be the first to be injured. That is, if the corvette does not turn your ship into splinters.

"You treacherous bastard!"

"Instead of impugning my heritage, I suggest you strike your colors or the approaching U.S. Navy ship will be obliged to open fire."

Hornsby saw the man turn and issue a stream of orders. While he did not hear them all, he saw the result. *Drake's* sails were sheeted home, and the ship fell off to port. Men started to climb the rigging carrying muskets and bags of powder and shot for what Hornsby assumed were swivel guns.

As *Drake* tacked, it crossed the corvette's bow and, at about 500 yards and opened fire.

ON BOARD *RATTLESNAKE*, 3.58 P.M.

The fact that the brig opened fire was a surprise to Micah. This was peacetime, and he made the rash assumption that a British ship would not open fire. But then again, war could have been declared after they left New York.

Three of the six 9-pounder balls hit *Rattlesnake.* One whizzed down the deck and plowed into the bulkhead that was the front wall of where the officers' cabins were forward of the captain's. From where he stood, he could hear the ball shattering wood. Another ball hit the bulwark, right next to the bowsprit, destroying the wood where the martingale and the bob stays attached to the hull.

The third ball penetrated the hull just beneath the bowsprit. It caved in two planks dissipating its energy. Splinters, however, wounded three men on the #1 gun on the port side.

Micah bent over the railing and bellowed. "Tack to port on my command. New course so' by so' west." Looking at the brig, Micah allowed self-recrimination to flow through his mind. *Damn, I should have anticipated that the brig would fall off and might open fire. Now we must exchange broadsides at 400 yards or less.* "Fire as your guns bear."

The #1 gun on the port side bellowed. The effect on the brig was immediate. A large section of its bulwark flew through the air. The #2 18-pounder spit fire and smoke. From the quarterdeck, Micah could see a hole in the brig's side between the #4- and #5-gun ports. He forced his mind not to imagine what it was like on the brig's gundeck.

Numbers 3 and 4 of the port 18-pounders fired, and both balls penetrated the brig's side. The ball from *Rattlesnake's* #5 cannon slammed into the brig, almost in line with the ship's mainmast. Number 6 fired before Micah could yell cease fire when he saw the Union Jack flutter down.

Now, Micah turned his attention to *Confederation.* He brought *Rattlesnake* around to the merchant ship's stern. With the bow of the corvette just 50 feet from *Confederation's* stern, he called out. "*Confederation, I am captain of the Naval Escort Services Corvette* Rattlesnake. *Sorry we are late. Do you need any assistance?*"

Hornsby shook his head before yelling, "No. Nice work!"

"Thank you."

"*Rattlesnake,* I have twenty-four of *Drake's* crew on board, including their captain and third lieutenant. What do you suggest?"

"Keep the captain and third lieutenant and take them to New York. Send the rest back to their ship. Please wait until we determine if their ship is sinking."

Hornsby waved.

Micah maneuvered his corvette so the bow was less than 50 feet from *Drake's* stern. He steadied himself on the undamaged section of bulkhead just aft of the bowsprit. "*Drake,* are you in danger of sinking?"

The man looking at Micah looked to be much older than he was. There was a shake of his head. "No."

"Excellent. Your crew members on *Confederation* will be sent over to you. Your captain and third lieutenant will be taken to New York where we will let an Admiralty Court determine what action to take."

The man nodded.

"May I ask why you opened fire? To my understanding, we are not at war."

The man said nothing, which said it all. The privateer captain wanted to keep his prize. Micah asked, "Do you have a doctor on board?"

"Aye. He has plenty of work to do, and I have a ship to save."

"I wish you decent weather. Good luck."

By dark, *Confederation's* helmsman was following the green lantern hanging from *Rattlesnake's* stern. New York was four weeks away.

WASHINGTON, FIRST WEEK OF MARCH 1812

Neither Darren nor Jaco knew what to expect in their meeting with Secretary of the Navy Paul Hamilton. They came prepared with what N.E.S. could do in the way of training new officers and seamen, to new ship concepts, to tactics. Each set of ideas was outlined on a sheet. What they didn't know was what specifically Secretary Hamilton wanted to discuss, other than the vague reference to the future growth of our Navy in the invitation.

Neither man was in uniform because technically, they were not on active duty. Waiting in the office was Commodore John Rodgers, the most senior officer in the Navy. Another Commodore, Alexander Murray, who was senior to Rodgers, declined the invitation.

After a warm greeting from both Rodgers and Hamilton, the Secretary of the Navy pointed to the table in his office, suggesting this was going to be a more formal than casual conversation. After he sat down next to Darren, Jaco pulled the stack of documents from the leather pouch and put it on the table between them.

"Gentlemen, I apologize for the vagueness of what I wished to speak about, but my goal was to let the discussion take us wherever. I do, however, have some specific questions."

A nod from both Darren and Jaco told the Secretary of the Navy to begin. "Let's start with an easy one. Assuming I authorize it, how fast can N.E.S. get its four frigates – *Eagle, Goshawk, Kestrel,* and *Osprey* – ready for sea?"

"They will sail within thirty days from the date we receive your authorization. It would, as per our contract, come with a letter stating that N.E.S. transfers them to the U.S. Navy. We did that for the war against the Barbary Pirates.

"And the corvettes?"

"Same. We keep four deployed overseas, plus two of the frigates. Right now, two are based in Ponta Delgada in the Azores, along with two of the frigates, and two more are based in Naples. Two are back in New York or New

Hampshire being refitted. And we are building up an inventory of powder and shot in several neutral countries so we can replenish what we fire."

"Deployed? How, why?"

"Sir, N.E.S. has contracts with several ship owners to protect their ships. We do so by escorting convoys and by patrolling areas where the Royal Navy likes to stop ships. Our presence has slowed down but has not ended their practice of stopping our ships. My point is that we can recall them at any time or simply send them new sailing orders. We have four small, but very fast schooners that sail back and forth on a regular basis."

"Would you put those ships to work for the Navy?"

"Of course." Jaco looked at Darren, and then said, "Sir, all the N.E.S. officers and mates hold reserve commissions in the U.S. Navy, as do many of our sailors. Most of the Fonseca-Laredo officers also have served during our revolution, our brief war with France, and the Barbary Pirates War. We, Darren and I, can ask them if they want to serve their country. I suspect most would say yes."

Secretary Hamilton looked at Jaco. "How come I didn't know all this?"

"Sir, we keep the Commodore informed on our operations. I suggest you come to New York and visit Naval Escort Services' offices as well as those of Fonseca-Laredo's. You would find it very informative."

"I shall do so very soon. Captain Smythe, assume we go to war with Great Britain, what do you think the Royal Navy will do?"

"Same as it always does. Blockade our ports, attack our merchant ships, and then land troops on our soil either as raids or a full-scale invasion. I suspect most of the British Army is occupied in Europe, so we can expect raids on ports. Parliament will issue letters of marque to almost any consortium that applies."

"Captain," Commodore Rodgers put his coffee cup down, "How would you counter that strategy?"

Darren had a ready answer that made sense to Rodgers and Secretary Hamilton. That led to a discussion as to where he thought the Royal Navy was most vulnerable.

Rodgers asked how Jaco and Darren would employ a Navy that is numerically inferior and has no ships with more than 44 guns. Jaco's answer was in two parts. One, our ships are faster and handle better, so we can control how the engagement unfolds, or we can simply sail away.

When Hamilton and Rodgers ran out of questions, Jaco asked, "Mr. Secretary, when do you think Congress is going to declare war?"

"Why?"

"I'd like to have our ships at sea within a day or two afterwards. This way, the Royal Navy doesn't have time to react, and we can begin protecting our coasts without having to fight through a line of blockading ships."

Hamilton looked at Rodgers and then at Darren and Jaco. "Think June. For planning purposes, you need to have your ships that are not already at sea, ready to sail by the first of June. Those at sea should be fully provisioned by that date."

LONDON, SECOND WEEK OF MARCH 1812

When Vice Admiral of the Red Stacey Davidson submitted his resignation, the First Naval Lord accepted it and then asked him to stay on until a replacement was found. It would be announced at the end of June along with all the other flag postings.

The respite in the war against Napoleon, at least from the perspective of supporting the British Army in Spain and Portugal had given Vice Admiral of the Red Stacy Davidson time to do some long-range planning. He had his staff assess the age of the Royal Navy's 600 ships and reached a startling conclusion.

If the service decommissioned the oldest 10 percent of its ships, it would have enough officers and men to fully man those that remained and crews for over half the newer ships being built. He had just ordered the two officers who did the calculations to create the next level of detail. Davidson wanted the names of the ships to be broken up, where they would send the crews based on how soon they could get the ship to the breaker's yard, and when the new ships would be commissioned.

He was not ready to take the idea to the First Naval Lord until he had enough details about how to execute this plan. Davidson was looking at the list, which included some ships on which he served, when the First Naval Lord appeared in his doorway holding a newspaper that he laid on Davidson's desk.

"Have you seen this?" The newspaper was the *Bristol Mercury,* whose headline read "Privateer Drake Mauled by U.S. Navy."

"No, sir, I have not."

"It was delivered to my office by a courier from the MP who represents Bristol. The note said, "Did we, meaning the the First Naval Lord, meaning me, know about this, and the answer is no."

Davidson read the story whose subhead noted that 12 of *Drake's* crew were killed, 22 more wounded. The reporter, who interviewed the ship's First Lieutenant noted that *Drake's* captain and Third Lieutenant were taken aboard a ship called *Rattlesnake.* The American ship's captain said Captain Fitzmaurice would be turned over to an Admiralty Court in New York.

Admiral Bickerton waited until Davidson read the entire story. "What do you make of it?"

"I would say a privateer got his hand caught in the cookie jar. He tried to capture an American ship, and *Rattlesnake* came along and put an end to it. And, if I may, sir, privateers are not the responsibility of the Royal Navy. They operate under letters of marque issued by Parliament. I am sure that, in good time, the Foreign Office will hear from the Americans about this."

"What if the MP makes it the Royal Navy's problem?"

"Sir, I don't think that will happen. Privateers are an independent lot and do not like to be constrained by the same rules under which we operate. They have a letter of marque for one reason and one reason only, and that is to capture ships and sell their cargoes to make money. *Confederation* fits that bill to a tee."

Bickerton stood for a few seconds. "*Rattlesnake,* why does that name ring a bell?"

"It's one of the Naval Escort Services corvettes that saw action against the Barbary Pirates."

"What do you know about them?"

"Captain Rathburn has been on one. From what we know, they are fast, very maneuverable three-masted schooners armed with twelve long 18-pounders."

"Is that American chap we met with Captain Smythe involved with them?"

"Aye, sir, he is. I believe Naval Escort Services operates six of them. They have a contract with several ship owners to provide armed escorts for their merchant ships, and legally, they can engage a privateer or pirate that attacks one of their ships. In time of war, they are seconded to the American Navy."

"Clever idea."

"Aye, sir, it is. If it comes to war with the Americans, N.E.S. will provide trained and experienced crews to the U.S. Navy."

The First Naval Lord made a face, saying, "That is not good news." as he walked out of Davidson's office.

NEW YORK, THIRD WEEK OF MARCH 1812

When Jaco arrived just after eight in the morning, the man at the front desk said, "Sir, there are at least six men in the conference room. All of them say it is important that they speak to you, and Mr. Geiger is in your office."

"Is Darren here yet?"

"Yes. He arrived moments ago and is speaking with Mr. Geiger."

Jaco took a deep breath and went up the two flights of stairs to the third floor, where American Shipping & Passenger Lines had its offices. Naval Escort Services offices were in the building next door.

Morton Geiger was smiling as Jaco hung up his coat. He held out a cup of hot chocolate, and as he took it, Jaco asked, "Are we ready for Secretary Hamilton and Commodore Rodgers?"

"We are. But before they arrive, you need to go into the conference room and answer questions."

"Who's in there?"

"I'll give you three guesses, but the first two don't count. The rumor is out that we're going to war with the English."

Jaco rolled his eyes. "Let's get this over with. Is there a place in the agenda where they, assuming I have guessed correctly who they are can meet with Commodore Rodgers and Secretary Hamilton?"

"We'll make room."

"Good, Darren, come with Morton and me. You are about to watch me melt in front of some very good people."

Jaco opened the door to the conference room, and Ezekiel Winters said, "Attention on deck." Ezekiel and the six men in the room – Cato Cooper, Abner Jeffords, Colin Landry, Brandon Grantham, Jeremiah Smythe, Micah Jacinto – stood and came to attention.

"At ease, gentlemen. Let me guess. You have heard that the United States may go to war with England, and you want to captain a ship."

Abner Jeffords, the oldest of the six, and along with Colin Landry, were the most senior of the nine men in the room who had served with Jaco, spoke. "Sir, please do not be angry with us. We just thought that if the Navy is going to war, and you and Captain Smythe were going to captain a frigate or two, you would need a few good men."

"All of us who fought the British the first time are now in our fifties, and we have families and even grandchildren. War is a young man's game."

Colin Landry held up his hand, "Sir, we all know that. Cato, Brandon, Abner, Morton, and I gave the Royal Navy a good licking. With all due respect, Captain Smythe, it took us over eight years to get our freedom, and by God, sir, I will fight the British for another eight if I must to keep what we have."

The Irish brogue of Brandon Grantham came out whenever he became emotional. "Sir, my parents didn't bring me to Boston as a wee lad to become British again. I would rather die first. Sorry, Captain Smythe.

Smiling, Darren said, "I understand completely. I'm with you. I don't want to be an Englishman again. The Royal Navy thinks I am a traitor."

"Aye, sir," Grantham was grinning, "We're all traitors in the eyes of King George III, but he can go to bloody hell. I would rather die before I swore an oath to be English."

Jaco waved his hands. "Gentlemen, what I am about to tell you cannot leave this room. Understood." He pointed to each man, and each said, "Aye, sir."

"According to the Secretary of the Navy, unless the British Parliament changes its laws and policies, President Madison is going to ask for a declaration of war sometime in June. We – Fonseca-Laredo, AS&PL, and N.E.S. are waiting for a letter from the Secretary of the Navy asking us to transfer our frigates and corvettes to the U.S. Navy. That same letter will inform those of us who have reserve commissions that we are now on active duty. We, that's Darren and me, have ordered all the corvettes that are at sea, along with *Kestrel* and *Osprey*, to return to either New York or Boston. Then, the day war is declared, we shall sally forth from several ports. Darren and I must select the officers and crews between now and then."

"Sir, no need." Colin Landry waved his hand in the direction of the others, "We have a list for you to review for each ship."

"Where is the list?"

Cato Cooper took it from his pocket. "Sir, it is not complete. We didn't know how many ships we needed to man. Give us a day or two, and we will have the muster rolls down to the mates and gun captains. Then, Captain Smythe and you can review it."

There was a knock on the door. It was someone from the operations center. "Mr. Jacinto, the Secretary of the Navy, and Commodore Rodgers are here."

"Tell them I will be with them shortly." Jaco waved at the men in the room. "Don't go anywhere, this afternoon you are going to join Commodore Rodgers and Secretary Hamilton for lunch. Mr. Geiger will redo the seating chart so that half of you sit with our guests. Then, after lunch, Captain Smythe and I will meet with our guests and hopefully learn more about our future tasking."

As Jaco headed to the door, he could feel the excitement in the room as Ezekiel Winters intoned, "Attention on deck."

After the tour and lunch, Commodore Rodgers and Secretary Hamilton sat in the conference room with Darren and Jaco. The discussion turned to tactics when Secretary Hamilton asked, "How do you see us employing the N.E.S. ships?"

Jaco and Darren exchanged glances. It was a subject they'd been discussing off and on for weeks. "Sir, I would form two small squadrons, one with *Kestrel* and three corvettes, and one with *Osprey* as the flagship and three corvettes. Use them to escort convoys of merchant ships to France, Spain, or wherever. That's what the corvettes were designed to do, and the two small frigates, if properly sailed, are a match for any frigate the Royal Navy has. *Eagle* and *Goshawk* should be turned loose on the Royal Navy to find and capture what they can."

"Pardon me for interrupting Jaco, but before I did that, I would use the four frigates to sweep up and down our coast to drive off or capture any Royal Navy ships. It will take the Admiralty months to figure out what happened and to respond. By then, the first two convoys will be well on their way to European ports."

Jaco could see Commodore Rodgers's eyes as he took in what Darren and he were suggesting. "Captains, are you suggesting that one of you take *Eagle* and the other *Goshawk* and act independently? Don't you think it is better to operate in squadrons?"

"Sir, Darren and I agree that we will never have enough ships to match what the Royal Navy will send our way. We think that the best strategy is to force them to chase us with frigates. When we encounter one, we think *Eagle* and *Goshawk* will carry the day."

"Not *Kestrel* and *Osprey?*"

"Properly sailed, they can defeat any Royal Navy frigate, but by including them in a convoy escort squadron, we can fend off any Royal Navy attack unless the convoy blunders into a fleet of first and second raters."

"How do you avoid that?'

"By using one of the corvettes to scout. "

Secretary Hamilton leaned forward. "Please, gentlemen, allow me to change the subject. I gather the men who dined with us will be some of your captains?"

Darren nodded, "Aye, sir. They have all shown their mettle in battle."

"And, Jeremiah, Micah, and Ezekiel, are your sons?"

"Ezekiel is the younger brother of my first wife. The other two are our sons, but I wish to point out that every man in that room, with the exception of Morton Geiger, has one or more sons either in Naval Escort Services or sailing on Fonseca-Laredo or American Shipping and Passenger Lines ships."

Nodding, Secretary Hamilton said, "I see. And they have all been vetted and graduated from your academy?"

Darren, who was responsible for training, quickly responded, "To be an officer or a mate, it is a requirement, so the answer is yes."

Hamilton looked at Rodgers. "Thank you, Captains. I think I can speak for Commodore Rodgers when I say we are impressed. You shall be hearing from me soon. Plan on sometime in June."

"We'll be ready by June 1st."

Secretary Hamilton stuck out his hand. "I shall so inform the president. Commodore Rodgers will need muster lists shortly after I officially notify you that we want to induct N.E.S. back into the Navy.

Jaco was the first to take it. "Sir, we'll be ready."

When Darren shook Commodore Rodgers's hand, he said, "Sir, you can count on us."

CHAPTER 14

SHOWING THE FLAG

KINGSTON, NY, THIRD WEEK OF MARCH 1812

One by one, the Fontaine clan filed into the small courtroom in the Ulster County seat. They were there to watch Didier and Cesar Fontaine sworn in as members of the Second Squadron, Second Cavalry Division of the New York State Militia. Their commitment was that they agreed to spend a week twice a year drilling. And, if called to active duty, they would provide their own horses and, at their option, swords.

Even though he was 47 and two years over the age limit, Cesar was allowed to join on the basis of his cavalry experience, albeit it in the French Army. Captain Newkirk and Captain Milsbough both signed a waiver letter after seeing copies of his French Army commission.

Three generations of the Fontaine clan as Sophie Fontaine referred to her family had become American citizens in 1799. Now, with war clouds on the horizon, they were committed to do their part to defend the United States. The fact that the war would be with England, France's traditional enemy, made the decision easier and sweeter.

So far, Girard had not been asked to give up his title as the Marquis de Gironde. He would do so only if asked by the American government. When he passes, his oldest son, Cesar understood that he would inherit the title and would be the leader of the Fontaine Clan.

VICINITY OF 44°N, 63°W, THIRD WEEK OF APRIL 1812

With the approval of Commodore Rodgers and the Secretary of the Navy, *Eagle, Goshawk, Kestrel,* and *Osprey* set out with full crews, a full load of ammunition and provisions for 10 weeks at sea. The squadron rendezvoused 10 miles off the tip of Cape Cod and, as planned, formed a scouting line as it headed nor' east by north.

Jaco's sailing orders as the squadron commodore were to show the flag to America's British friends. Sailing at a leisurely seven knots, they were 50 nautical miles east, so' east of Nova Scotia's southeastern tip, when lookouts spotted a Royal Navy frigate. Jaco ordered a change in formation to a diamond with *Eagle* leading and *Goshawk* trailing, and the smaller frigates out on the wings, before leading to within a half a mile of what looked like a 32-gun frigate headed eastward.

From the glints from spyglasses, it was clear that their formation, flying large American flags, was noticed, and Jaco was sure that the captain would make a note of their sighting in his log. If its destination was Portsmouth, England, Darren believed he would mention it when he reported to the Commander, Channel Fleet. If the Royal Navy frigate was headed for Halifax, then he would report their sighting to the Commander, North American Station.

Later in the day, when they were about five miles from the entrance to Halifax, Jaco's lookouts spotted two ships of the line, two frigates, and a sloop of war. The Americans watched signal flags go up and down the halyards of the larger of the two ships of the line that had 74 guns. The sloop-of-war peeled off from the larger ships and headed toward the American formation.

While the sloop-of-war was en route, Jaco ordered his squadron to tack to port and sail so' west and slow down. The Royal Navy sloop-of-war closed to within hailing distance of *Osprey,* which was the starboard point of the diamond formation. From his quarterdeck on *Goshawk,* Darren recognized the vessel as *H.M.S. Liber,* 12 guns, his first command.

"What ships are you?"

Cato Cooper, captain of *Osprey* came to the side of the quarterdeck. "United States frigates *Eagle, Goshawk,* and *Kestrel.*" He decided to let the Royal Navy captain figure out by reading the gold letters on the stern of his ship that he was talking to *Osprey.*

On the quarterdeck of the three-masted sloop, Cooper could see two midshipmen with slates he suspected were making notes on the four ships. *Liber* fell off, and Jaco ordered the squadron to increase speed.

Task one of the mission had been completed. The Royal Navy now knows that there are at least four U.S. Navy frigates at sea, two with 24 guns and two with 36.

Once south of Cape Cod, Jaco had the squadron spread out into a scouting line with *Kestrel* five to six miles from the U.S.'s Atlantic coast. The other ships from west to east, *Goshawk, Eagle,* and *Osprey* were spaced about 10 miles apart so their lookouts could see the topsails of the ship next in line.

TWO MILES EAST OF THE ENTRANCE TO CHESAPEAKE BAY, FOUR DAYS LATER

A flare from Kestrel alerted the formation that its lookouts had sighted a Royal Navy frigate. Jaco had a flare fired from Eagle to let Osprey, the frigate to the farthest east of the formation, know another Royal Navy ship had been sighted.

The problem was that the wind was from the nor' west and they would have to work their way directly west to reach the Royal Navy ship or ships. Within an hour, *Kestrel's* sails were seen by *Eagle's* lookouts along with the sails of two other frigates. From what the lookouts reported, *Kestrel* was still over a mile from the other two frigates that were less than a half mile apart.

Turning to his first lieutenant, "Signal other ships, *Eagle* will approach. Plan A. Then, clear the ship for action, load ball but do not run out. No drums."

Plan A was that *Eagle* would come alongside the Royal Navy frigates and Jaco would communicate with the Royal Navy's senior officer. The other American ships would maneuver so they were in position to rake the Royal Navy's ships if shooting started.

"Sir, signal from *Goshawk.* Larger frigate is *Minerva.*"

"Acknowledge with thanks." *Darren just told me that Minerva had, if I remember, 38 guns, twenty 18-pounders, and ten 9-pounder carronades. If Martingdale is still the captain, be careful.*

The two Royal Navy frigates were sailing so' by so' west at a leisurely five knots when *Eagle* took station 100 feet from *Minerva's* starboard side. Jaco stood in the forward port corner of the quarterdeck, resting one foot on the bottom crossmember of the rail. He was where crewmembers on *Scorpion* dubbed Perfecto Corner.

"*Minerva,* this is American Frigate *Eagle.* You are in U.S. waters. State your business." Jaco knew that *Minerva,* which was accompanied by another frigate, a little smaller named *Circe,* was not inside the three-mile limit, but Jaco suspected they were there waiting to pounce on a U.S. merchant vessel to impress some sailors.

"I am Everett Martingdale, Captain of *Minerva.* We have a right to sail these waters."

"Captain, I am not going to argue with you. At the direction of my president, I am ordering you to leave U.S. waters, NOW!"

"The Royal Navy and King George III don't recognize the authority of your president, so bugger off, rebel."

"Captain Martingdale, I am authorized to use force to compel you to leave." Jaco lowered the speaking trumpet and ordered. "Run out!"

The wooden gun ports thwacked against *Eagle's* hull, and the sound of wooden wheels rumbling across the planks of the gun deck were the loudest sound on *Eagle* until Jaco spoke again through the trumpet, knowing that if *Eagle* fired, it would be an act of war. But this was Martingdale, the Royal Navy captain who arrested Darren for no reason other than that he was born in England.

"Captain Martingdale, my cannons are all loaded. At this range, I suspect they will all hit your ship before you can fire a shot. Within short order, your ships will be raked by my squadron. Again, I am authorized to use force but would prefer if you sailed away on your own and did not come back."

"My government will protest your aggressive action that threatened *Minerva* and *Circe.*"

"Please do. It will get the same amount of attention as our protests of Royal Navy ships taking American seamen against their will received from your government."

Martingdale gave Jaco a dismissive wave and started giving orders. Before the sun had set, the four American ships had followed *Minerva* and *Circe* 60 or so miles into the Atlantic.

ONE MILE OFF BERMUDA, FOURTH WEEK OF APRIL 1812

The weather, as Darren wrote in his log, was brilliant. The skies were blue, no clouds and the temperature was warm but not hot. Ahead, on the port bow and to the nor' east was the island of Bermuda.

Jaco led the four U.S. frigates to the north side of the island, careful to stay a mile offshore to avoid, shoals and rocks. Unless one knew Bermuda and its harbor well, it could lead to an unpleasant experience for the captain and crew. There were, Darren warned the other captains as they planned this voyage, the bones of many ships on the reefs around the island.

Bermuda is part of a coral reef that formed atop an extinct volcano. The island is oriented northeast/southwest, and there was deep water close to the shore on the south side of the island, which would allow the U.S. Navy frigates to sail within a quarter mile of its shore.

Their visit, line astern, did not go unnoticed. As the frigates sailed at about five knots with flags flying, they could see the Royal Navy officers on the beach looking at the ships with spyglasses. Once the lookouts could no longer see the island, Jaco signaled for the ships to form a scouting line and set a course as close to the prevailing wind from the nor' west as possible.

With *Eagle* sailing nor' by west at nine knots, the squadron would reach a point about 100 nautical miles east of the entrance to New York Harbor so they could tack to the west and reach the harbor the next day. The mission to show the flag and to show the Royal Navy that the U.S. Navy had more frigates than just the six that were built just before the turn of the century had been, in Jaco's mind, a success.

It was clear that the squadron was noticed off Halifax and Bermuda, and soon, Martingdale's report will reach the Admiralty. What will happen now, was anybody's guess, but in his mind, they had sent the message to the Royal Navy - the U.S. Navy exists.

LONDON, FIRST WEEK OF MAY 1812

Vice Admiral of the Red Stacey Davidson had been wondering what had happened to his letter of resignation that he had submitted back in March 1811. Each time he brought up the subject with the First Naval Lord, Bickerton had an excuse that ended with, "Be patient. These things take time." The last time, the excuse was "We haven't found a replacement for you yet."

That response got a smile from Davidson because the personnel side – assignments and promotions – was a thankless task. Who got what frigate or ship of the line, or who was promoted and who was not, made some happy and others angry or frustrated. And then there was recruiting. Davidson was convinced that England was about out of manpower and the only answer would be conscription. That had its own risks, though, i.e., taking people out of the fields that produce the food the Royal Navy consumed or out of factories and shipyards that kept the Royal Navy and British Army supplied.

Now it was almost a year later with still no response from the First Naval Lord and Davidson was surprised when the new First Naval Lord, Robert Dundas, the 2nd Viscount Melville, tapped on the door frame. Dundas had been in office since late March 1812.

Normally, one went to the First Naval Lord, not the other way around. The civilian commander of the Royal Navy was carrying several sheets of paper in his hand. Davidson stood when the First Naval Lord entered. "Good afternoon, sir."

"Stacy, what do you make of Martingdale's encounter off Virginia and the sightings off Bermuda and Halifax?"

"The Americans are flexing their muscles. They want us to know that they have a Navy and are willing to use it to defend their country."

"How many ships do you think they have?"

"Sir, I only know what I read in the papers and reports. My guess is that they have maybe fifteen frigates ranging from twenty to forty-four guns. Add in some sloops and brigs, I estimate their fleet to be about thirty ships. Why?"

"And their crews and captains?"

"Equal if not better than ours. They are all volunteers. Why are you asking me this?"

Dundas laid the three letters he had been carrying on Davidson's desk. "Admiral, as the First Naval Lord, I am adamant about not accepting your resignation. In fact, the PM won't hear or discuss it, and he told me that he wants you to replace me when the time comes. It's in one of the letters on your desk. So, Admiral Davidson, I'd batten down your hatches because your job, sir, is to make sure our ships are up to the task of facing the Americans. Training, if I remember, is under the purview of the Second Naval Lord, and I, like you, think that the Americans and their ships will be an ugly surprise to some of our captains. So, now you have your orders, I suggest you set loose your Royals, topgallants and staysails, and get on with it."

Stacy Davidson leaned back, stunned. Then, training and custom took over. "Aye, aye, sir, I will do my best."

"Lad, I'd expect nothing less. If you wish, I will tell Belinda so you don't get a broadside."

"Not necessary. She is torn between leaving London and living in the country where one is a bit isolated from gossip and the goings on in society in the country."

Dundas smiled, "Aye, that it is, but then again, you don't have to sort the nonsense from the important. Let me know when you have a plan. If you need to cashier a few people, let's discuss it. We can do it as part of the flag promotions we announce in July."

KINGS POINT, NY, FIRST WEEK OF MAY 1812

When the muster lists for the officers of each of the N.E.S. ships were returned to N.E.S. neither Jaco nor Darren was surprised at the changes. All N.E.S.'s recommendations for captains were accepted, and almost all his suggestions for First and Third Lieutenants were replaced by officers from the U.S. Navy's ranks.

Plus, all the ships now had Marine detachments. On *Eagle* and *Goshawk,* a Marine captain, a lieutenant, two sergeants and 40 Marines were assigned. *Kestrel* and *Osprey,* a lieutenant, two sergeants and 30 other ranks. The corvettes each had 20 Marines led by a lieutenant and a sergeant. It would crowd the gun deck on the corvettes but was manageable. Darren's and Jaco's biggest fear was that on a corvette, 22 extra mouths to feed would strain its already limited supply of food.

With all the N.E.S. ships either anchored or tied up to piers on the Long Island side of the East River or at the Fonseca-Laredo/N.E.S. school at Kings Point, Darren and Jaco took a ferry from Manhattan to Brooklyn and then a carriage to the school.

By now, all the officers from N.E.S. were back from their various assignments on merchant ships or on the corvettes that had been deployed to Naples and the Azores. Over the next few days, the officers and crews assigned to the N.E.S. ships that were now part of the U.S. Navy would start arriving. Commodore Rodgers promised that they would all arrive in New York the third week of May. His note also said that any declaration of war would be in mid-June, if it happened at all.

The school had a large room that they used when the weather was inclement, and the instructors wanted to walk students through a task. Hung from the ceiling on one side of the room, there was a spar on a section of a mast so students could practice tying the gaskets that held a furled sail in place. They would do this while standing on the rope that stretched between the mast and the end of the spar.

For today, the school had set up the chairs for a meeting of a large group of students. In the front, there were three large blackboards with cloths covering the front where names were written.

Just before they entered the building, Jaco put a hand on his friend Darren's shoulder. Both men stopped, and Jaco said, "You realize that once we walk into that room, we are committing not only our sons and our friends to war, but those of hundreds of other parents. We, that's you and I, cannot fail them."

"Aye, Jaco, that has been weighing heavily on my mind as well. Marijke and I have been talking about it often in our private moments."

Nodding, Jaco smiled, knowing he was about to share some black humor, "At breakfast this morning, Reyna reminded me that at her age, she can easily replace a husband but cannot replace a son!"

"Aye, the good news is that all our captains have been through the grist mill and know what we may be undertaking. My comfort is that the last time, you Americans were ill-prepared to take us in the Royal Navy on. However, this time, I think the scale has been leveled. We still won't have the numbers, but we will have better quality."

"Captains, the officers are waiting...." The voice of Morton Geiger, who was the senior captain below Darren and Jaco interrupted the conversation.

Morton Geiger stood at the doorway, and as Darren, then Jaco paused outside the door, he said in a very loud voice that make many a bo'sun proud, "Attention on deck."

Jaco and Darren climbed up the two steps onto the platform, and Darren put the muster sheets on the podium. He then stepped back, and Jaco stood in the center at the edge with his hand clasped behind him.

From the personnel records of the 28 men in the audience, they knew that there were six men who were either freed slaves or sons of freed slaves, at least four Jews, two Mohawk Indians and sons of Dutch, German, Italian, Irish, French, and English immigrants. It was in Jaco's mind a solid representation of the population of the United States.

"Good morning. Today, all of you will receive your ship assignments. Some must change ships. That's the good news. The bad news is that now that we are part of the U.S. Navy, Commodore Rodgers and Secretary Hamilton have a say as to who mans our ships and where we sail. Every one of you in this room was picked by Captain Smythe, Captain Geiger,

Captain Cooper, Captain Landry, and me. We think you are the best of an excellent group of men who have served N.E.S. well."

Smiling, he said, "More good news. We will be able to take prizes, and the prize money formula will be explained to the crew once we are all on board. For the older hands, it is the same formula we used during our war for independence and when fighting the French. Had we taken a ship worth anything during the Barbary Pirates War, then prize money would have been paid. Instead, N.E.S. took a portion of its profits and gave every officer and sailor a bonus. And N.E.S. pays much better than the U.S. Navy, so as part of our agreement, the government will pay its sailors the same as you, so there will be no cuts in pay."

Jaco could see lots of smiles. "Now the bad news. Some of you will not get the assignments you expected. Do not worry, wars create opportunities for advancement. If you are being paid as a first lieutenant in N.E.S. and are assigned as a second lieutenant, your pay will not be reduced. Any questions so far?"

No hands were raised. "Perfecto. Commodore Rodgers wants the men they have recruited and those who have some time at sea in all the first and third lieutenant positions, partly so we can train and evaluate them. The assignments made today are for the first six-to-eight-month cruise, after which we will go through this exercise again. All of the captains expect you to work well with these new men. They will have experience you don't have and vice versa."

Another pause.

"Now, Captain Geiger pull the cover off the slate board, and Captain Smythe will read out an officer's name, ship assignment and billet. That officer will then walk to the slate board and write his last name next to his assignment. After that is done, we will share with you how we plan to operate, at least initially."

Nodding to his friend, Darren Smythe started with *Eagle,* then went down the list of frigates alphabetically, and then the six corvettes. Then, when they were finished, Darren asked, "Gentlemen, please sit with each of your captains. Captain Jacinto's and my crew will sit in the back two rows. As you move around, if you don't know each other on your ship, please introduce yourselves and then sit."

Jaco waited until the movement had stopped and stepped forward and said loudly, "Listen up!!!"

Those who were still standing sat down, and all eyes were on Captain Jacinto. "What I am about to say cannot leave this room. For those of you who sailed with N.E.S. in the Mediterranean against the Barbary Pirates, this organization will look somewhat familiar. Captain Smythe and I think it will enable us to be flexible. Notice that there are two escort groups led by Captain Cooper in *Kestrel* and Captain Jeffords in *Osprey.* Their mission, assuming war is declared, is to escort one convoy to a port in northern Europe that has not yet been picked and one to Naples. *Eagle* and *Goshawk* will be operating independently in the Atlantic, hunting Royal Navy frigates. We suspect that once the House of Commons learns war has been declared, Royal Navy frigates will be leaving Europe like rats on a sinking ship. All will be headed to our country to blockade our ports. We hope to reduce that number."

"When the rest of our crews arrive, we will begin training, and the best place to do it is at sea. We will start with some classroom work, then spend about three weeks at sea working on tactics and then come back and re-provision. Again, do not discuss our plans with anyone, even your girlfriends, mistresses, wives, and children. It is time for you to move your sea chests if your ship is different, and if your ship is not ready for your new shipmates, get it so. That is all."

Neither Darren nor Jaco wanted to take questions and left the room, followed by the officers from their respective ships. Tonight, and tomorrow night will be the last ones many of them will have time off.

WASHINGTON, SECOND WEEK OF JUNE 1812

The debate in both Houses of Congress continued, and the sides weren't drawn along party lines. Speaker Clay knew he had the votes in the House of Representatives, and it wouldn't be close. However, he wanted both sides to have a strong voice, so he asked Javier if he would speak.

Given his time in the House of Representatives, Javier Jacinto was now the minority leader. The Federalists only had 36 of the 142 seats, yet Javier knew that many Democratic-Republicans were against going to war with Great Britain.

The divide in the house was not about party loyalty; it was mostly about economics. Those representatives who had many constituents involved in international business and who had extensive trading relationships with English firms knew a war would bring a halt to that business. And, when peace finally came, hopefully they could re-establish those ties.

The lectern where one spoke to the members of the house was in the center of the arc around which all the desks and chairs for the individual representatives were arranged. When Javier slowly and deliberately walked to the podium, he was not sure exactly what he would say. Yes, he had some notes, but he wrote them down more to help organize his thoughts rather than write the specific words for a speech.

When Javier looked around, the House chamber was full, and he could see in the back area where spectators sat, there were at least half a dozen Senators from both parties. Apparently, someone in the House had let the Senate know that Javier Jacinto was about to speak.

"Members of the House and our guests, thirty-seven years ago, I sat, along with many of you, in a small room in the Pennsylvania State House as a member of the Continental Congress. We had gathered to decide how to gain the independence we now enjoy. When the shots were fired in Lexington on April 19th, there was no declaration of war. The Continental Congress had no such power, yet that very morning, we – the Thirteen British Colonies – declared war on the richest and most powerful nation in the world. At that moment, we didn't have an army or a navy, yet we were prepared to fight and die for our independence. I feel obligated to remind you that it took eight years and four months before Great Britain signed a peace treaty."

Javier looked around the room, making eye contact with both proponents and opponents of the declaration of war. "Yet, here we are again. We have a very small army that is strung out on the Western frontier. It is under-equipped and doesn't have the men for the missions and tasks assigned."

"Then, there is the Navy. Again, just nine years ago, we conducted and won a war four thousand five hundred miles from our shores. And, yet President Jefferson deemed it necessary to reduce it to just a few frigates, not all of which are ready to go to sea."

"Yes, gentlemen, here we are again. The difference between 1775 and 1812 is that we have a government elected by the people. We – that is, both members of the House of Representatives and the Senate are sitting here deciding if *we, the people of the United States,* are again going to war with the most powerful and richest nation in the world."

He looked around the room and could see that he had everyone's attention. "Do we have reasons to go to war with England? By God, we do, and we all know what they are. The British have arrogantly ignored or rejected any form of diplomacy to resolve our differences. This will be, just like our War for Independence, about our rights to determine our own destiny. It means that we cannot tolerate British soldiers inciting native tribes to kill our settlers. It means that we can no longer tolerate Royal Navy ships stopping our ships and kidnapping our seamen. It means we have the right to trade with whom we wish, when we wish, and wherever they may be." Javier stopped and let his voice drop. "We are, I am afraid, almost back to 1775. So here is where I stand."

Javier paused, "If we go to war, it will be costly in terms of blood and treasure. I do not want to hear from any of you or your constituents that the war is taking too long, or that the war is costly, and we need to sue for peace. When one goes to war, there is only one acceptable result, and that is a victory that preserves our democracy and our freedom."

"So here is what I demand from each and every one of you and my fellow citizens. We will suffer defeats, but we must persevere. We must do what we need to win, no matter what the costs. Anything else means that we have failed our constituents. It means our Republic has failed."

Javier was on a roll. "If we fail, that means all the blood and treasure to win our independence thirty-seven years ago will have been wasted."

He was tapping the lectern as he spoke to emphasize his points. "If we go to war, we are committing our sons and grandsons to battle, and unfortunately, some may be maimed, or worse, die. For those of you who don't know, I have a son and grandson in the Navy, and they will be amongst the first to go to sea to sail into the mouth of the lion to take on the Royal Navy. As a father and grandfather, I fear I may not see either again."

"We must be totally committed as a nation, each one of us must be totally committed, body, soul, and bank account, because if we are not, then we will lose, and that, my fellow members of the House and Senate, is not something I will tolerate."

Javier paused to glance down at his notes. He really wasn't doing it to look up a point he'd missed, but to gather his thoughts. "Speaker Clay asked me to announce my position. So here it is. As you know, my family is one of the owners of one of the largest businesses in the United States. We have already funded the acquisition of four frigates and six corvettes to protect our merchant ships. Approximately sixty percent of U.S. Industries' revenue comes from English customers. War will bring that down to zero. War with England will be financially painful and could be worse."

"Gentlemen of the House, I pledge to you that I am committed to victory. I shall vote yes to support our President if he asks for a declaration of war so *we the people* of the United States can say to the British, we are committed to enjoying our God given rights without the interference of your House of Commons or your damned King!"

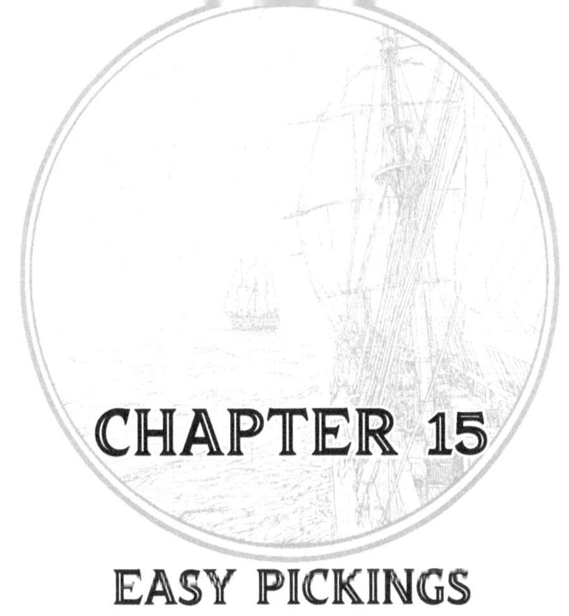

CHAPTER 15

EASY PICKINGS

NEW YORK, FOURTH WEEK OF JUNE 1812

On Thursday, June 18th, 1812, the House of Representatives voted 79 to 49 to approve a declaration of war against Great Britain. Later that day, the Senate passed the document 19 to 13 and the declaration was signed the next day by President Madison.

It took three days for the word to get to New York via a messenger riding on an AS&PL packet ship that stopped in Philadelphia before heading on to New York. Oddly enough, in the hold of the packet, there was a canvas bag of Royal Mail that contained the diplomatic pouch from the British Embassy in Washington. It was transferred to the three-masted AS&PL schooner *City of New York* that would deliver it to London 12 – 14 days hence.

So as not to show preference to their position, the word was passed that none of the officers, mates or sailors, even those who had families nearby, went ashore until Sunday. Then, Jaco granted those who lived in the New York area, one night of shore leave. They had to be back on board their ships by noon on Monday. While not said, the crews knew that anyone who did not return would be treated as a deserter.

Early Monday morning, the Smythes – Darren and Jeremiah – and Jacintos – Jaco and Micah rode across the East River to Brooklyn, where the 10 ships were tied up. No one said much, and when they arrived at the shipyard in Brooklyn, they took turns hugging each other and wishing the other good luck when they parted just before the First Watch began.

The mood at breakfast on the day the N.E.S. squadron – 6 corvettes and four frigates – sailed from New York was subdued, but confident. They had trained hard as individual crews as well as in exercises in which there were one-on-one duels, two-on-one duels, and even a three-on-one in which the corvettes were required to deal with either *Eagle* or *Goshawk.*

Escort Group A under the command of Cato Cooper on *Kestrel* led his three corvettes, *Cobra (*Colin Landry), *Copperhead (*Brandon Grantham), and *Rattlesnake (*Micah Jacinto), south to rendezvous with those merchant ships wanting escort from Norfolk to Amsterdam. Once they approached 20°W, they planned to go north around Scotland, then down through the North Sea to the Dutch city.

Abner Jeffords on *Osprey* would lead Escort Group B north with four merchant ships from New York to Boston with *Cottonmouth (*Ezekiel Winters), *Venom (*Jeremiah Smythe), and *Viper (*Morton Geiger). They were expecting another four merchant ships to join their convoy that was headed to Naples.

Eagle and *Goshawk* had different but supporting missions. Once out of sight of land, they headed north toward Halifax. If they found no Royal Navy frigates, *Eagle* would sail east so' east along the planned convoy route for the ships headed toward Amsterdam. *Goshawk* to the south by the same distance until the frigate rendezvoused around 38° N, 50° W with the convoy headed toward Naples.

Neither Darren nor Jaco wanted to be tied down to the two convoys, but by the same token, they wanted to provide protection. The strategy proposed and approved by Commodore Rodgers would accomplish two objectives. One, placate merchants who were fearful that the Royal Navy would make it impossible to trade with their customers in Europe. Two, it would get more U.S. Navy ships to sea.

Once *Eagle* was headed nor 'east, Jaco left the quarterdeck to make his log entry for the departure from New York. The log had a thin wooden plank on the back and on the cover that protected the pages. As new pages were added, he would slice open a small hole with his hunting knife and slip the eight-inch hemp rope through the hole.

Waiting for him was a letter from Reyna, who instructed him to read once he was at sea. He debated for a second or two whether he should read it now and get the emotional pain over with or wait until after dinner. He couldn't wait and popped open the wax seal.

My beloved husband,

I write this letter with a heavy heart, knowing that this is the fourth time in our marriage that you have gone off to war. Yes, I am counting!

First, it was to fight for our independence. Then, it was to deal with the French, who, in many ways, betrayed us. Next came the fight against the Barbary Pirates.

Each time you left, it was harder than the last. And what makes it worse this time is that our oldest son, Micah, is with you, in command of his own ship. While that makes me proud, I am also fearful.

Cannon and musket balls and splinters have no soul. They wound, maim, and kill whomever they strike.

You, my love, have braved the fire from the British, the French, and the pirates. And now, for the second time, the British. This time it is much different. Back in 1775, we thought we were immune to death, but now, we are parents, and I, like you, want to live to be a grandparent.

I know that you do your best to avoid fighting side by side with the enemy, but the odds, I fear, are against you. Keep that in mind as you plan your battles with the British.

You may think you are immortal, but we both know that is not true. I pray to God that he has written Micah and you in the Book of Life for 1812.

Come back to me safe. I will love you forever.

Reyna

What Reyna was telling him was that she was afraid that he would be killed. He could feel the tightness in his gut as he understood the impact of her words. She was right, every time he stood on the quarterdeck in a fight, he was risking death.

He poured four-fingers of port from the decanter of port he kept in his cabin. Before he wrote in his log, he downed most of the glass.

After dinner, Lieutenant Gordon Islip, the second in command of *Eagle's* 40-man Marine Detachment, something under N.E.S., the ships didn't have, did the honors by refilling each officer's glass before he read their sailing orders aloud to the ship's officers. Jaco popped off the seal from Commodore Rodgers' letter.

Captain Jacinto,

Eagle and the rest of your squadron's tasking for this cruise is three-fold. One, take the war to the Royal Navy by denying them control of the seas along the coast of North America and forcing them to defend English bases and ports.

Two, convoy U.S.-flagged merchant ships to ports in Europe.

Three, disrupt British commerce wherever you find it.

The Secretary of the Navy and I are giving you latitude on how you accomplish these goals. Good luck and Godspeed.

John Barry
Commodore
United States Navy

Thanks to several long conversations with Commodore Rodgers and Secretary of the Navy Hamilton, both Jaco and Darren understood the underlying intent of his sailing orders. One desire - convoying merchant ships and gaining control of the country's Atlantic coast - was based on U.S. politics, and they could say to citizens whose livelihood depended on foreign trade that the Navy was protecting them.

In short, his orders were to make the anticipated blockade ineffective. Even with the addition of the 10 N.E.S. ships, the small U.S. Navy could not accomplish the goals set out in the first two paragraphs of his sailing orders.

The Royal Navy was already maintaining a blockade of French ports and those in countries that had declared war against Great Britain. It was effective enough to keep the French and Spanish navies along with those fighting England in port. Was the Royal Navy large enough to do the same to the U.S.?

In planning this two-convoy effort, Commodore Rodgers agreed that by the time the ships returned to the U.S., the Royal Navy blockade would have begun. Once it was in place in the major ports, trying to assemble enough ships to justify a convoy would draw the Royal Navy to the port like bees to honey.

The compromise was that once they returned, then the frigates individually and corvettes in packs of three would be turned loose to hunt for British privateers and prizes. That day, God willing, would come, Jaco thought, either this fall or next spring.

LONDON, FIRST WEEK OF JULY 1812

Outside the carriage carrying Vice Admiral of the Red Stacy Davidson, dark clouds told the Royal Navy officer that rain was in the offing. He did not know why he was summoned to meet with the First Naval Lord Dundas, but, since the First Naval Lord was the head of the Royal Navy, both Davidson and the officer who came to his house climbed into the waiting carriage.

The lieutenant who came to the Admiralty building on Admiralty Place would only say that the meeting was urgent. Once inside the carriage, the young officer sat facing aft, and the two men rode in silence for the mile and a quarter from Admiralty Lane to the Parliament building.

Davidson walked to Dundas' office, who seeing his deputy, pointed to an overstuffed chair with worn leather. The First Naval Lord closed the door and then went to the buffet where decanters of whiskey, port, and madeira rested. "Drink, Stacey?"

"I'll have whatever you're having."

"Scotch it is." Dundas poured four fingers of a smoky malt scotch into a crystal glass and handed it to Davidson. "The King and our Navy."

Davidson tilted his glass and then said, "King and the Navy." After Davidson took a sip. "Sir, may I ask what is so urgent?"

"You may, but first you must tell me how a document signed in Washington on June 18th and delivered to our ambassador that same day can arrive in London on July 2nd."

"Easy, sir. An American company called American Shipping & Passenger Lines has ships that sail from New York to London on a schedule, and they guarantee, weather permitting, under fourteen days. Usually, they make it in twelve. The ships carry Royal Mail as well as U.S. Mail, diplomatic pouches, passengers, and some cargo. The passenger cabins on these ships, I must add, are quite nice, as is the food and service."

"What type of ships are they and how fast do they sail?"

"Three-masted gaff-rigged schooners, and they make ten to twelve knots on the crossing and can, with decent wind and sea state, sustain fourteen."

"And you know all this about this line, how?"

"I know both the managing directors. One is a former Royal Navy captain who is now an American citizen."

Dundas turned to his desk. "Here is the reason for my summons." He handed the declaration of war that was included in the ambassador's diplomatic pouch, along with his thoughts. "What do you make of it?"

"I'm not surprised by this, sir."

Dundas' eyebrows raised. "Pray tell, why not. It makes no sense to me. Just so you know, the sloops with the war warning left for Port Royal, Halifax, and Bermuda this morning."

"Sir, if you were sitting in Washington and are frustrated because they have tried diplomacy and informal contacts to get Britain to change its policies…"

Dundas interrupted, "Which are?"

"For at least fifteen years, they have been asking the Royal Navy to quit impressing its seamen, end the policy of insisting that any ship headed for a European port not on this island, stop so we can inspect them and charge duty. And last, end giving arms and ammunition to Indians from forts on U.S. sovereign territory so they can kill American settlers. What they get from us is rejection. We don't even want to talk to them about these issues, which, I may add, had they involved Englishmen, we'd have gone to war on any one of these issues. So, sir, they have a right to be pissed. Pardon me, sir, but I believe the declaration of war came about because they were at wits' end."

Davidson took a long swig of his scotch and enjoyed the burning sensation going down his gullet. "Sir, if you wish for me to resign, you already have my letter; I shall. However, to find the causes of this war, the House of Commons only has to look into the mirror."

"Is the Royal Navy ready?"

"Yes. We have a respite from Napoleon because we have the Spanish and his fleet bottled, but fighting the Americans will take ships away from that task."

"How many?"

"The North American Squadron in Halifax has eighty-five ships assigned. Where they are, I do not know. They will need another thirty or forty. Some to blockade their major ports, some to protect our merchant ships, and some to hunt their navy and privateers."

"How many frigates and ships-of-the-line do they have?"

"All their ships are fourth and fifth raters, and at most, they will be able to put to sea about two dozen, maybe thirty."

"And we have?"

"At last count, we are manning just under six hundred."

"Numbers alone are in our favor. Don't you agree that we should put this U.S. Navy out of business in short order?"

"Sir, what I am going to say will be unpopular, but I feel I must say this. I believe that the U.S. Navy, small as it is, will be an ugly surprise to the Royal Navy. They started their War for Independence with no navy, and by the end, the ships they sent to sea were a handful. Since then, they took on the French and in every ship-to-ship action, they won decisively. Between 1803 and 1805, the U.S. Navy conducted a campaign against the Barbary Pirates that would earn baronies for the succession of commanders 'were they in the Royal Navy. Today, I believe their ships are equal to ours and maybe even, in some ways, better. They will be sailed by skilled captains who know how to take advantage of their ships' sailing qualities."

Davidson was on a roll, and Dundas let him continue. "The Americans will not quit, they didn't during their War for Independence, and I suspect we will find them to be determined and innovative in the way they fight us. So, sir, we need to be prepared for a long and, I'm afraid, costly war."

"What about their crews?"

"They are fighting for themselves and their freedoms. Many of the men we will fight are veterans of their War for Independence. They will die to ensure they are not ruled by a king."

"Admiral, you know this how?"

"I have been on several of their frigates and have met their officers and men. When I had a squadron in the Mediterranean, I met with their commanders fighting the Barbary Pirates. Trust me, this will not be like fighting the French or Spanish."

The First Naval Lord put his glass of scotch on the table. It was now empty. "Thank you for your forthright opinions. I gather you have not shared them with others."

"Only one, sir."

"Who may that be?"

"Rear Admiral of the Blue Drew Rathburn. He was my chief of staff and, like me, fought the Americans. Rathburn is en route to take over Jamaica Station. In quiet moments when I had Jamaica and the West Indies, and then as Commander of the Channel Fleet, we talked about this eventuality."

"Wasn't he on the most recent flag list?"

"Aye, sir. I think he is perfect for this posting."

"And Admiral Sir Hubert Sawyer, the head of the North America Station?"

"Sir, may I assume my comments do not leave this room?"

"Yes, of course. This is why I am asking. Your comments are a breath of fresh air compared to the blather I get from MPs, the Secretary for War and the Colonies, and some of my other subordinates. Bickerton told me that you were not afraid to speak your mind and your opinions were well-reasoned and based on facts.

"I think Admiral Sawyer will manage what we give him but will struggle if the Americans get creative."

"By creative, what do you mean?"

"Taking his ships. Punching holes in his blockade. Interfering with British commerce with Canada and the Caribbean."

"Would you replace him?

"Yes, but not now. It would send the wrong message because it would not be a regular rotation. I think if you give him clear direction and he fails or has a setback, then we can make a change."

"Do you have a replacement in mind?"

"I do, sir."

"Would you care to share his name with me?"

Davidson thought about it for a few minutes. "Only if the First Naval Lord promises not to interfere with the madness that is personnel assignments and pluck him out from where he is."

Grinning, Dundas said, "You have my pledge, but I, as First Naval Lord, reserve the right to enquire as to when the change may happen and encourage you to increase the pace at which it will happen."

"Understood."

"And the name, sir?"

"Sir Alexander Inglis Cochrane would be perfect. He is not afraid to make changes."

Dundas went to the buffet and poured himself another glass of scotch. Shaking his head, "Stacey, there will be captains and some of your fellow flag officers who will have apoplexy if Cochrane is appointed as the commander of North American Station."

"Aye, sir, but he is just the man to root out the incompetents that I can't see and fight the Americans."

"Noted." Dundas took a sip of scotch. "I need to tell the PM how many ships and when will be heading to North America. When can I have that?"

"Tomorrow."

VICINITY OF 40°N, 20°W, FOURTH WEEK OF JULY 1812

After waving goodbye to Jaco on Eagle, Goshawk headed to where Darren believed he'd find Royal Navy frigates headed to either Bermuda, Halifax, or Port Royal. When he was a captain in the Royal Navy, when he'd deploy in the summer, once clear of the English Channel and well west of the tip of Britanny to where Goshawk was right now, 40°N, 20°W or about 600 miles west of Porto, Portugal.

Depending on the month, it was in this area that the winds would shift from mostly out of the nor' west to from the nor' east. These favorable winds, known as the Northeast Trades, would push his ship across the Atlantic to the Caribbean with hardly a tack. If he was going to New York or Halifax, then somewhere west of Bermuda, he would tack to nor' nor' easterly course and enjoy favorable winds from the starboard side of the ship.

Darren believed, as did his friend Jaco, that this would be a rich hunting ground for Royal Navy frigates rushing to North America. Again, knowing the Royal Navy, the ships would leave Portsmouth as soon as they were supplied. It was unlikely that they would sail as a group. The frigate captains wanted to get to sea because they had dreams of easy pickings of American merchant ships that would, once sold in an Admiralty Court, make them rich men.

He sat staring out at *Goshawk's* wake. Arriving in this area early this morning, he had let out some of the sails and turned north, hoping to find a Royal Navy ship. Darren was under no illusions about what his fate would be if he were captured. In his lock box were letters to each of his children, Emily and Marijke, that were to be delivered only if he was killed.

Once they were written and locked away, it gave him the freedom to think about the future and the various ways he would fight *Goshawk* against the Royal Navy. Frustrated by waiting, Darren left his cabin, and as he walked onto the main deck, one of the bo'sun mates stopped abruptly in front of him.

"Beggin' th' captain's pardon, but Mr. Graz sent me to tell you that we have a ship in sight."

Levi Graz, son of a German immigrant from the area around Hannover, was *Goshawk's* First Lieutenant and one of his officers assigned by Commodore Rodgers to the frigate. He began as a midshipman on *Constellation* during the Quasi-War and had seen action against the Barbary Pirates. Since then, he'd spent half the time on half-pay working for his father in their dry goods store in Philadelphia and the other half of the year on a U.S. Navy ship.

"Captain on the quarterdeck." Darren waited until the announcement was made before he approached the 26-year-old. "Mr. Graz, what do we have?"

The Philadelphia native handed Darren the Dollond spyglass. "Sir, look two points off the starboard bow at about three miles. I believe, as do the lookouts, that it is Royal Navy. I've never seen a ship like this before because it has the look of a three-decker, but I can only see two rows of gun ports."

Goshawk's bell rang, and the bo'sun's mate on watch intoned loudly, One Bell of the Forenoon Watch."

To Darren, it meant that they had all afternoon for this fight that would take place under sunny skies with a steady breeze. The Atlantic's three-foot swells were causing *Goshawk* to gently corkscrew as she angled through the dark-blue sea.

While Darren studied what he could see of the Royal Navy ship, he said, "It's a razée. Most likely a sixty-four third rater whose upper gundeck was removed to turn her into a heavy frigate with about forty guns. The gun deck will have twenty-four pounders, the main deck twelve-pounders with a few large carronades. The bow will have twelve-pounders and again, a carronade or two."

"Aye, sir. That tells me she may be, compared to *Goshawk,* a clumsy sailer and several knots slower."

"Splendid answer, Mr. Graz, you are correct, Mr. Graz. Hoist our largest Stars and Stripes and the Don't Tread on Me flag at the top of the mainmast. Then, pass the word to have all the officers join me at the aft end of the quarterdeck, forthwith after you order the bo'sun to clear the decks for action. Load ball, but do not run out."

Leaning against the rail, Darren looked at his officers. They were, except for Quartermaster Nutt, who was 32, and 34-year-old Bo' sun Digby, all under the age of 30. At 54, Darren was old enough to be their father.

"Gentlemen, this will be our first action together. We have trained well, and that training, especially the gun crews, will put us in good stead. Focus on the gun drill, get your aiming right, and our long twenty-fours will serve us well. My job, as well as Lieutenant Graz's, and if we fall, Lieutenant Wolcott's is to maneuver *Goshawk* into position so your guns can do the most damage."

"Mr. Islip, your men have the maintops. First target for the swivel guns are the officers on the quarterdeck, then the gun crews that are in the open.

Captain Lynn, your Marines will help Bo'sun Howard with sails, and then, when the action gets close, your men will be in pairs on the main deck, just as we have trained. One shoots, the other loads."

Nodding heads told him they understood their roles. Now it was time to share his plan. "Gentlemen, this is how we plan to take apart this beast. If we play our cards right, we should be escorting a prize into Funchal. I have a letter from the Portuguese ambassador saying that if we go to war against England, Portugal will be neutral."

The men left the aft end of the quarterdeck. Darren took a look at the former 64-gun ship-of-the-line. It was now two miles away, and *Goshawk* was angling toward the Royal Navy ship.

"Mr. Radcliffe, a word."

The son of Edmund Radcliffe and Sophie Fontaine was on his way to the gun deck when he heard his captain's voice. He stopped at the forward end of the quarterdeck so Darren could lean over the railing.

Born in Martinique, he had just turned 20. Old to be a midshipman, but he was determined to serve his country. He had just graduated from the Fonseca-Laredo/N.E.S. Academy in the spring of 1811 and volunteered to serve on one of the N.E.S. ships.

"This is your first action. Your job is to encourage your gun crews, help them with aim, and if need be, help if a man goes down. Focus on that, and you'll be fine."

"Thank you, sir." Each time Jaco saw the young man, he said he looked just like his father. The only difference was that he had a much better personality, and it was Darren's job to keep him alive since Jaco killed his father when Edmund was the captain of the French privateer, *Rapier.*

Darren didn't need a spyglass to work out how he wanted to proceed. "Mr. Graz, I believe the Royal Navy captain wants a fight. He is altering course towards us so we exchange broadsides at about five hundred yards as we pass. I want him to think we are afraid of him and don't want to fight." Then, in a louder voice, "Mr. Nutt, ease your helm to nor' west."

ON BOARD, H.M.S. *KING EDWARD*, 12:42 P.M. LOCAL TIME

Captain Marcus Honeycutt stood with one foot braced on the bottom railing of the quarterdeck rail as he saw the large American flag stream from the aftmost halyard attached to the mizzenmast. "I'll be damned, an American frigate. Bo'sun, clear the decks for action, load ball and run out."

As he studied the ship approaching his ship that was originally designed to take the pounding from ships with 70 and 80 cannons. Honeycutt tried to remember what he read on the sheet of paper signed by the Second Naval Lord.

It was a very interesting read in that it outlined the tactics the American frigates were likely to use, that their gunnery was excellent, and their ships seemed impervious to 18- and 24-pound balls. When he read that, Honeycutt thought that was all well and good when fighting the French or the Barbary Pirates, but his ship was part of the Royal Navy that had vanquished every foe by closing with the enemy and delivering devastating and rapid fire.

He wondered why the American ship had not, like *King Edward,* shortened sail. His next look at the American frigate told him that his angle of view had changed slightly, suggesting the American had fallen off to starboard to extend the range. *Ah, yes, the Americans like to fire at long range because they are afraid of my ship.*

ON BOARD *GOSHAWK*, 12:59 P.M. LOCAL TIME

Darren smiled as he looked at the Royal Navy ship and ordered, "Quartermaster, ease off your helm another half point to nor' by nor' east. Mr. Digby, trim the sails accordingly."

"Mr. Graz...."

Graz, who was, by order of Captain Smythe, to stay diagonally opposite to wherever the captains stood to minimize one ball from killing both of them, came over to where Darren stood at the edge of the deck. "Stay with me until the shooting starts, and I will share my thoughts as we maneuver."

"Aye, captain, thank you."

"Don't thank me, thank Captain Jacinto. We have spent hours using our children's toy boats, making moves and counter moves. During the War for Independence, I was on the receiving end of his tactics, and I can assure you that it wasn't pleasant."

Graz didn't say anything and looked at the bow of the Royal Navy ship. "Sir, I believe they are going to fire one of their bow chasers."

"Let them. At this range, a hit, even from a twelve-pounder, is unlikely." Darren waited and watched how the masts were lined up. Right now, he could see a gap, but if the Royal Navy frigate turns toward *Goshawk,* the gaps will close. If it turns away, the gaps will open.

"If the Royal Navy captain takes the bait, he will alter course to try to cross our stern. If he does, then we will turn nor' west and threaten his. I suspect *Goshawk* will turn much better than his bluff-bowed former third rater." Darren was about to say something and stopped. The bow of the third rater was coming around faster than he anticipated, and the range was now within 1,000 yards. "Mr. Nutt, ease off to a course of due east. Mr. Digby, trim our sails as needed."

Goshawk's bow had already turned a few degrees when both men saw the flash from the British ship's two bow chasers fire. They didn't have to wait for the boom. The splash behind and short plus the turning frigate told Darren what he needed to know.

ON BOARD *KING EDWARD*, 12:08 P.M. LOCAL TIME

The first question in Captain Honeycutt's mind was, American frigate, what are you doing? You are run out, so are you going to stay and fight, or are we going to dance, or are you going to run?

He told this quartermaster to keep the ship turning to port until it was parallel to the American's new course. With the wind from the north, Honeycutt was confident that he had the advantage since he was upwind.

ON BOARD *GOSHAWK*, 12:30 P.M. LOCAL TIME

Standing with his hands on the aft railing of the quarterdeck, Darren turned to his first lieutenant, "How far behind us do you think our adversary is?"

"Half a mile and I suspect we are gaining."

"Splendid. I concur. Turning to the bo'sun's mate on the quarterdeck, "Pass the word for Mister Landry, Wolcott, and Radcliffe to join me on the quarterdeck forthwith."

All three men came up. "Gentlemen, we are about to slacken our sails a bit to let our enemy close. We will then tack to port and sheet home the sails. Range will be under one thousand yards. I want aimed shots, and out of the sixteen guns, I want at least a dozen hits. If he turns, then you will have a bigger target. Understood?"

The young officers nodded and departed.

"Mr. Graz, I'll let you time the turn. Quarterdeck, Mr. Graz has the deck for the tack to port, on his command." After hearing the acknowledgements of his orders, he said softly so only his First Lieutenant could hear. "No pressure, Mr. Graz. Do it right, and we cross the T. Do it wrong, and we could have a bad day."

Graz rolled his eyes at his captain and then turned his eyes toward the Royal Navy ship. "On my command, come left to nor' nor' west. Bo'sun, get those sheets home smartly." Walking to the front of the quarterdeck, Graz cupped his hands and yelled but didn't need to. "Mr. Landry, you may fire when your guns bear. Range eight to nine hundred yards."

ON BOARD *KING EDWARD*, 12:32 P.M.

Honeycutt, when he saw the bow start to come to port, said under his breath, "You bloody American bastard." Even if he had said it loud enough to hear, gunners on Goshawk were adjusting their aim.

He now had two choices, both bad. Choice one - continue the turn to port and tack through the wind. If he chose that, he would slow, but present his port side to the American, which might give his after guns a chance at hitting the American.

Choice two - fall off to starboard, regain some speed, then either tack to port or wear to starboard and re-engage. Bad part was that he was exposing his stern to the enemy.

"Quartermaster, fall off to starboard. Bo'sun, get men aloft to loosen the topsails and top gallants."

Hopefully, this would give him some more speed and separation from the American.

The words were just out of his mouth when the first 24-pound ball slammed into the port bow chaser. Shards of shattered cast iron from the disintegrating cannon barrel and the ball flew down the gun deck, killing and maiming Royal Navy sailors.

Ball two, hit the figurehead, and the wooden sculpture of King Edward II disappeared in a shower of fragments. The ball didn't penetrate the hull, but the impact caused the 1,400-ton ship to reverberate like a bell. Honeycutt felt the vibrations in his feet.

Ball three sang overhead, parting a few stays, and splashed into the water about a half a mile behind *King Edward.*

The ball from *Goshawk's* #4 port gun missed the hull but slammed into the end of a barrel of the #1 24-pounder on the gun deck. The impact caused the barrel to start to spin like a top. As it did, the barrel ripped out the bulwark between its gun port and that of the #2 gun. Five men fell, gored by large splinters and chunks of metal.

The sixth and seventh balls passed harmlessly through *King Edward's* rigging, but number eight thudded into its foremast, about six feet above the deck. The mast was strong enough to stop the ball that lodged itself in the two-foot diameter section of oak. From the bow, it didn't look bad, but the survivors of the splinters that came out from the mast could tell it was coming down.

Honeycutt could see the damage and didn't pay attention to the rest of the balls that slammed into his ship which was now starting to turn. Men were hauling braces around, and before he could yell stop, the foremast gave way.

Thankfully, the netting strung above the main deck caught most of the debris, but the spar for the mainsail was heavy enough to rip the netting down and crush several sailors.

ON ONBOARD *GOSHAWK*, 12:34 P.M. LOCAL TIME

Impatiently, Darren said to his First Lieutenant, who he could see was staring at the Royal Navy ship. "What next? Mr. Graz. You still have the quarterdeck. This is no time for lollygagging!"

"Sorry, sir." Graz thought for a second, "Mr. Nutt, Mr. Digby, stand-by to come about to port on my command. New course due south."

Goshawk came around, and Darren leaned over so he could speak to his Second Lieutenant, Isaac Landry. "Once the port guns are loaded, have the gun crews come up two at time, so they can see the result of their work. This is not over, so they need to get back to their guns quickly."

Graz adjusted *Goshawk's* course so that it was offset by about 200 yards to port. This would, he believed, enable *Goshawk* to cross the stern of the Royal Navy ship.

"Deck, name of the Royal Navy ship is *King Edward.*"

Darren looked up, "Deck eye." Turning to Graz, "What's your next move?"

"Close to about three or four hundred yards and then wear to port and hit her with the starboard battery."

"Concur, Mr. Graz, you still have the deck. A word to the wise. You need to plan at least two moves, if not three ahead and have alternatives. Once the enemy makes a move, you must decide if you are going to counter and then what that move is. Hesitation will get your ship hammered, and you killed."

"Aye, Captain."

From the quarterdeck, Darren could see the crew of *King Edward* clearing away debris, much of which went over the side. At the aft end of the deck, a portly man wearing the coat with two gold epaulets of a Royal Navy captain watched *Goshawk.*

Captain, are you going to let me pour a broadside down your ship, or are you going to attempt to turn and fight? If you turn, so will I, and you will not get your chance to try to cripple Goshawk. *Or are you going to strike?*

Darren heard Graz's voice. "Bo 'sun, Quartermaster, stand-by to wear ship to port on my command. New course due east."

Once Graz heard the order acknowledged, he said, "Wear ship now!"

The bow of *Goshawk* started to turn to port. Once the ship was into the turn, the man at the aft end of *King Edward's* quarterdeck untied the halyard to the Union Jack and let it flutter down. Before the two Royal Navy seamen could catch it, Darren bellowed, "Cease fire, Cease fire!!!"

He heard Isaac Landry's acknowledgement. "Mr. Graz, I have the quarterdeck. Well done."

"Aye, aye, sir."

"Mr. Digby and Mr. Nutt, I want to fall off to starboard and for you to put the bowsprit fifty feet from the starboard, aft corner of *King Edward's* quarterdeck. Then maintain station while I have a chat with its captain."

ON BOARD *KING EDWARD*, 1:36 P.M. LOCAL TIME

Darren was the first officer from Goshawk to climb up King Edward's side and onto its main deck. Many of the Royal Navy sailors ignored him and the other six men who followed as they went about clearing the mess on the main deck.

The portly man came toward Darren followed by two other lieutenants. "Captain, I am Marcus Honeycutt, captain of *His Majesty's Frigate King Edward.*" He held his sword horizontally.

Darren took it and then said, "I shall return this when we get safely to a neutral port. Who is the best navigator of your officers?"

Honeycutt pointed to a young Lieutenant. "I am Clarence Chauncey, sir."

"Splendid. You will remain on board after Captain Honeycutt buries your dead. The other officers will join us on *Goshawk.* While you are preparing your dead, we will transfer your powder to my frigate. Then, when *King Edward* is ready to sail, you, Chauncey, will follow *Goshawk* to where I tell you the ship will be sold as a prize. Captain Honeycutt and the rest of *King Edward's* crew will be kept there as guests until they are returned to England."

Turning toward Honeycutt, Darren asked in a polite tone that was really an order. "Captain, I need your ship's papers and muster roll."

Once in Honeycutt's cabin, Darren spoke. "Captain, I will ask this question only once, and I expect the truth. How many Americans are aboard *King Edward?*"

"None, Captain Smythe, they are all Englishmen."

"We shall see. If I find any impressed seamen, instead of enjoying a lieutenant's cabin, you will be clapped in irons and kept in the hold until we return to a U.S. port where you will be tried for kidnapping."

ON BOARD *GOSHAWK*, 8:23 P.M. LOCAL TIME

Dinner, or supper, as it was known in the Royal Navy, was difficult. At the table were two Royal Navy officers – Honeycutt and Smithson, his First Lieutenant – plus four of Darren's own – Radcliffe, Graz, Jeffreys, and Digby. His surgeon was on King Edward helping tend to the two dozen sailors maimed by shrapnel from Goshawk's 24-pounder balls and splinters from wood shattered by their impact. The Royal Navy officers' mood was also darkened now that the two ships were underway after burying 32 of their shipmates.

Darren had two problems he was wrestling with. One, where would he take *King Edward?* Theoretically, he could take the frigate to Lisbon or Porto in Portugal. The Madeira Islands were out of the question because the British had reoccupied the islands in 1807.

The Canary Islands? They were a possibility, but were controlled by Spain, which was aligned with the British. They were the next closest port. His other choices – the Azores and Rabat - were at 800 nautical miles away, equidistant from their current location.

Portugal owned the Azores, and the governor allowed N.E.S. to base its ships in Ponta Delgada. Now that the U.S. was at war with England, and Portugal aligned with the British, the Azores were not the answer.

This left Rabat, which had its own risks in that the ships would pass close to Gibraltar. However, Fonseca-Laredo had agents in Agadir, Casablanca, Rabat, and Tangiers, and the Moroccans had a commercial treaty with the U.S. that had been in force since the 1770s.

Problem two was that *Goshawk* was now a floating powder keg. Tied down at the aft end of the berthing deck and in the hold, outside the magazine, were two tons of gunpowder taken from *King Edward.*

The powder, along with the shot, muskets, pistols, and swords, would be stored in the Fonseca-Laredo agent's warehouse in Rabat. Hopefully, he would have a building large enough to keep these supplies so that any American Navy warship can use them to replenish its magazine.

From the captain's cabin on *Goshawk,* the men at the table could see the dark shape of *King Edward* about a quarter mile behind. The former Royal Navy frigate was sailing under its main and top sails on its main and mizzenmast. Before they got underway, Darren was assured by his and *King Edwards'* bo'sun that the two remaining masts would stay up unless they ran into a gale.

Honeycutt topped off his glass of wine, "Captain Smythe, where are you taking my ship? There are no friendly ports within a thousand miles."

"Captain Honeycutt, that is not true. We're going to Rabat where the Sultan might pay handsomely for your ship and its cannon."

The Royal Navy captain's eyes opened wide, and his lower jaw dropped. "You are going to turn us over to bloody heathens who will sell us into slavery!!!"

"I doubt that. The Sultan may dislike you British, but he is not stupid. He will, however, take great delight in filling his coffers with gold sovereigns for a frigate crew King George III would like to get back." Turning to his Second Lieutenant, Darren asked, "Mr. Landry, how long will it take us to reach Rabat?"

"At most seven days at our present five knots."

"Splendid. Let us enjoy the voyage, shall we. Captain Honeycutt, as our guest, what would you like to chat about?"

CHAPTER 16

OLD FRIEND, NEW BASE

RABAT, MOROCCO, FIRST WEEK OF AUGUST 1812

The day before *Goshawk* and *King Edward* arrived off Rabat, Lieutenant Clarence Chauncey signaled that he wanted Darren to come on board *King Edward.* The two ships were making just enough speed so their rudders were effective. With the temperature in the low 80s and no clouds, the weather was pleasant and the seas relatively calm, which made the transit via rowed longboat easy.

This was not the first time Darren had been on *King Edward.* Each time they signaled that they needed to bury a sailor who had died of his wounds, Darren accompanied Captain Honeycutt to the Royal Navy ship, not to officiate, but to show respect for the fallen sailor.

Today, however, he was alone and asked Lieutenant Chauncey to muster the crew aft of the main and mizzen mast so he could speak to them. Darren was unarmed, and even though there were still muskets, bayonets, swords, and pistols on board *King Edward,* there was no powder or lead balls. Darren believed that the Royal Navy sailors would not attack him.

The men parted as he walked from the hatch in the bulwark to the quarterdeck, where only the two helmsmen and Lieutenant Chauncey stood. Given the fact that they were prisoners in their own ship, he expected a more sullen reception than he got. Then he realized that for them, at least until they were returned to the Royal Navy, their war was over.

"If Lieutenant Chauncey has not told you, tomorrow we, God willing, will anchor in Rabat, Morocco. My country, the United States, has had a treaty of peace, friendship, and commerce with Morocco since 1787. That treaty was reaffirmed in 1803."

Darren could see the men were paying attention. "Before this war began, my employer was a trading firm that bought spices from Morocco, and it has an agent in Rabat. My plan is to enlist his help in finding an acceptable place for you to stay until you are paroled. How long that will take, I do not know. I will ask the Sultan if he wishes to purchase *King Edward.* Again, I do not know. Captain Honeycutt and I expect your cooperation."

Nodding once meant that Darren was finished speaking, at least for the moment.

A voice from the second rank yelled out. "What about our sea chests? What's in them is all me and my mates have."

"When you are transferred ashore, I will do my best to ensure that you can take your chests with you. But I do not know if the Sultan will allow it. You can be assured, I will ask because it is a reasonable request."

When *Goshawk* glided to a halt about a quarter mile from the shoreline where his chart said there was plenty of water under the keel, there was already a boat headed toward the two frigates. *Goshawk* was flying the same large American flag, and *King Edward* had a large white flag made from sailcloth from its halyard over a Union Jack. Darren hoped that it would signal to whoever was watching that the larger *King Edward* was a prize.

Standing next to Captain Smythe and Honeycutt was one of his gunner's mates, Ray (short for Raythane) Mebarek, who had walked on board the first Fonseca-Laredo ship that called on Tunis and asked for a job. After he became a citizen, he enlisted in the U.S. Navy. Mebarek was there because he spoke fluent Arabic.

The two men who came onto the deck were wearing white, loose-fitting pantaloons and red, double-breasted coats. The first man up had a blue sash with a large emblem pinned at the top. On his head, he had a pot-shaped hat that Darren learned later was a fez with a blue tassel.

Once Bo'sun Howard blew "all call" on his pipe, he bellowed out, "Morocco, arriving." The first of the two men nodded and walked between the two lines of U.S. Marines, resplendent in their dark blue coats, white trousers, with their rifled muskets held vertically.

Darren waited until the man stopped in front of him then nodded slightly. "I am Darren Smythe, captain of the United States Navy frigate *Goshawk.* Next to me is Captain Marcus Honeycutt of the Royal Navy frigate *King Edward,* which I captured in battle."

The pause allowed Mebarek to translate. The man smiled and then said in accented English, "I am Colonel Amir Harrak and a member of Sultan Mawlay Sulayman bin Mohammed's staff. Welcome to Morocco. I am to take you and one of your officers to meet our Sultan. We do not need an interpreter since the Sultan speaks English and French."

Captain Harrak turned to the man standing next to him, "May I present Captain Hamza Bensaid. We assume you need supplies, and he will guide you through the markets when your officers are ready."

Turning to his First Lieutenant, Darren said, "Mr. Graz, you have the ship. Mr. Landry, you come with me. Mr. Wolcott, you take Mr. Radcliffe and Mebarek with you on a detail to buy food."

After hearing the "aye, aye's," Darren pointed with his outstretched palm toward the hatch, "Colonel, we should not keep the Sultan waiting."

Walking next to Colonel Harrak, Darren's nose was filled with the pleasant scents of cinnamon, cumin, and sesame mingled with the more pungent paprika and turmeric. Melody had used these spices that she bought in the Charleston Store, and now, Marijke got them in New York for cooking. Yet here in Rabat, the smells seemed stronger.

"Captain, have you ever been to my country?"

"No, Colonel Harrak, I cannot say that I have."

"You do know that our Sultan's father was one of the first countries to recognize yours?"

"Aye, that I do." He knew of the relationship and that Laura Fonseca Laredo's mother was Moroccan. But for him, Morocco was a strange and very foreign land.

The streets were narrow and winding as they climbed the steps toward the palace. Every so often, they would walk down a street that was lined with merchants selling their wares. Harrak stopped abruptly at a shop where a baker was removing round flatbreads from an oven and then drizzling olive oil on top, which was followed by a sprinkle of dried garlic, ground coriander, and sesame seeds.

Harrak handed one to Darren, another to Colin Landry and then took one himself. After giving the merchant several coins, the Moroccan folded the warm bread in half and took a bite.

Following the Moroccan colonel's example, Darren did the same. His nostrils were filled with the strong aroma of freshly squeezed olive oil, the pungency of garlic, and the earthy citrus aroma that had a hint of lemon and pepper. "This is delicious."

Landry mumbled the same, and they continued onto the palace. Once there, the colonel led them through corridors made from stone in which the air was noticeably cooler. Harrak stopped in front of two guards who had muskets with fixed bayonets. They came to attention, and Harrak held up his to wait for a third guard to open the oak doors that Darren guessed must be 15 feet tall.

"Please, when you are in our Sultan's presence, do not sit unless told to do so. Captain Honeycutt, you will stand on my right side to show that you are a trusted visitor. Also, you are not allowed to touch His Excellency. Speak only when spoken to. If the Sultan is speaking, we must listen. He values the truth in simple terms. As the junior officer, Lieutenant Landry, you will stand off to the side of Captain Smythe so His Excellency can see you and one step back."

Splendid. Why would I lie to a man who could have my ship destroyed, my crew imprisoned, and my head lopped off on a whim?

"Thank you, Colonel."

Harrak said something in Arabic, and the sergeant opened the door. At the far end, Darren could see Sultan Mawlay Sulayman bin Mohammed sitting on cushions on a raised platform at the far end of the hall. Six men, three on each side, dressed in long-sleeved, cream-colored *djellabas,* stood waiting for his commands.

Harrak stopped one stride from the six steps that led up to the platform where Sultan Mawlay Sulayman bin Mohammed waited. Before speaking, Harrak bowed slightly. "Your Excellency, may I present Captain Darren Smythe, commander of the United States Navy frigate *Goshawk.* With him is Lieutenant Colin Landry. He captured His Majesty King George III's Royal Navy frigate *King Edward* in a recent battle and wishes to ask His Excellency if he is interested in purchasing the Royal Navy ship."

"Captain Smythe and Lieutenant Landry, welcome to Morocco. Before you won your independence from England, my father negotiated a commercial treaty with your Continental Congress. Then, in 1787, the new Congress ratified it. My merchants tell me that they do good business with your traders."

"Thank you, your Excellency, if may suggest a course of action that will cost Morocco nothing and will generate profits for its merchants."

"Please, I am always interested in ways to benefit my people."

"Send a note to our government in Washington that in times of war with Britain, our warships can stop in Moroccan ports to buy naval supplies, food, and beverages.

Captain, you mean powder and shot as well as food."

"Yes, your Excellency, that is correct."

"I shall have a letter sent on the next merchant ship that calls on Morocco and give you a copy as well." The sultan turned to a man next to him and spoke in Arabic before facing Darren. "Tell me about your conquest."

His explanation took just a few minutes, and he did not glorify his decisions or note the mistakes that Captain Honeycutt made. The Sultan nodded. "What do you propose?"

Morocco didn't have Admiralty Courts like those in the United States, Britain, and its colonies. He had long decided to see if the Sultan was interested in a business transaction. "Your Excellency, what I propose will add to Morocco's wealth."

Before he could continue, Sultan Mawlay Sulayman bin Mohammed, said, "How so?"

"Sir, I mean, Your Excellency, I propose that you buy *King Edward* from the United States. Then, you contact the British in Gibraltar and ask them if they are interested in buying the frigate from you as well as paying a ransom for its crew."

The sultan smiled. "I like the way you think. I presume you are speaking for the United States?"

"Aye. I do not believe we have a consul here, so yes, as captain of *Goshawk,* in matters such as these, I represent my government."

"Agreed. What do you want for the ship?"

"Before I answer, please allow me to explain how I came to a price."

Sultan Mawlay Sulayman bin Mohammed nodded as if to say continue.

"My ship, *Goshawk,* cost approximately £35,000 (~£3,231,047 or ~$4,038,809 in January 2026) to build and carries thirty-six guns - thirty-two 24-pounders and four 18-pounders. It is smaller than *King Edward,* which was originally built to carry sixty-four cannons in a mix of 18- and 24-pounders. Therefore, it costs more, probably £45,000 (~£4,154,203 or ~$%,192,754 in January 2026) to build. According to its captain, it was launched in 1799, and then in 1805, the Royal Navy eliminated the upper gun deck. Now it carries 44 cannons, eighteen 24-pounders, sixteen 18-pounders, and eight 12-pounders."

The sultan didn't sound impatient when he said, "Including the cannons, how much?"

"£13,000. (~£1,181,509 or about ~$1,476,886 in January 2026)."

"What do you suggest I ask the British to pay?"

"I'd start with £20,000 ~(£1,817,706 or ~$2,272,132 in January 2026) and then agree to any number above eighteen."

"And the crew?"

"It is, thanks to its captain, a well-trained lot." *They're more valuable to the Royal Navy than the ship.* "I'd ask £20,000 (~£1,817,706 or ~$2,272133 in January 2026)."

"You are telling me that the Royal Navy will pay me £45,000 (£4,089,839 or ~$5,112,299 in January 2026) for *King Edward* and its crew."

"Aye. Buying the ship back from you is much cheaper than building a new one and finding a new crew. You would have to shelter and feed the crew well while they are waiting for transport to return them back to England." *Now with war declared, England has to find a new source of high-quality oak, something the U.S. has in great quantities and England does not.*

"And if the English refuse?"

"Then you can use the cannons in your fortresses and the wood to build what you wish."

"How do you wish to be paid?"

"English gold coins, French gold livres or francs, Spanish dollars, Dutch guilders."

The sultan's head went up and down. "I like the idea of the English paying me. But, before I make such a deal, I would like to inspect the ship."

"We are, your Excellency, at your service. My ship will need a few days to purchase and load supplies."

"How about tomorrow morning?"

"Splendid, Your Excellency. We would be honored to have you as our guest. Should you come out in the morning, we could give you a tour of *King Edward* after which, we could retire to *Goshawk,* and if you wish, conclude the transaction."

"Excellent. Colonel Harrak, see to it that the arrangements are made."

"Before you go, is this the only prize you will bring to Morocco, or if I buy this one to sell back to the British, there will be more?"

"There can, if His Excellency wishes, be more. You, sir, would have to notify my government and Navy that you welcome prizes that can be resold to not only the British, but also to the French and Spanish."

Smiling, "I shall include that in my letter to your President Madison." Sultan Mawlay Sulayman bin Mohammed turned to an aide, signaling that the meeting was over. Darren left, not surprised that the Sultan knew the name of the American president.

CHAPTER 17

INTO THE HORNET'S NEST

VICINITY 35°N 12°W, FIRST WEEK OF AUGUST 1812

For three weeks, the convoy of eight ships sailed along a base course of due east from New York to the middle of the Straits of Gibraltar. As they worked their way through the Horse Latitudes and a wind on their bows, they would tack to the nor' east by east and sail for six hours. Then, on a signal from *Osprey*, they would tack back through the wind to sail a course of so' east by south.

At night, they would sail the same course in formation from just before sunset to sunrise. The first tack in the morning would match the time of the night transit.

The tacking back and forth added days to their transit, but so far, other than a few squall lines, the weather had been fair. Only an occasional merchantman had been spotted.

On the table in his cabin, Captain Abner Jeffords, Escort Group B's Commodore, maintained a plot based on two sightings a day. One was taken at noon and the other at midnight. The positions were marked on the chart so Jeffords could see how far off or close his convoy was to the planned route.

Given the time of year and the number of tacks the convoy would have to make, he estimated his straight-line speed was four knots. To cover the 3,400 nautical miles from Norfolk, Virginia, to Gibraltar, his original estimate was that the convoy would need about 35 days to make the journey.

They had been at sea for 29 days, and his plot showed that he was about five days ahead of schedule. The faster transit would make the merchant ship captains happy and their owners even happier. The faster they reached Naples, the sooner they could offload their cargo, reload, and sail back to the U.S.

Jeffords had been counting the days since the declaration of war. He assumed that the British government received the declaration on either July 3rd or 4th. Today, six weeks had passed. Given where the convoy was, according to the last sighting, in the waters where Darren Smythe said Royal Navy frigates and ships of the line sailed when deploying to North America in the summer.

Each morning, one of the corvettes would leave the convoy and sail a triangular track that took them roughly 30 nautical miles ahead of the convoy, then two hours in the direction the convoy was sailing before returning.

Today was *Venom's* turn. *Osprey* set the pace and course, and the other two corvettes, *Cottonmouth* under Ezekiel Winters maintained a position about a mile to starboard of the convoy, and *Viper* under Morton Geiger maintained a similar position to port.

Jeffords felt restless because in his bones, he suspected they would not sail into the Mediterranean without some sort of fight with a Royal Navy ship. Rather than sit in his cabin, he went out onto the main deck and walked to the forecastle and then back to the companionway that led to the quarterdeck.

He was in the midst of his second lap when the lookout called out, "Deck, *Venom* is returning."

To Jeffords, *Venom's* early return meant only one thing. *The Royal Navy had just raised its ugly lion head.*

On the quarterdeck, Jeffords asked, "Where's Mr. Denbow?"

The officer of the watch was Linus Smith, one of the regular Navy officers and *Osprey's* First Lieutenant. "Sir, he is in the wardroom studying. I'll send a mate to fetch him and the signals book."

Jeffords nodded. He did not speculate what news *Venom* would bring. He would find out soon enough.

Two bells rang, reminding Jeffords that it was an hour into the Forenoon Watch. The new chronometer on his desk said it was just after nine in the morning.

VICINITY 35.2°N, 12.3°W, ON BOARD *EAGLE*, 9:07 A.M. THE SAME DAY

Before they left New York, Jaco promised that he would shadow the convoy when it went through these waters in case Escort Group B ran afoul of the Royal Navy. *Eagle* had scouted the areas south of Ireland looking for prizes and Royal Navy frigates and found neither.

In his cabin, he had the planned track of Jeffords' Escort Group B plotted and deliberately sailed to the west on the track before he started working *Eagle* to the east. Jaco wasn't sure, but his gut told him that they were within a day of his old shipmate Jeffords and Escort Group B.

The two men first met when Jeffords was a quartermaster mate and Jacinto was a midshipman on *Providence* way back in 1776. The two men became friends as they worked their way up the ranks with Jeffords always being his first choice to be his ship's quartermaster. Now, Jeffords was one of N.E.S. and Fonseca-Laredo's more experienced captains which is why he was the commander of Escort Group B.

"Deck, flotsam in the water, one point off the starboard bow."

"Mr. Howard, slack all sails to slow us down. Mr. Turner, steer toward the debris."

Once he gave the order to untie the sheets to let the sails flap, Howard ordered four men to get boat hooks and then turned to the quarterdeck. "Captain, do you want to put a boat in the water?"

"Only if you see a survivor. Get some stuff on board so we can tell what type of ship."

Jaco could feel the frigate slowing. "No sign of survivors, sir, but it looks like several spars and a section of a mast."

"Captain, aye."

Eagle was barely making steerage way when it entered the flotsam which was a mix of sections of planking, two spars and a large log that looked like a section of a mast. Two sailors managed to hook a section of rope that was tied to a spar.

It took a half a dozen men to get the large piece of wood onto the deck. "It's Royal Navy, sir."

"How do you know?"

"Crown with KG and three I's are stamped on several of the fittings."

"Good enough. Salvage anything you can and then dump it back into the water. His carpenter's mate said, "Sir, the section of spar is not waterlogged. We could secure it to the deck to dry out and add it to our spares."

"Perfecto." Jaco turned to the black man who was the officer of the deck, "Mr. Cooper, get us underway again. We have a convoy to catch."

Mr. Cooper, *Eagle's* second lieutenant, was the 20-year-old Elias Cooper, son of Cato Cooper, *Kestrel's* captain. He was another of "the" many sons of men he knew that he was leading into war.

ON BOARD *OSPREY*, 9:28 A.M.

With the naked eye, it was hard to read the signals *Venom* was sending because the three-masted schooner was heeled well to port. Jeffords could see it had its topsails raised and both jibs set.

"Sir, *Venom* is signaling. Two frigates, one two-decker sighted."

"Understood, is that all?"

"No, sir. *Venom* is hoisting another signal." Denbow paused as he studied the onrushing corvette. "Enemy three points of port bow, distance twenty."

"Understood."

"Last signal. *Venom* may not have been spotted. Sir, more information is coming."

"Well done so far, Mr. Denbow. Have you written this all on a slate?"

"Aye, aye, sir. Last signal, Enemy on course to intercept, shadow?"

"Mr. Denbow, do you take that last word as a question?"

"Aye, sir, I do."

"Signal *Venom,* decoy if possible, do not engage. Turning convoy to nor' east by north."

Both men could see *Venom* tacking. By decoy, he meant for *Venom* to try to get the Royal Navy commander to follow him thinking he would lead them to a convoy. If not, they were in for a fight.

Jeffords wondered what young Jeremiah Smythe, *Venom's* captain would do. He was known to be cautious and calculating but he was not afraid to take risks if it meant surprising the enemy.

"Mr. Denbow, signal convoy, tack to port immediately, new course nor' east by north."

Once that was acknowledged, he ordered, "Now signal, escorts form on flagship."

"Keep an eye on the other ships for a signal." Jeffords strode to the forward edge of the quarterdeck and cupped his hands around his mouth. "Lookouts, be alert for sounds of cannon fire. Now, Mr. Denbow, we wait."

ON BOARD H.M.S. *EQUATION*, 9:51 A.M.

In Captain Hugh Gibson's mind, his 50-gun fourth rater didn't knife through the water, it bludgeoned its way along. Each time the bluff-bowed frigate plowed into a swell more than two or three feet high, the 1,300-ton vessel sent spray off to the side. If there was a moderate wind blowing, the spray would blow back onto the deck, making her, in Royal Navy parlance, a wet sailer.

Spray would drop down through the gratings onto the gun deck, making it slippery. When it dripped onto the berthing deck, the added moisture kept hammocks and clothing in the forward end of the ship damp.

Equation was the "flagship" of a three-ship squadron being sent to Bermuda for further assignment in either the North American Station or Jamaica Station. If he were given a preference, he would prefer Jamaica. The weather was nicer and there were more chances for prizes.

The other two frigates, *H.M.S. Godfrey* and *H.M.S. Persistent,* were both members of the *Flora*-class of 36-gun frigates. Their primary armament was twenty-six 18-pounders. For bow and stern chasers, the 870-ton frigates were equipped with two 6-pounders at each end.

Gibson, as the senior captain of the three, was appointed as the squadron commodore for the purposes of the transit to Bermuda. He was looking out his cabin windows at the smaller frigates, trailing *Equation* on either side of the V formation, while he contemplated his future.

Knowing the Royal Navy as he did, the three ships would be allocated in some fashion. He had spent most of his career on frigates, usually off some French, Spanish, or Dutch port. The 10 prizes he'd captured, four of which were warships – two Spanish and two French – earned him notice. He thought that being sent to North America to fight the Americans was another chance for him to show his mettle and might even earn him a promotion to Rear Admiral.

A tap on his door caused Gibson to turn around. "Come in." Seeing the young pimple-faced midshipman who was just 12 years old, he said, gruffly. "What?"

"Sir, Mr. Williston wanted to let you know that the lookouts have spotted that three-masted schooner again. He thinks it is one of the American corvettes and maybe shadowing us."

"Tell Mr. Williston, I will be up presently."

The midshipman, Jerome Vessey, left, and Gibson put a cork on the ink bottle and closed his log. This gave the midshipman time to get back to the quarterdeck.

Williston, who was 6"3" had to stoop when he walked through the interior of the ship. Coming out of the aft companionway, he stretched his back, now able to stand up straight. He tucked the spyglass under his left armpit and touched the back of his hand to his forehead. "Sir, about every twenty minutes or so, we catch a glimpse of a three-masted schooner that is roughly on the same course as *Equation.* There are a few rain showers about, and the schooner seems to be using them as cover. By what the lookouts say, it may be one of those American corvettes that was described on the sheet that accompanied our sailing orders."

"Assume this ship is a rebel, Mr. Williston, what is its captain's intent?

Williston didn't hesitate. "Sir, it is acting as if it was scouting. Our information says these are used to escort convoys. If so, one may be nearby. Or it could be scouting for a rebel squadron of frigates."

"Pray tell, what would you do if you were commodore?"

"Dispatch one of our frigates to follow it."

"For how long?"

"The rest of the day."

"You do know our sailing orders require us to proceed to Bermuda with utmost haste. Tacking to the nor' west to see what this schooner is about will lengthen our sailing time to Bermuda."

"Aye, sir, but our orders do not give a date by which time we must be in Bermuda. That tells me that we have some latitude. If this turns into nothing, at least we know. But, sir, what if it is a convoy escorted by these schooners. Our frigates could make short work of them, giving us a covey of prizes for His Majesty."

"Williston, I like your thinking. We've seen this schooner on different courses, correct?"

"Aye, sir, we have. Mostly staying within sighting distance."

"I think the ships the schooner is screening are north of us. Order a course change to the west, as close to the wind as you can, but still make our best speed. Tell *Persistent* and *Godfrey* to make all sail to investigate this schooner and rebel convoy ahead."

ON BOARD *VENOM*, 10:03 A.M.

Jeremiah Smythe resisted the temptation to climb the rigging to the lookouts' platform to see for himself. What he had just heard was that the Royal Navy frigates had tacked to the nor' nor' west, one was headed toward *Venom,* and all were hanging their royals. From *Venom's* position relative to the convoy, he knew that in an hour or two, they would spot the masts of the convoy.

One of the advantages schooners had over full-rigged ships was that they were generally faster and could sail much closer to the wind, i.e., within 20 degrees versus 60 for a square-rigged ship. The big disadvantage the schooners had was that they heeled more than a square-rigged ship whenever the wind was coming over either beam.

The question rattling around in Jeremiah's mind was how could he send a warning to the convoy without firing a flare?

He cupped his hands, "Lookouts, how far is the nearest frigate?"

"Four, mebbe, five miles."

He wasn't sure if the others on the quarterdeck saw him smile, but he said softly, the word that his Uncle Darren's best friend would use, "Perfecto."

Jeremiah went to the railing and, spotting his First Lieutenant, he called out. "Mr. Packwood, get ready to wear ship to the east on my command. Mr. Pimm, you still have the deck."

"Aye sir." Pimm's papers said he was 13, and was big for his age, but he would be that when he entered the Fonseca Laredo Naval Academy, he wasn't a day older than 12. But then again, all the officers on *Venom* still hadn't reached their 30th birthday.

Jeremiah studied the three Royal Navy frigates through a spyglass before collapsing it. Looking up he yelled, "Have the Royal Navy frigates finished their tacks."

"Aye, sir. Looks like they are heading east."

"Captain, aye. Mr. Pimm, Mr. Packwood. We'll hold our course for another few minutes until we see if there is a widening gap between the largest Royal Navy frigate and any of the others."

"What's the plan, sir?"

"Create a distraction to alert our friends."

"How?"

"Good question. Gunfire. Our ships are downwind and the sound will carry farther and faster. If we fire a flare, *Osprey* will never see it, and then the British will know there are our ships nearby."

"You devious bastard."

Smythe was smiling, "Aye, Mr. Packwood. That's why we'll win."

ON BOARD *EQUATION*, 10: 21 A.M.

Gibson was making a note in his log justifying his decision to deviate from the fastest course to Bermuda when he heard a pounding on his door. It was Midshipman Vessey. "Sir, Mr. Williston respects, sir. He would like you on the quarterdeck quickly."

"Good God, man, what happened?"

"Sir, the American corvette is heading straight for our squadron."

"I'll be there presently."

Calmly, Gibson walked from his cabin and then up the companionway, outwardly trying to portray an aura of calmness. Inside, his stomach was churning away, just as it always did before any action.

As soon as he saw his captain, Williston pointed at the corvette that was heeled over to port, sailing about 20 degrees off the wind. "There, sir, two points broad on the port beam."

At first, Gibson thought the American captain was stupid, exposing his ship to the superior weight of *Equation's* broadside or even the two other frigates, now about half a mile ahead of *Equation.* Looking at the American ship through a spyglass, he could see only four on the quarterdeck and about half a dozen on the main deck. Its gunports were closed, and as heeled over as the ship was, it would be impossible to fire the guns on its starboard side. Even then, at this range, what could it do with 6- or 9-pounders.

Without dropping the spyglass, "Mr. Williston, have the ship cleared for action. Tell the men to be quick about it. Load ball. I think we're about to teach an American Navy captain not to fight one of His Majesty's ships."

"Sir, do you want to alter course?"

"Not yet. I wish to let him get well inside one thousand yards, and then we will wear ship to the so' east and give him a taste of a Royal Navy broadside from about three hundred yards. That ship probably only has popguns that will nary cause a crack in our hull.

"Captain, our information says those corvettes have 12-, maybe 18-pounders."

"I doubt that. No ship that small has the scantlings that will allow it to fire anything bigger than a 12-pounder."

ON BOARD *VENOM*, 10:39 A.M.

Venom was sailing as close to the wind as Jeremiah dared. The wind was coming over the starboard bow, and he bent over the railing to talk to his second and third lieutenants. "Mr. Lincoln, have your men on the starboard battery ready, we'll be inside seven hundred yards when I give the order to fire. I want six hits. Then, a few minutes later, the port battery will have its chance. Have Mr. Pimm stand just forward of the quarterdeck so I can use him to pass information to you."

Jeremiah didn't need a spyglass to tell the range. What he was working out in his mind was how long should he wait to fire. His gut screamed, NOW!!!

As loudly as he could but without screaming, he bellowed to his bo'sun, "Mr. Stanton, luff all the sails, now!!! Repeat NOW!!!"

Venom leveled as it slowed. "Mr. Lincoln, fire!"

It wasn't a simultaneous broadside, but it was close. The starboard side of the corvette was enveloped in an acrid-tasting, gray-white smoke.

"Mr. Law, wear us around to a course of so' east. We'll adjust when we get around. Mr. Stanton, get the jibs through as if your life depends on it."

The jibs came through the stays cleanly as *Venom* had enough way for the rudder to be effective. With the push of the jibs and now with the booms of the main and top sails being pulled in, the corvette began to accelerate.

"Mr. Stanton, let go the sheets on the main sails. Mr. Shelly, it is the port battery's turn. Fire as your guns bear."

One after another, all six guns fired, and the men on the gun deck were reloading when Smythe ordered the sheets to be pulled in on the mainsails. Everyone on board could feel *Venom* accelerate.

"Deck!"

With the large two-decker now behind and off to its port side, *Venom* was well out of range. Jeremiah looked up. "Deck, aye. How'd we do?"

"No misses, sir. We saw all the balls strike home."

"Excellent."

"What's next, sir?"

"Mr. Packwood, let me catch my breath, and then we will make our next move."

"Which is?"

"Good question. Besides defeating our enemy and not getting killed in the process, not sure."

ON BOARD *EQUATION*, 10:44 A.M.

The size of the flash of flame was a surprise to Captain Gibson. So was the impact of an 18-pound ball coming from a long-barreled 18-pounder. Each time *Equation* was struck, the ship quivered as if hit by a giant hammer.

He had his quartermaster stop the turn so *Equation* could launch a broadside at the fleeing corvette. But by then, it was out of range, and only a few guns could bear. Silas Williston said the lookouts said the name of the corvette was *Venom.*

"What's the butcher's bill and what's the damage, Mr. Williston?"

Gibson was now in a quandary. *Equation* was now headed north, the corvette east, and the rest of his squadron headed due west.

"Mr. Williston, "Fall off the wind and let us head nor' west to catch up to our other frigates. Have the lookouts keep an eye on *Venom,* for I think he is going to come back for another bite of the apple."

"Aye, sir. Fifteen of our men were wounded, four were killed outright, and two of our upper deck 12-pounders and one of our 24-pounders are out of action. If I may so, sir, those popguns on that corvette rang our bell very hard."

"Mind your tongue, Mr. Williston. We will get our chance."

ON BOARD *VENOM*, 10:48 A.M.

Jeremiah Smythe's brain said he, which meant both Venom and his opponent that he now knew to be Equation, needed to make more noise. To do that, he had to entice its captain to fire a broadside. The question was how to do that without his ship being demolished, and he, along with most of his crew, either killed or maimed.

"Mr. Packwood, Mr. Stanton, we're going to wear about to starboard, then run down our friend. I want as much speed out of *Venom* as possible without risking losing a mast. We are going to run parallel to *Equation* at over 1,000 yards."

Venom's First Lieutenant looked askance at his captain. His look said, *you want to do what?*

"On my command, Mr. Packwood. Wear ship to port. New course, nor' west."

While *Venom* turned, Smythe walked over to his first lieutenant. "*Equation* has normal length 24s, which means that at long range, they are not accurate. I will bet you a gold sovereign that *Equation's* gunners won't register six hits on *Venom.*"

"I'll take that bet."

"You're on, Mr. Packwood." Smythe leaned over the forward quarterdeck railing. "Mr. Stanton, I want everyone on the gun deck except you and one of your mates. Mr. Packwood and I will remain on the quarterdeck with Mr. Law."

Seeing his second lieutenant come on deck, Smythe ordered, "Mr. Lincoln, once your gunners on the starboard side can see *Equation* they are to open fire. Range will be about twelve hundred yards. I want rapid, accurate fire. I expect a full broadside in return."

Lincoln cocked his head, "Aye, aye, sir."

Looking at the larger Royal Navy frigate, Smythe estimated that it was making about seven knots, and his corvette between 10 and 12. At a three-knot closure rate, he was gaining just over 100 yards a minute. At four, *Venom* was gaining at about 125 yards a minute.

The rate of closure was noticeable, and his helmsman eased off to port to increase the range between the ships. The aftmost cannon on *Equation's* lower deck spat out a tongue of flame. The ball splashed into the water about 200 yards short, about the same time that the retort reached *Venom.*

Smythe spoke in a loud enough voice so those on the main deck could hear. "Ranging shot."

Another gun fired, and this ball sent up a column of water a bit closer before it skipped twice and disappeared. "Mr. Law, ease off a bit more."

Venom's bow was now abeam the captain's cabin of *Equation.* Smythe was thinking, *any time now, Mr. Lincoln, any time* when the port #1 gun fired. The ball landed short.

The corvette's #2 gun on the starboard side fired, and then the #3. The lookouts called out hits when starting with the aft-most cannon on *Equation,* one after another, they fired. The noise from his long 18-pounders was mixed with the broadside fired by *Equation.*

Cannon balls screamed overhead, some splashed into the water, and a dozen hammered into *Venom's* hull. The thumps when they hit the layered wood that protected the gun deck were mixed with the screeching of oak and pine in the upper bulwark around the main deck being ripped asunder.

One splinter stuck into the oak planks on the front side of the binnacle. Others whistled by Jeremiah's head. "Mr. Law, ease us off another hundred yards or so."

When a ball went through one of the sails, it made a distinctive popping sound. The integrity of *Venom's* sails was vital to Jeremiah's plans. Intact sails are what gave the corvette speed, and speed, along with maneuverability, gave *Venom* its chance to survive.

Equation fired another broadside. This one was more ragged than the first and mixed with the firing from *Venom's* long 18-pounders, Jeremiah couldn't differentiate between the noise of his corvette's firing and the frigate's guns. What was noticed were the thumps on *Venom's* hull.

"Mr. Law, Mr. Stanton, on my command, let us fall off two points to port."

There was a ripple of gun blasts, and subconsciously, Smythe's brain counted six. The return fire from *Equation* continued, but it was ragged as was the fall of shot.

"Fall off now!!!"

There was a loud crash and Jeremiah ducked instinctively as a cloud of splinters filled the air. He heard Law grunt as he was speared just inside the shoulder. Jeremiah yelled out. "Mr. Packwood, get Mr. Law below. I have the helm."

Suddenly, the only sound was that of air rushing through the rigging and water rustling past the hull. Over his shoulder, he could see *Equation* trailing the other two Royal Navy frigates that were now tacking.

Seeing his first lieutenant come onto the main deck, Smythe called out, "Mr. Packwood, what's the butcher's bill and the damage?"

"First, Captain Smythe, you owe me a gold sovereign. Given the number of cannon balls that came our way, *Venom* is in good shape." He pointed at the gap in the bulwark where a 24-pound ball tore a three-foot-wide gap, "Other than the new hatch in the bulwark, we have ten men with minor splinter wounds. The surgeon is working on Mr. Law who has the nastiest wound."

A quartermaster mate replaced Jeremiah at the *Venom's* helm. "Mr. Packwood, I hope we made enough noise that our friends could hear. We're going to stay about two thousand yards off *Equation's* port side for the time being."

Jeremiah ran some numbers through his head. If he were a betting man, the lead Royal Navy frigate was about five to six miles from the convoy, maybe a few more. He began to formulate a plan that would harass the Royal Navy ships and hopefully give some assistance to the rest of Escort Group B.

ON BOARD *OSPREY*, 10:49 A.M.

Abner Jeffords was staring at the sea off to his frigate's front starboard quarter wondering where Venom was. A distant rumble flowed across the water. Instantly, he knew it was the sound of gunfire.

Cupping his hands, he looked up, "Lookouts, did you hear the rumble?"

"Aye, somewhere off our starboard quarter. Hard to make out."

If there's one cannon being shot, there's a high likelihood there will be others. Then he heard the sound of several cannons being fired in the sounds that wafted toward his ship.

"Deck, I make out the sound to be broad on the beam."

"Captain, aye."

He was sure the deep booms were from the long 18-pounders on *Venom,* and the sharp barks that were distinct reminded him of 12-pounders. Then there was a deep rumble that he assumed was a ship firing a broadside.

Jeffords worried for a few seconds about Jeremy Smythe and what he would say to his uncle, Captain Darren Smythe that his nephew and sister Emily's son was killed in battle. He put that ugly thought out of his mind and decided to wait. Soon he believed, they would sight the Royal Navy ships.

ON BOARD *EAGLE*, 10:50 A.M.

From the sea rushing past the hull, Jaco could tell his frigate was going fast. The wind from the nor' east had *Eagle* heeled noticeably to port. His quartermaster of the watch had just told him that the frigate was making 10 knots and probably couldn't go faster with these winds and on this tack without risking bringing down a mast.

Jaco was enjoying listening to the repartee between his midshipman, August von Korbach, and his Second Lieutenant Elias Cooper as he wondered if he had made the right choice for a course that would enable *Eagle* to find the convoy. He'd promised Jeffords that he would rejoin the convoy well before it approached the Straits of Gibraltar.

Von Korbach, who was a midshipman, had just turned 14 and was teaching German to Cooper, and the Bostonian was having trouble with the pronunciation of some of the words. Cooper was the third son of Cato Cooper, captain of *Kestrel* and the commodore for Escort Group A.

The midshipman was the son of Heinz von Korbach, a captain in a Waldeck infantry regiment shipped to fight in the British Army during the American Revolution. When he arrived in Charleston, Heinz von Korbach and 70 other men in the regiment defected to the Americans. They helped Amos Laredo and the 4th Carolina Dragoons harass the British Army every time it ventured out of Charleston. By the end of the war, there were over 200 German soldiers under von Korbach's command.

All wanted to stay in the new United States, and von Korbach, like the rest of them, married a woman from South Carolina. Von Korbach senior insisted that each of his sons either join the militia, the U.S. Army, or Navy. They didn't have to make their service a career, but had to serve, and August chose the Navy.

Javier Jacinto managed to get him an appointment as a midshipman and admitted to the Fonseca-Laredo/N.E.S. academy in Kings Point. This was August von Korbach's first long deployment on a ship.

Jaco and several others stopped what they were doing when they heard a distant rumble. Most, like Jaco, looked at the sky and seeing no clouds, were sure the sound was gunfire.

"Maintop, did you hear that?"

"Aye, captain."

Jaco went to the forward edge of the quarterdeck railing. "Quiet on the deck. No talking."

He didn't need a threat because they all heard the sound. Then there was a stronger rumble followed by more sounds of gunfire.

"Deck, we make it out to be ahead on our starboard quarter."

"Deck, aye. Keep a sharp lookout for other ships."

ON BOARD *EQUATION*, 10:53 A.M.

From where he stood on the port side of the quarterdeck, Captain Hugh Gibson could clearly see Venom. To him, the corvette was more of an annoyance than a threat. Yes, it had powerful cannons but not many. His attention was on what would they find ahead and was it worth pursuing?

"Mr. Williston, I shall take a tour of the gun decks to see the damage firsthand. You have the deck."

"Aye, captain."

On the upper gun deck, the men had already cleaned up debris and were cannibalizing three of the gun carriages to see if they could get one that would replace one of the three 9-pounders that were out of action. As Gibson walked along, he could see where the 18-pound balls hit the side of the ship by the sections of wood that splintered on impact. The splinters coming from the inside of the hull's planking did most of the wounding.

On the lower gun deck, the damage was less because the hull was thicker, but there was significant damage as well. After short conversations with his gun crews, during which he congratulated them on their good work, he climbed up the companionway to the main deck and then onto the quarterdeck.

"Mr. Williston, how much longer do you think we should continue in this direction?"

"Dark, sir. *Venom* was either scouting for a squadron or a convoy. And the fact that she is running just a mile off our port side tells me that there's a fight ahead. It is most likely a convoy because our information says that the Americans have less than thirty ships in their Navy. So, my hypothesis is that there's a convoy up ahead somewhere. We just need to find it."

Gibson nodded, still not convinced, "I have half a mind to turn toward the so' west and resume our course to Bermuda. What say you?"

"Sir, I would wait. It costs us nothing, but then again, we might find several fat merchant ships to take as prizes. If the Americans follow what the

Royal Navy does, convoys of merchant ships are escorted by a small frigate, and two or three sloops of war or brigs. We should be able to defeat them."

Prizes!!! As the commodore of this squadron, he was entitled to the admiral's share of 12.5% plus his 25% as a captain. That would, he thought, make him a rich man.

"Mr. Williston, let's continue on this course. I shall go to my cabin to write in my log. Please send for me if anything changes."

ON BOARD *VENOM*, 11:09 A.M.

To Jeremiah Smythe's practiced eye, Equation was at least two miles behind its two consorts. Within a few minutes, Venom would be less than a mile behind and about mile to port of the middle Royal Navy frigate.

"Captain, what are you thinking?"

"Why do you ask that?"

"Sir, we have sailed together long enough so I can tell when your mind is working hard on a plan. You have that glassy look in your eyes!"

"O.K., Mr. Packwood. Before I do, how is Mr. Law?"

"Resting. The surgeon says he believes he got out all the wood, and by following Dr. Laredo's practices by keeping it clean with rum and fresh sea water, he may be able to keep it from getting infected."

"Good. When he is able, move him to his cabin, and the watch can ensure he is fed."

"Aye, sir. So, what is the plan?"

"My estimate is that the lead Royal Navy frigate is about to spot our ships. I want to put a spoke in their wheel, so to speak."

"Pray tell, sir, how would you do that? We've already traded broadsides with a 50-gunner, albeit at just over one thousand yards, and lived to tell our children. Now, what mad scheme have you worked up?"

"Simple.... Watch, and you, my good friend, will get to see the master at work!"

"As long as he doesn't get me killed, this should be fun."

"Quartermaster and Mr. Stanton, standby by to tack to starboard. New course will be due north, and the wind will be over our port fore quarter so we will be close hauled. The course may change slightly. Mr. Pimm, please ask Lieutenants Lincoln and Shelly to join me on the quarterdeck."

Seeing that the bosun had the men in position to handle the sails, Jeremiah ordered, "Tack to starboard, now. Bring us around smartly, quartermaster. New course due north."

Venom's bow came around smartly, and the two jibs slipped through the halyards and stays one right after another. Men holding the sheets to the booms let them play out as they went from over on the port side of the corvette's centerline to the starboard.

Jeremiah looked at *Equation* and then at the second Royal Navy frigate once *Venom* was steady up on its new course. He was trying to gauge when the corvette would cross the *Equation's* bow and *Godfrey's* stern.

ON BOARD *EQUATION*, 11:11 A.M.

There was confusion on Equation's quarterdeck. The midshipman of the watch was trying to relay the signals while at the same time Gibson was debating if he should ignore Venom's turn to pass between his ship and Godfrey.

"What did *Godfrey* signal?"

Gibson's impatient tone had flabbergasted the young midshipman named Standish who finally stammered out, "Sir, *Persistent* has spotted two of those corvettes and a small frigate as well as a convoy of eight merchant ships."

The pimply faced midshipman was standing by the railings with signal book resting on the rack containing the signal flags. "Standish, what have you signaled back?"

"Nothing yet, sir."

"Send disable frigates and corvettes first."

"Aye captain."

Gibson then looked at *Venom.* "Cheeky bastard, I'll say. He's going to shoot up *Godfrey's* stern. Standish, signal suggest you turn port to defend your stern."

Even after the signal flags were run up and acknowledged by *Godfrey,* the frigate continued straight ahead. Gibson, having engaged *Venom,* ordered his midshipman, "Signal, urgent you tack to port. Corvette has a nasty bite."

"Sir, there are no flags for nasty bite."

"Then spell it out."

What went up were "Urgent, tack to port" which was followed by "Corvette bites."

Still *Godfrey* hadn't turned.

"Deck, three enemy ships, one point off the port bow. Estimate five miles."

"Captain, aye. Mr. Standish, let loose our royals. We need to get *Equation* to the party."

ON BOARD *OSPREY*, 11:14 A.M.

The knot in Abner Jeffords stomach got tighter when he could see the sails of the Royal Navy ships. His ships in Escort Group B would be heavily outgunned in terms of the weight of broadside. However, the captains of his ships were well versed in the tactics they were to employ – maneuver, speed, long-range gunnery – against bigger ships.

"Mr. Denbow, signal *Viper* to engage lead frigate, *Cottonmouth* to take second ship. *Osprey* will engage both enroute to largest ship. Once they acknowledge my signal, send "Leave formation when *Osprey* tacks to starboard."

"Aye, sir."

"Let me know when they have responded."

"Deck, *Venom* in sight!"

"Where away?"

There was a noticeable pause, "Broad on the beam at about three miles."

"Is she damaged?"

"Only a few holes in her sails." Then the lookout added, "Sir, she's going between the last two British frigates and sailing due north."

It took a few seconds for Jeffords to process what he just heard and not only work out the geometry but also the impact it may have on the Royal Navy captains. It changed his plan.

"Mr. Denbow, signal *Cottonmouth,* tack now, engage first frigate."

About the same time as he heard his midshipman say *Cottonmouth* acknowledged the signal, he could see the corvette's bow starting to turn.

"Send to *Viper,* Tack on my command."

ON BOARD *VENOM*, 11:18 A.M.

Through a spyglass, Jeremiah could see blue-coated men looking at him through spyglasses. So far, *H.M.S. Godfrey* had not made a move to turn, and he wondered why. He found it hard to believe that the ship would let him cross its stern. What was he missing?

A glance to his starboard side and *Equation* was firing its port bow chaser at *Venom,* but the balls were falling short. Other than that *Equation* now had its royals unfurled, there was no change. And, even with the additional sails, the 50-gun frigate wouldn't be able to close the gap.

Jeremiah shifted his study to the stern of *Godfrey* trying to discern what size cannon it had in the stern. He handed the glass to his first lieutenant, "What size stern chasers does *Godfrey* have?"

Augustus Packwood studied *Godfrey's* stern carefully. "Two 6- or 9-pounders."

"That's what I think. Should we double-shot? We're at four hundred yards."

"Let's stick with a single ball. If we can put four balls down her gun deck, they will cause damage."

"Four hundred it is. Pass the word to Mr. Lincoln. I'll have Mr. Stanton let out the sails to give them a more level platform. Tell him I want six hits in the captain's cabin to break up his crockery! We open fire in about three minutes."

ON BOARD *H.M.S. GODFREY*, 11:20 A.M.

From the quarterdeck, Captain Simon Cuthbart looked down at the onrushing corvette with growing horror. Already, his ship was hampered by several broken ropes that connected the wheel to the rudder. Rats had gnawed away the hemp, and it broke. They were steering with the rudder bar, but it was, at best, cumbersome. Any turn would stop the work splicing the ropes.

Damn, those are big cannons! Cuthbart had never seen a small ship with such large guns that had to be 18-pounders. *Godfrey* was commissioned in 1799, and the 137-foot-long, 820-ton frigate was armed with twenty-six 18-pounders in her main battery. They were supplemented by four 9-pounders on the quarterdeck, but his bow and stern chasers were only 6-pounders. In his mind, they were noise makers.

He was wondering if the corvette would try to shoot heeled to port. That question was answered when he watched the crew release all three booms simultaneously. The American ship was level for only a few seconds when the first cannon fired.

The gunner's aim was good, and Cuthbart heard the splintering of glass as the ball went into his cabin, down the main deck, sending splinters flying just before it blew out the bulwark in the forecastle, just to the left of the bowsprit.

Ball two hit the stern of the ship, and Cuthbart heard and felt the impact. What damage it did was unknown. He could, however, hear the screams of wounded seamen. One of the 6-pounders in the stern barked, and he saw the ball hit the top of the corvette's bulwark. It sent splinters flying, but little damage.

Ball four from the corvette punched through the stern and ended its flight against the barrel of *Godfrey's* starboard #6 18-pounder. Shards of cast iron from the destroyed cannon and the ball itself shredded eight men.

Ball five hit near where ball four hit and widened the hole made by four. It too ended its flight against the breech of an 18-pounder, and more chunks of metal ripped men apart.

It was ball six that did the most damage. It hit about three feet to the right of where balls four and five punched through the planking and plowed into the rudder bar, breaking it in two. Knocked off course, it cut two men in half and took with it as it entered the aft hold, the ropes that would have connected the wheel to the rudder bar.

Now, *Godfrey* had no control over its rudder. Down below, the surviving carpenter and bo'suns mates were frantically trying to get a line from the ship's wheel to the broken rudder bar. Until they could get something attached, *Godfrey* couldn't steer.

Slowly, the frigate began to weathercock, and Captain Cuthbart ordered the sheets on all the sails to be let go. None of this was known to those on *Venom* that continued until it was 2,000 yards on *Godfrey's* starboard side. At that point, Cuthbart heard his lookouts tell him that the corvette was tacking to parallel his ship.

ON BOARD *EAGLE*, 11:26 A.M.

The singular aimed firing by Venom's gunners sent pulses of noise in all directions. For the lookouts and those on the Eagle's deck, they helped hone the direction to where the battle was being fought.

"Deck, three large sails, just above the horizon, three points forward of the starboard beam." There was a pause, "They're bloody English by the cut of their sails."

"Captain, aye. Distance?"

"Ten miles, no more."

"Deck, one of our schooners is in sight. Same bearing."

"Captain aye." A wave of relief flushed over Jaco Jacinto. He'd found Escort Group B, but it would be at least an hour before *Eagle* would be able to join the fight. Jaco wondered if he was too late. "Bo' sun, clear *Eagle* for action, load ball."

"Do you want us to run out?"

Jaco thought for a second. "No, not yet." Then he turned to the junior quartermaster's mate on the quarterdeck. "Please pay my respects to the officers when you ask them to join me on the quarterdeck."

ON BOARD OSPREY, 11:28 A.M.

Everything in Abner Jeffords' body – his gut, his brain, and his heart - said it was time. He started to spit out commands. "Mr. Barnsley, Mr. Otley, standby to tack on my command to starboard, new course due east. Mr. Denbow, signal Viper, Tack now."

Jeffords waited a few seconds so the 34-year-old Hosea Barnsley from Kittery, Maine, ensured his men were in position. Then he gave the order to tack. Once *Osprey's* bow started to turn, he glanced behind. The corvettes turned much faster than the bigger frigates, and the *Viper's* captain anticipated where he wanted his ship positioned, i.e., slightly to the inside of *Osprey's* track.

Once the frigate was headed east, Jeffords ordered, "Mr. Otley, keep us about one thousand yards from the first Royal Navy frigate."

Otley, who was a big, burly man from Savannah, Georgia, could control the ship's wheel with one hand. He responded with an "aye, captain" in his soft accent. He was the second-oldest man on the ship, with Jeffords being 56 and Otley 20 years his junior.

Jeffords stepped to the forward railing and not seeing his second lieutenant, yelled out. "Mr. Smythe!"

A blonde-haired young man appeared in the aft companion way. "Sir!" The 27-year-old lieutenant was a spitting image of his father, Darren. For him, the role of second lieutenant was a demotion of sorts since he had captained American Shipping & Passenger Lines schooners on trans-Atlantic runs. Darryl Smythe's choice was either accepting the billet or sitting out the war until a captaincy became available.

With the small number of ships in the U.S. Navy, the next round of captain assignments would go to those who had proved themselves in 1812. Both his father and Captain Jacinto told him to do his job with excellence, and he would have his chance because more ships were being built.

"Mr. Smythe, we're about to have a passing engagement at one thousand yards. Have your gunners aim and then reload smartly. I'd like two shots before we move onto the next target."

ON BOARD *PERSISTENT*, 11:42 A.M.

With three ships headed toward H.M.S. Persistent, Captain Benedict Robinson believed the advantage was his. As the American ships passed down either side, he could fire both his port and starboard batteries, each with thirteen 18-pounders. Once passed, he could wear to port and restart the action.

He had one of those small American corvettes bearing down on his port side. It had started angling at his ship, a move that would bring the three-masted schooner closer to *Persistent's* 18-pounders. The small frigate and the other corvette looked to pass his ship about 1,000 yards, right at the maximum effective range. However, he believed his starboard battery could get off a broadside at the frigate, reload, and then fire at the smaller corvette that was about a quarter mile behind.

Behind him, he could see *Godfrey* dead in the water with its sails luffed. What the problem was, Robinson didn't know other than it wasn't his to solve, at least at this moment.

Equation was coming under full sail, and in a few minutes, it would join the battle. It was still a mile away and wouldn't affect what happened in the next few minutes.

Robinson ordered his starboard battery to fire at the leading frigate almost at the same exact time as the American did. He was surprised when five 24-pound balls hammered into his ship, and the balls from his 18-pounders punched a few holes in the frigate's sails. He could not tell if they had any effect.

The American's gunners reloaded faster than his which also surprised Robinson, and more American balls hammered into *Persistent's* side. He could feel the ship shudder with their impact, and then that ship was past.

When the corvette was alongside, its gunners were firing, and so were his. He saw several balls hit, and then the foremast came down bringing the main with it. The small corvette slewed into the wind, and Robinson heard the cheers from the gun deck, which were followed by more cannon balls. The American had not struck his colors, so Robinson felt he was allowed to keep shooting.

"Sir, the American ship to port is tacking to port."

Robinson spun around and went to the port railing of the quarterdeck. *You're going to cross my bow at close range and hit my ship with your popguns hoping to force me to wear to port and expose my stern to your friends. However, I am going to foil your plan and will continue straight ahead and send cannon balls up your arse.*

The bellow of the #1 gun from *Cottonmouth's* starboard battery startled Robinson. He felt the impact when half the ball ended its flight in the base of his mizzen mast after passing through the port bow chaser gun port, turned three men into a pile of bloody pulp, and glanced off the breech of his #4 starboard 18-pounder. Shrapnel cut up a half dozen sailors.

Ball #2 took out the port bow chaser and the four other men remaining from the gun crew. It was ball #3 that did the most damage. After the ball shattered on the barrel of the #2 gun on *Persistent's* port side, a chunk of cast iron ripped open the gunner's flask of priming powder that floated down into the tub of slow match. At the same time, a piece of shrapnel ripped open the ready charge before goring its holder. As the man fell, the powder in the tub with the slow match exploded.

Embers set the dry canvas of the hammocks hung in nettings along the bulkhead on fire and very quickly turned the port side of *Persistent's* gun deck into an inferno. Men started running out of the confined gun deck as more ready charges of gunpowder began to burn.

On the quarterdeck, the first explosion, then the smoke, then the men running, the series of explosions that followed is what alerted Captain Robinson that his ship was in serious trouble. Quick-thinking men on the starboard battery fired their guns in a ragged broadside at the American ships and tossed the ready charges out the gun ports before they ran topside.

On deck, *Persistent's* bo'sun had already rigged the pumps, and he had the canvas hoses in the water so several men could hold the hoses and spray salt water on the flames. Meanwhile, the officers and bo'suns mates were swinging the ship's boats over the side so that they had better access to the fire.

Robinson went down the aft companionway only to see that the fire had spread down the entire port side of the ship. He could see the streams of water hitting the flames, but to him, it was akin to pissing into a stiff wind. His ship was doomed, and it was only a matter of time before the flames reached the magazine.

Climbing up the companionway, he knew that he didn't have enough space on the boats for his entire 260-man crew. But he hoped to save those he could. On the quarterdeck, he untied the halyard so the Union Jack would come fluttering down.

ON BOARD *VIPER*, 11:44 A.M.

The splinter wounds in Morton Gieger's right arm and leg were painful, but he had a ship to save. One of the balls from the British frigate's 18-pounders must have hit the foremast in the right place because it snapped cleanly in two. As it came down, it snapped the mainmast off at the lookout's position.

Viper's deck was covered with debris from where the 18-pound balls shattered the bulwark along the edge of the main deck. His second lieutenant, Henrik Kopf, emerged from the gun deck to report that two of the guns were out of action, and while no balls penetrated the layered wood, shrapnel from the balls that broke up when they hit the gun barrels killed four men and wounded eight more.

Geiger was weak from loss of blood and looked around for his first officer, Lawrence Vance. He spotted his body with its back against the aft railing of the quarterdeck. A large length of wood had speared him in the upper chest. Given the position of his head and hands, Geiger knew he was dead.

"Sir, let us get you below to your cabin. I'll have the surgeon come up to treat you." The voice was from Henrik Kopf.

"You're the captain now."

"Aye sir, *Viper's* hull is sound. The carpenter says he can fix the mainmast so we should be sailing soon."

Geiger nodded weakly, and then Kopf detailed two men to help their captain to his cabin and to fetch the ship's surgeon. Kopf found *Viper's* third lieutenant who reported the gun deck was ready for action, minus two guns on the port side.

The small shelter around the wheel looked like a porcupine with all the splinters stuck in its side, but the quartermaster was, except for a few splinters he plucked out of his body, unhurt. Kopf's inspection of the main deck found none of the ship's boats had survived. He told the bo'sun to save them as firewood.

ON BOARD *EQUATION*, 11:48 A.M.

From the port forward corner of his ship's quarterdeck, Gibson surveyed the scene ahead of him, first with his naked eye, then, when he found something of interest, his spyglass. The column of black smoke rising from Persistent told him why Captain Robinson hauled down his flag. Its long boats were rowing toward Godfrey, which was also lowering its boats.

For reasons he did not know, *Godfrey* had struck its colors. Knowing Cuthbart as he did, Gibson thought he must have had a good reason.

This left *Equation* alone against two corvettes and a small American frigate. This was, he thought, going to be a very nasty action. He ordered a tot of rum to be given to the crew immediately.

"Deck, another frigate approaching, two points off the port bow, under three miles."

"Can you make out its flag?"

"No, but by the make of its rigging it is not French, Spanish, or one of ours."

Gibson turned to his first lieutenant, "Apparently we have stuck our hand into a hornet's nest and are about to be stung."

"What sir, do you plan to do? We're outnumbered now four to one."

"Give a good account of ourselves. We have time before the American frigate arrives." Gibson ordered a slight change of course toward the larger of the three ships now bearing down on *Equation.*

ON BOARD *OSPREY*, 12:08 P.M.

A slight course alteration enabled Osprey to pass close astern of the ship he now knew as Godfrey. Jeffords didn't want to slow to discuss Godfrey's surrender, so he had his midshipman dip the Stars and Stripes in acknowledgement that Godfrey had hauled down its colors. He also steered clear of the boats that were going between the burning frigate and Godfrey.

How to attack a two-decker was his next problem. *Eagle* was in sight, but still too far from the fight. For a second, Jeffords debated whether he should wait for *Eagle* but decided against it. Escort Group B, less *Viper,* had the initiative.

"Mr. Denbow, signal *Venom,* you cross the stern. Then signal *Cottonmouth,* you take the bow." This was right out of their doctrine and left *Osprey* to exchange broadsides with the two-decker at over 1,000 yards.

Immediately after acknowledging the signal, Jeffords saw *Venom,* which was the closest ship to the Royal Navy ship-of-the-line, tack to starboard.

ON BOARD *EQUATION*, 12:17 P.M.

Gibson knew his ship was about to take damage. His calculus was that the six 18-pound balls from the corvette were a fair trade with the chance to exchange broadsides with the smaller frigate, which after counting the gunports, could only bring 12 guns to the fight.

This was also the first opportunity to get a close look at the corvette bearing down on his stern. The man who was the captain was young and, from the way he moved around the deck, confident. He also noticed for the first time, the corvette's narrow, raked bow and lean lines that told him the ship was fast.

"Mr. Standish, make sure the gun decks know that we need rapid, accurate fire to carry the day."

"Aye, captain, I already have, but I will go below to remind them."

"Do that!" *In order for us to survive this action, we must damage the small frigate to even the odds.*

Gibson looked at the approaching American frigate. It too had a narrow bow and from what he could see, a relatively narrow hull. He admitted to himself that the Americans built good-looking ships.

His study of the larger American frigate was jarred when the first ball from the American corvette crashed into *Equation.* It was followed in rapid succession by five more, each one causing his two-decker to shudder.

Gibson watched as the corvette passed astern and almost immediately, its captain was tacking to port for another pass. By the time the corvette arrives, he will be engaged with the small frigate.

To Gibson's relief, Standish appeared. "We've lost two more guns, but they are on the port side. Our gunners should give a good account of ourselves. I told them to fire as soon as their guns bear. The 12-pounders will be firing at maximum elevation."

"The butcher's bill?"

"Sir, I don't know. I suppose many."

The first 12-pounder fired, then the first 24-pounder. Smoke drifting aft obscured his view of the American ship. However, he knew *Equation* was being hit by the sound of hard oak being shattered. Its screeches were totally different and distinct from the sounds of cannon firing and the pain of wounded men.

The cannonade between both ships was furious and was nearing its end when a 24-pound ball from *Osprey* hit the planking just below the quarterdeck. Splinters flew as planks buckled. Three speared Gibson, who staggered back with one in his belly, another in his chest, and a third in his thigh.

Standish caught his captain before he fell to the deck. Both men could tell that Gibson was mortally wounded. "Standish, apparently I have blotted my copybook. Do with the ship what you feel best to save the crew. They're good lads...."

Thinking that continuing this fight was nonsense, Standish lowered Gibson's still bleeding but lifeless body to the deck and strode aft to haul down *Equation's* flag.

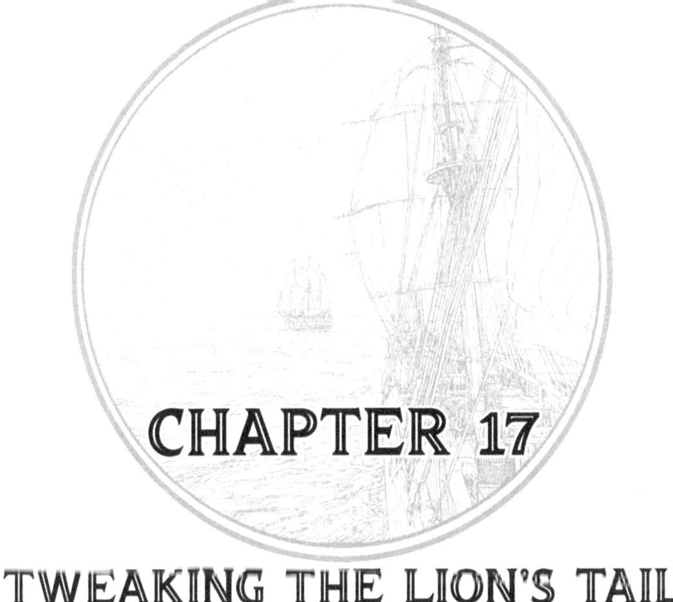

CHAPTER 17

TWEAKING THE LION'S TAIL

VICINITY 35°N 11°W, SECOND WEEK OF AUGUST 1812

The first tough decision Jaco had to make was what to do with the convoy. After talking with Abner Jeffords and the other captains on *Eagle,* the two relatively undamaged corvettes – *Copperhead* and *Venom* along with *Viper* would continue to Naples as planned.

Kestrel and *Eagle* would stay with the two remaining Royal Navy ships. *Persistent* had blown up, scattering planking and debris for a mile around the ship. Once they escorted them to a port to be sold, they would sail at best speed for Naples.

With the plan made for the convoy, the corvette captains left with instructions that Ezekiel Winters would be the escort group leader while Captain Geiger recovers from his wounds. Then, it was time to meet with the Royal Navy. Captains Robinson and Cuthbart and Lieutenant Williston had been waiting outside on the main deck and were now ushered into Jaco's cabin.

Jaco offered them a glass of port or Madeira and then pointed to the chairs as a way of saying this is going to be a discussion rather than he, as the victor, dictating terms.

"Captain Robinson, I understand you have taken command of *Equation,* is that correct?"

"Is the ship seaworthy?"

"Aye, 'tis. And also, I might add well-provisioned."

"Perfecto. *Godfrey,* what's the status of its rudder bar?"

"Cocked up, I'm afraid. We've tried splicing a spar, but where it is broken is by the rudder hinge. It needs to be hauled out of the water to be fixed properly. We have it in neutral now."

"Can your ship be towed?"

"I believe so if the weather and the seas cooperate."

Jaco nodded. "Here's what I propose. *Godfrey* transfers as many men to *Equation* as the fourth rater can accommodate. This way, if *Godfrey* flounders, we have fewer to rescue. I'd transfer any needed supplies as well. We will transfer the shot we can use and all the powder out of *Equation's* and *Godfrey's* magazines to *Osprey* and *Eagle.* Once that's done, we will get underway with *Equation* towing *Godfrey.* If that doesn't work, we shall set *Godfrey* afire. Agreed?"

The three Royal Navy captains nodded their heads.

"Gentlemen, I don't mean to be difficult, but I would like to hear the words aye or yes to come out of your mouths."

The Royal Navy officers said, "Aye, aye." Then, Captain Robinson asked, "Pray tell, where are you taking us?"

"That is an excellent question. Gentlemen, my first choice, given where we are, is Rabat. It is, according to my chart, about seventy miles away. If we tow at four knots, we should be there by supper tomorrow."

They had been underway for only three hours when *Eagle's* lookouts spotted a familiar-looking frigate. Darren maneuvered *Goshawk* alongside and said he had important information for Jaco. Once he was on board *Eagle,* both American frigates sped up while Darren told Jaco about his meeting with the Sultan. Then he said, "I have been working on a plan that will hurt the Royal Navy in ways they can't imagine."

After listening to Darren explain that there are no Royal Navy ships in Gibraltar. He believed that the Royal Navy is fitting out what is in ordinary in Portsmouth and the Medway to go to North America. It would, he opined, be months before they can be made ready for sea. Then he explained how he would give the Royal Navy a bloody nose.

Jaco nodded his head and smiled. "I like the plan. Are you asking my permission for this raid? And do you need *Eagle?*"

"Technically, both Medway and Portsmouth are in the area where I am supposed to be escorting the convoy to Amsterdam. My preference would be Portsmouth because that is the Royal Navy's main base. So, permission, no. Approval, yes. Want *Eagle,* yes. Need *Eagle,* no."

"Do it but be careful. If the Royal Navy captures you, if you aren't hung in a few days, they will put you in a dungeon so deep, no one will find you, not even me."

"Of that, my good friend, I am aware. But I have a few tricks up my sleeve that will make it difficult for my former comrades to find *Goshawk,* much less catch her."

RABAT, THIRD WEEK OF AUGUST 1812

As a teenager on board one of Max Laredo's ships, Jaco had been to Rabat and Casablanca. He'd also been there after the war as the captain of a merchant ship, so the harbor was vaguely familiar. Darren's notes on where to anchor were helpful. Both Equation and Godfrey managed to anchor without hitting each other.

When they stopped, Jaco could see *King Edward* tied to the end of a pier. He could see the Royal Navy sailors lining the deck of what was their prison. The xebec with an emissary to the British admiral commanding its Mediterranean squadron based in Gibraltar had left the same day as Darren. By now, Jaco thought, it was already there, if not approaching the British fortress.

Colonel Harrak was grinning as he enjoyed the honors as he boarded *Eagle.* After being introduced, he asked, "Captain Jacinto, do you know a Captain Smythe?"

"I do. He had just left Rabat when I saw him a few days ago." What was unstated was that now you know I know the deal Darren worked out with Sultan Mawlay Sulayman bin Mohammed.

"Excellent. His Excellency would like to meet you. Have you been to my country before?"

"I have, three times as a younger man. I love tagine." Harrak smiled. "Let us not keep His Excellency waiting."

When ushered into the throne room, Jaco could smell what was being cooked. He didn't know what was being made, but the spices reminded him of the dishes his mother often made using recipes from southern Spain.

The negotiations followed the same pattern, and the Sultan agreed to pay £12,000 (~£1,090,624 or ~$1,363,280 in January 2026) for *Godfrey* and £18,000 (~£1,635,936 or ~$2,033,920 in January 2026) for *Equation.* When he walked out of the palace, he had the same letters for *Kestrel* and *Eagle* that Darren carried. When he reached Naples, he would have them put on the fast N.E.S. owned packet ships that were now going from New York to Naples with occasional stops in Pauillac.

Three days after they arrived in Rabat, *Eagle* and *Kestrel* departed. *Kestrel* had enough wood taken from the Royal Navy ships to repair the damage to its bulwarks. Half of the powder and shot that they could not safely store on board the ships went into the Sultan's magazines. He would not allow private citizens to have gunpowder, but agreed that when U.S. Navy ships arrived, if they needed powder or shot, he would sell it to them at the price Darren negotiated.

ARCACHON BAY, FRANCE, FOURTH WEEK OF AUGUST 1812

Goshawk glided to a stop just before six bells rang, saying it was three hours into the Morning Watch. From the quarterdeck, the first hints of light were on the eastern horizon.

When *Goshawk* dropped anchor just outside Arcachon Bay, thirty or so miles so' so' west of Bordeaux, no one paid attention to the American frigate. On the main deck, the men lowered the long boat into the water and raised the sail.

Darren Smythe, Third Lieutenant Oliver Cranston, Midshipman Hugo Radcliffe, and seven other sailors stepped into the boat. Once it pushed off, the long boat with mainsail and jib sheeted home, the 20-foot-long boat headed into the harbor. Destination - the fishing village of Andernos-les-Bains.

While the boat was sailing in, they waved to the fishermen heading out toward the Bay of Biscay to fish. Whatever they caught, would be sold that afternoon in the market.

The long boat with one of the quartermaster mates at the tiller, crunched gently onto the sand just south of the fish market. Cranston, who was from

New Orleans and spoke French, along with two sailors, jumped out and headed into the city. Their job was to buy eggs, cheeses, and smoked meats.

Darren was on another mission. With Radcliffe's effortless and rapid-fire French, they were quickly directed to a man who had several fishing boats for sale. Leonard Gaskins, *Goshawk's* carpenter mate and grandson of Leo Gaskins, who was *Scorpion's* carpenter, looked over each boat in succession.

When he found two seaworthy boats that were at least 20 feet long and had a small, covered area in the front, the haggling began. At first, the seller only wanted to sell the hulls and the masts. Sails and even the rudder cost extra, but Darren didn't care.

The price, two 20 Franc gold Napoleons that were minted in Bordeaux, was more than reasonable. They were finishing when Lieutenant Cranston walked up with two of his sailors pushing large wheelbarrows full of food and a man with a horse-drawn wagon.

The newly purchased boats were pushed into the water, the sails rigged, and both were sailed around close to shore for a few minutes. Satisfied, Darren handed the boat broker two 20 Franc Napoleons. Another 20 Franc Napoleon went to the man with the wagon.

By the beginning of the First Watch, men at the capstans were pushing hard to a sea shanty to pull the starboard anchor up first. Then the port anchor came up, and *Goshawk* fell off to port and headed into the Bay of Biscay.

OFF PORTSMOUTH, U.K., FIRST WEEK OF SEPTEMBER 1812

Goshawk glided to a stop just after the tones from the ship's bell ringing eight times and the bo'sun's somber announcement that the Second Dog Watch had ended and the First Watch had begun. On the darkened ship, the first of the two boats bought in Andernos-les-Bains, were hoisted over the side. Already under the covered area, improved with additional wood to keep the five 50-pound barrels of course gunpowder dry, along with four oars, was a tub of slow match that was already glowing.

Once it was in the water, Midshipman Hugo Radcliffe followed the other two sailors down into the boat. They raised the sail and then pushed off. When the second long boat touched the water, four men climbed down into it, raised the sail and jib, and pushed off.

Sitting on Hugo Radcliffe's lap was a crude chart copied from an Admiralty chart on which Darren had written notes. He sat at the aft end of the boat just forward of the quartermaster so he could easily direct him.

With the wind from the nor' west, the fore-and-aft rigged boats sailed close hauled and slightly heeled over. Ahead, all the men could see the lights of Gosport, the town where their captain grew up, on their left and the Royal Navy base to starboard. The lanterns that lit the streets of the naval base and the edge of the docks made it easy to navigate.

To help understand where he was, Hugo looked left and right. Coming up on the third buoy on the right side of the channel, the lights in Southsea Castle burned brightly, as did the light at Southsea Common.

The buoys, Captain Smythe told him, were red-painted barrels tied to an old brass cannon sitting on the seabed. He could barely make out the barrels on the far side, over 100 yards to his right. Occasional glints of moonlight on the paint made them easier to see.

Getting into the harbor was not what worried Hugo, it was finding *Goshawk* on the way out. The land narrowed, and suddenly, they were in Portsmouth harbor. Dead ahead were four ships, which he recognized as frigates rafted together. He couldn't see the hawsers connected to their anchors, but he was sure they were present. To their right, there were three larger ships, also anchored, and in the moonlight, their crosstrees were bare, telling Hugo that they didn't have any sails. The four frigates had furled sails on all their spars.

He crawled forward and laid a thick run of fine gunpowder down the keel of the boat. With that done, the quartermaster aimed the small fishing boat at the four frigates.

The long boat was only a few feet away when the sailor in the bow slipped over the side and was quickly picked up. Next over the side was the quartermaster. Hugo lit the cloth stuffed into the top of a bottle of rum and nestled it against a rib. It flared and then burned like a candle. To make sure, he lit a candle, melted the bottom, and stuck it to the keel.

Gently, he slipped over the side and was hauled onto the second longboat that tacked around and raced toward the harbor entrance. Hugo, along with his two shipmates, was grinning as they shivered in the cool night air.

The fishing boat sailed true. It hit the bow of the third ship in the raft, a 36-gun *Flora*-class frigate. The impact caused the bottle of rum to fall over, and its flame, along with that of the candle, lit the fuse. Just after the boat wedged between the two ships, the 250 pounds of gunpowder exploded.

Both frigates now had large holes in their hulls at the waterline, and, in addition to burning, they started to sink. The fire spread to the other two frigates, whose skeleton crews began jumping over the side to swim to shore.

Radcliffe had found the first buoy on the right side of the channel when they heard an explosion. All they could see was the glow of the fires.

Hugo spotted *Goshawk's* silhouette and had the quartermaster who had the tiller steer straight for the frigate. He wasn't worried about the depth of water that averaged seven to nine feet.

Darren Smythe greeted them as they came on board. *Goshawk* was just starting to get underway when the magazine on one of the frigates exploded. It set off sympathetic detonations of the other three.

What none of them could see was the rain of debris landing on the streets of Gosport, Portsmouth, and the Royal Navy base. Darren wondered if his father's house and the Smythe & Sons factory were damaged by the falling wood.

By the time dawn broke, *Goshawk* was 60 miles to the so' east, well past Bournemouth in the south of England, and headed into the Celtic Sea.

LONDON, FIRST WEEK OF SEPTEMBER 1812

To say that the First Naval Lord was angry was an understatement. It had been a bad two days. Yesterday, the sloop-of-war arrived from Gibraltar with the demand notes saying that if the Royal Navy wanted the three ships back, the price was £70,000 (~£6,361,972 or ~$7,952,465 in January 2026) and plus another £50,000 (~£4,544,266 or ~$6,580,333 in January 2026) for the crews. Payment was to be in gold sovereigns, and the PM told him that he would have to take the payment and repair costs for the ships from the Royal Navy's current accounts.

Vice Admiral of the Red and Second Naval Lord Stacey Davidson stood outside the First Naval Lord's office to let the commander tell his boss that he was here. "Good morning, sir. What is so urgent?"

"Read this!"

Admiral Dundas handed his deputy the report that he had just received from Portsmouth. It detailed the sinking of the four frigates but also of three 74-gun third-rated ships-of-the-line that were damaged waiting to be pulled to a dock to be readied for sea. As he watched Davidson read it, he said, "I know it is early, but would you like to join me in a stiff drink. I need one."

"I'll join you. Scotch, sir."

While the First Naval Lord poured from the decanter, Davidson put the report on the Admiral's desk. As he slid it to the center with the tip of his index finger, he said, "Sir, I am not surprised. Captain Jacinto made it a habit of raiding our ports. If I remember correctly, he burned Aberdeen and Stornoway on one visit. Then, he set fire to a squadron getting ready to escort a convoy forming in the Caribbean during their War for Independence."

"So, you think this is Jacinto's work?"

"Or Captain Smythe."

"Aye, a man several of my predecessors refused to keep on active duty."

"He was just one of many, but yes. Captain Smythe was, at the time, one of our best young captains."

"You do know that their *Constitution* sank our *Guerriere,* to name just one other frigate we lost to these Americans."

Davidson didn't say anything. Instead, he sipped from his drink to keep himself from saying what was on his mind.

"Stacey, go ahead and say it, I told you so."

"You said it, sir, so I don't have to."

"What do you recommend?"

"Sir, the only two things we can do that will work. Blockade their major ports – Boston, New York, Philadelphia, Chesapeake Bay, Charleston, and Savannah. We let our privateers hunt their merchant ships. For those frigates that escape the blockade, we must accept the losses and hunt them in small squadrons. This will not be easy, and you, as the First Naval Lord will bear the brunt of the complaints from the House of Commons. I fear one on one, our ships will be found wanting."

"Captains or ships?"

"Both, sir."

Dundas took a sip of scotch, and Davidson took the opportunity to ask, "Sir, how many men is the Sultan holding in Rabat?"

"Eight fifty, give or take."

"And the ships?"

"Repairable. *Godfrey* will need to be pulled into a dry dock to fix her rudder."

"Then pay the Sultan. We can have those three ships back at sea and crewed faster than we can bring ones out of ordinary."

"I suppose you are right. I'll authorize the payment, but it will mean cutbacks elsewhere. Where I don't know, but everyone will feel the pinch. The PM is not going to the House of Commons to get the money. He says this is a Royal Navy problem."

Davidson put down his empty glass. The alcohol was making him feel a bit lightheaded. "Sir, let me pull the muster sheets of *King Edward, Equation, Persistent,* and *Godfrey,* and see what ships that are coming off the ways that need crews. Or, if it is best to keep them on their ships."

"When they are returned, I want to talk to the captains."

"As do I. We may learn a thing or two. Along with their sailing orders, I sent a printed sheet that gave my best information on the American ships and their tactics."

"I'd like to see that."

"I'll have my secretary bring it to you as soon as I return to my office."

Davidson started to leave when the First Naval Lord spoke, "Stacey, do ever want to go back to being the captain of a frigate and only have to worry about your crew and how to defeat an enemy?"

"Aye, sir, I do every day."

"Me too."

CHAPTER 18

KEEPERS OF THE FAITH

NEW YORK, SECOND WEEK OF SEPTEMBER 1812

The annual planning event went on as planned without those who were on active duty. Many of the men who served on the Fonseca-Laredo and the American Shipping & Passenger Lines ships were on the frigates and corvettes that had gone to sea.

As planned back in June, Laura Fonseca Laredo had taken over management of AS&PL, which was, despite the war, running a ship to London every other week. So far, none of its schooners had been stopped. And, so far, none of the English papers they brought back mentioned any Royal Navy losses to the U.S. Navy. But then again, everyone at the table understood that the papers the AS&PL schooners brought to the U.S. were at least two weeks out of date.

The two convoys, each of which contained four Fonseca-Laredo ships, were expected back by mid-October. They were only eight ships out of their fleet of 22.

Another four were in the Caribbean collecting barrels of rum and molasses and crates of coffee, cocoa beans, and raw sugar. Two more were en route to Morocco to pick up spices in exchange for rice via a southern route that they hoped wasn't patrolled by the Royal Navy. Two were in Charleston, one in Savannah, loading lumber, cotton, and indigo, while two more were in Hampton, Virginia, loading crates of dried tobacco leaves. All were destined for ports in Italy and Sweden.

Only one ship of the firm's 22 was not at sea carrying cargo. It was being refitted in a yard in Baltimore.

Already, they could see the blockade because every two or three days, a Royal Navy frigate would sail by the entrance of New York Harbor. They assumed its lookouts were taking inventory of the ships anchored in the harbor.

The captains of the AS&PL ships reported that there were typically one or two frigates loitering three to five miles off the harbor mouth. The AS&PL captains who sailed the packets from Boston to Savannah and then around to New Orleans reported seeing Royal Navy frigates off the entrance to Delaware and Chesapeake Bays as well as Charleston and Savannah.

Given the entrances to the harbors, the merchant ship captains were confident that they could enter and leave New York, Boston, and both the Chesapeake and Delaware Bays at night. This would mean that if they neared the entrance just after dark, by dawn, they would be 50 miles at sea. The only risk was if, at dawn, they stumbled on a Royal Navy frigate.

Both Max Laredo and Javier Jacinto understood the risks. They were the same as they faced during the War for Independence. Laura remembered that her father's firm was close to bankruptcy due to the loss of ships to the British. The decision on how many of their ships they would risk was up to Laura, but both Max and Javier wanted to discuss her plans with the understanding that they may change.

From a U.S. Industries perspective, they had the most financial risk in the shipping company, which was highly profitable. However, without cargoes to carry, they would still have to pay their loans, storage, and docking fees for ships and crew salaries.

Financial services were also affected by the war. It too had risk from outstanding loans and investment in firms that might be affected by the war.

But the real cash and profit cow was the import and export business. Last year, sensing that war was coming, Javier had directed his son Gento to find other products to sell that were not imported or exported. Over the year, he and Amos Laredo suggested businesses to either acquire or negotiate contracts to buy or licenses to make their products.

As he sat listening to Gento describe his plans, he could feel himself getting angrier by the minute. Gento had done little of what was suggested. Yes, there was a deal with the Rittenhouse and Wilcox paper mills in

Pennsylvania and another one that took half the wine produced by the Fontaines and one of their neighbors who started making wine.

What Gento called his flagship deal was the expansion of American Saw. It now made hammers, nails, saws, chisels, hatchets, axes, and adzes that were shipped to every state. But that, in Javier's mind, wasn't enough.

Controlling his anger, Javier asked, "What else have you investigated that has promise?"

Gento rattled off two that were, to Javier, pie in the sky. "Have you contacted the Lowell's in Massachusetts. They are looking for investors, and I believe the bank is discussing that venture right now."

His son said nothing, and Javier slammed the palm of his hand on the table. Few of the people at the table had ever seen him display this much anger. He, like Max Laredo, was the calm no matter what storm was brewing around them. "Damn you, Gento. This is a golden opportunity, and you have done nothing. You should have traveled with Rafer and said to the Lowell's that we'll take a quarter or half of what they produce!"

"But father, we don't have customers."

Javier's words spat out of his mouth like shells from a rapid-fire cannon. "Then find them. Every general store like the one in Charleston sells cloth. We can make money by bringing the ginned cotton from Charleston and Savannah to Boston. Then make money again when the cloth is sold."

Javier's words hung like a sword. Gento's face was bright red as he flushed with embarrassment from the power of his father's words. "I'll look into it, Father."

"No, by God, you will do it. And if you can't figure it out, I'll find someone who will!"

No one said anything at the table until Javier said, "I apologize for my outburst. Rafer or Greg, would you please introduce Gento to the Lowell's. Turning to Nathan, he asked, "Nathan, ask your friend Philippe to talk to Gento and explain how he built his wine distribution business. I suspect that many of the stores that buy the wine he peddles also sell other things, like cloth. If not, maybe they can make some introductions. I suspect that somewhere in U.S. Industries, there is a young man or two or three who would like to make a living selling cloth to stores and tailor shops."

55 NM EAST OF SABLE ISLAND, FIRST WEEK OF OCTOBER 1812

The long, crescent-shaped island that was about 165 nautical miles east of Halifax was visible to Goshawk's lookouts. From back when he was in the Royal Navy, Darren knew about the uninhabited Sable Island claimed by the British and considered part of Canada. If nothing else, it was a landmark confirming that they were about 550 nautical miles or four and a half days from Boston.

Escort Group A had, while they were in Amsterdam, collected a dozen more ships owned by Americans plus eight from Fonseca-Laredo. The captains managed to get out of Edinburgh, Southampton, and London before the British government, upon receiving the declaration of war, seized their ships and cargoes.

Others, Darren suspected, were either seized in Bristol and Liverpool or were making their way back to the U.S. After its raid on Portsmouth, *Goshawk* doubled back through the English Channel that night and pulled into Amsterdam to resupply and wait for the convoy.

Again, since it was early fall, the convoy went north and passed through the gap between the Faroe and Orkney Islands before heading west so' west into the Atlantic. Luckily, the weather was fair as they tacked back and forth against the prevailing westerlies.

Ahead of the 20-ship convoy, *Rattlesnake,* commanded by Micah Jacinto, was today's scout. As per their doctrine, he would take the corvette out to 25 – 30 nautical miles ahead on the base course and then turn downwind, if possible, or in this case, crosswind for two hours or about 20 nautical miles. Then, unless his lookouts had spotted a Royal Navy ship, he would sail back to the convoy.

The four warships – *Goshawk, Kestrel, Cobra,* and *Copperhead* – sailed at each of the corners of the convoy box that was five rows of four ships each. They were entering the area where, if the convoy was going to run into a Royal Navy squadron, this was it.

Darren was sitting in his cabin debating how he should rank his officers, warrants, and mates. Before he left, Jaco and he had told the crews that, assuming the U.S. Navy had more ships, there would be promotions. Also, the plan was to give the crews a break before the next deployment.

Then, there was prize money to be paid out. In the magazine, there were two chests filled with gold sovereigns totaling £13,000. The U.S. Government would keep 12.5% or £1,625 (~£147,688 or ~$184,610 in January 2026). As the captain, Darren would pocket 25% or £3,250 (~£295,377 or ~$369,221 in January 2026).

His three lieutenants, two Marine officers, and surgeon would divvy up 12.5% or £1,625 or £270 16 shillings per officer (~£59,292 or ~$74,115 in January 2026). His warrant officers – the bo'sun, quartermaster, carpenter, sailmaker, gunner – would split an 12.5% or another £1,625 or £325 each (~£71,159 or ~$88,949 in January 2026).

The 12 mates and midshipman divide another 12.5% or £1,625 and receive £125 each (~£27,368 or ~$46,585), and the remaining 25% or £3,250 would be divided amongst the remaining 200 members of the crew. Each man would receive £16 4 shillings (~£3,558 or ~$4,448 in January 2026)

For all on board *Goshawk,* it will be a very nice payday over and above their wages.

ON BOARD *RATTLESNAKE*, THE SAME DAY, 12:03 P.M. LOCAL TIME,

Rattlesnake had been running so' east for almost an hour on the bottom of the triangle after tacking when the lookout called, "Deck, small ship, two points broad on the beam at four miles."

"Deck, aye. Can you tell what type?"

"Either a really small frigate or a sloop-of-war."

"What course?"

"Roughly so' west."

Same base course as the convoy which means ...

"Deck, she's setting her royals."

... she is Royal Navy. Probably a packet carrying dispatches which means she is worth chasing.

"Gentlemen, we're about to give chase. On my command, standby to come about to new course, so' by east."

Micah waited until his bo'sun had the men in place to handle the sheets for the main sails and jib before he gave the order to tack. Once *Rattlesnake* was steadied up on its new course, he ordered a second jib to be flown. Whether or not it gave the corvette more speed, he wasn't sure, but every tenth of a knot counted.

From the reports from the lookouts, *Rattlesnake* was angling toward the unknown ship and gaining. By now, those awake had come on deck to see why the ship had changed course. It was time to awaken those who were still asleep.

Micah saw his First Lieutenant Melvin Norburg. He was a native New Yorker, and his family was a member of the same congregation as the Jacintos. Norburg looked like a male version of his Aunt Shoshana, well over six feet tall with long blond hair. He looked like a Viking because his family emigrated from Malmö, Sweden, just after the War for Independence. "Mr. Norburg, clear for action, load ball…"

"Deck, ship just broke out the Union Jack! We're about two miles on her starboard quarter."

Micah yelled, "Deck, aye." Then he looked at Norburg, "As I was saying, load ball and run out. I want to show the Royal Navy we're ready for action."

Norburg nodded, and already he could see men readying the ship for a fight. He took the speaking trumpet from the binnacle and looked up. "Lookouts, how many gun ports?"

"Eleven. She's run out, sir, and they look like 9-pounders! There are what look like three 24-pounder or 32-pounder carronades on the quarterdeck."

"Deck, aye." *We won't get close enough for them to be effective.* Micah could now see the ship clearly with the naked eye. Its captain had staysails set along with his royals telling him that the captain really wanted to get away, not stay and fight. Staysails meant that his crew had more sails to handle which meant he couldn't tack or wear his ship as easily.

Rattlesnake was catching the sloop at an angle that was probably making eight, maybe nine knots. *Rattlesnake,* according to the log taken at the beginning of each watch, was making 10. Now that they were close, the gain, which was about 30 – 40 yards a minute, was barely noticeable.

"Mr. Norburg, we're going to maintain this heading, cross her stern at I think about four or five hundred yards." Norburg went forward and spoke with the two lieutenants on the gun deck and re-emerged.

Just as Micah was about to give the order to fire as your guns bear, the sloop began to wear to port. Micah ran to the forward quarterdeck railing. The Royal Navy crew had dropped the staysails to the deck and were hauling its yards around so that the sloop would run with the wind. Micah could now read the name on the stern. The sloop was *H.M.S. Gar.* "Fire if your guns bear!"

Two of the six balls hit, and those on the deck could see wood flying from the impact of the 18-pound balls from their long 18-pounders. Micah cursed at himself aloud for not anticipating the move by the Royal Navy captain.

Once past *Gar's* stern, Micah ordered his crew to wear *Rattlesnake* to port. Again, it was going to be a game of catch-up. He stood next to the shelter around the wheel and told his quartermaster that he wanted to stay about six to seven hundred yards to *Gar's* port."

Gar's gunners manning the carronades on her quarterdeck and the big balls made huge splashes as they fell about 100 yards short of *Rattlesnake.* The bark of the 6-pounders on *Gar's* quarterdeck sounded like, in comparison, that of a small yappy dog.

Micah felt as if he were bulletproof as he watched the Royal Navy sailors reload the two carronades. The aftmost one was being pulled into battery when the #1 cannon on *Rattlesnake's* port side bellowed. Seconds later, large chunks of wood flew as the ball hit *Gar* just below the quarterdeck between the two carronades.

Micah could see the quarterdeck sagging, and when the gunner yanked on his lanyard to fire the carronade, the recoil ripped the restraining ropes out of the weakened planking on the aft side. The gun's momentum and the ropes on the forward side caused it to turn. First, the wheels and then the entire gun fell through to the deck below.

Gar's gunners fired its 9-pounders. Nine of the 11 balls managed to reach *Rattlesnake.* Those that hit the hull didn't penetrate. Two went through the mainsail on the mainmast, and one splintered the top longboat in the stack of three between the fore and mainmasts.

Suddenly, *Gar* started turning to starboard. Surprised, Micah watched the ship turn toward his. Alarm bells went off in his mind. "Bo'sun, tack to port, NOW!!! Quartermaster, turn port to nor' nor' east."

Rattlesnake's port cannons continued to fire until there was no target. The corvette's bow came about, and the ships missed hitting each other by about 50 yards. Musket balls from Royal Marines filling the rigging filled the air. Many of them were aimed at the quarterdeck, and Micah heard more than one smack into the planking around him. The two swivel guns at the lookout position on *Rattlesnake* barked, each sending 25 one-ounce musket balls down at *Gar.*

He turned to see his first lieutenant holding what was left of his right arm lean over the edge of the quarterdeck railing and yell. "Starboard battery, Fire!!!"

Norburg slumped to the deck, and the quartermaster mate rushed to tie the scarf he wore around his neck around Norburg's upper arm to stop the bleeding. Micah didn't hear the mate yell for someone to help Norburg to the ship's surgeon.

The lieutenant's command was drowned out by the blast and the bellow of the #1 cannon on the starboard side. Flying glass, wood and other material could be seen on *Rattlesnake* as the ball hit the corner of the captain's cabin. One right after another, the remaining five cannons fired with each ball doing its best to turn the sloop into a floating wreck.

Once *Rattlesnake's* stern was past *Gar's,* Micah waited. The question in his mind was how long he would wait until he wore his corvette around to starboard to re-engage, and at what range. He ordered the ship to turn to starboard so that it would come parallel to *Gar* at about 400 yards.

After the first two cannons fired, someone on *Gar* hauled down its flag. Micah ordered his quartermaster to allow *Rattlesnake* to get within 100 yards when he picked up the speaking trumpet. "*Gar,* Heave to immediately!"

"Aye, we will luff up into the wind."

Micah could see smoke curling out of the forward grating. "*Gar,* are you on fire?"

"Aye, we think we have it under control."

The ships glided to a stop, and Micah boarded the longboat that took him to *Gar.* Once on the deck, a man not much older than he came up to him. His coat was bloody, and Micah was not sure if it was from his wounds or helping others. "I am Captain Piers de Vere, commander of His Majesty's sloop-of-war *Gar.*"

De Vere held out the hilt of his sword. Micah took it and unsheathed the weapon to see the inscription and the etching that said it had been made by Wilkinson for an Anton De Vere. "Was this your father's?"

"No, great-great-grandfather. It was given to me when I was made lieutenant."

Micah slid the sword all the way back into the scabbard. "I cannot take this. Just don't attempt to use it on either my men or me, or you will not be able to present it to the next generation of De Veres."

The Royal Navy officer bowed and hooked the sword back on his belt. "For that I am grateful."

"My Lieutenant Jude Smithson is about to search your cabin while we discuss what will happen next."

"Captain Jacinto…." Micah turned and walked to the bulwark. "Sir, lookouts have spotted the convoy. Looks like *Goshawk* has detached and is heading our way."

Micah went back to Captain De Vere who was holding out two keys. "What you are looking for and what we tried to defend is in my cabin, assuming that your cannon balls did not blow them away.

The American's surprised look on his face told De Vere to explain. "There is a large sea chest with twenty-five thousand pounds in notes (~£2,272,133 or $2,840,166 in January 2026) under my bunk. The other is the dispatch box with correspondence for the Commander of the North American Station as well as a red Royal Mail bag."

Smithson took the key and disappeared with one of the other sailors who came on board with their captain. "Is *Gar* seaworthy?"

"I think so. Your cannon ripped us apart, and I am amazed that our masts are still standing."

"Dead, wounded?"

"I do not know yet. I suspect many of both. Do you wish to inspect your prize, and we can find out from our surgeon?"

"That is not necessary. Here are my terms. You will keep your ship until we arrive in Boston and will sail with our convoy. There, it will be turned over to either my Navy or a prize court for sale. From Boston, my government will arrange for your men to be taken to Halifax. How, or when I do not know." *I am not going to tell him that once in Boston, each member of his crew will be asked if he wished to become a citizen of the United States.*

"And any funny business on my part will result in an unpleasant retaliation."

Micah smiled. "Aye. Then you understand. Assuming you have two officers who survived, you will be my guest on *Rattlesnake* until we reach Boston."

"Aye captain, I do. I have been in your shoes before when I took a French privateer in the Caribbean."

Micah held out his hand. De Vere took it. "I wish our countries were not at war."

"Me too."

A man with a bloody shirt came up to the two officers. "Begging the captain's pardon, sir, but the surgeon asked me to bring you to Lieutenant Harrow. He's in a bad way."

De Vere nodded. "Did the surgeon tell you how many wounded?"

Aye, sir. We have sixteen dead and thirty-one wounded, six, including Mr. Harrow, won't see the morning."

"On that happy note, Captain Jacinto, if you'll excuse me."

"Go. Take your time, I shall wait."

NEW YORK, THIRD WEEK OF OCTOBER 1812

Escort Group B arrived back in New York two days after A arrived. It had escorted 18 ships back from Naples, which was 10 more than it took eastward. When the convoy arrived off the mouth of Chesapeake Bay, after dropping four ships off in Charleston, there was a Royal Navy frigate loitering 12 miles off the coast.

The Royal Navy frigate was estimated to be eight miles away when it was spotted in the middle of the afternoon. Jaco headed in its direction in *Eagle,* and the Royal Navy ship sailed east into the Atlantic. Given the time of day and where they were, Jaco decided not to pursue since the chase would continue into the night.

He thought it odd that this frigate was the first Royal Navy ship he had seen since leaving Naples. Considering that it passed through the Straits of Gibraltar and sailed about 100 nautical miles south of Bermuda, his convoy was fortunate.

After a joyful reunion with his family, the post-deployment work had begun now that the crews were paid off. *Eagle* was on the opposite side of a pier to *Goshawk. Kestrel* and *Osprey* were in Kittery. Three of the schooners are being refitted in Baltimore, and the other three in Philadelphia.

They, Darren and Jaco, were waiting for the answer to the letter they had sent to Secretary of the Navy Hamilton. The letter from the First Naval Lord laid out what the senior officer in the Royal Navy expected the Commander of the North American Station to do, i.e., aggressively blockade American ports, sink or capture U.S. Navy vessels when and where found, encourage privateers based in Canada to take American cargo ships.

The dispatch from the Fourth Naval Lord, the Rear Admiral of the Red who was responsible for building and repairing ships, stated the Royal Navy was short of hemp and planking. Yards under the North American Stations purview needed to conserve naval stores of all types and if they purchased needed naval supplies locally, ensure they met Royal Navy standards.

What the two officers were most interested in was the response to their letter that suggested a plan of action for 1813.

Secretary Hamilton

In light of our experience from our two squadrons, we would like to recommend the Navy consider the following courses of action against the Royal Navy. These take into consideration that we cannot build or acquire, nor have the desire to man enough ships to equal the number that the Royal Navy will send to our waters. However, we can make it extremely difficult for their blockade to be successful. These suggestions will also affect the purses of English businessmen and the tax revenue on which British government depends to fund this war.

Any of these recommendations can be implemented early next year with the ships that we recently commanded. Our premise is that the Royal Navy cannot be everywhere. War with us will stretch it thinner than it has been as it focuses on keeping the French, Spanish, and other navies from countries at war with Great Britain in port.

First, in late January or early February, frigates Eagle, Goshawk, Kestrel, and Osprey should sally forth in pairs to attack any Royal Navy frigates lurking off our coasts. With our harbors clear, our merchants can safely send their ships to sea.

Two, the six corvettes should be sent south into the Caribbean to capture His Majesty's merchant ships filled with rum, molasses, sugar, coffee, and cocoa, all of which are meant to fill the pockets of the British merchants as well as the Chancellor of the Exchequer.

While the corvettes proved their worth against the Barbary Pirates and privateers, with only 12 long 18-pounders, they are no match for the larger frigates in a one-on-one fight. Therefore, we recommend they hunt in small squadrons of three. We have the option to include Kestrel and Osprey in these squadrons. Their captains have demonstrated that they know how to defeat a large frigate.

Three, Eagle and Goshawk are allowed to roam up and down the Atlantic coast, or go to the Caribbean, where we think we can wreak havoc.

While U.S. Industries has agents on many of the islands in the Caribbean, the question of where our ships could be resupplied needs to be answered. Without one, Savannah or Charleston are the closest, but they are a week from the northern Caribbean. The Danish islands of St. Thomas, St. Croix, and St. Jan, or St. Ignatius could be used if either country will have us.

Please advise with instructions.

Very Respectfully,

Jaco Jacinto	*Darren Smythe*
Captain	*Captain*
U.S. Navy	*U.S. Navy*

The courier with their letter, their reports as well as those of all the captains, receipts for pay, prize money, and recommendations for promotion left two days after the ships docked. Both men wondered if the Secretary of the Navy would come and when.

NEW YORK, FOURTH WEEK OF OCTOBER 1812

Attendance at Friday night dinners was not optional for the Jacinto children. Jaco's younger sister Shannon, four years his junior, was married and had just announced that she was pregnant. Joshua, two years younger than Micah, already had a son who was two, and his wife said at dinner that she too was with child.

That left Micah. Unmarried and not courting. After dinner, when his siblings had left to go to their homes, Reyna asked, "Micah, when are you going to find a woman to marry?"

"Mother, last I checked, I just spent most of the year at sea. It is hard to court if one sees ocean during the day! That is unless you want me to look for a mermaid!"

"That's not an acceptable answer."

"Mother, who would I court?"

Jaco, who was sitting in his favorite chair in the corner, was trying not to become part of the conversation, but he knew it was coming. Reyna had been asking him to encourage Micah to start looking for a wife.

"I could think of many, all come from good families, either here or in Charleston. Do you want me to start making introductions?"

"No, mother, please don't. I will start looking."

"When?"

"I don't know. Tomorrow, the next day. Who knows!"

Reyna knew when to push and when to stop. "You know, your father and I knew we were going to marry ever since we were in Hebrew school."

"Yes, and I went to religious school in Charleston, and now we live in New York."

"That's why I will put out feelers if you agree to at least meet an eligible woman. You would be quite the catch. Not many men come with several thousand pounds of prize money and the potential title of managing director of a successful shipping company, to say nothing of being a war hero."

Micah knew his mother would not let go. *I don't want to be a catch. I want to love the woman I marry.* "Mother, I will agree if you agree that if I don't like the woman, then no courtship."

"How do you know you will like her if you don't court her?"

Micah rolled his eyes. "Aye, mother, but if after a few meetings, I will know, just like Darren and Marijke and you and father. So, if I say no, it is no."

Reyna decided to change the subject now that she'd gotten at least a partial victory. Micah took the opportunity to go up to his room. As he did, he thought about buying a house, but then again, when he was at sea, who would take care of it?

NEW YORK, THE NEXT DAY, 1:22 P.M.

Each day since Rattlesnake returned, Micah visited the members of his crew being cared for in a small boarding house. He felt it was his duty to do so since they were under his command, and therefore, his responsibility, when they were injured.

That was one of the reasons he was knocking on the door of the Norburg's house. Since he was from New York, Reyna and the ship's doctor agreed that it would be better for Melvin Norburg to be with his family.

A woman he'd never seen before answered the door. She was cradling a toddler in her arm and had lovely green eyes that Micah felt were looking into his soul. The woman's tone was not hostile, but direct, as if she had more important things to do. "Who are you and what do you want?"

"Micah Jacinto."

There was a look of recognition in her eyes, and the features of her narrow, but attractive face softened. "Ahhhhh, Melvin's captain, who comes every day. Please come in."

"Yes, ma'am. If this is a bad time, I can come back."

"No, Melvin is in the parlor. We just treated his arm, or to be more correct, what's left of it. Mother is putting a clean bandage on it now. Come." A nod of her head with thick brown hair tied in a bun at the back of her head.

Micah followed the young woman who had a petite figure that was narrow at the waist. Melvin Norburg brightened and started to stand. "Don't get up."

Norburg's mother nodded as she said, "Good Shabbos, Micah. Thank you for coming." Helga Norburg turned to the young woman holding a baby as she put the soiled bandages into a basket. "We'll leave you two alone, come Frieda. We can attend to your children."

Micah's eyes and head followed Frieda as she walked out of the parlor. Then he turned to his friend. "How are you doing. My mother says the infection is down."

"It is. I am beginning to feel much better and the pain is lessening each day."

"Good." Micah had come to talk about one thing, and now he was distracted.

Noticing his captain's interest in Frieda, Melvin volunteered, "After her husband died last winter, Frieda sold their farm up in Poughkeepsie, and she and her two boys moved in with us. She is now working in my father's apothecary and taking classes in chemistry and biology at Columbia."

Micah's head went up and down.

"She's six years older than me. Would you like to be properly introduced?"

The word couldn't come out of his mouth fast enough. "Yes."

Norburg pushed himself up and started to the door of the parlor. It was clear to Micah that the fever he had after the doctor finished the amputation a musket ball began when it ripped his arm off had weakened Melvin. He could see that over the past few days, Norburg's color had improved.

He came back with his older sister, who was wearing the same light blue busk she was wearing before. This time, she wasn't holding a baby.

"Freida, may I present Micah Jacinto, captain of the corvette *Rattlesnake* and a future Managing Director of American Shipping & Passenger Lines."

The woman curtsied and held out her hand. "We met a long time ago in Hebrew school. Thankfully, you didn't recognize me because back then, I had pimples all over my face."

"And I wasn't interested in girls."

"Not exactly true. You had eyes for Michele Greenberg and followed her around like a lost puppy until she told you to get lost!"

"Ouch. I had forgotten about Ms. Greenberg."

Frieda started giggling as she remembered Micah, the teenager. "You were so awkward around girls."

"I was." *And still am.*

"Please, let's sit so we can talk." Turning to her brother, "Do you think you can get us some wine?"

"I can." Laughing, he said, "It may take me a few trips."

"Micah, before this goes any further, you must know that I am a widow with two children, Harald is about to turn three, and Moses, is eleven months. My husband, Michael Blumberg, died of pneumonia last December, and we sold our farm so I am not without means. So, my last name is Blumberg."

Micah nodded. What Freida said made sense and he didn't know what to say.

"So, I gather, this conversation is about whether or not you could court me, am I correct?"

Micah nodded definitively and managed to say, "Yes."

Frieda started giggling, again. "Micah, you are the one supposed to be asking questions."

"My apologies, but I have been taken in by your beauty. And to be honest, I am floundering a bit." *Because I have never seriously done this before, and I don't know what to ask!*

"Interesting. So, the fearless captain of the corvette *Rattlesnake* and scion of one of the wealthiest families in New York, if not the country, is adrift. Did I use the correct nautical term?"

"You did."

Melvin stood up. "I think I will get mother to make some refreshments. I suggest you two sit on the porch out back, and I will act as your servant."

Frieda held out her hand. Micah took it and found it to be soft and warm. She led them to the porch that overlooked a well-kept yard and garden. There was a wicker seat that could seat at least four. Frieda sat on one end and wedged her back against the corner so she could face Micah, who sat at the other end.

NEW YORK, THIRD WEEK IN DECEMBER 1812

While it might have been cold outside, inside U.S. Industries' large conference room, the temperature was red hot. And the heat didn't come from the fireplace; it was anger.

On the conference table was a letter from the Secretary of the Navy. It was first read by Jaco Jacinto since it was addressed to him. He then passed it on to Darren Smythe, who handed it to Javier Jacinto, who had just arrived from Washington. Congress was on its holiday break.

The other two in the room, Max Laredo, Shoshana Jacinto, and Greg Struthers, also read the letter which now sat in the center of the table, untouched as if it was poisonous.

Secretary Hamilton wrote:

Commodore Jacinto,

It is my duty to order you to cease any repair and refitting efforts on the ships under your command. Please send receipts along with a statement of what work has been done and what will be needed to return the vessels in your squadron to full readiness.

Once the Congress either appropriates the money or borrows it, and I am assured that the shipyards will be paid their due, the work will resume. Please advise soonest that this order has been carried out.

One further note, I have resigned as the Secretary of the Navy effective December 31st of this year. My successor, as of the writing of this letter, has not yet been named.

Paul Hamilton

Secretary of the Navy

The first to speak was Greg Struthers, who, besides losing a leg during the American Revolution on *Alfred,* was the head of the financial services group of U.S. Industries. Under Greg were the Bank of South Carolina, the New York Bank of Commerce, U.S. Investments, and the recently formed business U.S. Industries Real Estate. He pointed to the letter, "This is all about money, or the lack of it. The Congress agreed to declare war but didn't want to appropriate money to pay for it. So, Congress can or will not appropriate the money, and we shall lose to the British. Or we, U.S. Industries, can act on behalf of our country."

Missing from what was the "inner circle" of U.S. Industries were Emily Smythe, who was home ill, Laura Fonseca Laredo, who was in Charleston on business, and Reyna Laredo, who was tending patients. Inside this room, they were co-workers and friends and were comfortable with forgoing formality. Javier, as the co-chairman of the board of U.S. Industries, spoke first. "Greg, what are you thinking?"

"Loans or bonds or both." Greg paused for a few seconds as he gathered his thoughts. "We could loan the Federal government sufficient money to pay for new ships or supplies for the Army and Navy to be paid back over, let's say, ten years with interest. Or we could issue bonds to sell which would be a loan but be held by an individual. Again, the term I suggest is ten years. Either or both would be paid back with tax revenue."

Greg wasn't finished. "The government benefits because we could make the loan quickly with funding pending Congressional approval. The bonds may take Congress to approve, but here's how the bond would work. Each one thousand dollar bond the New York Bank of Commerce sells on behalf of the government costs the bondholder eight hundred dollars. Bondholders would collect the full one thousand when the bank is paid back by the government plus four per cent interest. The bonds would be guaranteed by the Federal government, so there is little risk to the bondholder."

Javier was smiling. "I like it, and I think I can get our Democratic-Republicans friends to back this."

"And I think we can approach many of our wealthy depositors to invest in their freedom. We could call them Freedom Bonds."

Jaco leaned forward so he could see his father. "What do I do in the interim? This letter is a direct order."

"You comply with the instructions in the letter. We can use the information to decide if we want to send the ships to sea as either privateers or as part of the Navy. Our contract says if the Navy does not employ them, we can have them back."

"And the crews who are coming back to where the ships are expecting to sail in February?"

"Let's sort out the funding first. I shall leave early for Washington on the next packet and meet with the incoming secretary, whomever he may be, Speaker Clay, and the President. Then we will know what to tell the men."

CHAPTER 19

BIRDS OF PREY

WASHINGTON, FIRST WEEK OF JANUARY 1813

Immediately after arriving in Washington on the sixth of January, Javier contacted President Madison and Speaker Clay ostensibly to see who the next Secretary of the Navy would be. He was surprised when he was asked to come to the White House.

In the President's office, Javier was surprised to see two other men. Besides Speaker Clay and the President, there was an old friend from Charleston, William Jones. Jones also ran a successful import and export business, mostly bringing manufactured goods in from England before he moved to Philadelphia.

William Jones greeted Javier heartily. After shaking hands, Javier put his left hand on Jones' right shoulder. "Pray tell, Mr. Jones, what are you doing here?"

Jones turned to the country's leader, "Mr. President, I think it best you explain."

Madison waved to the couch and waited until each visitor was served a cup of coffee or tea, whichever was their preferred morning drink. "Congressman Jacinto, your enquiry was quite timely. I have officially nominated Mr. Jones to be the next Secretary of the Navy. While I know you do not sit in the Senate and cannot vote on his candidacy, what say you?"

"Mr. President, without hesitation, I would vote for Mr. Jones's confirmation as the next Secretary of the Navy. May I tell the Federalist leader in the Senate of your opinion."

"Please do. There are only seven Federalists in the Senate so you don't need your votes. However, I shall endeavor to speak with each Federalist in the Senate when Congress reconvenes."

"Thank you."

"Sir, if I may, I have two other pressing matters that I would like to discuss. Both involve Mr. Jones, assuming he is confirmed, and Speaker Clay. The topics should interest you, Mr. President."

"Congressman, if they concern defeating the British, then they interest me."

Javier looked at Speaker Clay and then at William Jones. Then, he decided to address the most senior member in the room. "Mr. President, the topics are one, funding the war, and the other is how best to employ the ships Naval Escort Services has seconded to the Navy."

Madison's body language and facial expression said continue, and Speaker Clay was listening. Even though they opposed each other on many issues, Speaker Clay respected Javier and the ideas he brought to the House of Representatives.

"We, that is, U.S. Industries, through New York Bank of Commerce and the Bank of South Carolina, are in a position to help the government fund the war via two methods. One would be an outright series of loans that the Federal government would pay back through taxes. The other would be a series of bonds."

He then explained the ideas discussed in New York. When he was finished, Madison looked at the Speaker of the House. "Congressman, do you have any documents I can review that cover these ideas?"

"I do. Back at my house, I have a preliminary loan document and a sample bond for the Ways and Means Committee to review. Mr. Speaker, if you wish, I can bring it to your office either this afternoon or tomorrow."

"Tomorrow at nine. That will give us all day to haggle! Then we can take what we think is right and have Ezekiel Bacon look at it, which will start the negotiations all over again!" Henry Clay laughed as did Javier Jacinto. Bacon was the chairman of the House Ways and Means Committee and a representative from Boston. He was a lawyer who championed the war and was also known to be a tough negotiator.

Madison sipped his coffee and then said, "Good, now that we may have found a way around the money issue, let's talk about ships. For the sake of this discussion, please assume that Mr. Jones is the Secretary of the Navy."

William Jones nodded, and the president continued. "Congressman Jones, I presume you read the letter that Captain Smythe and Javier's son, Captain Jaco Jacinto, wrote last October to Secretary Hamilton."

"Yes, I am aware of that letter as well as all the other documents that were sent to Mr. Hamilton."

"Good. So, what say you?"

"Mr. President, assuming I am confirmed, my first priority is securing the Great Lakes. We have not done well up there, and if I were the Secretary of War, I would be demanding heads on platters. Mr. Hamilton has started a program to build, equip, and man ships. I intend to continue and expand it. That is my first priority."

"Second priority is sticking needles into the Royal Navy. We don't have, even with the N.E.S. vessels, enough ships to prevent the British from blockading our ports. So, what I propose, again if confirmed, is to get our large frigates to sea to make life difficult for the Royal Navy."

Without hesitating, Jones continued with what Javier believed was what he wanted to discuss with the President and Speaker when he arrived. "Last, I want to go after their merchant fleet in the Caribbean. That's where you and I know the money is in the cargoes of sugar, rum, molasses, et cetera. Again, if confirmed, I plan to ask Congress to issue letters of marque to well-funded consortia. N.E.S. would be at the top of my list that would meet that criteria."

Jones took a sip of his coffee, and Javier assumed the potential Secretary of the Navy was about to tell him what he wanted from N.E.S.

"'Twere I the Secretary of the Navy, I would be issuing orders to Captains Smythe and Jacinto to take *Goshawk* and *Eagle* into the Atlantic and create what mayhem they can. Specifically, I want them hunting and either sinking or capturing Royal Navy ships wherever they find them."

"My second set of orders would be to dispatch half of the remaining ships N.E.S. owns, the corvettes, and the smaller frigates to Charleston and the other half to Savannah. Their mission is to sally forth into the Caribbean and hunt like packs of wolves. Merchant ships are the target, and if in the process, they have to defeat a Royal Navy frigate or two, so be it. What I have not figured out is what to do with the prizes."

"Mr. Jones, I have a possible solution. U.S. Industries Exports and Imports has agents on the Dutch islands of Aruba and Sint Eustatius that have been stocking munitions and other supplies since the middle of 1811.

They are locally owned, and neither country is at war with England. Plus, what complicated things for the British is that the Dutch are either neutral or on the side of the English, which makes it uncomfortable if one of their ships raids one of these ports. The same is true for the Azores and Madeira Islands, which are owned by Portugal, and the Canaries, which are controlled by Spain. While these may not be our first choices, they do give us options."

"Brilliant! So, is N.E.S. willing to support my plan?"

"Aye, the orders must come from you, but yes. They will do this eagerly and well."

Jones turned to Madison, who was smiling. "So, now we have a plan, and we have participants who can execute the plan. All I need to do now is get Mr. Jones confirmed by the Senate. This meeting has been most beneficial. So, I propose we have a drink to celebrate!"

60 NM NOR' EAST OF CHESAPEAKE BAY, SECOND WEEK OF MARCH 1813

The plan to spring the ships out of the harbors where they were refitted was both sequential and simple. The first ships to slip into the Atlantic were Kestrel and Osprey. They sailed east into the Atlantic and avoided the British ships blockading Boston.

Four days later, *Eagle* and *Goshawk* sortied into the Atlantic. They were spotted by a Royal Navy frigate late in the afternoon, and while the two faster American frigates gave chase, the Royal Navy ship was allowed to disappear into the darkness and inform the Royal Navy that two American frigates had sortied from New York.

This was according to the plan. The next stop was to rendezvous with the three corvettes – *Cobra, Copperhead,* and *Rattlesnake* that were in Philadelphia. They sailed down Delaware Bay and then into the Atlantic at night. At dawn the next day, they made the rendezvous with the four frigates at 73°N, 35°W.

Jaco's and Darren's assumption was that the Royal Navy would have three or four ships loitering in the vicinity of the entrance to Chesapeake Bay. To prepare for their escape, the three corvettes refurbished in Baltimore – *Venom, Viper,* and *Cottonmouth* – moved down to Norfolk.

Expecting a fight, the four frigates and two of the corvettes sailed south in a scouting line with *Cobra* scouting ahead. The only Royal Navy ship they spotted was a brig that beat a hasty retreat when they spotted the American ships. While they were anxious to do battle with the Royal Navy, the primary goal of the first part of the deployment was to get all 10 ships out into the Atlantic.

This time, the organization and tasking was different. What used to be Escort Groups A and B were now Hunting Groups A and B. While Hunting Group A and B were what the squadrons were designated on their sailing orders, the crews and commanders referred to their squadrons as Wolfpack A and Wolfpack B.

The flagship of Hunting Group A (Wolfpack A) was Cato Cooper on *Kestrel.* Assigned to him were *Cobra, Copperhead,* and *Rattlesnake.* Their task was to sail to the Southern Caribbean, take prizes back to Willemstad in Dutch-held Aruba.

Hunting Group B (Wolfpack B) with the corvettes - *Venom, Viper,* and *Cottonmouth* - and under the command of Abner Jeffords on *Osprey,* were assigned the Northern Caribbean and would use Sint Eustatius as their base.

Once the escape was made, *Eagle* and *Goshawk* would sail east. Their mission, capture or sink Royal Navy frigates whenever possible, and take prizes. Ultimately, when they split up, one would go to Amsterdam, the other to Rabat. Secondary base was Punta Delgada in the Azores.

There were some other changes. One, Secretary of the Navy Jones, confirmed on January 19th, took all the regular Navy officers back and sent them to the Great Lakes. The quartermasters and bo'suns remained.

Laura Fonseca Laredo and the other owners of the consortium that owned N.E.S. provided a new cadre of officers. Those who hadn't been to the N.E.S. Academy went through it during the weeks before what they were calling the "Great Escape."

Morton Geiger, who had recovered from his wounds, gave up his command of *Viper.* All the officers who were second lieutenants on the 1812 cruise were now first lieutenants, and the second and third lieutenants on all the ships were brand new, right out of the academy. Those with more than three years of sea-going experience were made second lieutenants, those with less became the third lieutenants.

The sun was high overhead, and the tones from the eight bells died away. The bo'sun mate on watch bellowed. "Forenoon Watch has begun." It was time. Jaco ordered his midshipman, August von Korbach, to hoist the signal, "Good Luck and Good hunting. "It was followed by "Godspeed."

With the signal given, Jaco ordered, "Stand by to wear ship, new course, east."

Eagle slid away from the formation, and Jaco took the time to look at *Rattlesnake.* He could see his son on the quarterdeck and hoped it would not be the last time he saw him.

With the Wolfpacks over the horizon and everyone enjoyed the warm sun, Oswald Stanwix, his new second lieutenant who worked for Bay Colony Shipping, said, "Beggin' the captain's pardon, sir, there's a signal from *Goshawk.* The flags spelled out the word whereto. How do you want me to respond?

"One word, Lieutenant, Bermuda. We're about to cruise around the island and see what we can see. And we want to make sure that the Royal Navy knows we are there."

VICINITY OF 40°N, 17°W, THIRD WEEK OF MARCH 1813

Before they deployed from New York, Darren and Jaco pored over both Admiralty charts as well as ones from the French Dépôt des Cartes et Plans de la Marin of the waters off the West Coast of Africa as well as Europe. Both men had ruled out going down toward the Cape Verde Islands looking for prizes, and Darren showed Jaco the typical routes British merchant ships coming from India and South Africa sailed.

Darren felt more comfortable hunting in the Celtic Sea and the waters south of Ireland, while Jaco took the area west of Morocco and the Iberian Peninsula. When they split up after sailing about halfway across the Atlantic, the two captains agreed to meet in Rabat in the middle of June.

Eagle had weathered a squall line that had battered the frigate with heavy rains, high winds, and 10-foot waves that broke over the bow. The storm forced Jaco to shorten sail so that the ship was sailing under just its main sails on each mast. Each of the mainsails had been reefed so that only about half the sail was being used. It was enough to push the frigate along at about five knots, more than enough for the rudder to be effective so that the quartermasters kept the frigate sailing downwind.

By six bells on the Middle Watch, the storm had passed. Dawn brought clear skies, a steady wind from the so' west and a gentle, long, two-foot swell. Bo'sun Howard inspected the hull and the rigging for damage. There was none, but the sails were soaked. To prevent the canvas from rotting, it had to be dried. At dawn, Jaco ordered the main, top, and top gallants released and sheeted home.

When the sailors on the Afternoon Watch came on duty, the now dry top gallants were furled, and the gaskets holding the royals tight to the spar were released. Under this odd, but necessary sail configuration, *Eagle* loafed along at nine knots.

Jaco, who had been on the quarterdeck throughout the storm Once it passed, he walked through the ship and hold before going to bed. This was something he did at odd intervals during the day, speaking with members of the crew. His, as he called them, meanderings around *Eagle* were really an informal inspection.

If he found something not to his liking, and had to do with the physical condition of the ship, he would find Harold Howard, *Eagle's* bo'sun to have it taken care of. Or, if it had to do with any of the cannons, then Second Lieutenant Elias Cooper would be asked to "see to it."

While the officers dined together, they ate the same food as served to the crew. The only difference was that they had whiskey, port, and Madeira to go with their meals. The crew was served a weak beer.

Once a week, Jaco and the officers dined with the crew rather than in their own mess. The meal, generally supper, was served just before the First Dog Watch ended so that the officers could dine with those taking over the Second Dog Watch. They would then sit and talk with the sailors from the First Dog Watch as they ate.

Normally, hammocks would be rolled and hung from the rings on the beams above the berthing deck. Given the amount of water that seeped into the berthing deck, Jaco had the word passed that anything wet was to be hung out to dry unless they had to clear for action.

He was coming up from the hold after seeing how much water had collected in the bilge. There was barely enough to pump, but any water in the bottom of the ship was, in Jaco's mind too much, and he ordered the pumps rigged to get the water over the side.

Jaco leaned over the side to see the ugly smelling bilge water being pumped over the side when he heard, "Deck, three ships, starboard quarter, mebbe five miles. I can only see the top sails."

"What type?"

"One's a frigate and the other two are much larger. Probably East Indiamen."

"Captain, aye." Jaco noticed that the lookout's call had stopped the pumping action. "Keep pumping, gentlemen, and then when you have the bilges dry, flush out the hoses by putting the pickups in the sea. There's plenty of time before we see about filling your pockets with prize money."

His walk back to the quarterdeck allowed Jaco to formulate a plan. The British East Indiamen were big ships, generally about 1,200 tons or more, and usually armed with 20 or more 12-pounders. Some of the new ones had 18-pounders. However, they were not, according to Darren, very maneuverable or fast, or manned with very large crews.

The trick would be to defeat the frigate without letting the East Indiamen into the action. The how was what he was trying to work out as he climbed the companionway to the quarterdeck. "Mr. Howard, have the watch set the top gallants. Once they are set, on my command, we will wear ship to starboard. Our new course will be due east."

"Bo'sun, aye." Howard's voice was followed by Quartermaster Turner's acknowledgement. Apparently, he'd come on deck and was about to relieve one of the quartermaster mates when they cleared *Eagle* for action. The other three quartermaster mates would take up station on the berthing deck so that if the ropes from the wheel were shot away, they could insert the tiller bar into the steering mechanism, something that Captain Jacinto had them practice every week.

With the ship now headed on an intercept course to the three ships, all his officers were gathered at the aft end of the quarterdeck. "Gentlemen, we are chasing three unknown ships, probably British but in these waters, they could also be Dutch, French or Spanish. If they are the latter, then we dip our flags and sail away. Should they be English, we have a tall task ahead of us in that we must separate the frigate from her charges and then defeat her first. If the frigate is escorting British East Indiamen, we must assume they are armed with at least twenty 12-pounders, maybe more, and possibly 18-pounders."

"Deck, ships have set their royals and are wearing to the east."

Jaco looked up and cupped his hands around his mouth. "Deck, aye."

"We are going…"

"Deck, frigate is tacking to the west… Appears to be heading nor' west."

Without taking his eyes off his officers, Jaco shouted, "Deck, aye." Then, in a more normal voice, Jaco said, grinning, "I know this sounds odd coming from me, but we are going to let the frigate make the first move. I need to know what his intentions are before we commit to a fight. Right now, we have the wind gauge, and I intend to keep it for as long as we can. Let us clear for action, load ball, but do not run out until we know they are British. Mr. Preston and Mr. Stanwix, I suspect discipline to ensure we fire accurately and rapidly will carry the day. You must be prepared to engage with both batteries. That is all. Gentlemen, carry on."

While the ship was clearing for action, Jaco walked to the forward right corner of the quarterdeck, the crew of the *Scorpion* dubbed Perfecto Starboard. The other side was Perfecto Port, and during battles, he was on the side facing the enemy ship. The moniker came from his use of the Spanish word *perfecto.*

With the Dollond spyglass that his father bought him when he was selected to command *Scorpion,* he studied the three ships. They were still hull down, but now he could see all their sails, from mainsail to royal. All were set, and the frigate was running on a reach, as close to the wind as it could. He guessed that its captain was attempting to run north of *Eagle* to gain the wind advantage and tack to port to come at his ship.

"Mr. Turner, fall off starboard to a new course, so' east. Mr. Howard, trim the sails accordingly. Then, hoist our colors so they know who we are."

Jaco figured that *Eagle* was making about 10 knots and the other frigate about eight, giving the ships a combined closure rate of about 18 knots, or about 620 yards every minute. The other ship's hull was coming into view, which meant they were within two miles. In just over six minutes, they would be side by side.

He could see black cannon barrels poking out on each side of the Royal Navy frigate. It had already run out, telling Jaco that whoever the captain was, he was ready for a fight. Leaning over the railing, Captain Jacinto called out, "Mr. Preston, Mr. Stanwix, run out."

"Deck, frigate is Royal Navy. Other ships look like East Indiamen."

"Captain, aye." Rather than use the word deck indicating it was the officer of the watch, Jaco used his rank and position to let the lookouts know that he was the one communicating with them. "How many guns?"

"Thirteen aside, plus two carronades, one up near the forecastle, the other aft on the quarterdeck."

Thirty guns. Probably 18-pounders. Eagle *has 36 guns, twenty-six long 24-pounders – 13 on each side - and two long 18-pounders in the bow and two more in the stern. Mr. Royal Navy captain, if you want to play the maneuver game, please do.. This is the fight I prefer.*

"Mr. Howard, Mr. Turner, wear ship on my command to new course, nor' by east. We may have to adjust."

"Bo'sun aye!"

"Quartermaster aye."

"Wear ship now!"

Eagle was turning about 90 degrees, enough in Jaco's mind to threaten the Royal Navy frigate's stern. They were now inside 2,000 yards, an extreme range for their long 24-pounders. Leaning over the edge of the forward quarterdeck railing, Jaco called out. "Mr. Preston, your port guns will bear in about two minutes. Range, eighteen to two thousand yards. Can you give me seven or eight hits out of thirteen?"

Each time Jaco gave an order to his Third Lieutenant Emerson Preston, he thought of the man's late father, who was his bo'sun for many years. Preston was not the only son of someone he fought with during the American Revolution. There was his Second Lieutenant, who was the spitting image of his father, Cato Cooper, and just as big. He stood a good six feet two and was easily 200 pounds. And, last, there was Midshipman August von Korbach, the son of a Waldeck German officer who didn't like being paid to fight for someone else's king.

It was bad enough that the Graf von Waldeck zu Bergheim was so broke that he contracted with the British government to send two 600-man regiments of his fellow citizens off to fight for the British in North America. What made it worse and the reason that this father, Captain Heinz von Korbach, along with 70 of his men, deserted was that the Americans were fighting for what they wanted, i.e., to get out from under the thumb of a ruler who had absolute control over their lives.

The blast from port #1 long 24-pounder caught everyone on the main and quarterdeck by surprise. Those who didn't cover their ears felt the pain an extremely loud noise makes and felt the concussion.

Jaco and others still on the quarterdeck turned to see if the balls hit. There was no splash of water. "Deck, hit amidships."

Jaco was more prepared for the #2 cannon. He saw the tongue of flame that extended at least a foot from the end of the barrel, and while he couldn't see the ball, he did see it splash a few yards from the Royal Navy frigate.

Balls from the #3, #5, #6, #9, #12, and #13 all hit their target. Jaco bent over the railing and yelled at Elias Cooper, who had long, thick black hair, unlike his father, who was bald as a cannonball, "Excellent shooting."

The Royal Navy frigate passed over 1,000 yards from *Eagle's* stern as she turned to so' so' east. If neither ship turned, they would collide. A turn to the west would let the Royal Navy cross *Eagle's* bow.

If Jaco fell off more to the south, *Eagle* could be forced to luff up. If he fell off to port, then the two ships would battle it out side by side.

His third option was to break it off now and use *Eagle's* superior speed to pull away. Also, a move in that direction would also threaten the transports which were now sailing nor' nor' east. It was also what the Royal Navy frigate captain wanted which was to box *Eagle* between the two East Indiamen.

"Mr. Howard, Mr. Turner, standby to wear ship on my command. New course due east."

Out of the corner of his eye, Jaco saw Elias give him a questioning look. He grinned back as if to say, "Watch, the old master has a trick up his sleeve."

"Mr. Howard, Mr. Turner, I want *Eagle* to turn smartly as you can while maintaining our speed."

In the turn made with the wind coming over *Eagle's* stern, the sails, particularly the jibs, came through the stays without snagging. "Well done, lads! Now, stand by, we're going to let our Royal Navy friend get closer."

Just as Jaco had anticipated, the Royal Navy frigate had closed the gap and was now about 500 yards behind *Eagle* and offset on the downwind side. Given its track, its captain ordered its helmsman to steer a course that would, if the two ships continued without turning, position it upwind of *Eagle.* Or he could tack to port and fire a broadside into *Eagle's* stern.

Jaco now had the option of waiting, which gave him a choice. Once the Royal Navy captain made his decision, he would make his. The British frigate began to tack to port. Given the tracks, Jaco thought they would be, if *Eagle* turned to port, about 800 yards between the ships. Since the Royal Navy Captain was choosing to exchange broadsides, it suggested that his ship had 18-pounders or long 12-pounders.

Or he could continue this dance and fall off to starboard and keep maneuvering. Or take a chance that the Royal Navy's gunners were not as good as his at long range and extend and then turn and shoot at over 1,000 yards.

"Mr. Howard, Mr. Turner, standby to wear ship to starboard, on my command. New course due south."

Once *Eagle* was steady on its new course and accelerating, Jaco watched the Royal Navy frigate fall off and head back toward the two East Indiamen. Jaco then had his ship wear off to the east and then the nor' east as he was now on a course that might enable *Eagle* to cross the Royal Navy ship's stern. The British frigate started to wear off to the south when there was a crack, loud enough to be heard on *Eagle.*

Slowly, one could say, majestically, the top section of the frigate's foremast started to come down. Some stays and halyards popped as the mass of its royal, top gallant, and then its top sail yards and mast crashed into the netting rigged above its main deck.

Immediately, the frigate slowed as the captain had his helmsman steer a course that put minimum strain it its remaining masts. Everyone on *Eagle's* deck could see men on the Royal Navy frigate trying to get the mass of sails and rigging out of the way. Some of the wood was dumped over the side, and other pieces were pulled onto the deck.

"Mr. Howard, Mr. Turner, we're going to sail up the enemy frigates arse and I am going to ask its captain if he wants to strike. Let's start by wearing *Eagle,* so we come its wake on the port side. Fly a white flag off our starboard side so he knows we want to parlay."

Turning to his First Lieutenant, "Mr. Cooper, if the captain doesn't strike, we fall off and pound his frigate into splinters."

The Royal Navy frigate, which they now knew as *H.M.S. Esteem,* was making about four knots when *Eagle* took station. During their approach, they could see where their 24-pound cannonballs hit. There was a hole in the frigate's starboard side where one of the gun ports was enlarged by a 24-pound cannonball. Two chunks of the main deck bulwark were missing.

A man in a blue coat with gold epaulets on either shoulder stood at the aft railing. Jaco held up the speaking trumpet to his mouth. "Captain, we can end any more bloodshed now. All I need you to do is come over to my ship. I will give you a letter to take to your Admiralty, and you can do what you need to repair your ship and sail it home."

"What about the two merchant ships?"

"I will take them as prizes. You have the damage to your ship to show that you tried to defend your charges."

"And if I don't agree?"

"*Eagle* will fall off, pound *Esteem* into splinters, and then run after the East Indiamen. It is up to you as to how large you want your butcher's bill to be."

The man spoke to two other men wearing blue coats, one of whom handed him a trumpet. "I agree. Can you send a boat over?"

"Aye, we will fall off a few hundred feet and lower a boat."

Jaco was waiting by the mainmast as *Esteem's* captain climbed up the ladder on the side. When the Royal Navy officer came through the bulwark, there were two rows of U.S. Navy sailors to provide a path to where Jaco was standing. As soon as the officer was on the main deck, Bo'sun Howard blew "all call" and then announced, *H.M.S. Esteem,* ARRRiving!!!!

Somewhat surprised, the captain stopped and then strode toward Jaco, who was wearing a Navy-blue coat and white breeches. His coat was a darker blue than that worn by the Royal Navy. Extending his hand, "Welcome to the United States frigate *Eagle*. I am Captain Jaco Jacinto, the ship's commanding officer."

The Royal Navy captain unhooked his sword and handed it to Jaco horizontally. "I am Captain Ewan MacGregor, Captain of *H.M.S. Esteem.* I am giving you my sword as a symbol of my surrendering my ship."

Jaco took it and then handed it back to MacGregor. "Sir, you keep this for your children and grandchildren."

"Thank you, sir, I am the fifth man in my family who has had the honor to carry this sword, but only the first to offer it in surrender."

"I can imagine how painful it must be. Please, will you join me in cabin. It will only take a few minutes."

Once in the cabin, Lieutenant Cooper joined the two captains, and Midshipman von Korbach poured each man a port. When they were full, Jaco held out his and said, "To friends lost and that we may meet again in happier times."

"I'll bloody well drink to that." MacGregor's accent was similar to Rafer Muir's. After he took a sip, he said, "What kind of cannon do you have? You hit us from a thousand yards. The first ball took out a chunk of our foremast. We were trying to splint it, but it finally failed."

"Captain, the man to whom this letter is addressed asked me the same question, and I will give you the same answer I gave him, which is accurate, long-range ones!"

The Royal Navy captain looked at the letter sealed with a U.S. Navy emblem. He looked at it and said, "This must be some kind of joke."

"No, Captain, I know Vice Admiral of the Red Davidson quite well. Currently, he is, I believe, the Second Naval Lord. My terms are simply this. *Esteem* makes the best speed to Portsmouth, and you deliver this personally. He won't bite, I assure you. In it, among other things, I gave you credit for making it hard for me to defeat you."

"Thank you, captain, but that is not necessary. There will be a board of inquiry, and that will determine my fate."

"Well, I hope Vice Admiral Davidson of the Red makes sure the board knows what is in this letter."

The Scotsman finished his glass of port, "Thank you for your generosity."

"My pleasure, sir. Now, if you'll excuse me, you have a ship to repair to get underway, and I have two prizes to catch."

"They won't give in easily."

"Of that, I am sure. Good day, Captain MacGregor."

VICINITY OF 38°N, 8°W, FOURTH WEEK OF MARCH 1813

The fog that hung over the Celtic Sea was thick as pea soup. It also meant that there was little or no wind, and Goshawk was barely making way through the water. Yards that normally creaked with pressure from the wind were silent, and the loudest sound on the ship, other than those who were talking, was the clacking of pulleys, which normally had lines holding them tight, and the tension kept them silent.

Darren had passed the word that while they were in the fog, no one would be allowed on the main deck, and there would be no talking or even ringing the ship's bell to signal the passage of the watch. Inside the binnacle, his bo'sun, Jonas Digby, had an hourglass with thirty minutes of sand. Each time the glass emptied and was turned upside down, the bo'sun mate on watch would leave the quarterdeck and walk through the gun and berthing deck, reciting the number of bells that were rung. His last stop was the wardroom and then the captain's cabin to announce the same information.

The reason for the silence is that noise carries a long way over water, and if there was a Royal Navy frigate out there, Darren didn't want noise to give away his position. Also, since the normal lookout station at the top of the topsail yard was still in the fog, he had a lookout stationed, or actually sitting, on the royal's yardarm.

For the past hour, he too was in the clouds, and while the fog was thinner almost 100 feet off the water, he still could not see anything but the gray murk. Sometimes, the lookout could barely see the ship below him. To relieve the lookout's boredom, Darren ordered that every hour, the lookout be relieved.

Besides almost no visibility, the fog brought a cool dampness that gave a chill to the air. Darren's experience was that these fogs were common in the spring and would, in a few hours, blow away.

Suddenly, there was a faint sound of a bell ringing. Looking at the chronometer, he noticed that it was 11:30 in the morning, or seven bells into the Forenoon Watch. Darren slowly stood and opened the window to his cabin just in time to hear the last gong as it died away.

Out on deck, the relay of lookouts from the main top had just dropped to the deck. "Sir, we heard it and think it is off our port bow, but we didn't see no ship."

"Aye, lads, good work. Pass the word to keep a sharp eye and ear out. Go get a tot of rum to take off the chill."

In 30 minutes, they and the other ship would be at eight bells. If the tones were stronger, it meant they were closer. If they were fainter, then the ships were on a diverging course. Now, it was just a matter of waiting.

Sure enough, those on the deck heard the eight bells distinctly. Again, the lookout from the maintop scampered down the ratlines. "Sir, we're pretty sure the ship is one to two points off our port bow, or thereabouts. Up ahead, we can see blue sky, and we'll be able to see."

Darren walked down onto the main deck where he saw his first lieutenant Jake Kahn, and Midshipman Hugo Radcliffe. Speaking just above a whisper, "Gentlemen, pass the word to clear for action. Load ball, but do not run out. Do it quietly, no drums, no yelling, no banging of wood. If you need, put several layers of cloth under the wheels of the gun carriages to minimize the noise as they are pulled back."

Looking up, Darren could see the sky brightening. Soon, he hoped, they would see the unknown ship.

When *Goshawk* came out of the fog, it was if they had walked from a darkened room into bright sunlight. And there, not 500 yards away was a Royal Navy frigate sailing on a parallel course. A count of gun ports told him that the ship had at least 36 guns. On the quarter deck and near the forecastle, he could see the bulbous breeches of carronades.

The smack of gun ports opening brought him back to reality. He was about to yell, "Fire," when the first three cannons on *Goshawk's* port side bellowed. Then the other 10 followed suit.

Now it was the other ship's turn to return fire while his gun crews went through the loading drill. Sponge the barrel, stuff the powder charge down into the barrel, and ram it home. Then came the ball, which was pushed hard into the wax on the end of the wad. As that task was going on, the assistant gunner poured fine gunpowder into the touch hole and the small indentation at the top of the breech while the gun captain adjusted the elevation of the gun. Satisfied with his aim, the gun captain yelled 'clear' to make sure all his men kept their feet back from where the gun carriage would recoil, then touched the slow match to the powder in the pan.

If done right, the cannon would fire and slam back against the ropes with the back of the carriage about halfway across the deck. Then, the process of reloading began all over again. Within minutes, the men were sweating from the heat generated by hot gun barrels and the effort needed to pull the 4,600-pound cannon back into battery.

In the middle of all this, the Royal Navy ship got off a ragged broadside. Clearly, when *Goshawk's* first cannon fired, the British ship was caught by surprise, but its 18-pounders hammered into *Goshawk's.* Unless one of the balls hit a weak spot in the planking or found the edge of a gun port, the 18-pound balls slammed into the 12 inches of hard oak, which would then push into the six inches of softer pine, which would compress as it pushed against the inner six inches of oak that was screwed to *Goshawk's* ribs and crossmembers.

The result was that most of the 18-pound balls thumped into *Goshawk's* hull and dropped harmlessly into the water. One slammed into the side of the gunport, and splinters mowed down half of the gun crew. Another went through the gunport, pulped the gun captain who was just standing up after aiming his weapon, and then ended its flight in the hammocks hung in the nets inside the gun deck's bulwarks.

On the main deck, the balls from the Royal Navy frigate turned one of the stacks of boats into firewood. Another hammered into the bowsprit, and Bo'sun Digby and two of his mates were already replacing the stays that were cut and wedging splinters from the damaged boats into place to keep the bowsprit in position.

ON BOARD H.M.S. *APOSTLE*

Captain Everett Martingdale was as surprised as anyone on his frigate when the American frigate emerged from the fog. No one had any idea it was there. There was no time to clear for action.

Martingdale ordered his men to load and fire ball as fast as they could get their cannons into action. While they were doing this, he exhorted his crew to keep firing no matter what happened around them.

From the quarterdeck, he could see that his ship was taking a pounding. A large section of the starboard bulwark was missing. He already knew that four of the ship's 18-pounders were out of action. The forward carronade on the right side exploded when it was hit by a ball from the American frigate, and the carronade behind him was unmanned. He sent a powder monkey down to get a bag of canister and a powder charge. Like a maniac, he went through the loading drill, and men on the main deck saw their captain struggling to pull the heavy carronade into battery.

They managed, and Martingdale yanked the lanyard attached to a frizzen that worked like a musket. A flint scraped along a piece of metal that looked like a file, and sparks flew.

The gun didn't fire. Martingdale poured more powder into the touch hole and yanked again. The carronade fired and jumped back just as a 24-pound ball from *Goshawk* arrived. It destroyed the gun carriage and sent shards of metal and wood flying around the quarterdeck.

ON BOARD *GOSHAWK*

This was the type of fight Darren didn't want to fight, but it was the fight he had. The canister fired by Apostle's carronade was like what came out of a shotgun. At 500 yards, the balls were not very concentrated. Some ended in the water, most smacked harmlessly into Goshawk's hull. The sucking sound Darren heard told him that the ball had found someone, and he turned to see a Quartermaster mate staggering away from the wheel, bleeding from a wound in his side.

From where he stood, he sensed the battle was going *Goshawk's* way. While he had many wounded and dead, all of his cannons were firing, and only a few on his enemy's ship.

ON BOARD *APOSTLE*

When the 24-pound ball hit the gun carriage of the starboard 32-pounder carronade, the first to go down was Martingdale. One of the wheels that had been shattered had severed his right leg above the knee and drove two large splinters into his stomach.

Quick work by his first lieutenant who put a tourniquet around what was left of his leg stopped Martingdale from bleeding out. When he finished, Gabriel Newsom, the ship's First Lieutenant, was the only man left alive on the quarterdeck. A new quartermaster's mate was running up the companionway to take the wheel.

As Newsom surveyed the scene on the quarterdeck, he stopped counting the bodies when he reached six. Newsom felt another ball hit *Apostle* as he untied the halyard so the Union Jack could come floating down. While it was on the way down, he yelled, "Cease fire, cease fire, we have struck."

The ship's third lieutenant staggered up the companionway from the gun deck. "About bloody time. Don't go down there, sir, it is a shambles."

ON BOARD *GOSHAWK*

Darren ordered the ship to close slightly to the Royal Navy frigate. Of the *Goshawk's* six boats, only three were seaworthy. He brought with him his second lieutenant, Miles Lombard.

When he stepped onto *Apostle's* main deck, there was debris everywhere along with bleeding men, some of whom were dying. The bodies of the dead, most of whom had been dismembered, lay where they fell.

"Sir, I am Lieutenant Gavin Newsom, *H.M.S. Apostle's* First Lieutenant. My captain is on the quarterdeck but is mortally wounded and doesn't have long to live."

"Let us go pay our respects, Lieutenant."

Darren recognized the man lying on the deck, bleeding from the stomach and what was left of his right leg. Martingdale was propped up against the railing.

Bending down, Darren spoke softly to the dying man. "Captain Martingdale, do you remember me?"

Everett Martingdale's eyes opened and got wider as he recognized the blond-haired man crouching down next to him. "Do you remember what I said to you when they hauled me off *Minerva?*"

Martingdale nodded. "You said that one day, you would send me to hell."

"Aye. And now, I will let you die knowing that a man you unjustly called a traitor has not only defeated your ship but killed you as well."

"Go to hell, Smythe."

"Maybe, maybe not. But Martingdale, you are going there sooner than me."

Darren stood up. Before he could say a word to Newsom, Martingdale gasped and went limp. He was dead.

"Lieutenant Newsom, gather your wounded together along with your surgeon. They are going to be transferred to my ship. Then, you will bury your dead, all except Martingdale. He will remain where he died. Then, my men will come aboard and set fire to *Apostle.*

"Where are you taking us?"

"That, Mr. Newsom, will be decided in the next day or so. Now, get on with the task of caring for your wounded and preparing the dead for burial.

CHAPTER 20

LESSONS TAUGHT TO OUR ENEMY

RABAT, FIRST WEEK OF APRIL

Unlike his prior visit to the Moroccan capital, this time, there were two U.S. flagged merchantmen tied to the pier where former prizes were kept waiting for sale. Flying from the top of the mainmast, both had Fonseca-Laredo flags.

Today, the ceremony of piping aboard Colonel Amir Harrak and his assistant, Captain Hamsa Bensaid, was a little different. Instead of just sailors, Jaco had the sailors and Marines in the line of side boys.

A smiling Colonel Harrak asked, "What have you brought to us this time?"

"Two East Indiamen, each with five hundred tons of tea and spices."

"My Sultan will be pleased. The British have been most eager to get their ships and crews back. We now have, what I think the British say, an arrangement."

"Excellent. I will need some of the powder and shot we have stored in Rabat."

"Captain Bensaid can take care of that with your victualling order. Come, let us meet with the Sultan. As you can see, we have two ships from your country. They brought us rice, cotton, dried corn, and some dried beans. We will help their captains now helping them buy spices."

"I suspect they could buy some of the tea."

Harrak nodded. "That too is possible. Come, my Sultan is waiting. He will decide."

In the throne room, once the pleasantries were finished, Sultan Mawlay Sulayman bin Mohammed smiled. "Captain, your war with England is good for Morocco. My coffers are now filled with English gold sovereigns. What have you brought me?"

After listening to Jaco list what was on the manifests of *Queen Anne* and *Queen Elizabeth,* the Sultan said, "We drink tea, so I will give you four thousand pounds for all the tea and another two thousand for the spices which I do not want."

Jaco decided on the spot that negotiating prices for commodities was not something he wanted to do. "Your Excellency, may I suggest Colonel Harrak speak with the merchant ship captains from my country to see if they wish to purchase the spices."

Mawlay Sulayman bin Mohammed had a hushed conversation with a man standing next to his throne. When they are finished, he turned to Jaco. "I think it better that I sell the spices back to the British. What do you want for the ships?"

"Eleven thousand pounds for each."

Before he could explain his price, the Sultan said, "Eight."

Haggling was a way of life in Morocco. It was, his father once said, of a game of "I come up, you come down." "Your Excellency, to replace either of the ships will cost fifteen thousand pounds. I think ten thousand each is a fair price, and you can have whatever you can get for the crews."

Again, there was a discussion with the man standing next to him. "Nine thousand five."

"Agreed. Payment in the usual manner."

"It will be delivered with your supplies."

Perfecto. Eighteen thousand pounds for the ships and another six for the cargo will make a very nice addition to the men's pay at the end of the cruise.

265 NM DUE WEST OF BREST, FIRST WEEK OF APRIL

Once Goshawk had the surviving men from Apostle on board, the next task was moving half of the powder and enough food from the Royal Navy frigate to Goshawk. The American frigate now had 156 more mouths to feed.

Once the transfers were complete, Goshawk's second lieutenant, Miles Standard, remained on board *Apostle* along with *Goshawk's* bo'sun, Jonas Digby. They walked into every compartment on the frigate searching for anyone who might have remained on board. Finding none, the two went about building piles of splintered wood on each of the decks to get the fire going. Once that was done, Standard waited until Bo'sun Digby emptied a barrel of gunpowder to create an inch-deep trail of gunpowder from the berthing deck to the magazine.

With this done, three bottles full of rum, corked with cloth that was also soaked in rum and sprinkled with gunpowder, were carefully handed up to Standard. When Bo'sun Digby was on his way down to the boat, Standard blew on the last remaining section of slow match, a rope soaked in a solution of potassium nitrate and then dried.

The slow match flared, and Standard touched it to the cloth on one of the bottles. When flared, he tossed it toward the forecastle, where it broke and started a fire. One was thrown on the aft pile and then on the wood by the mainmast.

Satisfied that the fires were burning, Standard climbed down the ladder and into the rowboat. One of the rowers released the line that was looped through a ring and started pulling strongly toward *Goshawk.*

The boat was barely out of the water when Darren gave the order to sheet home the sails and set a course to the west. After six hours heading westward, *Goshawk* tacked through the wind to the so' east. Destination Rabat.

Goshawk was about two miles from *Apostle* when the 250 pounds of gunpowder in the magazine blew the frigate in half. The bow and stern floated for a few minutes after the debris landed in the water, then disappeared below the surface, taking Martingdale's body with it.

THE NEXT AFTERNOON

As they pulled away from where Apostle went down, Darren drew a line on the map to show his watch standers the course he wanted to take to Rabat. The route, against the prevailing winds from the so' west would keep the frigate well clear of the nor' western tip of the Iberian Peninsula.

At about 35°N, 13°W, the ship would head so' by west until *Goshawk* was well west of the Straits of Gibraltar where it would sail east so' east to the Moroccan capital. Hopefully, the route would avoid any Royal Navy frigates.

The call, "Sail ho, Royal Navy frigate, one point off the port bow, five miles," brought Darren up to the quarterdeck. When he arrived, the lookout had called out that the ship was missing most of its foremast and the top third of its mainmast. Thinking it might be an easy target, Darren ordered *Goshawk* to change course and head toward the unknown ship.

Goshawk had what Darren called its talons out, i.e., its long-barreled 24-pounder cannon, as it approached the Royal Navy frigate, which had run up a white flag over its Union Jack. Not sure of the Royal Navy captain's intent, even though the frigate had not opened its gunports or run its cannons out.

Through a spyglass, Darren could see men lining the ship's main deck bulwark. Still, wanting to be cautious, Darren swung wide of the frigate and then sailed up its wake until *Goshawk's* bow was even with the frigate's quarterdeck. They now knew that the damaged ship was *H.M.S. Esteem.*

By wedging his feet in gaps between where the bowsprit joined the forecastle, Darren was sure he would be able to maintain his balance. And unless he pitched forward into the water, if he fell, he would land unceremoniously on the main deck. Now that he was close, he could see the temporary repairs made by the crew. "Captain of *Esteem,* please heave to."

"Pray tell, why?"

"Please do not make me fire on you."

"Again, why? Do you intend to take me as a prize?" MacGregor's heavy Scottish accent made it hard for Darren to understand over the noise from the wind and the ship going through the water.

"Where are you headed?"

"Portsmouth, again, why?"

"We need to talk." Darren realized, as he said the words, that he sounded like his wife, who often wanted to discuss important things just after they climbed into bed. "I can force you to stop, if needed."

MacGregor turned to an officer, and the sheets to his remaining sails were let go. "I'll slow down rather than stop."

"Aye. I will come over on a boat."

"Mr. Kahn, you will have command of *Goshawk* while I am gone. Bring Mr. Newsom to me."

On board *Esteem,* MacGregor led Darren to his cabin. “Here’s why I wanted you to stop. I have one hundred and fifty-two Royal Navy sailors on my ship. I am happy to turn those over to you who want to return to the Royal Navy, plus sufficient food so you can all go back to England.”

“What do you mean by do not want to return?”

“Some of *Apostle’s* sailors have indicated that they would prefer to join the U.S. Navy and become U.S. citizens.”

“You can’t do that?“

“Says who?”

“It is bloody kidnapping?“

“No, it isn’t. It is not impressment or kidnapping, it is called immigration.”

MacGregor was silent. “Do you know a Captain Jacinto?”

Darren smiled, “Why?”

“After we struck our colors, he gave me a letter to give to the Second Naval Lord. He bloody well claims he knows the man.” MacGregor held out the document, and Darren recognized his friend’s handwriting.

“He does, and I strongly suggest you carry out his wish since I suspect your choice was becoming a prisoner of war.”

“Aye.”

“Splendid, I shall return to *Goshawk* and start sending over those who wish to return to England, officers and warrants last. They will come complete with a current muster list. The surviving officer, Lieutenant Newsom has a report written on our battle with *Apostle.*”

“Where is *Apostle* now?”

“On the bottom of the Atlantic. I shall take my leave and good luck, Captain MacGregor. When you see Vice Admiral of the Red Davidson who is the Second Naval Lord, please give him my best wishes.”

MacGregor’s mouth dropped as Darren headed for the door. “Wait, how do you know him?”

“Deliver the letter and ask him.”

LONDON, THIRD WEEK OF APRIL 1813

From what Vice Admiral of the Red and Second Naval Lord Davidson could tell from what little news they had of the war in North America, it was going well for England. The American attempt to invade Canada had failed, and the British Army had captured several forts in Michigan.

At sea, while the Royal Navy was losing more ships than the Americans, they had more to begin with. The blockade was in place, but the Royal Navy still didn't have enough ships in North American waters to lock down all the ports, so, to use the First Naval Lord's assessment, the blockade was porous.

The biggest concern was privateers and the two small squadrons in the Caribbean that had taken almost 50% of the trade – rum, sugar, molasses, spices, coffee – coming from the British possessions. The ships and their cargoes were being sold to American traders who were, he presumed, smuggling them into the United States. His wife Belinda told him pointedly that the price of a pound of sugar had tripled in the past two months.

There was a knock on the door. It was his senior secretary. "Sir, there is a Captain Ewen MacGregor on the quarterdeck saying he has an important letter for you from an American captain by the name of Jacinto. What should I do?"

"Bring Captain MacGregor here forthwith. And we shall see how the letter will either ruin or brighten my day."

MacGregor stood at attention in front of Vice Admiral of the Red Davidson's desk and stuck out the letter. Davidson took it, "Take a seat, Captain while I read this. A taste? I suspect we may need it."

"Do you have any whiskey from the Highlands?"

"I do. Single malt?"

"Aye, that would be perfect."

Davidson poured three fingers of a light-brown liquid into two crystal glasses, then handed one to MacGregor. "To absent friends and shipmates."

"Aye, Vice Admiral, I'll always drink to that."

"How did you acquire this letter?"

MacGregor gave Davidson a précis of the battle in which he lost his charges. Where they were now, MacGregor did not know.

He would guess, given where the battle happened, that Jacinto took the ships to Rabat. This meant that after the British government paid thousands of pounds, the ships would be returned with or without their cargo. Popping off the seal with a small dagger, Davidson opened the folded document.

Vice Admiral of the Red Davidson,

By now, we - that is, you and I - and our respective navies and our countries are again at war for the second time in thirty-eight years. And the reasons we fought the first time are the same ones that started the first fight. We the People of the United States want the freedom to choose what profession we pursue, who we wish to marry, where we want to live, and with whom we do business.

As you and I discussed, British policies over the past decade have attempted to restrict our trade, kidnapped my fellow sailors, and incited the Native Tribes against our settlers on our sovereign land. There were several attempts, directly and indirectly, by my government to get England to change. Unfortunately, our entreaties were either ignored or rebuffed which left us with only one resort - declare war.

However, this time it is different. In 1775, the Thirteen Colonies did not have an army or a navy. Yet, we declared war on the battlefield of Lexington and Concord on April 19th, 1775, knowing we were taking on the richest and most powerful nation known to man that also had a well-trained army and navy. It took a long time - eight years and four months - to finally get England's leaders to realize that they would never defeat us.

This time, we have a small navy and an army. We will lose battles, but we will ultimately prevail. England, no matter how many soldiers and ships it sends to America, will never conquer us.

Why? We have been free and independent now for 38 years. The men like me who fought England in our War for Independence now have sons and grandsons who never want to go back to being an English colony and ruled by a king.

What's different now? England still has a larger Navy and a bigger Army and is a wealthier country. But when President Madison asked for a declaration of war, the Congress agreed. This was not about a king or a duke who wants to restore a relative to a throne. No, this is about the will of we, the American people.

We the People who elect members of Congress want to be treated as an equal. We want to be respected for who we are and what we represent, which is freedom and equality in a country where a noble class does not determine what we will do with our lives, who we can marry, what profession we follow, and then, without asking, send us off to war.

The United States is a country where you can arrive on our doorstep with little or no money, with a dream that, with hard work and a bit of luck, one can succeed. And one can own as much land as one can afford. This is the magnet that has drawn and will continue to draw thousands of Europeans to our shores.

This is a principle worth fighting, even dying for. It is why, no matter how many soldiers England sends to our shores or ships to blockade our harbors, we will find a way to win, no matter how long it takes or what it costs in terms of treasure and lives.

Sir, I suggest you take my words to heart and realize that this is just the beginning. No American wants to be ruled by another country. We will eventually prevail because, for us, there is no other acceptable choice.

Unlike the continental armies which are drafted into an army to fight in a war they don't understand, we are fighting because We the People have chosen to again fight for our independence. That is the difference between the soldiers and sailors who fight under the American flag and those who fight under the Union Jack.

My fervent hope is that this war will end soon and we can again break bread together as friends. But I suspect that the road to get there will be difficult. Many sons of America and England will die on this road. We the People are prepared to fight for years. Is England?

Jaco Jacinto
Captain
United States Navy
Managing Director

American Shipping & Passenger Lines

Davidson took a long swallow of his scotch and handed the letter to MacGregor. He could see the Scotsman's eyes open wide as he read Jaco's words. When he looked up, the Second Naval Lord asked, "What say you?"

"As a Scotsman or as a Royal Navy officer?"

"Both."

"As a Scotsman, I have empathy and sympathy for Captain Jacinto's words. After all, I have family members who fought English kings. I also have envy because the Americans achieved what we Scotsmen didn't." MacGregor took a long swig of the scotch. "But, as a Royal Navy officer, my sworn duty is to defeat men like this Jacinto any and every time we meet."

"Good and truthful answer."

"Admiral, sir, how did you come to know this Captain Jacinto?"

"That, Captain, will take some time to tell. How about a refill, and I will share the tale of Captain Jacinto and Royal Navy Captain retired and now U.S. Navy Captain Darren Smythe."

Holding his glass and tilting to the Second Naval Lord, "Sir, I will sit here for as long as it takes. There is nothing like a true sea story to capture one's attention."

SERIES EPILOGUE

U.S. INDUSTRIES

After the War of 1812 ended, the food fight for control of the company began. Both Max Laredo and Javier wanted to ensure the company they created survived, stronger and better led than before.

What emerged was a formalized triumvirate that would lead the company. The organization remained the same as did the board with the stipulation that once one was elected to be a member of the leading triumvirate, one could not drop back to run one of the companies.

Initially, there were many candidates who politicked for one of the three seats on the "triumvirate" who would be elected for terms of five years and could be reelected only twice. No one could serve if during their term, they would turn 70.

The leading candidates initially were Reyna, because she stayed out of the corporate politics, Shoshana, Greg Struthers, Amos Laredo. In the end, the three elected were Jaco, Greg Struthers and Shoshana.

Greg said, upon election, he will serve one term and was followed on the board by Amos Laredo. Shoshana wanted to travel after one term and was replaced by Emily Smythe-Muir, thus setting the precedent that at least one seat of the triumvirate would be a woman.

The firm continued to grow and becomes one of the largest companies in the U.S.

AS&PL

Once the Treaty of Ghent was signed, AS&PL's passenger business exploded. It became the leader in passenger service and by 1818, it was running regularly scheduled service between London, Amsterdam and Hamburg to the U.S.

When Jaco moved up to the Triumvirate, Darren became its sole managing director. He continued to run the company until 1825 when he turned it over to Micah Jacinto and Jeffrey Smythe.

Marijke died in 1837 and Darren passed away in 1840.

U.S. PUBLISHING

The publishing company released its first books in June 1800 under three imprints – Fleur de Femme for romance novels, Castle for history, biographies and memoirs and Oak Tree for fiction. Within two years, it was immensely profitable with a catalogue of over 30 titles.

After Naomi retired in 1832, Alain Fontaine continued building the company into one of the largest publishing houses in the U.S. Alain died in 1843 and left a strong management team that continued is growth.

SMYTHE & SONS

Esau Labatto ran Smythe & Sons until 1846 when he turned over the management to his son, Benjamin. Under his leadership, the firm broadened its customer base into cutting tools and inexpensive cutlery. By 1820, the revenue or turnover, of the firm was twice what it had been when Emily asked him to be president.

PEOPLE AND FAMILIES

VICE ADMIRAL OF THE RED, AND SECOND NAVAL LORD, STACEY DAVIDSON

Stacey and Belinda Davidson, the Duke and Duchess of Somerset made good their promise to visit the United States. They booked a one-way passage in May 1816 on the AIS&PL schooner Westerlies. When they left England, they were planning to stay a month, maybe two, in the U.S.

They were welcomed by both Jaco and Darren who introduced them to New York society. Morton Geiger hosted them in Boston. In the end, after a short visit to Philadelphia in August, they returned to New York and left in early October 1816.

When he returned to England, Stacey Davidson stood for election to Parliament and won. While he could have been a member of the House of Lords, he chose the lower house. There, he lobbied and made speeches for a closer relationship with the former British Colony called the United States. He was on record several times saying that impressment was wrong and the Royal Navy needed to end the practice.

Belinda passed away in 1830 and Stacey died in 1836.

THE FONTAINE CLAN

Sophie Fontaine kept writing even after Greg Struthers retired from U.S. Industries in 1830. They both died in 1836.

Marguerite Fontaine passed away in 1812 and Girard Fontaine died in 1813, so the title Marquis de Gironde passed to Sophie's oldest son Hugo. At the time, Hugo was running the family winery along with Didier and Cesar who did not want the title. When Hugo learns that Napoleon has been exiled to St. Helena and the Bourbon's are back on the throne, he decides to return to France against the wishes of his American born wife, Audry Stemmons, the granddaughter of Jacob Stemmons.

Hugo sells the U.S. winery and buys Red Rapier winery which is a mere shadow of itself. Audry refused to move to France and divorces Hugo who then marries the daughter of Sebastien Dubisson,

Edmund, Sophie's son and his sister Rose are joined by Félicité in France and rebuild the Red Rapier winery to its former glory. Hugo dies in 1869 and Rose follows him into the ground in 1873. Félicité passes away in 1866.

Sophie Fontaine Struthers and Greg Struthers remained married until their death. They had no children together and Sophie's wealth, charm and fame as an author and Greg's position within U.S. Industries enabled her to join the "upper crust" of the growing city's society as Greg's wife. Greg Struthers passed away in 1821 and Sophie remained active socially and sexually until she died in 1848 at the age of 95.

THE JACINTO CLAN

After moving to New York, Jaco and Reyna lived quietly and modestly in a small three-story house on 5th Avenue. Reyna continued practicing medicine until she realized that she had cancer. She died in Jaco's arms in 1825. Jaco passed away in 1841.

Their daughter, Shannon Jacinto married Seth Geiger, one of Abraham Geiger's grandsons and moved to Boston. Their son Micah married Frieda Norburg and ultimately became the president of AS&PL.

Joshua attended the University of Pennsylvania and graduated from its law school. He joined his aunt Shoshana in the U.S. Industries office of the General Counsel. There, in 1817, he convinced the board to acquire all the beach front property it could in Florida, SC and New Jersey. After the Civil War, Joshua used the financial power of U.S. Industries' financial arm to help southern farmers who were members of Shayna Enterprises to get back on their feet.

Shoshana Jacinto and Naomi Moreno stayed together as life-long partners. After retiring from U.S. Industries in 1825, the couple traveled to England, The Netherlands, France, and Sweden. Shoshana died in 1845 in the arms of Naomi who passed away in 1846.

After she retired, Shoshana, along with Anita Hastings and her partner Gloria Oglethorpe, helped create a network of women with the same sexual preferences and she provided pro bono legal assistance to those who needed it.

Nathan Jacinto and Philippe Dubisson continue their business and romantic relationship. In 1817, Nathan resigned from U.S. Industries so he can fulfill his lifelong dream as living and dressing as a woman, something that he could not do as an employee of U.S. Industries. Philippe passes away in 1829 and Nathan lived alone as Natalie, as a woman, until dying in 1840.

Saul Jacinto became a professor of literature at U. Penn and married a local woman, Eleana Cohen. They had four children. He passes away in 1843.

THE SMYTHE AND MUIR CLANS

Rafer Muir died in 1826 and Emily followed him into the grave in 1839. The couple left a large estate to her children and those they had together.

Jeremiah went west and ultimately settled in St. Louis running a dry goods store. Jonah became a midshipman in the U.S. Navy and served during the War of 1812 before retiring in Boston after the Mexican War in 1848. He did not marry and died in 1863.

Rafer and Emily's son Laclan married Morton Geiger's youngest daughter Ruth and converted to Judaism. They lived in Boston until they both passed away in 1862.

THE LAREDO CLAN

Amos and Laura Laredo live in New York. Laura died of cancer in 1836 and Amos died in 1842. Both of their sons went to Columbia University and join the U.S. Industries Financial Services group.

ABOUT THE AUTHOR

MARC LIEBMAN, CITIZEN SAILOR, ENTREPRENEUR AND AUTHOR

Marc retired as a Captain after twenty-four years in the Navy and is a combat veteran of Vietnam, the Tanker Wars of the 1980s and Desert Shield/Storm. He is a Naval Aviator with just under 6,000 hours of flight time in helicopters and fixed wing aircraft. Captain Liebman has worked with the armed forces of Australia, Canada, Japan, Thailand, Republic of Korea, the Philippines and the U.K.

He has been a partner in two different consulting firms advising clients on business and operational strategy, business process re-engineering, sales and marketing; the CEO of an aerospace and defense manufacturing company; an associate editor of a national magazine and a copywriter for an advertising agency.

The Liebmans live near Aubrey, Texas. Marc is married to Betty, his lovely wife of 57+ years. They spend a lot of time visiting their seven grandchildren.

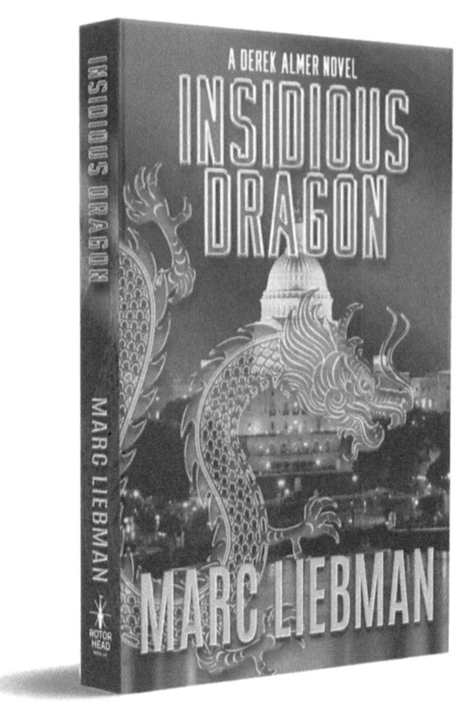

Insidious Dragon

With a doctorate in virology from the University of San Diego in hand, Jun Lin, a native of Guangzhou, returns to the People's Republic of China. In 2002, an ambitious People's Liberation Army Senior Colonel Fang Sun got approval to create and test a biological weapon, and Lin was ordered to help develop the toxin. Horrified, she confides in her cousin, a second-generation U.S. citizen who is also a Naval Intelligence Officer, to help expose and stop the program.

The Red Star of Death

9/11 turned Janis Goodrich's world upside down. As Janet Pulaski, she was once one of the most feared assassins in the world and known as The Red Star of Death. 9/11 turned Janis' world upside down. Three former customers – CIA, Cuba's Dirección de Inteligencia, and Mossad – who have never met or seen her, want to retain Goodrich's services to kill known terrorists. To accomplish her mission, Janis has to deal with traitors in the CIA and Mossad and a rogue FBI agent who wants to put her in jail.

www.ingramcontent.com/pod-product-compliance
Lightning Source LLC
LaVergne TN
LVHW100511110826
845146LV00002B/596